Corrington, John William
    The bombardier; a novel. G. P. Putnam's
Sons, c1970.
    255 p.

I Title

THE BOMBARDIER

**Books by
John William
Corrington**

FICTION

AND WAIT FOR THE NIGHT (1964)
THE UPPER HAND (1967)
THE LONESOME TRAVELER (1968)
THE BOMBARDIER (1970)

POETRY

WHERE WE ARE (1962)
MR. CLEAN AND OTHER POEMS (1963)
THE ANATOMY OF LOVE (1964)
LINES TO THE SOUTH (1965)

ANTHOLOGIES

SOUTHERN WRITING IN THE SIXTIES:
   FICTION (1966)
SOUTHERN WRITING IN THE SIXTIES:
   POETRY (1967)
   Both with Miller Williams

John William Corrington

THE
BOMBARDIER

A NOVEL

G. P. PUTNAM'S SONS
New York

A M D G—

and for Barbara Steinberg and my students at the University of California, Berkeley

I

. . . I have never regretted my service
as a bomber pilot in World War II . . .

SENATOR GEORGE MCGOVERN

. . . I will do such things,—
What they are, yet I know not; but they shall be
The terrors of the earth. . . .

King Lear

Michaelis

—Bombs? You're out of your mind.

He stood up just then, turning toward Moseley, his face working, his arms flailing like broken wings. A waiter laden with a tray of drinks was passing, and an instant later the air was full of highballs sailing, curving through the air, falling on uniformed shoulders all over the room.

The Navy lieutenant from Pensacola sat back down unsteadily, his embarrassment turning into sweat and running down his forehead. Or was it the remnants of someone's bourbon and water?

Moseley was still grinning, holding out the pieces of flimsy from the signals room. —Read it for yourself, he said. —Go on, read it.

—The *Prince of Wales*? The *Repulse*?

I could see how much Buster Moseley was enjoying it. Not because he wished the British ill, but in the name of an old friend named Billy Mitchell.

The room was still in tumult, people moving in and out in uniforms I had never seen, some ill-fitting, a few that looked as if they had seen service in 1918. There was so much confusion that the lieutenant's contretemps with the tray of drinks had hardly caused heads to turn. Officers' clubs, I remember thinking, change considerably when you have a three-day old war.

—God bless those Jap bastards, Buster Moseley was saying, pouring another slug of bourbon into my glass from his bottle. The pitcher of water in the middle of the table remained untouched. We had been drinking for two hours now, waiting for people to fly into Barksdale Air Base for staff meetings. Before that, Moseley had had no sleep at all for seventy-two hours. I

11

had caught four or five in trains and planes and jeeps getting here.

—Those Jap sonsofbitches have handed us the moon, Moseley finished.

Luckman, a personnel officer, frowned. —They've run us out of the Pacific. We may need the moon for regrouping.

Moseley shook his head and poured Luckman another drink. —Don't be dense, Sid. When they bombed out Hickam and Pearl, they turned the war over to us. Mitchell spent his life trying to convince the Navy and War Department people what the Japs proved in thirty minutes. This war belongs to the Air Corps.

The lieutenant from Pensacola gritted his teeth. —Nothing has changed. Sea power is still primary.

Buster Moseley raised his eyebrows and grinned at me. —Right, Admiral Hornblower. Tell it to those guys down inside the *Arizona*.

—All right, we took some losses . . .

—No. No, you didn't take any losses. You just got phased into second—or third—place. You boys are going to get pushed out of the hog trough. No more fifty-million-dollar battleships. Not when those bastards in Washington know that their fifty million can be taken out by half a dozen two-thousand-dollar bombs. Naw, you didn't take any losses. You're just a victim of progress.

I had to laugh at that.

Moseley leaned back in his chair. He looked like a man who had it made. —Bombs, he said slowly, drawling out the word, making it sound like some arcanum of his profession grasped only by a handful. —Guernica. Rotterdam. The combined dive bomber-armor assaults on Poland and France. The saturation raids on Channel ports. There it is. Listen, he said, leaning forward, almost whispering. —Listen, you give me an unlimited bomber force with tactical support and I'll hand you the goddamned world. There's nothing that can resist a determined bomber offensive.

I caught his eye. —If Satan has bombers at Armageddon . . .

—You better believe it. He smiled, drowsy with fatigue, liquor and certainty. —If he does, God makes terms. Or else.

Luckman was first to use the pitcher of water. As he poured, you could see that his hand was a little shaky from lack of sleep.

12

—What do you plan to do with your budget? he asked Moseley. —The planes you can build, but where do you figure to get the men? Someone in D.C. has projected that we'll need twelve thousand pilots, nine thousand navigators, eight thousand bombardiers. Within two years.

Moseley sat forward. His high pleasure receded a little. —I don't know, he said. —We've got the money. Like you say, the planes are easy. We've got techniques and strategic planning. Staff work will be beautiful. But personnel . . . that's your department.

Luckman shrugged. He had been in industry a week ago. —I'm a clearinghouse. I can expedite. I can test. I can hustle the best material and channel it into the Air Corps. But I can't train them. I can't make them . . . good.

I sipped my whiskey and studied the two stars on Buster's collar. They looked better, less overstated than my eagles. —I can make a man into a bombardier, I heard myself saying. —In three months. Maybe four.

The lieutenant from Pensacola snorted. —You can in a pig's ass, Moseley said.

We had been friends, Buster Moseley and I, since the days when we flew Jennies and other cigar boxes. I had left the service and made a few dollars testing. I had flown the trimotor for Ford, the first of the flying boats for Pan American. Now, an apostate, I was back in the corps and Buster's ambivalence showed. No one doubts that, during the course of his first home-cooked meal, the prodigal son got a bowl of soup dumped into his lap. By an older brother who had never left. Who was tired of hearing about the kid's exploits.

—What kind of man will you need? Luckman asked me.

I shrugged. It may have been the whiskey: a mean contentious brand drunk chiefly by Old Army, a few retired wildcatters and others with twelve dollars to pay for a quart. All of whom, bereft of their money, would have switched to Sterno and hardly noticed. Or it could have been the loss of sleep, the peculiar state of my blood, as I realized, back in uniform again, that I was a colonel, Buster a major general. Anyhow: —I can make bombardiers, I said, —out of anything you send me. Only no draftees. I need volunteers.

—In less than a year, Moseley said. His voice was low and casual. The whiskey was nudging him, too. And I was coming

13

on strong. The Greek who had pulled out of the corps to pick up some of that easy money that could be plucked in the early days of commercial aviation. It was a voice I had heard over poker tables from Manila to Dayton.

—All right, I said, smiling.

—Make it six months, Moseley said.

—Fine, I said.

—How would you like to bet on that? he asked, still casual.

—All right, fine. What?

—Six months from the time you get a squadron group, you'll have me a bunch of bombardiers who register in the upper twenty-five percent on standard accuracy runs, right?

—All right, fine. For what?

—A star if you win. Five thousand bucks if you bomb out. If you don't come up with . . . how many?

—Half a dozen, I said. —My way, you have to do it in small batches. But you can make that the upper ten percent on the SAR's.

—Jesus Christ, the Navy lieutenant whistled. —Somebody put him to bed.

Moseley was hunched over the table grinning from ear to ear. —You got a bet. He turned to Luckman. —Sid, I want you to find Michaelis the best boys that—

—No, I cut in. —Random will do fine. Straight out of the hat. No picked people. Anybody who makes it through basic.

The Navy lieutenant shook his head slowly, as if, presuming Moseley was right and the Air Corps would be running this war, he were already part of a conquered nation. The other two looked at me without expression.

—Random, Moseley said. —Right out of the hat.

—Like magic, I laughed. Then we settled down to some serious drinking.

Boyd

I awoke that morning with an exceptionally bad head. We were working the Café Rouge at the Pennsylvania Hotel. After

14

the job, I had shook the fans, checked it to the boys and wandered up to a little bar in Harlem.

If you went on a Saturday night and luck was with you, the man came wading in about two or three o'clock. He would wave to those friends he knew and those he didn't. Then, as the house piano dragged his music together and moved off the stool, the man would sit down like a prince taking back a throne he'd left vacant for a while. He'd hitch up his trousers and lay his derby on the drummer's equipment case, smile and run up and down that keyboard so rapidly, with such perfect and invisible technique that you would wonder if he was actually touching the keys or if there was some kind of magic whereby he could call up music by simply waving his black hands over the keyboard.

Then, after a run or two, it was always the same.

No one to walk with, all by myself;
No one to talk with, but I'm happy on the shelf . . .
Ain't misbehaving . . .

There was no way to be jealous: he owned the song. He should have. He wrote it.

Like Jack Horner, in the corner,
Don't go nowhere, what do I care . . .

I wished that I could play that kind of piano, sound like Fats Wallder. But I couldn't. I played another kind, and so had taken over from Claude Thornhill playing for the most famous orchestra that had ever played—or ever would play—in America. It was a job five hundred other piano players would have given an arm—bass or treble—even to try out for.

It was late when Fats stopped. I had been drinking one after another, trying to follow him on the tabletop, playing one chorus after another as he did. I never missed. I could duplicate every note, his touch, each nuance of his style, his mind. Only I could never get one note ahead of him. I could sense the logic of what he was doing in "Bach Up to Me," I could see where he would have to take it. Only I had to wait for him. I think that's why I drank.

When he was done, he stopped by the table.

15

—'Lo, Al. You lookin' peaked.

—Soused, Fats. Down around low B-flat.

—Pull up your socks, boy. You got it made. They say you pounding it all around for the Big Man.

We drank a little. Fats lit a cigar.

—How do you like him? I hear he's hard.

—He's hard, I said. —He told me you get good by being hard. He drives. He dumps it on you.

Fats shrugged. —It sounds sweet. Sounds fine. I heard that one youall cut last month, Jerry Gratziano's thing. Hear it all over. String . . .

—"String of Pearls"?

—Ummm. Fine . . .

—Fine. But what?

—Hard. Lonesome. Everybody's right there, but they come in and they go out like it was a stage play. Nothing easy in it. That alto and tenor that keeps swappin'—they friends?

—They work together. They get along fine.

—Un-huh.

—Somebody in *Billboard* called it . . . The Heaven Machine.

—Uh-huh. I can see why. That "Moonlight Sonata"—

They were piling up the chairs on top of the tables. Black men in white aprons who kept their eyes on Fats' glass—and on mine because I was with him.

—I think sometimes I ought to move on, I said, finishing off my last.

Fats smiled and blew a cloud of six A.M. smoke up into the dark over our table. —Where you got to go, Al? Somebody waiting on you?

—There's a girl. And my family . . .

—You play mighty nice piano. You did them pearls good. That side is going to be around awhile.

—But it's not easy. I'm not easy, am I?

—No, Fats said slowly. —No, you ain't any way easy. You remind me of a little old boy over at the Roseland. Shines shoes. Does a fine job, you see, slaps 'em flat. Makes 'em glitter. But Malcolm don't get any pleasure out of it. He does it fine, but it's not easy . . .

—And if it's not easy, it's not right.

Fats smiled. An easy smile. —I never said that. That's my

way. When I come up on a tight corner, I love my way around it. That's my way. Maybe you got somewhere else to go.

I finished the latest drink one of the aproned waiters had brought us and laid a ten-dollar bill on the table edge. Nobody came for it. They would wait till Mr. Fats got up to leave. If he stayed till noon, somebody would be there to wait on him. That was the way people in Harlem felt about him. And it came easy.

—It's lonely one way and it's lonely all the others, I said. My tongue was getting thick.

—I don't feel so lonely up behind the box, Fats said slowly. —I feel warm and full. Like I was up against it and slid right in. You know?

We left then, he walking deeper into Harlem, I catching a cab driven by a sullen nervous white and heading for my apartment in the Village. It was getting light when I paid him and started upstairs. Dawn and chill December and lonely there in the only city I really knew, only blocks from Sandy, who, for all I knew, I loved and might love me. But she had no use for what I was doing, for what I was trying to find.

So I pulled down the foldaway bed, stripped off my clothes and pulled the drapes tight. As I moved toward sleep, I could hear, in my mind, another one of Jerry's tunes: "I Dreamt I Dwelt in Harlem."

Monday morning I caught a cab down to the Victor studios. We were cutting six new sides. I had slept the clock around, and even so, my head was very bad indeed. I lay back in the cab and almost passed out. The cabby tried talking.

—Whatchu think about the war?

—It's a war, I said, and he let it go. I was trying to remember our arrangement of the *Pathétique* Symphony. We would be cutting it this morning. Called "The Story of a Starry Night."

Upstairs, the studio was a mess. I walked in and Marion was squealing like a cheerleader, as always. She was a special kind of girl. She made me think of Sandy.

—Al, isn't it the biggest thing? she was saying.

Then Glenn walked in and everybody quieted down. The band-boy was passing out fresh manuscript for a couple of the tunes. Glenn raised his arms.

—Look, I know it's going to be hard to work this morning. But let's get it done and then we can talk about what to do, what we want to do. All right? So get up "Moonlight Cocktails."

Which was a good tune made great by one of the smoothest arrangements we'd used. It was silk, and Ray Eberle, who did very little for me, came together with the Modernaires and made the best side he ever cut—except possibly "Spring Will Be So Sad." It was as we reached the vocal coda, half-time, very nice arranging, that my eye landed on a newspaper. It said, JAPANESE BOMB PEARL HARBOR. Which I thought was someplace in China. Till I looked at the next column: FDR ASKS FOR DECLARATION OF WAR.

—For Christ's sake, Al, have you been juicing? somebody asked in a stage whisper. Miller was staring over at me, cutting the band off. I looked back at him, shaking my head as the voices and horns trailed off.

—I'm sorry, I said. —It's . . . this thing . . . this war. I didn't know . . .

When they found out I didn't know we were in a war, everybody laughed. Even Miller. Then we settled down and finished the session. The fourth tune we cut was an instrumental with a lot of trombone. Called "Keep 'em Flying."

We finished the Tchaikovsky adaptation, and I leaned over the keyboard. The rest were talking about Army bands, about whether the band could survive. Paul Tanner offered me a cigarette.

—Thanks. What are you going to do?

He put down his trombone and blew a long tight cylinder of smoke across the studio. —Whatever looks right, he said. —Anywhere we go from here will be down.

Which was true. We had it made. We were, taken together, the greatest unit of pop musicians that ever existed. Sure, the faddists like Tampa Red or Bessie Smith. They bent my ear in the after-hours places about Herman and some kid out in Balboa Beach named Kenton. Or it was Les Brown. But Miller was the age. We were a machine, yes. It was a machine age. But we were, together, great. No one of us was that alone. Once some columnist asked Glenn who the star of his outfit was. He waved at the whole band. —That's the featured performer, he said. Four trumpets, four trombones, five saxes and rhythm. A vocal group and two vocalists—not counting Tex—all of which, one by one, amounted to no great thing. But put together with Finegan's or Gratziano's arrangements, we were the summit of fifty years' musical growth. We had found a new magic, a way to make the whole band greater than the sum of its parts. None of us would go anywhere better from here, I thought.

But it was time to go, anyhow. Maybe, having arrived, one sees that arrival is only a preface to going on. And somewhere it galled me to know that the perfection we had constructed belonged to none of us because it was indivisible, the possession of us all. I envied Fats in his late solitude, inventing alone, constructing by himself, bound by no arrangement, answerable to no one—except those who paid to hear him laugh off big bands, collective greatness. Even when he played with a group, he was single. Born a solo artist. Which is the way a man wants to work. Outside any rules but those the box places on him by its very construction. I wanted that, and knew that I couldn't have it. Because, alone, without the driving power of the band, I forgot. I froze, I couldn't remember what I meant to say, and my hands became sly counterfeiters, robbing Jess Stacy and Carle, even other instrumentalists—Berry and Jenny and Hawkins, Benny Carter. Once, while I was working on a chorus of "Falling Leaves," I discovered myself reconstructing a mad pastiche of "In a Mist" and "For No Reason at All in C." The living and the dead plagued me, and every note, each cadence that I built belonged to someone else.

So it was time to go. The Japanese provided a good excuse. I walked up to Glenn.

—Notice, I said.

He took off his glasses and rubbed the red welts on either side of his nose wearily. He was waiting for the engineers to play back "Starry Night" and "Fooled." If they sounded perfect, without any detectable flaw either of note or dynamic, balance or blend, we might go home for a few hours. Till time for the *Chesterfield Supper Club* air shot from the hotel. If they were not perfect, we would be recording them again. And again. The way to get undiluted perfection from a machine is through absolute ruthlessness. Brute repetition—in the hands of a genius—equals craftsmanship. Every Miller band, no matter how many changes of personnel, sounded like every other one.

He looked at me for a moment. —Notice what? he asked shortly.

Then the studio filled with our sound. Everyone stopped talking. It was, I used to laugh to myself, apotheosis. We had created this music just moments before. Now it came back to us from some distant place where our skills, our work and sweat were no longer required—or even recognized. It was, of course, quite simply beautiful. No one could imitate that sound. It was, they say, a million-dollar sound.

"Cocktails" began with a nice eight-bar piano introduction. Miller's face clenched. He cupped his hand around his ear and leaned into the speakers.

—That's all right, he whispered grudgingly. —That's fine.

I watched him and the others. It was as if they had never heard the tunes before. Each man was locked in on his own work, his section's playing, the overall sound of the band. I saw Eberle ease forward on his stool. He had never sounded better. "Moonlight Cocktails" was one of his triumphs. Then they played back "Fooled." It was passable—until the vocal began. Eberle's face changed. He knew that he had lost it on this one. He heard himself reaching for the pitch, losing it, quavering into it again, his phrasing gone to hell as he tried to conquer the bad intonation.

Miller paid no attention. I remembered when Tommy Mercer tried to take Ray's job. It was no use. Miller could have picked anyone he wanted. He could have taken Sinatra from James. But he stuck with old friends.

Then we reached "Starry Night." Like "Cocktails," it was nearly perfect. The brass was crisp, stinging, vibrant. Eberle was on it again. It was a fine piece. I sat back and snuffed out my cigarette. It was a good way to go out.

—Notice of termination, I said. —I think it's time to move on.

He was still hearing the music, the sound of his band. It was a long way from Clarinda, Iowa, and the University of Colorado. It was a long time from Ray Noble, the Dorsey brothers and Schillinger's practice studies. It was a very long way for an indifferent trombonist who could hear, imagine, arrange music more perfect than he could ever execute by himself. It had been a long lonely way and time, and now, half a world away, new things had been set in motion.

—It happened in Hawaii. I laughed without humor. It was

20

the name of a tune we had cut just a couple of weeks before. —Maybe we're psychic.

—What are you going to do, Al? he wanted to know.

I shrugged. Then I thought of that little piece of a chorus I had stolen from Jess Stacy just twenty minutes before. —I think I'll help keep 'em flying, I said.

Boileau

That afternoon I was to have cocktails with Ursula Rougon and some friends over on Marengo Street in uptown New Orleans. But before I could finish dressing, the Japanese Imperial Navy changed my plans. My father came upstairs and walked · into the room as I stepped out of the shower. We lived alone. My mother had died long before. My elder sister was married and gone to live in Baton Rouge.

—It's started, my father said.

—No, not till five, I told him. —There's plenty of time.

—They're bombing Hawaii.

—They're . . . what?

—Bombing, he said, leaning against the wall of my room, staring past me out into the pale winter sunlight. I followed his gaze. An elderly woman was walking her spaniel. The window was open, and a light breeze chilled me as I rubbed with a towel. —The Japanese are bombing those people out there.

I frowned, my ears still ringing from the shower. —What the hell for? I asked. My father said nothing.

So I phoned my regrets to Ursula and asked her to convey my compliments to my classmates just graduated from the Tulane Law School. We would not be seeing each other again.

Then we sat listening to the radio, a little Philco my father had carried into the solarium. It was strange listening to the end of one world and the birth of another among plants and ferns and a few rubber trees in pots. We rarely listened to the radio. I could remember the last time. It had been the evening

21

last year when we heard that Leon Trotsky had been murdered in Mexico. My father had, in his own peculiar fashion, admired the old revolutionary. He had been moved by his death. —It's over he had said. —The Russian Revolution is dead now. I had been a senior in law school then and had not understood either his interest or his remark. I would not be understanding it for another five or six years. I am not very fast in such things. But I always arrive.

Now we listened again to the violence and confusion from out there as it flowed into our house through the radio. Simultaneous attacks had been launched on various British and American bases in the Pacific. Total casualties at Pearl Harbor, Schofield Barracks and Honolulu could not be fixed, but they clearly ran into the thousands. The Pacific fleet was in ruins except for a few ships that had not been at anchor. The west coast of the continent was open to assault. As I listened, I began nursing a vague and uncentered animosity toward that world outside, forever in chaos, that had at last spilled over into mine. I did not hate the Japanese especially. I reckoned they had their reasons—or what passed for reasons. My father judged that Roosevelt's arrogance had been nudging them toward war for quite a while. I countered by asking what nudged them into flaying China alive. My father answered that concern for China, coming from a Westerner, seemed a little belated. But now things were clarified. The luxury of reason, weighing fault and counterfault, was quits. Goddamn the Japanese. The Germans. The British. And the Americans—those in New York and Washington who made the decisions and the errors that would catapult me into their sprawling bleeding world, of which I wanted not the smallest part.

As the sun went down, my father stirred in his chair and went for a bottle of wine. When we were not hungry enough to cook or vigorous enough to go downtown for dinner, we drank port. We had a stock which had almost cost my father his life as he brought it out of Spain in 1938. He was never sure who had shot at the train. I liked to think it was the anarchists, for whom my father had a good deal of sympathy. Being twenty-two, I was exceptionally cynical. It was given to me to see the idiocy of every posture and attitude. Except my own.

—I wouldn't mind going, my father said. —If I could serve in the infantry. He had been in the French Flying Service in what we called then the Great War. Later we would refer to it as the last war—not in the sense of a conclusion, but as the next most recent in what appeared to be an interminable series.

—Not this time, I said, opening the port. —This one is mine.

He sat down again and stared out into the dusk. The old lady was passing again, taking her spaniel home. She paused for a moment in front of the house and studied our camellias. My father had kept them up for more than a decade at considerable expense. My mother loved them. After a moment he looked over at me. His eyes were moist.

—Once when I was flying in the Amiens sector, he began and paused. I passed him a glass of wine.

—I've told you about that, haven't I?

—About seeing them bring in von Richthofen's body? Yes.

—He was very young, my father went on, as if he could not stop even though he had told me the story before. —They carried him on a stretcher. There was a crowd of airmen and soldiers walking with the bearers. Next to him, Ludendorff and Haig and the rest were ciphers. You . . . can't imagine how . . . his face was bruised a little, but that was all. What I remember is that his eyes were still open, and there was an expression—something like an expression on his face. It was as if he were thinking, is that all there is to it? To living and dying? What a fraud.

—You still don't like to fly, do you? I asked him.

—No, he said, draining the wine. —I remember thinking . . . it was ridiculous . . . but I thought, they didn't kill him. It was coming down out of the sky, back into the world again. No, I . . . can't like to fly. But that's what you'll be doing, isn't it?

His last words were, for him, loud. Almost defensive.

—I expect so.

—So I'll have to get used to it. I'd rather fly myself. I'll be working on a brief or whatever, and I'll think, right now, right now, he's up there. In a P-40 or a B-19 or whatever. And I'll feel that same cold I've carried locked in a hamper all the way from France twenty-five years ago. My God, how much we have to get used to. I'm tired of it, really. There's no point to it.

—What?

—Being reconciled to . . . all this. By the time you've finished the job, drained yourself of pity or fear or whatever,

23

it's over. You've debauched yourself for nothing. Goddamn this age, these people.

I smiled. My own thoughts coming back in another form. That was the way it was between us.

—I have to go, I said. —I have to go right away.

My father slammed his glass down on the small table between our chairs. —Of course you have to go, he almost bellowed. —Go and be done with it.

He reached for the second bottle of port he had brought, broached it and filled both our glasses.

—But then, you don't have much experience in that, do you?

—What?

—Being reconciled, he said. —It isn't like missing one of Ursula Rougon's soirees without going all to pieces.

I looked away from him. Sometimes I wondered if there was Calvinist blood in the family. At best, we were not French, not even Gaulish or even Teutonic. Somehow we were the preserved and unaltered Roman stock, genes absolutely oblivious to the experience of those who bore them. Austerity above all.

He sensed my resentment. —Do you recall . . . the problem of mortmain? he asked.

—Of course. Why?

—Nothing. Absolutely nothing. I was just thinking, how many dead hands released those bombs this morning. In Germany, the sixteenth century invading the twentieth. In Japan, the eighteenth telling the twentieth what it has to do . . . the samurai . . .

—We learn what we have to. Our hands against every man's. Living and dead.

—My God, what did they teach you at Tulane? I thought you did classics and law.

—That's what they taught me. From Cicero to Coke. On the sea and in the sky.

My father shuddered. —Stay on the ground.

—It's all the same. Killing is killing.

My father looked at me as if so late he had discovered he was rearing an imbecile. —Why don't you forget about joining the Army Air Corps and go along to the Rougons'? It would be better for everyone.

—What? What's the difference?

24

—How would you like to kill a man from a mile, two miles away?

I stared at him. I wouldn't care too much for that, I thought. It sounded like the next thing to hiring someone to do your fighting for you. Like sex, killing deserves to be personal.

—That's fighting in the air. Killing men you never see. Unless . . .

—Later?

—Yes. Or how does it strike you to fire a shotgun into a crowd of people—women, children—to kill one lunatic?

—I wouldn't . . .

My father stood up and walked into the parlor, leaving me with the stuttering radio and this:

—You will, he said, his voice beginning to fade under the hard urgent tones of the newscaster who crackled on about attacks on Wake and Midway, Luzon and other places I had never heard of. —Everyone will. You'll fire into crowds to blast out the evil, and the crowds will vanish, and the evil—

—What? I called after him.

—Won't be gone. You know why?

—No, I almost shouted. —No. Why?

—You'll know. You already do, only . . .

Next morning I was on my way. Through basic training and on to a place called Pilsbury, Texas, which, as it turned out, was for a few years the junction of St. Charles Avenue and the road to hell.

Michaelis

Think of loneliness given a place. That was the base. Think of sand and weeds, clumps of stunted growth sprawled toward every point of the compass under a sky larger, more naked than any other. Days, the sun played across that wilderness as if it sought some crevice, some shaded place in which a patch of moisture might have survived from the numberless days past in which it parched and burned. Even the lizards and

25

snakes seemed tinder-dry, like warped sand-hued twigs. At
night, that blast-furnace heat fell suddenly away and it was
cold. Then the sky raveled, and a million stars, tiny afterimages
of the sun, blinked chill and remote, and the desert, lifeless still,
lay quiet, resting, tranced in the ether of its tenantlessness, the
single howl of a coyote faltering, dropping, rising like the voice
of one singled from many, wrapt in loss, amplified by darkness
and the myriad angles of bush and sand grain and distant stars.

Amid all this, at the end of a macadam road stretching dark
and uncertainly from the west, was fixed in its place a concrete
building they called the Blockhouse. It was a hollow square
with an open center—what had been once a small courtyard or
patio now only a barren patch of sand and weed, microcosm of
what lay outside. In one corner, there was a barrel cactus, if I
remember, and here and there small hollows in the wall where
mice or rats made nests free from the sun. Against one of the
walls rested the broken frame of an ancient bicycle, ownerless,
dateless, inexplicable, preserved and purposeless, remnants of
its tires rotted away, leaving only a crust of rubber on each
wheel rim. The rest of the building was composed of rooms off
an inner hallway which skirted the patio. No, not rooms. Because they had, each of them, an iron door and bars on the outside windows. Even the room I meant to use for an office was so
arranged. It was as if, used once for a stockade, even the war-
den, the guards, had been under suspicion. No one at Main
Base could remember when or for what purpose the Blockhouse had been used. Main Base had been turned over to the
Air Corps in 1928. Before that, it had been a minor cavalry
post, but the Blockhouse had not been used in those days. Perhaps, someone said, in Washington they know.

The rooms were barren as the desert outside. I had cots,
tables, chairs placed in them. I had water basins and soap and
towels placed on small stands under ten-cent mirrors. Nothing
else. Once these rooms had been cells. They would be again.
The bombardiers in training would be alone. There would be
no radios, no newspapers, no communication with outside.
There would be no outside. And as the accustomed was gradually evaded, it would be replaced with mystery, with something
in which, out of their loneliness, the emptiness of all they had
known before, they would come to believe. They would be a
new kind of anchorites.

26

Down at the end of the back segment of the square—facing away from the road—was a room without windows, with a great double-width iron door. Inside, the room was completely vacant: no sign that it had ever been used or even entered. Except when I walked into it, I found on the floor a bent and tattered bit of pasteboard. It was a Bicycle playing card. When I turned it up, it was the ace of spaces. Which evoked in my mind that winter afternoon, alone in the blockhouse, the idea that won my gamble. The Dark Room. And when the Blockhouse and the Dark Room had done their work, I would send them on to Moseley. And they would begin the new life.

Jacobs

—That's fine, my mother said. So wait till they draft you. Go back to school.

She's sitting on the far side of a bowl of strawberries and cream. Uncle Morris is beside her. This is her younger brother. He's nodding, agreeing I should wait for the draft. If she said I should shoot Roosevelt, he'd nod like that. Morris isn't simple. She raised him, and somewhere between Poznan and Brooklyn he picked up the nod. How do I know? Maybe he's got intermittent Parkinson's disease. What are you going to do? They're killing everybody in Europe. They're wiping out England. Now they've started on Hawaii? So I should wait till they come after me in New York?

—That's stupid, I told her. —School? What school? Do they have a school for dying? You want me to end up in a camp? I'll go to an Army camp. Our Army.

—Whose Army? my mother wanted to know. —You go and they'll get you killed. Cannon fodder.

—You need to get out more, I told her. —Read a newspaper. Her face went blank for a minute. Morris frowned. She doesn't read any English, and she hates to be reminded of it. It's always a good lick. You tell her to read a good book and she may cry. Morris reads to her. She knows *Gone with the Wind* from Morris reading it to her three times. She calls the Northern Army Cossacks.

When my father came home, he listens to her, to Morris, who stutters something about cannon fodder. I wonder where he got that. Then he turns to me. He's nodding his head, only not like Morris. He nods when he thinks. Morris nods instead of thinking.

—So you want to quit at the school?

—No. I want to help the country.

—You want to help the country.

—So stay in school and make money and pay taxes, my mother put in.

—The government needs taxes, Morris whispers to me. —They got to have the money.

—I think everybody is crazy, I said. —Are all of you crazy?

My father has stopped nodding. He knows what he means to say now.

—When will you go?

My father has a halo of white hair. His face is lined and his hands are big and red. My father worked in leather. He bound fine books. He used to say, the school is good, but when you finish, learn a trade. Always learn a trade. When times are bad, you can always use a trade. As I look at him, I'm thinking all this, but what I don't know is that I'm not just going to join the Air Corps. I'm going to learn a trade.

—Tomorrow, I said. —I'm already enlisted.

Momma fainted. Morris nodded. My father shook hands with me and took me down to a bar in the next block. We drank a lot of bourbon whiskey and he told me what to look for if I should get so far as Warsaw. He gave me names, insisting that I should commit them to memory like I was a spy or something. People left in the old country. Even relations. He told me to be a good boy and respect women. Obey my officers. Do what I was told. Don't be a smart aleck, he tells me. They don't need any smart alecks. This is America.

So after what they called basic training, they sent me to Texas.

I could tell you about the place for six months, but you couldn't imagine it. Never mind, just think of hell. Desert. Nothing for miles except sand and heat and no clouds. Really, nothing. Except the . . . what they called the Blockhouse. It's this big square concrete building with rooms in it. We each had a room. And there was a wardroom and the office where Michaelis, the colonel, stayed when he was around. And down the corridor, one turn from my room, they had this other place. A big black door with an MP always in front of it. It got to bothering me. It wasn't a prison. Once in a while Michaelis went in. He had to show the guard his pass every time even though the guard knew Colonel Michaelis as well as he knew his name. When he came out, Michaelis would be shaking his head as if he were astounded by what he had in there. I don't know. It got to everybody. They talked about it a lot.

And the guard. A different one every day. As if they couldn't trust the one from the day before. And none of them would talk. You could go up to one of them and ask him for a match and he'd ignore you. He'd stand there at parade rest staring down the corridor into the sun as if only Michaelis could turn him on. Once I made as if I'd go past him and try to open the door. He snapped to attention and jerked his weapon to present arms, still staring down the hot hallway. He carried a tommy gun, and I stepped back and walked to my room, trembling.

I had gotten there ahead of the others. I was by myself the first night. I tried to talk to the guard, but it was no use. At six a jeep pulled up with a new guard and some water and K rations. That was supper, and the new guard looked exactly like the old one. Even when one of them came off duty, he wouldn't speak. It was as if they chose deaf-mutes for the job.

Anyhow I watched the sun go down over the desert. It was, I have to admit, beautiful. The sand and the sky changed color very slowly, subtly, as it came near evening. I remember thinking, you don't see things like this in the city. Make the best of it. Try to enjoy it, learn something.

Toward the south there was a huge white column of cloud that came out of the earth and reached to the top of the sky. It picked up each new color from the west, seeming to turn, to move like a tornado funnel in slow motion. And all around the sand, the emptiness, the silence. Only once in a while could I hear a motor cough or some other muffled sound from Main Base, which was some three or four miles away.

I shook my head. I had never been alone like this. Always in New York the house was full with people. My mother, my father, Morris. My older sister who was married to a man who smoked a pipe and sold something to the Navy yard and lived over in Fairlawn. Or my father's friends. Men who sat and talked, usually in Yiddish, laughing, slapping their knees, ignoring the time and the women until it was the hour for food. They all worked together in the district. One of them factored cloth, domestic and imported. Some of them were tailors. One was a runner. I don't know what he did. As a little boy I thought he must be very strong, running all day. Maybe when I'm grown, I can be a runner. But then, standing, sitting still, I was never alone. I didn't know how to be alone. In the Hebrew school they had dozens of us reciting the Torah by rote. Nobody ever took me aside and said, —Look, this is what it means. That was for later. First, among dozens, you get to know it by heart.

I missed the next part. I knew plenty of things by heart. I could memorize anything. But what does anything mean? Never mind what anything means, I thought sometimes. If you know it, that's enough. Maybe knowing a thing *is* what it means. You see, I was already a runner.

That evening I'm out there sitting in the sand. I just sat down and felt the sand cooling under me. I tried to put my mind on college. I had finished my sophomore year. When this business was over, I'd go back. To City College. I thought literature. Or political science. Listen, why not political science? Politics had gotten me into this uniform. Maybe you could study and find ways to keep people from wars anymore. Which sounds like a sophomore.

Then I came to think about the desert again. Sweet Christ, is this where my people came from? Is this the kind of place Judas Maccabaeus and his brethren fought for? No wonder they had rather be burned in Spain or spat on in England. What kind of God would you expect to come across in the middle of this? Sand and weeds and sun ten times the size it should be?

I lit a cigarette and studied the sun's going down. You wouldn't believe how big it was. And you could actually see it touch the rim of the desert and begin to slide downward. No buildings in the way. I had never seen it go down except behind the Woolworth Building or a block of apartments. I thought, stay inside from now on. Think of home. Go through your wallet. Polish your shoes. Take your mind off of it. Let the

30

goyim burn out their brains contending with it. Be a runner. Nod like Morris. Nod and don't pay any attention to anything.

I smiled and finished the cigarette. Some kind of weed was rolling past, caught by a spit of breeze. I flipped the cigarette at it and it seemed to consume the butt. In a minute it started rolling again, only it was smoking. It was so dry the butt had sparked it. I looked around as if I were afraid somebody would get angry with me for messing up the place, like they do in the park. It was almost dark now, and I watched the weed scuttle away, smoking, little snaps of flame here and there in the thin brittle parts that were dry.

It was suddenly cool. Then cold. And overhead the sky was a trail of stars. They were bright and distinct, and I thought, you're not going to stay inside. You're going to be out here a lot. Why? Never mind. Where are you going? Out to find what it was I memorized all about. An associate of my grandfather's. Something. Look, before anything, we're all Bedouins. This is what we do, that's all.

Oh, sweet. I'm in the great Texas desert one lousy afternoon and evening and I'm crackers. I'm the Foreign Legion and the Riffs all in one. I'm a walking desert song. I walk away from that ghostly Blockhouse a little way, the distance from midtown to the river, and it's as if I'd just lost twenty-five hundred years. That cloud had spread and broken up, and now there was a wind rising, whistling down from those stars and all I could think was: the shoes are polished. There's nothing in the wallet but twenty bucks, a City College library card and a picture of some girl you met on Long Island who lives in Queens and was never home when you called after the summer was done. There's nothing but this. Stick with it. Learn something.

Poole

Shagging in D.C. and a little drop down to Richmond with this passer. She was sweet, wanted all the good, and I said, black or tan, sug, whatever's right. But it was bad down in Vir-

ginia with this Zonk cop laying an iron on my neck, saying,
—You had your last white woman, coon. Can you hear me
laughing right there in the road, car pulled over, gal sweating
dark juice, not for me—no, figuring when Mr. Zonk has stashed
me, it's ass and a slab for her too? But I laughed. So far out and
just as well, saying, —Joke's on you, mister. She's light but not
white. And him looking, seeing the same woman—so good
you'd bring a spoon—but his face twisting, nose crinkling like
a rabbit, leaning over close. And knowing. Not believing. Zonk
never believed a nigger. Oh, no. He knew. Aside from wanting
to cut him a necklace of his nuts, I liked that. Never ease that
boy along. He could smell jig on her right past the expensive
car, the two-hundred-dollar dress, the French perfume (bought
on the *Normandie,* last time over). And he smiled. Laid his
iron back in his belt, that county badge shining like an eye.
   —Like to made a mistake, he said. —Boy, you got to rub off
on her.
   I thought, you can't kill him and she deserves it. Play him
like a foul hook, easy and greasy. —The way you got me sweating, I'll bring her down three shades before we make Alexandria.
   He smiled and I smiled. Between us it was said. —Not here
and now. Maybe there and then. Sure enough, one day and one
way. So I climbed back in and aimed dead north, thinking
nothing. Not really hating, because you don't hate what is invul-
nerable to you. How you going to hate a machine with a hundred million pale parts? No, I just grinned at her. —Why'd you
tell him that? my sweet lemon drop says. Oh, Lord, she's hurting. Not so much me saying, but him knowing. She knows what
I knew he knew, and from now on, crossing over is going to be
a little tougher. It won't be kicky, no. Because she will just have
to sweat every Zonk she lays eyes on. Wondering if that one is
going to figure out for himself without my help what this Virginia weed puller come to know with nothing but a light push
from one sorry scared nigger. Aha, the darky's revenge. Lay on
the black, don't hold back.
   —Don't let it crimp you, hon, I said, my hands steady on the
wheel now, and proud of that, lacking anything else. —He's
going to be driving that twenty miles of road back and forth for
the rest of his life. Everybody's somebody's nigger.
   Comes the Chinamen or whoever pumps it into old Pearl be-

fore we can get back into D.C. And I'm sitting alongside a hamper of ribs thinking, why don't you try some Army, dad? They got to give you a gun. How would it be to have a gun? Might pick it up and never lay it down. But the rules say clearly: They got to give you a gun. Worst come to worst, swallow a handful of bullets, squat and fart 'em back. It's got to beat this hanging up and dragging down.

Between the recruiting office and the Air Corps was the usual. It don't matter. Just that Virginia Zonk following me around like he had been since I was six and had that trouble with DeFatta because of my baseball and his kerosene drum. The Zonk had a thousand faces. Oh, Lord, he was the Shadow. Able to cloud men's minds, knowing the difference between good and evil, changing his face, his voice, his very mind. I mean his brain. No, he never changed his mind. He was the Army doctor, wiping off his stethoscope after he put it on my chest, trying not to touch my skin any more than he could help. I remember the way he looked when he reached into my crotch and asked me to cough. His face went flat, distant. Him thinking Zonk-like, I got my hand in this burrhead's nuts. Ugh. The only excuse is if I bring them out when I come. But I coughed, delicately, he winced, and I went through. No rupture. Not so you could notice. Not yet. The Zonk filled mess halls, barracks, seemed to have the whole world in his hands. My God, I thought, it's like being a fly in a turtle tank. Zonk snapping at every step. Who cares about the back of the bus? But how about the sweat? Does this bar look okay? Does he want your quarter? Or will he say this time, —We don't serve niggers. You can't count on him even for that. Toilets are a major decision, but it's death to draw a piss on Zonk's streets. You had as soon grab a sad thin tit or what passes for hip on Zonk's woman. And remember his power: If you get brittle for Zonk's woman, he will know. He will absolutely know. He has that power, among others. He knows if you mean, ever in your life, to resist him, turn your hand against him. I came to see for certain that Zonk had never ever wrongfully lynched a black man. No, he knew that nigger was percolating, simmering, getting hunched for a bull move. If you don't believe in magic, Zonk is beyond explanation. Listen:

On the way to Asshole Alley, Texas, the bus stopped, and I climbed down, eyes frozen solid, smelling my nigger neighbors:

33

Oh, real niggers. Busted all to pieces inside, Zonked out. Carrying little packages wrapped in newspaper, tied with secondhand string. Packages which should have been full of black powder and fuses, hand-grenades and surplus nine-inch blades from the Alamo. But no: You could smell the catfish and the okra, the little green tomatoes or a piece of ham too old for eating, but ready for a mess of red beans. We stood around. Somebody collected money to buy cold drinks at this kind of bar and general store across the road. I shook my head when the old man came up to me. —I'll get my own, I said. Then I walked behind him. It was a dump, put together out of weathered lumber and corrugated metal. There was a long sagging gallery supported by posts, with one false window above. The porch had a hole or two in it, and the screen door hung open, a big metal strip across the middle for a handle. It said:

SEVEN UP
You like it. It likes you.

The whole front was studded with other signs: Groves Chill Tonic, Nehi, Cherocola, Lydia Pinkham's Compound. And a new sign, a strip of brightly colored paper which said: LUCKY STRIKE GREEN HAS GONE TO WAR. There was a little pack of cigarettes marching along with a bayoneted rifle and a helmet perched over the stamp where you found De Witt Clinton scratching his wool.

I smiled. How about it? Zonk conjure a pack of smokes. Why not? One morning Hitler will awake to find a deck of Luckies going for his windpipe. Oh, Zonk, how you do come on.

The old man was inside. I stopped and lit a smoke. Camel. Seemed to fit me better than Luckies. I could hear the old man:

—Yessah, yessah. Fo' Coke an' three Doctah Peppah. Oh, yessah, sho', sho'. My guts did that little two step they always did about then, and I thought, it doesn't even bother him. He's seventy if he's a day, and he's in there shuffling, giving them a little smile, a little cringe. And they say, —Why sure, Uncle. You got a deposit for the bottles? —Oh, yessah. Heh, heh.

Heh, heh. I want to pick up the old bastard and break up the place with his head. Oh, shit. And shit. And shit. But pretty soon he comes easing out, still smiling, still leaning over in that crouch he picked up on a slave ship three hundred years ago.

34

The day they laid a banjo on him and found he knew how to play it without any lessons. He gave me the tag end of that smile and went on across the road to where the people stood around the bus waiting. They smiled at him. He had done a big thing. Savior of the tribe. Fo' Cokes and three Doctah Peppahs. You can always count on the elders, is what I say. For soft drinks.

I am pissed in my soul—over and above the stink I have got and can't get shut of ever. I am going in that place and walk out with a beer and ease over by the folks and ruin that old turd for at least the balance of this trip. Walk over sipping a cool brew, smacking my thick fine lips, saying yessah, yessah to Mr. Bud. Let's see what that feels like.

Inside it is dark. I must be vanishing as I move on in, hearing the screen door slam behind me. Oh, Lord, the magic is in here. I wish Lucky Strike hadn't gone. I wish that little motha was here with his shiv. There are four or five of him, the Zonk. Original model. One behind the counter and others here and there. In overalls, one with a wide-brimmed black hat. One chewing on a Clark Bar, the wrapper bright orange and angry in his hand. The others have bottles of beer. What are they doing? They are waiting for me. They know it is a mile, a clean mile, between the door and that counter. I have forgotten everything. I can smell the smell they smell of me. It is fear, and I can feel tears in my eyes and can hear a voice out of the back of my smashed head yelling out to the tribe, Good-bye, good-bye. He's got me. And, I'm sorry, old man, you did right. I knew but just couldn't believe what I knew. I stepped forward wishing to Jew Jesus I was outside rolling in the dirt.

—I'd like a Bud, I said. I fooled around with a "please," but it wasn't right. Zonk's woman liked "please." Zonk just thought that was "yessah" educated.

—We don't serve no beer to niggers, the one behind the counter said, as if it was recorded and is what he would have said even if I asked for a two-pound slab of High John the Conqueror root and two dozen blessed lodestones chipped from the subpavement of Mecca.

What next? Why not across the counter and into the icebox, grabbing a bottle, smashing off the neck, slobbering it down, fighting to the death with what's left in my hand? Because that isn't what gets done. Nosah, I shows mah money.

—I've got fifty cents.

—I don't give a shit if you've got fifty dollars, boy.

So I am whipped. That's all there is. There is no next step from my side. Absolutely none. But Zonk has a whole world of plays left. Hard or easy, it's all in his blood pressure and how the day has gone. What kind of shape he wants to cut for his friends. Who pay fifteen cents for their brew. When they pay.

—Boy, you off that bus?

Now what do I do? If it's not yessah or nosah, it's got to be a saying that yessah or nosah doesn't fit. If I want out of here.

—I come in on the bus.

—Whyn't you give some money to that old nigger when he come in and bought Cokes?

And three Doctah Peppahs. He knows. Part of his power. He knows what I thought out on his porch, how I felt on the way from door to counter. Knows what is in my head right now. He asks, knowing.

—I . . . wanted a beer.

—We don't sell no beer to niggers.

This is a relief. He hasn't carried me out. Maybe he has a registerful of money or a fine woman waiting, and no gorge on the rise. Nothing lost so far that I ever had.

—Boy, you ought to of give that old man your money. You could have got a drink.

We could go through the whole thing again. But I want to go. So I turn and start toward the door. It is said by some of the tribe that they won't take you behind because there is no fun cutting a man down if you can't see his eyes, watch him boiling away, going, drifting, as you shoot, stab, punch, cut.

I am at the door, hand on the screen, every tiny square hopping, the white shell and sand world out there like Eden, hot or not.

—You watch your step, boy, you hear?

I am on the porch. I don't have to answer. It isn't important enough to draw spiders out of the dark. He didn't say it loud enough to carry anything more with it. A close guess, but safe.

Across the way, the old man and the tribe watch me coming. It is time to go. The old man says nothing. The tribe watches. I shake out a cigarette and light it slowly. I am saying, —I bought a pack of Camels. Don't you know where Lucky Strike has gone? Heh, heh. They come in a white pack now. That's right.

Lucky is white, not green. Because if it was really green, you got to know fifty cents would buy a beer.

But the bus doesn't leave. There is something wrong with the fuel pump. We have got a night here. The tribe doesn't even shrug. The old man wanders off. He will find a sleepy corner. There is room all over for an old man. But I feel the temperature falling ten degrees a minute. You watch your step, boy, you hear? YesSAH.

It was somewhere along about eleven o'clock and I was still walking. They had closed up the bus. They wouldn't let me sleep on it. I was paid through to Pilsbury, Texas—riding. It wasn't a hotel, right? Right, if you say so, Zonk turned into bus driver.

It was cool, and I figured to walk up and down by the bus, even though the gas station was closed. I had my ticket in my hand, waiting for the sheriff's car. Which would come. A '29 Model A or a '35 V-8 or a '39 Plymouth. Roadster with Zonk pretending a county job. Before dawn, he would come. I stayed awake, watching one isolated car pass every fifteen minutes or so. I got to feeling disappointed when the cars' light loomed up, caught and held me, and then faded. Hey, I thought, youall come on. Don't you see this nigger, this suspicious nigger lurking around, about to steal a gas station? Or maybe he's going to rape that bus. Help. Was I a suspicious nigger? Oh, Lord, you got to know it. Suspicious of every shadow. Chilled by sounds that put other folks to sleep. I thought about how to get hold of it all, how to make a fine big play. But I dropped it as quick as I picked it up. I had fooled with that since old DeFatta kept my ball, saying, what does a zigaboo need with balls? Heh, heh. Dead end. Like trying to create the universe without any glue and stuff. So I come to feel how tired I was and chewed on that for a while.

But just after eleven o'clock by the flyspecked clock in the gas station window, I heard the door of the store slam across the way. I didn't look. I drifted around behind the bus. He might have counted up that register and come out fifty cents short. Never mind that, I thought. You've done had that storekeeper, haven't you?

Yes, I had, and no, I hadn't. As I watched from around the back of the bus, he fell down the steps. Just turned from closing

37

the padlock on the door and fell down on his face. It woke me up and made the last six or seven hours worthwhile. It was the next best thing that could happen. First best would have been if I had knocked him down the steps. But such was not given, and you got to like second bests. It is essential, since you're lucky to get a third best if you're darker than sun tans a leper.

For a long time he just laid there. I thought, heart attack. Comes and catches the good and the bad, specially since we're all bad. Stretched him like a fish on a tray. I can see him now, arms hung over his head, legs kind of pulled up under him like he was asleep. I must have watched him for ten minutes. A dead Zonk. Knew they died, heard they did. But never saw one stretched. Then while I studied him, he went to groaning.

At first I thought it was a cat mewing somewhere. It didn't seem to be coming from the Zonk. But I finally got a fix on it as he rolled over on his back in the dirt. —Wa-a-agh, he said. And it hit me like a side of fresh-killed shoat: that sonofabitch is drunk. On the beer he wouldn't sell me.

I nudged him with my shoe, and he looked up. Not at me. More at the moon over my shoulder. I was kind of outlined against the moon, and he couldn't tell who I was. Or what. I couldn't think of anything to say.

—What you doing lying in the road? I finally asked him.

He rolled his head from side to side. Sadder but wiser, it was supposed to say. I started to step on his face, but held up.

—You remember me, I asked him.

—Ah, he breathed, squinting up at me. And he smiled and reached up for a hand.

I had him almost home when the sheriff's car pulled up beside us. It was maybe another block, the old man was saying. The fat deputy got out, hands away from sides like he was ready for anything a tricky Indian might come up with.

—Whatcha doin' with Mr. Travis? he wanted to know.

—Not much, I said. —Trying to get him home.

The deputy sniffed at him suspiciously, kept looking at me out of what might have been a squint he couldn't help, had been born with. —I think he's been drinkin'.

—Umm, I said.

—Lemme have him, the deputy said.

I tried to pass him over, but he held on to me.

38

—You can count on a nigger, the old man blurred softly. —Ever' fuckin' time. Nigger'll never let you down.

The deputy was embarrassed. Or disgusted. Whatever a Zonk feels when another one is betraying his class, even drunk as a cricket on popskull.

I finally worked free of the old fool and stepped back to see a rare sight: Zonk bearing his own cross. Looked fine. Then the old man grinned a two-tooth-missing smile and beckoned me close. I leaned in, leery but wondering. He was fooling around in his trousers pocket, reached out and put something in my hand. By that time the deputy had purely enough and was dragging him away. When they had moved off, I opened my hand enough to let the moonlight fall into it. There was a fifty-cent piece, and I know the deputy heard me laugh or snort or howl or cheer. Or choke. Whatever it was. Because he turned, the old man's dusty arm around his neck, and stared at me like Esau dragging away his pottage, wondering what Jacob had in his mind.

Then it was dawn and the bus people got their part, the tribe gathered, the old black man yessah'd his way back on board, and we moved out. The last thing I saw was somebody on the front porch of the store waving, but when I looked just behind the bus, I could see somebody else waving back. Out of the sheriff's car. So I laid back and after a long while went to sleep studying on magic and knowledge and damnation, knowing if I lived to be four hundred and forty-two I might never really like or trust myself all the way again.

Jacobs

It was before dawn when I awoke the second morning. The room was white, no, a gray—off-white like the bones of a skeleton seen down in the water. Not that I ever saw any skeleton in water. It was my imagination. Outside I could hear voices. They were clear and distinct and disembodied as if they were floating on the desert air from all the way over at Main

39

Base. I got up, pulling my sheet after me, and went to the barred window. I could see a jeep parked and a man pulling a bag out of it. I listened to him talking to the driver.

—Do they serve food around here?

—Listen, old son, I don't know a goddamned thing about this place. I don't even know what youall do.

It was a Texas accent, I think. It was the driver.

—Well, I reckon we eat from time to time.

—Not with us you don't. Maybe youall are a secret weapon.

The other had his bag cleared by then, and the jeep started up and tore away back down the narrow concrete strip we had come in on. Then the yard in front was empty except for this man alone in his air cadet uniform. He stood there beside his duffle, hands stuck in his back pockets, palms out. I thought maybe he was a Texan, too. He had that strange blurred accent, that way of losing all his final g's and letting words slide into one another with hardly any space in between. Now he stood there watching the jeep's dust. Then he pulled off his garrison cap angrily and threw it on the ground. I found suddenly that it was very cold and that I had gooseflesh up and down my arms and legs. I wondered if I should go say hello to the new man. But I wasn't in charge. Don't take things on yourself, my mother had told me. If they want you to do something, they'll tell you. Don't worry, they'll tell you. Morris had nodded. He was in the First War, a typist at Fort Bragg. Whenever anyone asked him about it, he only shivered and said nothing. By then I was at the door, looking down the hall into the deep gloom. Down there, in front of the iron door, the MP stood at parade rest with his Thompson machine-gun just the way he had been standing when I went to sleep. At the other end of the hall, where the wardroom was, I could hear the new man walking back and forth now, and once in a while I could hear him curse in that flat, soft, blurred voice. Most of what he said I couldn't understand. But once he said, quite clearly, —Goddamned Yankee Army. Something made me close the door very quietly and climb back into bed. It was still gray outside and I pulled the sheet and the single thin blanket they had given me all around my shoulders and tried to sleep again.

When next I woke up, the sun was there. It was cutting big yellow squares across the floor of the room, divided by the bars in the window. It was already hot and I could feel myself sweating. It was the heat that had waked me up. I got to my feet and began to dress. There was a shower down the hall, but it wasn't working yet. There was no water except a big insulated tin can with ice water that was traded for a new one each time they changed the guard. I couldn't even shave.

But when I got to the wardroom, there was a table laid, and this other guy was sitting at the head of the table with eggs and toast and bacon and coffee spread in front of him. I guess I must have looked surprised. Like he was some kind of King of the Golden River who could make things appear. There were four or five other aluminum plates laid and some cracked dishes with what looked like it might be food.

—Reckon you'd better get some before it's cold, he said. —Breakfast is the only decent meal they send us.

I sat down at the middle of the table and poked in the dishes. I took some scrambled eggs that looked peculiar and white. And some bacon and toast. There was some white stuff that looked like cream of wheat, but no dish, no bowl for it. I put some on my plate and stared at it. The other guy had some and was spooning butter into it.

—Grits, he said. —Make you big and mean.

—I never heard . . . never ate any before.

He looked at me and went on eating, pushing the eggs and grits onto his fork with a piece of toast. —Don't tell anybody, he said. —Maybe they won't know. It's not your fault.

—Are you a . . . Texan? I asked him.

—Louisiana, he said, finishing his eggs and turning to coffee so black it looked like a hole in the cup. Over on the wardroom table was a hot plate and some water in a pan. Next to it was a coffee bag. It was kind of orange and said LUZIANNE or something on the side.

—All I could get, he said. —Generally I drink Lyons' with my own chicory. Since the war, you drink what you can get. Have some.

I got up and poured some out of the pan. From behind me I heard his voice soft with irony. —You might try pouring it through that handkerchief there. Unless you favor the grounds.

I poured it back into the pan and tried again. It was still pitch black. I drank some, and it almost strangled me. Jesus, I thought, what kind of people are these?

41

—My name is Jacobs, I said.

—Boileau, he answered, finishing his coffee, wiping his upper lip with another handkerchief and taking a long thin cigar from his shirt pocket. He bit off the end, lit it and turned in his chair to survey the yard outside and the endless silent sand. His back was to me now, or at an angle from me. I could see his profile in three-quarter perspective. It was sharp and thin. For all his self-control, he was still young. He had no flesh on him. My mother would have tried to feed him five or six times a day. But I felt that he would have turned it down. Politely.

—You'd be from New York, he said with that peculiar tone in his voice that I got used to as months and years passed.

—How did you know?

—Second sight, he said. —I can see into people. It's a gift.

His lip curled up, and he went on looking out into the sand and sun. He said nothing else. I was dismissed. He was thinking. I wanted to ask him about his home. I wanted to know about where he was from. But I couldn't think of what to say. He had said everything he meant to say to me. I was out of his mind. I felt that if I had said anything, he would have looked around at me suddenly as if he had never seen me before, never shared the breakfast or his own brand of coffee with me.

So I walked past him, and started out into the desert again.

I walked for maybe an hour—who knows? Out there, how do you find a referent for time? I had put on a golf cap Morris had given me with a handkerchief stuffed under it. I was the whole Foreign Legion. Or the Riffs. No, I was something else. Behind me, the Blockhouse shook and danced under the sun. It was a mirage. I was having a mirage. I thought, mirage or not, you've got nothing but this. This is what your people came from. The others own New York. They own San Francisco and Chicago. It's theirs. They lease pieces of it all to clever kikes for local color. The whole world is Germany except the desert. That you can have, because nobody wants it. You'll end up here anyhow, squatting at a fire in cracked sandals, toasting a lizard on a stick. Arguing with yourself, thinking God is out here having chosen you, stuck with His choice. How do you like that?

What was funny was that I liked it well enough. I remember Momma telling me, —Don't put your hand out too quick.

You'll lose your hand. Wait till you see if anybody else wants it, whatever it is. I thought, that's a hell of a way to live. Then I thought, but it's a way to live. What do you need? A way to die?

So I stood in that place, sharpening my eyes, forgetting and remembering. Then I started back, the whole tawny desert wobbling me under, parched for water, back to the fort. Where they had the camels, the palms, the oasis. *Mon capitain* . . .

When I got back, there were two new guys standing on the road with their duffles at their feet. One was medium tall with blond hair—no, pale hair—and not much eyebrows. He looked sleepy, like he was going to fall over and just go to sleep where he was. The other one was short and dark. He was hairy, and he couldn't stand still. You know what I mean? His hair was straight and so black that in the sunlight it looked almost blue. He squinted up toward the sun as if it were an enemy, and I thought, he's an Italian. They'll never get any work out of him. He won't work. He looked at me, and whatever passes between people who are bound to have no liking for one another leaped like a spark. I mean, I knew he didn't like me. And that was fine. Because I wasn't going to like him. He was going to be a big pain in the ass. Watch and see, I said to myself as if I had to convince myself. Watch who works and who doesn't. You'll see.

But he said hello—I mean the blond guy. The other one just stood and sweated and looked as if he wanted somebody to carry his bag. The blond guy was Boyd. He seemed all right, only not in the groove. It was as if he was always thinking of something beside what you were talking about. It turned out he had a fine education, Yale, and they wanted him to go to law school. But he went into music. Played with the really big bands. I asked him why, why not set himself up?

—It wasn't what I wanted, Boyd told me. —I wanted something else. I don't know.

We talked for a while, and then another jeep came and brought us dinner and a new guard for the Dark Room. It was nearly dark, and we were starting in when we heard something from inside. Like a chair turned over. When we stepped inside the wardroom, there was Boileau and the hairy one, named Krepinski, standing across the table from one another, both of them tensed like animals ready to spring at each other. Boileau's face was flushed, and his hands, spread on the table, were

43

white with the pressure of his body's weight. Krepinski had this kind of sick grin on his face, as if he didn't know what was going on.

—If you cross me again, I'll kill you, Boileau said to him without even raising his voice. —Don't talk to me, don't get near me. I'm not going to warn you again.

—What's . . . , I started to ask.

—Stow it, hebe, Krepinski said. —Just go eat your beans.

Nobody had ever called me anything like that before. You hear about it. You hear that maybe you go into a restaurant and a drunk sees you and calls you a kike. Or that you try to rent a house and the real estate man looks at you funny and says it's already taken. You hear what "restricted" means. But until it happens, you can't believe it will happen to you. It's always somebody else: some loudmouth who asks for it, who throws his money around. So help me God, I got a little dizzy. I felt hot, like I wanted to vanish and reappear somewhere else. I looked at Boileau. He was still staring at Krepinski, his face not flushed any longer. Pale now, and with an expression of hate so deep you wouldn't believe it. Boyd was just standing there, looking away from all of us. I don't know what Krepinski was doing. I couldn't look at him. I wasn't afraid. I even thought about hitting him, ripping into him and trying to hurt him. But I didn't know what to do. Was it enough to fight about? What would the others do? Did I have a chance, even a slim chance of beating him? Should that matter? Somebody insults you. What do you do?

I walked out. A great solution, you say? A man should stand on his own ground, defend himself. Fine. Where is my ground? Texas? Come on. New York? Who needs it? Wherever I stand is my ground? You say that. I don't know. I didn't know. Not then, not for a long time.

Out there it was dark now with the moon red and full and very close rising behind the Blockhouse. It was all different now. Cold and getting colder. I walked a long way, I think. I remember squatting and picking up a handful of sand. It was still warm an inch or so down. It felt alive, like blood fresh from an animal. It fell through my fingers like tiny diamonds catching the moon's new light, filling again the hollow from which I had scooped it. I put my eye close to my hand and watched the crystals falling, tumbling back to the earth. Then something be-

44

yond the cold made me shiver. All of a sudden something pulled my head up, and there above the sky was a mirror of the earth. The midnight blue was filled with patches of light like the campfires of different people, seeming to be close, and yet each one far distant from the rest. None of them knew the others were there, so much darkness stood between them. Only just above me there was a long band of stars, bright yet faint and far away like a path sprinkled with sand. It was like a negative of high noon on this desert. I thought, don't even think of it. Those aren't yours, either. Put your feet down, Moishe. A physicist you're not: which is to say a religious man dreaming of how God must have been born. And I thought still, tell the stars, if thou be able to number them. No, I can't number them. Not yet. So it was the end of the second day. And I had learned something.

Boyd

If you wanted to look at it that way, it was insane. An alumnus of Yale and the Glenn Miller orchestra signed up to learn how you drop bombs on people. But remember this: It didn't happen last week. It happened a long time ago and things flowed then. They weren't fixed. I had almost joined the John Reed Club in New York, but I joined a band instead, and from one thing to another. I wasn't really political, and given the choice of rapping for the Popular Front or rapping piano for a band, I went the way I wanted to go. I had to find out. Even today that's not hard to understand. If it had all happened thirty years later, I might have been whanging the guitar behind Donovan. Looking for Atlantis. And don't kid yourself. Donovan may end up yet in the IRA—bombing.

So they sent me to basic, and then on to this little dump in Texas. A village. A real village. The jukebox had people I'd never heard of: Ernest Tubb, Jimmy Rodgers. And one of our things. "In the Mood." Only it was three years old now. Maybe the mail was slow down there.

When I got to Main Base, I pulled my duffle off the bus and stretched. It was hot. The sun had a funny look about it. I couldn't figure it out. It seemed closer. As if it were an observer or a participant instead of the distant polite electric light it was in New York. I was in my air cadet uniform, a round black patch with wings and a propeller on my shoulder. My tie was tucked into my shirt. I turned in my orders and walked over to the officers' club for a beer.

It was dark inside and a little cooler. A rackety window fan pulled a faint breeze through the bar. I picked up a beer and looked around. There was an upright piano in the far corner on a low stage. I walked to it very deliberately, set my beer on top and picked out a few chords. I did one of the new Will Bradley things, "Celery Stalks at Midnight." It was a little ragged, but by the time I had enough of it, the technique was back. I was always fluent. I had a fine ear, very good hands and a sense of rhythmic balance that surprised everyone I ever worked for. There is no way to say how lonely you feel when you have every gift. Except originality. Except the capacity to make real use of the gifts. My mind wandered. I thought of how much resistance my family had offered to the music thing. Outside man at a broker's, law—even the Episcopal ministry. But for God's sake, you're not going to throw yourself away. No, Momma, I'm going to put all those piano lessons you insisted on to use.

A very square family. We didn't see much of each other. A friend from college met me in the Café Rouge one night. When I left his table and stepped up to join the band, he was rather put out. I could see it. He didn't even know why. The word he was looking for in his sophomore French was *déclassé*. He had been talking to an employee. Later, in a different mood, possibly aware of just how universally celebrated my employer was, he dropped me a patronizing note which mentioned a visit to my parents. He said my mother had sent out for the newest Glenn Miller album—carefully keeping it hidden between two of the Brandenburg Concerti. I chuckled thinking of my mother in an inevitable blue cocktail dress with a pitcher of martinis next to her. Alone, my father in Los Angeles or Boston. Listening, seeking some epiphany of her own Albert amid the strains of "Chattanooga Choo-Choo" or "Serenade in Blue."

I riffed off a chorus or two of Dorsey's big tune, Pinetop

46

Smith's "Boogie Woogie." I barreled it, dropped it an octave and moved the bartender. I eased it and put the place back together with my left while my right minded other business upstairs in the nonresonant keys. Then I stopped and smiled. I was a really talented pianist. And I was finished with it. Now I was going to try another trade. Why not? Maybe I would have genius as a bombardier. Maybe I'd be more than talented. Maybe I'd be the Fats Waller of bombardiers.

Then a noncom found me, and I finished my beer and followed him. Outside there was a colonel. He said his name was Michaelis and that I had been assigned to his section. When I told him my previous trade, I thought he was going to be sick. Then he shrugged and told me to bring my duffle and follow him.

Out there beside a jeep this short greasy-looking character was standing. He had thrown his duffle in back and was walking back and forth, looking this way and that, one expression after another passing over his face. He looked like an animal on a leash. Some kind of thing that hunted or raced for its keep. Colonel Michaelis introduced us. His name was Krepinski, and he was assigned to the special bombing section, too. He mumbled something and climbed into the back seat. Michaelis got under the wheel and I got in beside him.

We left Main Base and drove out into the desert. We spoke of the war, of the heat, but Colonel Michaelis looked straight ahead along the narrow concrete strip that vanished into sand. Then, ahead of us, I saw a jutting building that looked like one of Teddy Roosevelt's great white fleet under full steam or a presidio left over from some Alamo that had been solved by diplomats. As we came closer, its isolation closed on me, and I could see in my memory the distance between this place, whatever it was, and the teeming streets of Manhattan. I felt cold suddenly, as if I had made a great and maybe fatal error and couldn't even be sure what it was. Behind me, Krepinski was humming tunelessly. I think it was intended to be "In the Mood."

—This is the Blockhouse, Michaelis said as we stopped in front of it. —This is where you'll learn.

As we climbed out, I saw a man standing in the doorway. He was dressed in cadet uniform—with tie and cap. He watched Michaelis without any sign of recognition or warmth or even dislike. He walked out and disappeared around the building as I watched. When Krepinski and I had pulled our duffles out, Michaelis revved the jeep engine. If he isn't going to stay, I wondered, why didn't he have a noncom drive us?

His face, thick and healthy, had no expression. I would find that it rarely did. If he had emotions, they showed only in his small gray eyes. Now those eyes, under dark heavy brows, were bright, almost humorous, uninformative.

—Meet people, he said. —Have a nice time.

—Sir, I called out as he started to pull away,—when do we . . .

He jerked the jeep up short. —Very soon. When the last one comes. He smiled at me. —That's good. That's very good.

Then he drove on, leaving us standing next to our duffles in the dust and sand.

Before we could walk to the Blockhouse, another cadet materialized out of the desert. I turned and there he was: thin, his uniform fitting badly, smiling, almost grimacing. He had on some kind of cap with a handkerchief draped down his neck. He held out his hand and I shook it.

—I'm Jacobs, he said. —It's hell here.

—Is it always this hot?

—All the time. Listen, it never lets up.

He offered his hand to Krepinski, who managed to be looking the other way, out toward the simmering horizon.

—What did you do? Jacobs asked me.

—I was . . . a musician, I told him.

—Gee.

So we talked awhile. Krepinski finally picked up his duffle and dragged it to the Blockhouse, leaving us there in the sun, a couple of strangers two thousand miles from any place or anything we understood. After a while we went inside.

We ate cold beans and some Spam that evening. Jacobs seemed nervous but very bright. He was from New York, too. Krepinski told us about the choice pussy he had stashed in Jersey City. The other one was named Boileau, Jacobs told us, from Louisiana somewhere. There was trouble almost before we could open the beans. The Southerner told Krepinski to stay clear of him. Or he'd kill him. I never found out why. It happened like this:

I had started to eat my beans. You hear about the South.

That it's still back in the Middle Ages. You hear different things. I remembered seeing *Gone with the Wind* and thinking how much finer their way of life looked. Till I remembered it was a movie. They probably all had lice under the crinoline. But I was curious about this one that Jacobs was talking about. Maybe I was expecting Clark Gable or Leslie Howard.

He came in just as it got dark, looking like anyone else. He was almost six feet, on the thin side, all his face carrying you toward his eyes. Just at first they looked gray and genial. But as he looked at me, I could see that hardness, that certain petulant unconcern with what happened anywhere but inside of him that I had seen only twice before. In Glenn Miller's eyes and in my mother's. With my mother it was ordinary unvarnished selfishness. With Miller it had been the outward sign of an idea, a desire so large and consuming that he could not really grasp or focus on other things. With Miller, it was the band and nothing but the band truly mattered. I wondered what it was with Boileau.

Krepinski made some familiar crude remark to him. Boileau ignored him, stared at me, picked up a can of beans, opened them and started out again into the darkness. As he reached the door, Krepinski gave him a Bronx cheer. He stopped and turned, looking at each of us in turn.

—I know you people are raised to treat each other like animals, he said. —And that's all right. Youall do that to each other. But the next one who troubles me is going to get himself killed.

As he walked out, Jacobs shook his head. Krepinski laughed without much conviction.

—Thinks he's a bad ass, Krepinski said.

—I think so, too, Jacobs said. —I think he meant it.

Krepinski looked at Jacobs with a sneer on his face. —You would. You kikes don't like no trouble, do you?

Jacobs was transfixed. He looked away, out into the darkness, and then walked out in the direction Boileau had taken. I leaned back, cold beans in my mouth. What a collection of misfits. I should have stayed in the band. I understood that frustration, that mystery. It had to do with a certain lack of insight, a failure of intuition. There was no telling what all this would come to. And I hadn't even seen the enemy yet.

Boileau

He came in at dawn our third day there. Before Michaelis got there. So that we were what you could call complete before Michaelis ever began on us. Which, I reckon, was as it was supposed to be.

He was very black. Not vanishing, but perishing black. Good features—not one of those wall-eyed blubber-lipped comic creatures endlessly popping up to serve at table in *Gone with the Wind*. But black beyond the common gambit of Mexican or Puerto Rican. I was sitting on the porch considering the sand, sopping up the coolness of early morning against the rising sun. He got out of the jeep with the morning guard for the Dark Room and watched as the night guard climbed in, cranked up and turned back toward the base.

He stood there watching the jeep grow small, churning a wake of alkali behind. Then he walked very slowly up on the porch, not looking at me or even at the Blockhouse, only looking inward at whatever landscape a nigger manages to construct in his head. I closed my eyes again and studied wanting to know nothing. It went well. In a moment, I could smell the cool air and was ready for that day's evil. Then he spoke.

Not to me, rather at me. But not even that, really. Spoke rather at large, addressed the desert, the fuming risen sun, whom it might concern. A nigger's way. Avoiding the loneliness of no reply. He needn't have worried. I was too proud to ignore a nigger.

—Any officers hereabouts?

—None I know of.

He glanced at me, that one eye like a cock's, uncommonly coy. Aha, he thought. A Southern man. Well, what? I almost said aloud: Leave it be, Ike. There's nothing in it, I am studying on resignation.

—You from around here?

—Louisiana.

50

—Ah. Never was there. Never was. I come from Virginia.

Sounded like a man avoiding recrimination. Nobody had accused him of ever being in Louisiana. Then I remembered: All niggers are guilty of all crimes. They only wait around till a white man determines in his absolute judgment which one to hang on him. Or in him. Or him on. And I read the Virginia business quick enough. A nigger from Virginia reckons he's better than anything of any color from Carolina on South.

—Youall get anything to eat here?

—Time to time, I said. —They'll bring some eggs and bacon and grits after a while.

I reckoned he was a cook. I didn't feel so; I just reckoned it. I been wrong a couple other times. So it didn't get in the way of my resignation. I was letting go, sending the nigger and his questions off somewhere. He was all right. I just couldn't figure any use for him just then. Something said, anyhow, he wouldn't be very useful. You come across that kind now and again. We would have us a talk sometime.

Jacobs

I thought I would go out again, visit the sands, study the rocks and weeds. There was a glory in them. But I reached the concrete porch, and there he was. Black and tall, hands resting on the single wooden rail that looked like a hitching post for horses and cattle. I smiled. I had never met one before, personally. I wanted to shake his hand, but he only looked at me and then at the other, Boileau. As if they had been talking, talking about the rest of us, and I was the first specimen to crawl out. He had that same air of contempt, that certain wrinkling of the nose as if he smelled a disgusting thing. So I walked on, turning to face the sun, letting it brush my body, my face, with its talons. I loved it. Maybe if the war got over, I would come live here. Maybe I could build a little shack and learn all about the desert. What would Morris say to that? Behind me, I saw them when I turned my head, the black man looking to one side, Boi-

51

leau squatting against the wall, eyes closed, hands hanging down between his legs as if he were about to grapple with himself, despairing of the angel's descent.

Michaelis

The coffee splashed out, and the sugar fell into the eggs, and it was snafu. I paid no mind until we pulled up in front of the Blockhouse and then told the driver, who had also loaded the jeep, to put himself on report. On the porch, two of them were waiting. What the hell are you? I asked the black one.

Poole

What the hell am I? I never expected that. I looked over at Loosian. He still sat with his eyes closed, his fatigues looking more like where he lived than what he lived in. He never opened his eyes, but I could see that grin. I thought, okay, Loosian, I do believe we got to talk sometime.

—I'm a special bombing section candidate, I told the one with the oak leaves and the big black mustache. —Here's my orders.

He took the papers without even knowing I'd handed them to him. The other ones came out, a hairy dumb Zonk looked like he couldn't pee with printed instructions, a plain one with light hair, and that little squint-eyed Jew who looked like he wanted to find him a home. Oh, Lord, what a bunch. And this Jew coming out, sees the one with the leaves and yells, — Tent-hut!

The hairy one and the plain one popped to, with the Jew sticking out his chest, looking like some kind of off-brand

chicken which hadn't took to its feed but had a little grit anyhow. Loosian kind of turned away and lit up a smoke. I saw
him pull on it and blow a long stream out into the heat. He
dropped the pack beside him. It wasn't Luckies. It was Wings,
and I saw him look at the little airplane picture that came on
the pack. Then he put it in his pocket and went on squatting,
his back to us. I went on looking at his back, and there in the
heat, I come cross his mind. It was just as if he had said out
loud; only I knew he hadn't: Shit. Here I am stuck with three
Yankees, a Greek and a nigger. And the nigger is the only one
in the bunch could clean himself with a cob. I got all that and
laughed while the major fooled with my orders, trying to figure
out how I was a German or a Jap spy. Then Loosian sent out
his last message: I must of sinned against God to get stuck in
this. Or maybe that was my message. Or ours.

Boyd

The classes were hell. Michaelis kept us at the math until I
wished I'd gone to class, taken the calculus seriously. Every
kind of instant calculation, drift, windage, characteristics of
various bombs. The Southerner sat at the back, a pencil in his
hand that he never used, eyes almost closed. But he always had
the answer, gave it to Michaelis as if it were a great burden,
more because of its triviality than its difficulty. The Negro did
all right. I noticed, I couldn't help noticing, that he sweated a
lot. By noon his shirt would be dark with perspiration. He sat
just in front of me, hunched over his desk, scratching like a Jap
calligrapher, his shoulders rising and falling. I couldn't take my
eyes off him. And I couldn't help wondering, what's his stake in
this? Why do they have him here? Thinking like that pushed
me into the first conversation with Boileau. That was the price
I paid for my first mistake.

Boileau

—Stake? Same as you, huh? I said. He didn't know, but his question amazed me. I cannot resign myself to Yankee naïveté. I cannot become accustomed to the fact that they are all vicious children, each wholly ignorant of his father's doing, its implications and its consequences. —His stake was made the first day of January, 1863. Mr. Lincoln enlisted him, I said. And laughed just a little.

Boyd frowned at me. He understood my reference. He just couldn't digest it, fit it to his question.

—But . . . why would he want . . . to fight? He . . . hasn't much to fight for.

I shrugged. Play him for an ass, part of my mind said—the part as yet unreconciled, the deep Louisiana part which delighted in confusion, in twists curved in upon twists. Hint at some dark private knowledge shared between you and the nigger. Let him reckon there's ju-ju working. He will if you want him to. But shit, my stoic parts said, you don't know the nigger's game, and it's silly to front for him. Every nigger has his own game, plays with his own personally designed deck. You know that much. Explain patiently to Boyd that this Poole has not yet figured why he enlisted or even how he managed to get into the Air Corps, much less into a special bombardier training unit. Tell him that Poole doesn't know what he's up to yet. Won't know till he's in it. Because your proper nigger never abstracts even when he uses abstract language, and that is why when you, Boyd, and I, Boileau, have swamped ourselves, Poole will be mimicking events which have not happened. Tell him the nigger is a master of an as-yet-uninvented art form called, for the sake of differentiation, prior mimesis.

I blinked and wondered about the heat. I shook out a cigarette and said: —Well, you get patriots in every shape—and color.

And Boyd said: —I respect him for that.

54

I think I dropped the cigarette. And discovered when he drifted away that I had stepped on it, crushed it. I didn't want it anyhow. Poole, sooner or later, we will certainly talk.

Michaelis

Poole was his name. The black. I feigned surprise when I saw his papers. I acted as if it was a mistake. I could see him dwindle even as I looked at him. He lost size, tightened, and what was left when he went down the hall was stone. He would learn what he had to learn. Now.

The astounding one was Krepinski. He was like an animal with a calculator sewn into its head. He had been with the others hardly more than a day, and already each one hated or despised him. Something had passed between him and Boileau—I never discovered what—and they stalked past one another like gunfighters who have not yet decided where and when things will be settled. But the Polack might well be the best of all. It was grotesque, but that was all right, fine. The grotesque wins wars. The Nazis had forged a modern state and a great army out of materials and leaders unfit to floor a latrine. I would watch Krepinski carefully. He might be my star. Which would be no more than the rightful triumph of the grotesque.

The Southerner, Cajun, whatever you called him, was all right. I had seen young racehorses like him. They moped or twitched. He had no motivation, only style. He would do well because he could not really grasp how not to do well. The better bombardiers the rest became, the better he would do. He supposed himself a man of breeding, of superior imagination, but in the showdown he would dump ten tons of bombs on an orphanage and sleep the good sleep afterward. Or, even failing to sleep, would dump again. Because he did not know the grammar, the syntax, by which duty may be questioned or avoided or nullified. He cared nothing for what anyone thought—except himself. And that is where I had him. He was very lonely. Child of an aborted revolution begun and lost by men to whom

55

the very idea of revolution was unpleasant, he had a long trip ahead of him. Probably longer than he could cover. He would end either Rupert or Cromwell, but that was his concern. In the meanwhile he would learn to drop explosives on people with immense precision.

Boyd was a problem. No, I thought he was. I thought, this is the ringer Moseley threw at you knowingly or not. What can you do with a musician? But he enlisted, after all. Something was wrong with the music, then. It had played out for him, perhaps, or the weight of his family and his friends. Something. I had him between lives, and so he might be the easiest to handle. His motivation would lie in the future. When he had done fighting the war, he would find out why he had done it. There were millions like him. They needed the war and had no idea why. Boyd would follow orders. I knew nothing of music, but I knew well enough that no group of twenty men becomes successful by practicing anarchy. He had taken orders, lost himself, fused his own loneliness to that of the saxophones and the drums. Now his sidemen would be pilots and gunners and navigators. He would be just fine.

The black. Poole. He was my arrogance. He would be my virtuoso performance, my chef d'oeuvre. There could be no doubt that he had the seeds of psychosis in him. They needed only to be drawn out, fed. He already believed in magic, felt it, knew it was as real as a white man's rope. He and I knew that. He knew that looks could wound, words could kill. He knew that the forces that bend events are bodiless and serve those who believe in them. If he could do the classroom work, he would be very good indeed. And he would draw the others after him into the darkness. He would want into the Dark Room worse than any of the others, and when I let him in, he would force the others to accept it all as I intended they should. Without him, it could all end a shambles, a joke. Poole would see to that problem. And Moseley would never understand. I remember watching the black during classes. At first I thought he was nervous. It must be the competition, I thought, this proximity of whites. All I knew for sure was that he seemed to . . . get all over things. Not with enthusiasm but with a lunatic intensity that was almost frightening to watch. He did not work: He teemed; he hummed and pawed and scratched. He attacked each problem, each conception as if it were something to rape, to smother, to absorb. He would sit at his desk, his black face expressionless, bathed in sweat, hands twitching, long fingers curling in and out. As he delved for that morsel, that turn that led to his own portal on understanding, he went on seething and muttering, his face breaking into an instant's grin once in a while. *Um. Un. Huh-huh-huh. Aha. Sho. Um-hummmm. Sho. Yeah.*

I never called him down about it, because at the end of his frenzy he would bring me a sheet of paper that looked like a map of some distant galaxy drawn by a demented savant or a modern sketch done by inking the feet of fleas. But the answers were correct. At the end of his labyrinthine jottings, the answer would be right. It was his way. It was magic. Only once I laughed—thinking what a pilot might hear through his intercom along the path of a bombing run. Poole, you black sonofabitch, you will outlast us all, and enjoy the last atom of your being as the evening collapses better than we have savored high noon.

As for Jacobs, the Jew was playing man games. I could sense him trying to deepen his voice, deliver his answers in a clipped noncommittal tone. My God, you could feel him inventing an Anglo-Saxon under that skinny frame of his. I could imagine him on one of his long desert walks. Sitting on the hot sand inspecting those elements that made him what he was, trying to decide what should be kept, what tossed away for the sands to inundate. He feared his own mystery worse than he feared me —or the fetid hatred that smoldered in Krepinski, whose Polish blood signed warrant as one of the only authentic unabstracted anti-Semites on earth. Of them all, Jacobs was the only one I would have spent an evening with except from duty. Not because he was interesting or likable, but because he was human, fully human. His parts were soft. He might grow. If he feared long enough, he might outgrow his fear, learn to sneer at life and death alike in the name of that inner land promised to him once and forever. Of them all, he was the only one who might just possibly become wise.

It would have been a little pleasure to whisper Plotinus to him, suggest that he come quickly to hear the demiurge. But at last the difference between wood and marble, Israel and Macedonia, requires for its bridging a span longer than two lives, a shout louder than I had in mind. Perhaps next time I would be a Jew, he a Greek. Then there would be time for invention. This time, I thought, almost gasping for air in the broiling classroom, we are playing Americans. Which is a full-time myth calling for all the ingenuity either—or both—of us possessed.

I knew all the while what kind of men I had to have. Young men without faith. I wanted men who could lose themselves despite everything in the act of dropping bombs on cities thousands of feet below and who could, even doing it, see themselves as servants of justice. They would need to be, at the very center, potential murderers—or suicides. They would have to have, in some way, abandoned their humanity. I could use a beast or two—perhaps a philosopher, which is to say, a beast turned inside out. A lawyer who has sublimed away all values except those which can be codified. I could use a mathematician, better yet: an accountant. And aliens, I needed aliens. Men who, having no real bond with this American soil, would serve it all the better, hoping that wholesale violence against another country and people would bring them closer to their own.

If I was right, you could take disrupted men, parts and fragments of men unaware of their fragmentation, and press them up against mystery. Make them, in their vacuum of belief, come to believe in magic. Who comes to distrust material more than a materialist? Who realizes the limits of reason better than a rationalist? Who can tell you better the pathos of sensuality than a beast? Every man is lonely, dissatisfied with his life, and from that loneliness and dissatisfaction comes all political—and military—power. What if one were to choose those who, in some way dissatisfied, could be made whole for a little while, given the overwhelming power of, say, a bombardier?

How can you know you are in heaven unless you are actively contributing to the creation and continuation of hell? What they will understand is that they are saved—because they are there, above the sky, instead of down below in the exploding streets of someone's city. If one of them should fall, the others will know without asking that he, the one who fell, somehow lost faith, ceased to believe and so had no support but wings and engines and fuselage. If they come to believe that, they will be great. In the way of bombardiers. I leave it to others to train pilots and navigators, though the principle is the same. But my people will learn to bomb as no one has ever learned to do it before. And in the end, they will bring me a star.

They would never have been in just this shape before. They would never be this way again. Two weeks without anything to do. No balls or bats, no radios, no books, no movies, no women, just the Dark Room there at the end of the passageway with the impassive MP in front of the door who would answer no question, pay no attention to anyone or anything until time for his relief, only staring back down the corridor toward the screen door, toward the sun, the sprawled empty desert.

By the end of those two weeks they would be insane to know what was behind the door, would have determined by process of elimination that it was not money or a prisoner or the like. Would have settled on *weapon*. But what kind? The rest didn't matter. Let them sweat. All greatness is the offspring of discipline. Energies must be gathered, centered, conserved for use. Each bit of energy wasted means a lessoning of determination, concentration. For the next few months these spiritual basket cases would be anchorites, monks chanting mathematical formulas, studying aerial photos as if they were an illuminated *Book of Hours*. They would bathe in the chill dawn, eat sparingly, genuflect within themselves when they passed the Black Door. And when I was done, they would go overseas. To fly over Germany. To be ordained.

When I had chosen the last one, Moseley looked at their dossiers and sniffed.

—Why the nigger? he asked.

—The nigger may be supreme, I said. —He might be the best of all. If not the idiot.

—What idiot?

—The Polack. From New York. He's a classic.

Moseley shook his head slowly. —I think this whole crazy deal is going to bomb out. I should never . . .

—All right, fine. Want to call it off? I asked him. —Junk the bet?

—No, he said. I want to see what . . . happens. You're crazy as hell, but—

—But what?

—You're not stupid.

No, not stupid. At least perceptive enough to see that the

men I had chosen would all, in some way, some sense, have within them the shriveled seeds of psychosis lying, awaiting the magic warmth that could start them growing. How would it go? Why, the nigger would sweat buckets to learn how to bomb white men. The Southerner would discover how to hallucinate and dream that down there was New York, Grant's Tomb, Sherman's statue, and millions of Yankees to doom. The Jew would be, as such things go, sane. Bombing Germans. Only for God, not for the United Jewish Appeal. For that bearded monstrosity that had grabbed hold of him four millennia ago. The New Yorker would be the maddest of all: killing from an abstract thirty thousand feet enemies (abstract) of democracy— all of it as clean and distant and unreal as if it were happening inside his head, which is the only place his democracy exists. As for the Pole, no problem. The Pole was my straw man. What could I teach him? He was psychotic from the first. Violence was life to him. The beast magic would have him rutting and thundering to abolish life whenever I chose to point him. He was a slave as every man is a slave who cannot control what genetics has made him heir to. There was in him a hatred that burned in all directions because from all sides his blood had been abused, abased. He hated Jacobs most of all because of the motion, the sad freedom, the certain seeking the Jew represented. If it were not for the hatred, the Pole could collapse into catatonia.

But before that, before any of them was satisfied or ruined, we would be over Germany. Down there would be the canvas upon which my journeymen would practice their art. Until they were masters and I had my triumph and my star.

Krepinski

They sent us some beer and I matched Boyd for one of his and the coon-assed bastard ignored his till I took both of them. So I had five. It was okay. I drank till dark and then went out and sat on a crate just at the square of light falling beyond the door. You had to watch for the snakes. There were snakes everywhere. They waited for you. I counted in my head how many snakes might be within a mile of us. You wouldn't believe it. I tried to get one of the guards to lend me his .45. Or rent it. I wanted to kill one of them, just one.

Then the nigger came out. He stood in the square of light at the door. He didn't see me. Then he went off into the darkness, and before he had taken ten steps, he was gone. Not faded away. One minute you saw him. Then he wasn't. He never even saw me. Or didn't pay any attention to me. I drank the fourth beer. I thought about the nigger. You looked at a nigger and right away you wanted to do something. I don't know. Seeing a nigger made you want to. Hit him, call him over and tell him something he had to do. I thought how I'd like to take care of him, see to it he stayed put. Jesus, I don't know. In New York we knew how.

Then this Jew bastard comes out. He looks all around and then walks off. Like he was drunk. On two beers. He kind of staggers into the darkness. For a minute I didn't think anything. I had that last beer. I drank it. Then I felt bloated. I thought, if the nigger and the Jew will walk in the dark, you'll walk in the dark. There aren't any snakes. They stay in at night. You don't have to worry about snakes.

I walked, and when I was a little way from the Blockhouse, it was like they turned on the sky. It wasn't dark. The sky was full of stars. Not faded and fuzzy, but sharp, like thousands of little teeth shining up there. And the moon was down on the edge of the world like it was a weak sun rising. You could see everything outlined, see a long way. You could see bushes and rock and the folds of sand laying like a wrinkled sheet. I looked back, and the Blockhouse was small, white, alone back there. It looked like a dead skull you found behind the stock pens; only light came from its eye sockets as if it was dead but still could see and know what you were doing.

I must have walked a mile, not paying any attention to where I was going till I noticed I was headed for a big pile of rock, the only big thing in sight.

It was just a pile of rock, a lot of stuff sticking up out of the sand like a crashed plane. I got close to it before I heard. It was something funny. It sounded like a steam engine or something mechanical. Like the generator my old man ran to power the jackhammer back home. Maybe they're drilling for oil out here, I thought. Texas is sand floating on oil, the bastards. Hah. Somebody was drilling okay.

When I heard the sound, I moved out a way. I didn't want to come up hard on some guy. I moved out almost a block and then made the corner of the pile of rocks. And there they were. There they were.

The nigger was kind of sitting in an angle of the rock. His arms were thrown out on either side, resting on the rock. He was staring out into the desert, where if you looked, stars were drifting out of the sky toward where it met the sand. On his left hand, the moon was coming up, red and big. On his right hand, behind me, was the Blockhouse, white and little.

And there was the Jew. He was sitting in the sand a little distance from the nigger. He was talking, talking loud. He had his hands going, gesturing, pointing like he was calling on God to witness something. His voice was whiny, like he was trying to make an alibi for something. Shit, I don't know. It was like *Tarzan and the Secret Kingdom* where the black king sits up above with all the white people down there worshiping and twisting and turning. But the black king never smiles. Even doing that stuff, they couldn't make him happy. So at the end they killed him and Tarzan told them not to have a king anymore. That black sonofabitch.

But the Jew was down there. His shoulders moved, hunched and thrown back, jabbering, jabbering, going on and on. Up above, the nigger had his shirt unbuttoned and just stood or sat there. He didn't have any expression. It was like he was alone, waiting for something that would be a long time coming. What the Jew was saying didn't matter one way or the other.

It was the Jew I wanted to kill. The nigger wasn't human; it didn't make any difference. But the Jew was worse than the people in the movie. I thought, if the guard had lent me his .45, if I had it now, I'd shoot the Jew in his head. Then I laughed and started backing up, moving away toward the Blockhouse. Thinking if I hit the Jew in the head, I'd splash him all over the nigger. I laughed out loud then so they must have heard me, and I started running, laughing, till I saw that square of light at the Blockhouse door. Then I slowed down and walked up to it. He was still there, the Southerner. When I got to the door, he was looking out at the moon. I turned to look. It was high now, and white and looked cold. The Southerner looked at me. Even in the darkness, you could feel those yellow eyes on you. They looked like an animal's eyes. Or like water in the ocean, cold, not caring about anything. But I didn't hate him then. I looked back at him and laughed one more time. Then I went in and found somebody's glass still half full of beer. I drank it and went back to the room and fell asleep.

Boyd

In the evening sometimes, without notice, Michaelis would appear again suddenly from Main Base. He would have the current mute MP lug a 16-mm projector into the wardroom, and there against the wall he would display German propaganda films from the Spanish war and the beginning of the war against Poland and France. We sat silent, listening to the creaking of the sprockets and Michaelis' occasional comments as the Condor Legion blasted Guernica into rubble. As Rotterdam and Amsterdam and Warsaw and a million nameless towns and trains and aerodromes and truck convoys and road junctions and troop concentrations blossomed into grainy puffs of black smoke. Heinkels roared over by the hundreds. Stukas poised like hawks and then plunged downward, spewing out black bombs from under their wings. I would watch, fascinated, unable to believe so many planes had done this so often, were yet doing it.

—This is nice work, Michaelis was saying. —You can see planes on the ground, taxiing, if you look closely. Now watch.

And a dive bomber slithered down diagonally across the screen, spat its cargo and zoomed upward while the film followed that rack of bombs down, caught them exploding among the toy planes, blasting buildings and runways into clouds of dark smoke.

Then the film moved to a ground shot. It was a panorama of total and unmitigated destruction. The camera panned block after block of anonymous rubble, smoking, forlorn, untenanted. No one walked past or stood around. No one was looking for a child or poking among the piled bricks for a favorite lampshade or bathrobe. Block after block of nothing. Then the film stopped, froze on an intersection where a wall had toppled over on a small cab.

—Recognize it? Michaelis' voice came out of the dark. —Anybody know where we are?

There was a negative monotone as I looked around to see Michaelis, only a shadow behind the projector, smoke of his cigar floating out, breaking up and dissolving the projector's tight beam. Then he allowed the film to go on, and we saw looming behind smoke and mist and distance the bulk of a long building with a tower at one end.

—Parliament, Boileau said an instant before me. —That's London. You're looking toward the river from the north.

—Right, Michaelis said, as the film began its pointless searching again amid ruins, emptiness, total destruction. —This is what bombers have done to the greatest city in the world. This is only part of it. The film could run for ten hours and not survey all the damage. What's left of London is underground. They've driven the government virtually off the face of the earth. With bombs. No German soldier has set foot on English soil. They don't need to. No English infantryman has fired a shot at the Germans on his own land. He probably never will.

The lights went up and Michaelis was gone. The MP loaded the equipment and moved on. Leaving us there in the wardroom alone, studying one another, each thinking how it would feel to destroy a city one has never set foot in.

I went down to my room and turned on the radio one of the guards had bootlegged in. We took turns with it. It was late evening now, and chill as the day was hot. It made you wonder how in God's name people had ever settled down here. And why. Over the radio came Glenn Miller.

> Soldier, let me read your letter,
> Let me pretend it's mine . . .

I thought what kind of letter could I send from here?

Dear Sandy, I wrote to this girl I had dated in Connecticut when I could get off the band for a night. They've put me in a lunatic asylum. An ape tells me the resident kike is in love with the darky, and there is this Greek captain who thinks he's Agamemnon, and a shade out of the swamps who has complete recall of every event between 1612 and 1865, and who, if they train him well, would rather bomb Manhattan than Berlin. It's war, honey. It already is. The Huns or Japs—whoever draws us —will be a relief. It was Miller again, and I thought, Frank Dailey, thanks for the Meadowbrook. Glen Island, thanks for the Casino. Atlantic City, thanks for the Steel Pier. Thanks for the memory.

> . . . pink cocktail for a blue lady,
> And waiter, don't tell her it's from me.

What could have possessed that Austrian Charlie Chaplin to send me to Pilsbury, Texas?

I lay back and tried to forget the cold. I made believe I was in a steam bath or under a sun lamp. I tried to pretend I could hear the solid swat of a tennis ball on a clay court. Or Will Swartz's clarinet leading us into "Moonlight Serenade." But all I heard was the distant roar of planes landing or taking off at Main Base, and the cold wasn't the kind you paid for. It was free; it was Texas. My country, they said on the radio in a spot for war bonds and stamps. And I hated every inch of it.

> . . . lonely lovely lady was once
> the toast of Vienna
> when Vienna was gay. . . .

Boileau

I was going into the wardroom where the radio was playing some popular music when Michaelis came in the front.

—Get the others, he said. —Tell them to meet me at the Dark Room. It's time.

The Dark Room. He'd never mentioned it. That room had no name. But we understood that it was the locked room with the guard. I looked into the wardroom and saw Boyd lying sprawled in a chair, looking asleep and simpleminded. —Get the others. Michaelis wants us. In the Dark Room.

—The Dark . . .

—Yes.

He got up and walked past me. I turned down the other way and stopped at the room where Poole and Jacobs and Boyd stayed. Jacobs was there. He sat on the edge of his bed as if he were already expecting a summons.

—The Dark Room, I told him. Then I stood for just a moment longer trying to imagine what he knew or did not know. One of his textbooks lay open on the bed next to him. Its margin was covered with tiny ciphers. He looked up at me.

—Yes? he asked.

—Nothing, I said, and turned away, not knowing what, if anything, I had meant to ask. Or say. I was irritated by his "yes." I should have been gone before he uttered it. But there was something. Perhaps ju-ju was here and operating. I smiled to myself as I walked back toward the Dark Room thinking, that poor little creature has never heard of the Kabala. The witch of Endor and Samuel's shade would shake at the impious thought of him. He has drained the pottage to its dregs, and if Abraham has sons, they would be Poole and Boileau before Jacobs. That is a fact in 1942. Then I noticed that the course of my mind had placed the nigger ahead of myself. Which was curious, wasn't it? Then I had reached the Dark Room, and the sight of it open and unguarded, black door ajar, so took me aback that other magic was forgotten and I went inside to see what Michaelis the thaumaturge might have to offer his novitiates.

Michaelis

Nothing. That was the heart of it. It had been part of the deal when I said, —All right, fine. But my way. My way involved certain magic. The Dark Room. The locked door. Even the guard. Nothing was lost. The room was unneeded, the lock cost thirty-five cents, and the guard would have been playing solitaire in barracks if I hadn't found a use for him. The magic, unlike other shifts, was infallible. It could not fail because it was not exterior to these people. The colored and the Jew, even the Cajun in his way—all took it at face value. They knew it was magic. That a lock and a guard before an anonymous room certain not to contain money, jewels or a woman had to contain a great secret. Boyd understood it to be military security— which is to say the magic of foolish and disillusioned men who can already smell death in their civilization—if not in themselves. Magic of the machine. One deals with each tribe as it is given to one to deal. I preferred, I suppose, Krepinski, who would have seen the Dark Room as a place to be opened, to be violated in good season. And what I had to show them would please Krepinski immensely. You cannot keep a secret from the Krepinskis. They know where the magic lives. They know who the ghosts are, and if Krepinski were challenged to a séance, he would produce something to break a mystic's heart. What I had to show them would be all things to each of them, but Krepinski, understanding absolutely nothing, would use it as it was intended to be used, and then, staring down through thirty thousand feet of marvel, he would see the magic and smile and worship it sincerely, and please the father of spells. Which was me, or my agent who might be—who knows?—my superior.

—This, I told them, —is the Norden Bombsight. You will use it. You will guard its central optical component with your life and destroy it if your plane is hit. It is the chief secret apparatus of this government—no, this nation. It will wipe out Nazi and Japanese expansionism and clean the world of dictators. In your hands, it will do miracles. From thirty thousand feet you can obliterate anything you can see. Your training has equipped you for no earthly purpose but to handle this weapon. When you've finished aerial training, you will be worth a fortune. You will be part of the weapon. There will be a plane, a B-17 or B-24, ten men, tons of bombs, six guns—all to ensure that you do your job. Which is to fire those bombs into the target. You have to understand this. Do you understand this?

They nodded and make sounds of assent. I paused. Thinking that the Norden Bombsight was perhaps a better instrument than a two-foot length of hollow lead pipe, but not a great deal better. It was a collection of knobs and setscrews, lenses and cross hairs. It was bulky, easily jolted out of calibration. It was all right, no more. But, Oh, God, it was magic. You could see it in their faces. Boileau tried to resist. But he couldn't. This is what he saw: a room painted flat black, ceiling, walls and floor. Even the shelves along the wall were painted flat black. The sight itself was black, too. Perhaps twenty-four inches high, thirty-six long, eighteen wide. An eyepiece jutted upward from it, and there were various controls here and there. Only a glint or two of milled steel broke the perfection of blackness. Poole stepped forward to touch it, his face as somber as if the sight were a portal to the gas chamber. His hands vanished as he touched it. Behind him, Jacobs took a step. Then he stopped, head down, staring at the reflectionless black floor between his small shoes.

Krepinski was chewing on a match. He had heard nothing. He lounged, waiting for me to assign a sight to him. He could wait.

Boileau was sweating, looking mildly ill—or was it disgusted? Did he realize what was happening and realize too that it was irreversible? Now he surely knew why the Blockhouse and the isolation. He knew it, but he would say nothing because that oldest part of him, spawned in France and slit-eyed as Descartes, was gobbled in the new part, which was older still: gotten in heat and miasma, fever swamp and the scuttling of animals. A rationalist who believed in magic. The heretic could never win against the tribesman. He would go up into the sky for me. And then he would forget his mind for a while and be glad. And much later, if he lived, his sense of the ridiculous would give him stories he could never tell grandchildren, but which would carry him laughing in good humor wherever those latter days might lead. Someone said, Paris is worth a mass. But not a black mass, and Boileau knew that. Now. Not ten minutes ago. But now. A black mass is worth more than Paris—or Helen either.

Krepinski

They never let me have one in school. I wanted one. They gave my sister one. But they put me in mechanical arts and no biology, so you never got to use one without you took biology.

Now I had this thing. It was different, but it was like one. I remembered I had looked in my sister's. It was another world in there. —That's a paramecium, she said.

—What? I asked.

—Never mind. A tiny bug.

—Gimme something I can stick it with, I said.

—Don't be silly. It's too small. You can't touch it.

—No way?

—No way. Why do you want to always hurt things?

—I dunno. There's got to be a way.

Then she tossed her hair and pushed me away. You know I hated that thing. A long thing with little tiny legs. But you couldn't hurt it. Like a girl in the eleventh grade. It didn't even know you were there. Staring in at it. At least with the girl you could go by in assembly and let your hand cup her ass, or in a crowd between classes, you could feel her cunt, grab her tits and slide off before she could spot you. But this thing in there, it was alone, and you couldn't make it afraid or know you were going to do something to it.

The bombsight was different. It was fine, and pretty soon I'd be looking down it, seeing things. And I could get to them. I didn't care about biology anymore. Mechanical arts was just fine. I thought, Blow it, sis. And I thought of the nigger and the Jew and pretended I had them in the cross hairs, lined up against that low hot moon. It was fine. It felt good.

Poole

They had us drop bags full of flour into circles for two weeks, and then they give us some little piss-ant bombs and we dropped them on shacks they made out of lathe and canvas painted. In about two months, we was as good at it as we was going to get, and Michaelis come by one afternoon to the Blockhouse and says, —All right, fine. You are ready and done good. They going to give you wings and a assignment.

But no leave, that mother. Cause he knew. He flat knew. That major son wasn't no kind of Zonk at all. They didn't bring him up South or North, and I could tell ole Boil-o knew it too. No leave. Three days on the base, and we was going out. Wherever. I said to Boil-o, —Which way you reckon?

—Sun behind us, it'll be England. In front, Hawaii. You gonna know when we fly, boy. It's in the stars.

I laughed. We did all right, me and Boil-o. I wanted to ask and tell. But not yet. Wasn't near ripe. We was still tight. After a couple trips, over a pair of quarts. I'd know. I wanted to ask him how come he knew about that girl and what I was supposed to do with his fifty-cent piece. I might even ask him about what he wanted me to do with his Jew. But later. Truth was, on Main Base, I couldn't even go in the officers' club. I had a pair of gold bars and some silver wings with ole stud bomb in the center, but I had to drop it in a little kind of cutoff place for colored officer personnel, and I didn't want to yell at Boil-o through a beaverboard partition. Wouldn't fit. I knew what would be coming later. We would get closer, right through that beaverboard, whether we liked it or not. That was part of what I figured in the Dark Room. Lord, what all went on in there. In the meantime, I reckoned to drop me something hard on the way east or west. Three days and a hundred dollars. Town of Pilsbury a mile from Main Base, and what they called targets of opportunity. Little advance payment for what I was just naturally going to do when they sent me east or west.

Michaelis

It was Boileau, of course. And I never, in the next thirty months, remembered to brace him, squeeze him to find out how he found out. He was just there at my quarters in the early morning, leaning against the door. Candy woke me. —One of your people is outside. Lieutenant Boileau. He says it's important. I'd never thought of any of them as officers. Lieutenant Boileau. A creature I had constructed impersonating an officer. I got up, kissed her, pulled off her pajama top. —Wait for me, I said. —Just a minute.

It was two years and more she had to wait, and much later I found out she had not waited two hours. Which was expected. A beautiful woman who is faithful will end up killing you in your bed. One way or another. You've had the best, now take the rest, they say. Settle for looks. Never mind about her spare time. You should have more to think about than that.

—If you want your nigger to make the trip, you better go see to him, Boileau said.

He had gone to a white whorehouse. The girls didn't mind, but some of the troops objected plenty. Only Poole had thrown three of them out into the street. Then he whipped some wop who was trying to explain something to him, and finally the word hit the street, and then came the Marvin County sheriff's deputy whose job paid a little extra to keep order in that house, and who would have shot Poole without a word except that when he arrived, Poole was in bed with his (the deputy's) favorite playmate and anyhow still had on his jacket with the gold bars. The deputy would claim that Poole had gone crazy, and he had something going for him on that point.

Because only a crazy colored ever went to a white whorehouse in Pilsbury, Texas, to begin with. Not to mention the three troops he broke up—or the pimp he dispossessed from his own quarters. Or choosing the deputy's girl or not even taking off his tunic. Or that last little fillip that the guinea pimp told the deputy: about Poole standing over the girl, cupping his hand over his eye as if it were a bombsight, laughing like a lunatic, shouting "bombs away," and dropping into her like a ton of fragmentation.

When I got to the jail, I was glad Boileau had suggested taking the Military Police. Even with five of them, it was touchy. Until the sheriff saw their Thompson submachine guns, he wasn't even listening to me. —I thought they hired you fellers to fight the Japs, he said angrily.

—Whatever's right, I told him. —Right now I want my boy. So Pilsbury, which was wide-awake and ready, gave way. Otherwise it might have been a three-front war.

Then we were at the planes. It was time to go. They were all there. Except Boileau, who turned up only seconds before he would have been a fugitive from military justice. —How did it go? he asked, throwing his duffel bag up into the plane and climbing after it. I looked at him for a long moment.

—We brought him out, I said. —What did you expect?

—That you'd bring him out. You didn't take him this far just to let some Texas shit kickers do for him before you got a chance to see . . .

—See what? I asked, thinking about Candy, wondering why she had not at least called the ready room.

—Just see, he smiled. Then we buckled down, and the first part was over.

II

Boyd

They put us at Gatwick for a week or two. Later we would move to a field in Kent close to Maidstone, and before we had done, they would station us with the 203d Bomb Wing of the Eighth Air Force based near East Grinstead. But always within the great silent umbra of London. We all felt it: the nearness of that dim gigantic old city. She was wounded and still smoking here and there under the ruins of 1940. She had still to endure the buzz bombs. But she had great power. I went up every week. It was some kind of magic to arrive in Victoria Station and walk out past the statue of Foch, stroll toward Buckingham Palace. There were shops and stores, some with boarded fronts, but still selling. I walked down the Strand, stopping at the bombed-out churches, wondering why Charing Cross Station wasn't located in Charing Cross Road. Or why all the bookshops were.

When I went to London, I tried to put the base out of mind. Not just the missions: the whole business. It was very bad. Everyone was insane, but our group soon had the name of chief lunatics. One English officer swore to God he had heard one of us reciting magical incantations over the flight radio. And Michaelis, who was chief bombing officer, had said most casually, —Why not?

But we were very popular, too. Because we hit our targets. First time every time. No pilot wanted to go back to the same target two days running because on that second day, the Jerries would be ready with fighters and flak. Losses could run forty percent, sometimes more. So that bombing accuracy was considered in the same light with salvation. And Michaelis' group was the unit that could deliver it. The best, to my complete bewilderment, was Krepinski. He began to be something of a legend and within four months was a first lieutenant. He could see

75

through clouds, they said. Absolutely deadeye. Any altitude, day or night. Any flak density. Even fighters didn't trouble him. He bombed. And when he came home, he would eat for an hour, drink for another two, and go to bed. In a few months, he had become astonishingly fat. Someone nicknamed him Goering, and the name stuck. Goering over Frankfurt. Why not? It came to that, didn't it?

Jacobs

The first time. It was early morning when we crossed France, and there was no light except the dim blue of control panels. Finney, the pilot, kept telling us where we were. —Karlsruhe-Durlach, seventy miles. Clear. Haze gathering. I can see it, the Rhine. Looks like the maps. I sat out there ahead of them all, the first man crossing into Germany, thinking, I am Harold Jacobs, second lieutenant, United States Army Air Corps, serial 1736641. And thinking, no, you are an escaped Jew, and we know how to deal with escaped Jews. You escaped hidden in your grandfather's scrotum, arriving in that other place in 1889. But now you are back and we will see to you. Welcome to Germany. And thinking, no, no. This time I'm on top. Grandfather sends regards from Hebrew Rest in Queens, and in twenty minutes I will send down his judgment. On all of you. All of you. Then I heard one of the waist gunners: —Me 109's. Nine o'clock, coming in fast.

The whole plane shook. The sky and the earth trembled. I could hear the guns. I reached over the sight and tripped the fifty that swung ahead of me. It pulsed under my hands, and I was ready. Behind, more than one gun was firing. The top turret was going. I could hear the whine of its electric motor. In my earphone, there was a gabble of voices, parts of sentences. Someone called out "score," and then I saw a gray shape materialize out ahead of me, flying in the same direction. It was one of their fighters. It was smoking, and pieces of metal seemed to leap from its fuselage. On the sides were straight-edged black crosses trimmed in white. On the tail, in a white circle, was that other cross, twisted, like the claws of a hungry animal reaching out to destroy. Then the smoke widened, hiding the plane as it began to fall, turning end over end, falling down toward that light haze that covered the earth below. —Score, Finney called. —Good work. That's our first. All right, heading for the slot. Jacobs, forget the gun. Get set up.

I was set up. I was bent over the sight, a small aerial photo map beside me on a clipboard with the target area marked. It was an ordnance factory north of Karlsruhe. I leaned into the sight, turning, adjusting. Waiting for the forms on the clipboard to appear in my sight. Thinking, this is mad. What are you doing here? Is this the work of a wise man? And ready, hold it, Finney. Bay doors open. Hold, left two degrees. I see it. I see it. I see it. And, now, on it. Hold, hold, hold. Bombs. Away.

My hand dropped the bomb release toggle. I was lying across the sight, my whole body welded to it, loving it, feeling myself, the plane, the world, lightening, rising higher and higher. Deanna Durbin. Trombones. All the towers of New York falling on them down there. Breaking the Friedrichs and the Wilhelms and the Manfreds. I could feel those finned tubes of steel chalked with crewmen's illiterate obscenities, streaking down through the cold air, about to send them a new century. Then the picture on my clipboard, transferred into the sight, began to blossom like sick flowers, gray, white, black, with centers of throbbing red and yellow. Like the moon, with black all around, stars bursting, the Trylon and Perisphere booming over them. And in my ears, someone back in the plane yelling, —Jesus Christ, I swear I can feel it. But, no, he couldn't. It was flak he felt, the puffy mirror image of what I had sent down rising again to meet us. But the plane only bucked and shuddered and went on, beginning now to bank, to turn slowly back. So that I could see my picture beginning to fade, to fall away, its smoky blossoms tearing as they rose into a shelf of wind below us. Oh, God, I was relieved and ashamed. Knowing what I must have done, must have sowed. Then I stood up, almost tearing away my mask and equipment. Thinking as if it were revelation:

> This is why they have their cross,
>   twisting,

And we have the white star.
Christ is dying down there.
The universe is born.

Born in explosion, born like a child whose single-celled egg is
bombed by father's long tubular sperm falling at him from con-
tinents away. This is not killing; it is conception. Stars act this
way. Stars burn. Worlds live in the burning. And then I fell
backward on my stool and slept amidst the gray morning, awak-
ening to calls of distance and the names of places like Paris and
Calais, Dover, and a patch of ground where they did not shoot
and we did not bomb so that everyone agreed it must be home.

Boyd

Later I would be able to put it together like a narra-
tive. But not then. Before, it had gone so neatly, so precisely. I
should have known: not in the event. All those smooth prac-
tices are to keep you on the track so that no matter what happens, you know what comes next. So when the bomb bay doors
hung, and we lost a flight engineer who fell opening them, fell
and opened his parachute right into a flak burst so that the next
plane behind and down three thousand reported seeing something like a side of slaughtered beef float past in a parachute
harness, I kept moving on the checklist, watching the template,
spotting the railroad yards outside Durlach, dumping within a
fraction of a fraction of a second right on the money while a
dose of flak took off a piece of our port wing and flecked the
whole left side of the plane like a gigantic shotgun. It was all
right. It wasn't as frightening as I had expected, and you didn't
think of the people down there. Why should you? They'd
begged for it. Now they were getting capital and interest for
what they had done to London in 1940. This was our summer.
This was ours, and it was all right. That's what I wrote to
Sandy, saying, Sweetest, tell your father we use a lot of that gas
rationed away from him to broaden our education. Today we

visited Karlsruhe, a town on the Rhine in Germany. They'll
never ever forget us . . .

Boileau

It was cold. My God, even with the flying suit, the fur-
lined boots and gloves, it was cold as the bottom of Dante's hell.
Maybe, I thought, we are all betrayers and Satan has swallowed
us down. Was it this cold that December at Fredericksburg? Is
that where the engorgement began? But as we neared the
Rhine, I reached forward and cleared my gun, drew out the optical component from the chamois case we kept it in until we
were approaching target. I inserted it with a smooth satisfactory
click. The sound triggered something in my memory. What?
The sound of a rifled musket being cocked? The sound of a
door being opened? Or closed? Those and more, I thought, as
the word came through my headphones. We're on it, Frenchie.
Put your thumb in their eye. Then I saw him. The German.
Heading straight at us from perhaps a thousand yards off.
Fighter. Twelve o'clock. Dead on, I shouted, forgetting to press
my throat mike. As it got closer, I could tell: it was a Focke-
Wulf 190. And as I reached for my gun, he fired. Our tracers
crossed each other, moving up and down, seeking like long un-
certain fingers, like lines in a magic lantern show illustrating
the principles of Euclid. Above me, I could hear them yelling.
The pilot, the copilot. Then the turret turned, and another set
of tracers swept out to join mine. Out there, on or near the
fighter, my line and those from above met. The German plane
seemed to stop, to buck, to blur, all its edges becoming unclear.
Then it exploded, and our plane was passing through a cloud
of smoke and debris which rattled heavily against the plexiglas
nose pod. But I was already sighting, finding a focus on the
earth, matching lines and squares, roads and blocks of buildings. The flak began to rise, but it caused no problem. I picked
up the factory. Not because of the main buildings along the rail
spur. They had done something to them. But the outlying

79

buildings, the inventory sheds, the rail spur itself. You cannot camouflage the whole world, I thought. What it is will show through. How can you hide a single place when everything surrounding it points to where, in its very absence, it must be. I asked for a ten-second hold, got it, and they were gone. But I didn't sit up, move away from the sight. Because we were moving over another target area, a railyard, and the forward planes' bombs were just lighting, beginning to punctuate that stylized landscape I knew as well as a map of New Orleans, from studying it day after day. It was lovely bombing. The rails vanished. The roundhouse ruptured into smoke and rubbish. You could see rolling stock rising, turning slowly in the air, and falling back. It was slow-motion and graceful as a ballet. What you could not see was the brakemen and stationmaster and freight handlers dissolving like brittle flowers. Or the *Hausfrau* pushing her big shabby baby carriage down the Bahnhofstrasse on her way to shop as the world ended at eight thirteen on a June morning. But I could see it. And had seen it since that first day in the Dark Room. And was resigned to it. My apologies had been directed at first to God, then to mankind. At last I apologized to myself for the violence being done me. The apology was grudgingly accepted, and that was that. I had begun back at the base to read a volume about the Roman settlement of Britain, the destruction of Celtic art. It seemed more real than the destruction we were engaged in. Events become real only as time cures them, anneals them, melts them into perspective and place. I was still mulling Appomattox. I thought then that I would leave it to my great-grandchildren to search this mess, this second Great War, and despise or honor as they decided.

Then we banked and were ready to go back. And the flak hit. It burst below and behind the nose bubble, and I felt the plane buck and rise even as the fragments hit me, knifing through my suit like tiny needles, like birdshot catching up with a chicken thief on the run. Then, from behind me, came the roar of the explosion, an instant of silence broken only by the sigh of wind rushing into the fuselage through the hole blown out near the navigator's area. Then the shrieks of those wounded but not killed, howls of demons tasting the full certainty of damnation's loneliness, their voices more terrible because I could hear them both down the length of the fuselage and through my headphones simultaneously. As I tried to rise, to turn again and help, I could see an enormous billow of dark smoke spreading below, and I thought, they've got us. This is the price of the brakemen and the *Hausfrau*. And you can believe it or not, but still trying to turn, twisting loose from the rubber umbilical cord that bound me to the oxygen system, I was resigned to that, too, and proud to a fault in that instant that I could discover not the slightest desire to be squatting again amidst heat and strange spaces under the sun against the pocked stucco wall of the Blockhouse. Because, I remember thinking, I am beyond that. So I broke the rubber hose and climbed back to find the radioman's head gone, the navigator bleeding to death out of an empty eye socket, and the flight engineer dangling in his harness from the top turret, legs shot away, and swinging, gently dead, over a ragged razor-edged steel abyss at the bottom of which I could see all Germany in flames.

Then I felt myself falling toward that great wound, my hands and legs useless, and found, like a pebble lying in the front of my mind, resignation for that, too, and thought, now you've done it, and there's no way left to die, and then there was nothing at all.

Poole

One thing you got to give 'em. Them English didn't have no prejudice on color. They didn't have no use for me because I was a American. I laughed. You got to laugh. They come on with them heavy looks on account they thought I was what nobody from Bangor to San Diego was anywhere near letting me be. How about a case of mistaken identity? Youall both mistaken: I got no identity. Girl serving what they call stout in what they call pub says, —What you here for, answer me that? I kind of smile easy and lean over the bar. She ain't much, but she beats a hot towel full of Vaseline.

—I come to save you, honey, I said. —My idea is saving. She just look kind of stoned and drew another armful of pitchers with that stout stuff. I sat and drank till I couldn't feel my feet.

81

Then some more till my legs and knees went. When it got to my belly, I cut it and started out. We got the first trip the next morning, and I can't use no Zonk officer laying it on me about responsibilities. Makes you want to save some of the load and drop it as you come over for your landing approach.

But as I got up, there was this English with a eye patch and some ribbons. He kind of pushed me out of the way to get my stool ahead of somebody else. I said, —Watch it, buddy. It's all yours. And he come back with something, I don't know, you can't understand one word in ten the way they say them, but it ended with NIGGER. Which never bothered me. Boileau used it. Some of the others used it. It was just a word. But this English, he makes it sound bad, makes it sound like NIGAR, rhymed to cigar. And it hit me: I ain't no nigar, and I hit him. Caught him so fine right in the throat. He looked sad and tired and commenced throwing up all he'd drunk, which was plenty, and before anybody could go to taking care of me, this English I hit was throwing up on everybody. Caught the men on both sides, fella trying to hit me, barmaid who'd asked me what I was here for. I never in my life saw anybody toss like that. Must have been carrying a month's rations in his craw, and while he ruined the place, I kind of snaked on out of there.

Five A.M. and they start using me. See what I can do with that box. Like as if that son Michaelis didn't know all the way from his root to his snoot already.

It come on five A.M. unnatural soon. I had laid down still laughing over that English, and here was Jacobs, my old Jew roommate, shaking me. —Go on, I said. —Not now. Go on.

—It's time, he whispers, like we was planning to run off together.

—It's time when I say it's time, I told him. —I'm going to bust your ass, Jew boy. But then I come around and looked at the dial on that watch they give us. Sure enough. Time to mount up.

—How about some coffee? Jacobs says, trying to get his voice down to where it would sound hearty and man to man.

—Fine, I told him. —I'll see you in the ready room.

I stretched and looked out. It was daylight. In the summer over there, you hardly have any night. But the winter makes up for it. I pulled on the underwear and the flying suit and thought, well, now you gonna see whether that box is genuine gre-gre or jus a piece of iron where the Zonks clunked out again. What about that, nigar?

We come over Karlsruhe just the way it looked on the map. A lot of straight lines and stuff beside this river. They had me down for the docks, and I slipped in that little telescope and went to looking. There they were, and I started telling this pilot from Oklahoma somewhere how to move.
—What? he asks over the phone.
—Don't gimme no shit, I said. —You know what I'm puttin' down.
—Big bad wolf, he answers.
—Big enough to chew your pale ass, I said, finding the docks. Little bits of things kind of curled by the water. With teeny boats tied up. Even as I looked, some of the boats began moving out from the docks. —Hold, I told Okie Zonk. Over port. More. More. Hold. Steady on. Oh, goddamn, I kind of pulled that toggle, pulled, pulled. It felt like my tool was falling off, and I didn't think I could take it. It was good, and I kept kind of pulled down over that box, moving over it, knowing those rocks were on their way, going down, and me whirling along after them, going for those docks and boats. Hold your water, boys: It's judgment coming. Poole sending judgment. Been unbalanced and found wanting. So long, Hans and Fritz, so long, Captain. Been good to blow you.
—Damn fool, can't you shoot, for God's sake, shoot shoot?
I'm easy now, kind of unfolding and this Okie Zonk keeps pounding on my ear. Hey, man, I've shot. Ain't anything else to give . . . and then the whole nose in front of me blows up and I can feel something like a hornet chew through the loose meat of my arm and feel that cold wind just booming in on me like somebody had just sprung the world's biggest icebox. It's them German planes, and one has just took the Okie out, and I can hear the copilot squeaking like he knew who was next out, and I got hold of that gun and cut loose some. Never hit a thing. They was shooting from half a mile out, and I couldn't put anything on 'em.

Upstairs the copilot has lost whatever he come out with. He's yellin', —Mayday, Mayday.
And I says back to him, —Christmas, New Year's. What's all the shit, Charlie? Well, it's nothing. They done shot up the

83

front office and killed the Okie and let sunshine into my bubble, and that was all. Four engines ginning, radio perking. Once we got that poor Zonk in the copilot's seat leveled off, it was all right going to what they liked to call home. I just laid back and kind of rested, seeing those docks and little boats and going down inside my mind to the river and watching those Zonk sonsofbitches looking up, seeing me looking down, and yelling in that stuff they spoke, seeing a big black long thing dumping on 'em. Don't cry, I thought, don't be sad. It's got to hurt to be good. What they tell me, you all need salvation. Here it comes; eat it up. If it's good, it's got to burn and burn, and when it's done, your soul will be clean. Ain't that what it's about? I laughed, thinking how they was down there dying and maybe being born again, which is as likely as any other shit they hand around. Going down and coming up while Poole is loving it, firing off his black gadget, looking down through those hairs at the world spread for it and Zonks on the way to sweet judgment. Then I laughed so hard it hurt the navigator's ears, and I said, —Sorry; thinking, serving God's sweet justice beats stuffing them high yellow broads in D.C. When it comes time, I just got to re-up. 'Cause when this is done, they got to find 'em another war somewhere, and what they just naturally got to have is us bombardiers, ones with good eyes, fast hands, and the stuff it takes to lay it on the line.

Michaelis

They called me in. Much brass. Ours, British, and the sad little collection of French, Polish and other imaginary officers who, in the name of certain future political possibilities, were given space, chairs, pencils and pads at minor conferences.

—How do you explain it? Lieutenant General Moseley asked me. It was permitted, under the circumstances, that I grin.

—Training, I said. —The old kind. Absolute discipline. I did grin. Moseley just stared at me. It was a measuring. The British suspected. The Frenchman hoped something would blow. The Pole stared at his blank pad. I was very slightly sorry for the Pole. Those possible political futures were closing down for his people. It was very hard to be a Pole anyhow. I made a note to tell him about Krepinski sometime. If there was no better way to use him.

—Crap, Moseley put in at last, deciding to play it very brassy. —Just crap. For the last year your people have scored a good solid sixty percent higher than the next best bunch of men we have flying. They were consistently above the average accuracy of men who've been flying over here for two years. I've seen their dossiers. There are only two I'd let on the base if they weren't in uniform. You've got one with an IQ of ninety-four— just enough to wipe his ass with help from a nurse's aide. You've got a black who ought to be playing drums for the Congo Chorus. You've got nothing. But the dimwit is better than the nigger, and the nigger is better than any of the others, and even the bottom man . . . Boyd, it is—even he is above the average by a good twenty percent. Now talk.

So I sat down. Without asking. I lit a cigar and set my lighter on the conference table. And I talked. Oh, yes. I told the truth. I told Moseley and the others. I mentioned psychology and effected response. I did not use the word magic. I did not say anything about the dark gods or how you conjure them. I didn't say that I had picked my men because there wasn't an American among them, that every one, in some way, was an alien and believed in the Dark Room, the black box. But when I was done, Moseley smiled. —If you had come to me at the start with this baloney, I'd have had you up for a section eight. But you've got the stuff. You've laid it on the line.

And that was my star. I was excited. You get excited when it turns out that insanity is the tool of conquest as it was in the hands of Alexander or Nero. I wanted to tell him that psychology was horseshit, that my people were not conditioned, that they were adepts, and that, given the bleeding, guttering holes in their psyches, given a sense of how desperately they needed to fill those holes, there was no limit to what one could do. In war. Not in peace. Only in the midst of sustained hysteria can you conjure. I wanted to tell Moseley that I could have made them supersharpshooters—with a very special black rifle suitably equipped. Or master assassins capable of getting to Hitler himself. Or possibly pilots who could fly as well in fog as in the

85

clearest noon sun. But I wanted the star, the silver five-pointed star, and the price of that is twofold: results in the world. And a rhetoric by which one pretends to explain them so that they fit the world.

—Stick with them, Moseley said. —I'd like you to train us a thousand more. But we'd better hold what we've got. We may need them. For something special.

Boyd

I saw him one last time. He phoned me and we decided to meet in London. It was in late November of 1944, and we had been at it almost two years. I could not remember how many missions I had flown or the names of the towns we had blasted off the map of Europe. I was past being tired and knew that I could quit anytime. But suppose I quit and went home? What then? What would I do?

—Do, Glenn asked, his brows raising behind those rimless glasses of his. —Why, play. When this is done—with your talent . . .

—That's no good, I said. —It's gone.

—Hell, a month—maybe two months and you'll be playing like Rubenstein.

We were in the dining room of the Rose Court Hotel, a small place off Marble Arch. Nice food, considering rationing. They bootlegged a goose when I told them who it would be for. The English loved him, and he seemed to return the compliment.

—It's not the playing that's gone, I told him. —It's the caring. I know I'll never be great. Not big great or even little great. I'm no Stacy or Bushkin. Much less an Ellington. If I went back, I'd always be somebody's sideman. Out here, I'm . . . one of the best. I'm one of five, Glenn. When they have a big one, they send one of us. Special Bombing Force Forty-nine. Just five guys and a general commanding us. We've wiped out most of Germany.

He stirred his imitation coffee and shook his head. —I'm not
. . . what you'd call a great trombone. Sure, I can play anything. But Dorsey has the sound. And Bobby Byrne. Or that
kid who was with Goodman: Moe?

—Zudekoff . . .

— . . . but I had something else. I could hear my band before I ever brought it together. I could hear it while I worked
with Pollack and Noble. I knew what it should sound like. I
wanted to create a sound nobody had ever heard before, but
that would seem to be the only way a song could be played.

—You made it, I said glumly. —Because it was in you. You
force it out.

—What's in you, Al? he said. —What do you want so badly
that nothing else matters?

I sat thinking. What did I want? What had sent me away
from music—and to Michaelis?

—To be great, I said finally. —I want to tower above the
whole world. It doesn't matter how, but that's what I really
want. To do something that only I can do.

Glenn lit a cigarette, a Chesterfield. I wondered if they still
sent them to him like they did when we played the *Supper
Club*. Then he looked across at me and I have never forgotten
that smile or his hand on my arm.

—Al, he said, —you'll make it. Energy is the thing. It'll have
to come out. You'll find it sooner or later. I hope I can see you
when it hits. It ought to be quite a collision. Bigger than one of
your blockbusters.

And when we parted that night at Paddington Station amid
the steam and bustle, we shook hands for what seemed a long
time.

It was Christmas Eve when I awoke, got coffee and picked
up the *Daily Telegraph*. In a box on the front page it said that
Major Glenn Miller was missing on a flight from England to
France. He had been going to join the band. I put the paper
down and almost lost control. It was a long way from the Café
Rouge, the Meadowbrook, Lowe's Ballroom. I thought again of
those words that had tumbled crazily through my mind night
after night over Germany:

> . . . I stand at your gate, and I wait,
> and the song that I sing is of moonlight. . . .

Then it was one more chill English morning with a war roaring through the snow on the far side of the Channel, and any way you cut it, I still had a long way to go.

—To Dresden, Boileau said.
—Where they make the little porcelain figures? I asked.
—Just about there, Boileau said. —Seems they want us to take out that laughing piper and the little shepherdess.
—My grandmother had candlesticks. Meissen. She met my grandfather in Dresden, Jacobs said.
—She's lucky she come from there, Poole said, paying no mind, looking down the bar. —They'd be using her for the candle.
Jacobs looked hurt. —That's not very kind. Poole shrugged. Boileau, grinning, nodded. —It's not very kind, he repeated.
—When? Krepinski asked. He was always strung tight when a mission was on. You would imagine he had had enough. More than a hundred now. More than any of us.
—Soon, I said.
—It can't wait if they want this weather. What are they sending?
—Much, Poole answered, tapping a cigarette on his thumbnail. —Some English was saying they gonna ship it all over.
—All?
—What they got. The whole rack.
We sat and drank. That was absurd. Nobody sends it all. Not a place like that. What was there? —I didn't even know it was a target, I said.
—It's all a target, Boileau said.
—We don't just go bombing indiscriminately, Jacobs began.
—Shee-it, Poole laughed, his face shining in the dim light.
—They'd lay a blockbuster up a pussy if they reckoned to bring down morale. He pronounced it "*mo*-rale."
I looked at them. At Krepinski and Poole, Jacobs, Boileau. What holds us together? I wondered. In the States, we wouldn't be within a thousand miles of one another. We'd never be sitting in the same bar. We had no more in common with one another than we did with the Germans. Then Boileau rose, laid a ten-shilling note on the bar and turned.
—Work in the morning, he said. —I feel it. I can feel them loading and gassing. Youall want to bet? And I remembered what kept us together.

Boileau

I was too sleepy to realize, but they came by, all but the nigger Poole, and each laid a ten-shilling note in my hand. It was fifteen hundred hours, cold and gray, and there were some of those peculiar little WAAF's moving about. One handed me my mission pack and a paper cup of lukewarm tea. —Thank you, ma'am, I said, bowing just enough to crack her Leeds-flat face. She turned, and I considered what a girdle could do in the discipline of amplitude. I thought how fine if there were a girdle for the soul. So that you could go as far as the restraint allowed, loose and free, knowing you would be brought up at the limit. But the girl moved off and I opened the mission pack so that I would know what the briefing officer was going to say and could decently nap while he talked. With my eyes open. On the pack it said THUNDERCLAP. It contained maps and the usual photos. Only my target area was simply a square in the middle of the city. There were no rail lines or factories, no barracks or motor pools or petrol storage. Just a square bounded by a long straight avenue on one side, and a park on the other. In the center was a tall building. It had a steeple. It was a cathedral. It was not marked safe. The town was Dresden. I sipped my coffee and felt my face red and hot. So it had come to this again: Owing to circumstances beyond our control, it is necessary to obliterate your city. Stay tuned to this station for the day and the hour. Yankee mean time. I remembered Hood at Atlanta, trying to explain by letter to Sherman that his artillery was killing women and children in their homes. Surrender, Sherman told him. If you don't want your women and children butchered, surrender.

I dropped the mission pack, pushing the photos back inside. I could sleep through this briefing without trepidation. I finished drinking the cup of whatever it was and considered various duties and claims. I even considered girdles again. But my mind was made up. So I walked into the briefing. Resigned.

Poole

Four cups of that stuff and a look at the next go. Dresden. Going for another hometown. Felt like a visiting ballplayer. Them semipros who come in and dust the local cats, drink their gin, nail their gash and move on. Well, it's some kind of work. Beats Zonking that back road in Virginia from now till the horn blows. I kept looking. Looked some more. Boil-o come by and tapped one of them pictures. He looked at me and I looked at him. —Wipe-out, I said.

He kind of nodded. —What you going to do?

—Do? I didn't know what he was up to.

—I never signed up to go butchering, he says. —Even if they're Nazis, they're still people.

I kind of laughed and put the pictures in the bag. —They're white, ain't they?

Boil-o give me a long take. —Oho, he says. —We got us a leak in the boat, huh?

I shook a shoulder at him. —Boat swamped. Back in D.C. Long time ago.

He nods and kind of looks tired: —Git to the back of the boat.

—No place left to go. Next time they push, I got to jump out, I said.

—But you won't, Boil-o says. —No, I reckon you'll dive right through the bottom, won't you?

We was walking to the briefing room. —Been tried. Hard bottom.

He grins real big. —They say youall got the hardest kind of head.

So we went in and sat down and fooled around with this briefing thing for half a hour, writing down numbers and looking at weather maps and all. And I thought, Boil-o, you and me. One of these days.

Krepinski

That was the one all right. If you was in on that one, you wouldn't ever forget. No way to forget. Jesus, for years I would wake up dreaming I was there again with that town burning from one end of the world to the other. I would wake up yelling, —Jesus, Jesus, and Gertrude would say, —Eddie, it's okay. You're home. Don't be scared.

—I ain't scared, goddamn you, I told her. —I ain't scared. You don't understand. You never could understand.

We come in above thirty thousand. There was frost on the sight and the .50 caliber was seized up. They said the radioman passed out and didn't come around till it was done. We come in high and we was the third wave. Because they give us this oil refinery, and I was supposed to set it off across these two roads. After they got the town stoked. Something they called innerdiction of access. It meant we would take care of the firemen on the way in. And the people on the way out. It was fine. The moon was bright and I didn't even notice the cold. There wasn't no night fighters to speak of, and the flak was just what they put up to keep us honest. Because this Dresden wasn't no military target. It was just a town. Except like Michaelis said, every rabbit hole in Germany was a military target. Because what the Germans did to the Polish people. I mean okay, I'm a American, but the old man came from Cracow and the old lady from Poznán. They told how it was in those places and how the Germans and Russians and Jews made it so you couldn't live like a white man. So they left. Okay. So the Germans took care of the kikes and we take care of the Germans. Later for the Russians. We're the strongest country on earth coming out of this, and we'll get around to the Russians. Jesus, so many scores to settle. I thought, you'll be in this bubble till you're an old man. Taking care of these dirty sonsofbitches who don't want democracy. They're going to take it, though. Or get what they got in that town.

So about five miles out, we dropped twenty thousand feet. When we hit the city limits, we was on the deck. Yancy, the pilot, is from Chicago. We talked about me going back there afterward. He says, —All right, shits, is it warm enough now? How do you like this piece? Because the first two waves have cut the place in half. You can see ribbons of fire below and smoke rising almost as high as we were flying. It had been bad shaky bombing. The blast paths twisted and curled like snakes, side by side and across one another. Not straight like mine. Because they were jackrabbits. Dump and run. Anything to get out of gun range. It wasn't bombing. Only today it didn't matter. Because they didn't have targets. They were supposed to take out the town, and they were doing that. The secondaries were going off under us, and once we came in over the town, there was no more flak. The first two waves had knocked their ass off, and they were in the shelters. I saw the oil dump or whatever it was with fire markers bracketed around it and pulled us north, came in out of the smoke and laid a stick right in where they had the stuff in dozens of big tanks. It was that synthetic gas they made out of coal, and so the next rack went into the processing area. It looked like the place where my old man worked for Standard of New Jersey. The whole works went up almost under us. I could hear Yancy yell as a thermal and the blast pushed us back up two or three thousand feet. I laughed. I knew it was coming and grabbed hold. We rode it, and I called Yancy and said, —Make it around once more. I got another Christmas box for the squareheads.

—Forget it, Yancy yelled. —You goddamn cretin. We're socking it in. Look out and back.

I climbed up into the end of the blister and looked. The right wing was full of holes, with pieces of metal hanging off. —It's nothing, I told him. —We're okay. Gimme one more shot. He didn't even answer.

So on the way back, while I was watching the town vanish in the darkness behind the horizon with nothing left but a tall twisting chimney of smoke and fire to show where it was—or had been—I see this *Dorf* down below. It's what they call a farm village. It's nothing. A dozen houses, a beer hall, a church. But they're all down there, looking like they're holding candles or something all standing in the *Platz* in front of what looks like a church. So I drop open the bomb bays and Yancy yells, —You crazy or something? Put 'em up. The wing you got ventilated is drag enough. But I just eyeballed that *Platz* and let 'em go. Then I looked back. The whole place went up. Not the *Platz* or the church. Everything. I couldn't figure it. Then I figured it. I had two stacks left. They got maybe a ton of 250's. It rolled up the whole countryside there under the moon. I closed the doors and leaned back. It was good over the town, watching the whole map catch fire. But that *Dorf*. That was nice, too. Sometimes when I think of the war, that's what I think of. I don't know why. It wasn't important. It was kind of a mistake. But you got to see everything, and nobody else had a hand in it. It was just me. Even the pilot didn't do anything. I wish I knew the name of that place. I wanted to tell the old man how I squared it for Cracow and Poznán. But I never knew the name. I couldn't find it on the maps. It wasn't on the maps. As far as the maps were concerned, it didn't even exist. Which is a pain in the ass.

Jacobs

Up there it was clear and cloudless, and I could feel the plane's life pulsing around me. Four Cyclone engines pushing forty-eight hundred horsepower through the ship's frame, holding us aloft, circulating oxygen, sending power to the turrets, light to the navigator. Each of us was like an organ bearing no life except that which we shared with the ship.

Up there it was still afternoon, and the sky above was a faded threadbare blue that almost warned of the black immensity of all space that lay beyond it. I closed my eyes and tried to imagine us going up and up, beyond all this. There would be no ten hours in this frozen sky, no raid at the end of it. We would go on up. Then I shook my head. It was absurd. We had this job to do. We did it very well. They said we did it better than anyone else. Can't you be proud of being the best?

We crossed the Channel and moved across occupied France. Nothing was above us, someone said over the intercom. He meant that our service ceiling was higher than any of the German fighters. Unless the Messerschmitt 262's, the jets, were out. But he was wrong in another way. Everything lies above us, doesn't it? It was hypnotic riding in the nose of a B-17 with the plane just behind you, surrounded by plexiglas so that the pale light poured in from every angle and there was darkness only behind you. Out on either side you could see the blurred translucent disks of the props, feel the animal power of those engines as if your own blood and bone and brain and muscle were somehow entwined with that great roar and you needed it to live and do your job. And you did.

That afternoon, locked in the fur cocoon of my flying suit, I watched the evening grow ahead of us as we flew east. We had cut a little north, passing over Harwich and the Hook of Holland and now I could make out the flat leaden water of the Zuider Zee below, the treeless plains of the lowlands down there. The land was neatly divided into squares and rectangles, marks of law and civilization put on the earth by the remote and mingled descendants of those who had once hunted and fought in skins down there only a few centuries ago. The barbarians were gone, weren't they? Now we were flying toward a city far to the east where hundreds of thousands of civilized people waited not knowing that they had a date with a man named Harold M. Jacobs from the Bronx. Who is coming to kill them, to incinerate their houses and blast their children into bloody gruel. And this man is no barbarian. This man can read and write. This man knows sorrow and pain and loneliness. This man holds in him thousands of years of suffering. This man believes in freedom and justice; otherwise he wouldn't be in this plane heading toward your town to rain down hundreds and hundreds of fire bombs and high explosive.

As the sun fell behind us, the sky deepened, turned to a rich midnight blue strewn with those same stars I had seen in another life a thousand years ago in Texas, two thousand years— no, four, in Ur of the Chaldees when a voice called me out to them and sent me on my way. Droplets of water condensed out of a string of high cloud and streamed back across my bubble. Down below I could see the last rays of sun dying on the spires of churches and post offices and courthouses down there. Hollanders and Flemings and Germans were looking up, hearing the faint purr of our engines from five miles up, counting us, wondering where we were bound. Listen, this is Jacobs, you hear? Bringing freedom and punishment. I wish I could separate them, send each to the right parties. But they come together in steel casings with fins and impact fuses. Is it that way with God? Does He level a city of a million ordinary people to punish fifty evildoers? Doesn't He? Could we fly if He willed otherwise? Sustineo Alas. For the sake of twenty—no, thirty-six—just men in Germany would He silence the cyclones, dissolve our bombs? No, the wheat and the tares are harvested together, Jesus said. And maybe they all go into the oven. Maybe . . .

It was hours later. I had slept and wakened in absolute darkness, the blue instrument lights illuminating the Norden sight in front of me with a strange glow I would never become accustomed to, a cold gleam, soft and very distant, like the icy shine of acetylene burning, burning.

—Jacobs, you asshole, wake up. Snap to . . .

—Huh? What, I answered Finney.

—One tens at ten o'clock low. See 'em?

They flew below and heading north like angry hornets with their navigation lights shining. Why the navigation lights? Don't they know we're here?

—It's the Window. Finney laughed, talking about the radar interference foil the marker planes ahead were still dropping to turn the German screens into snow storms. —They're wasting gas.

—Heading for Dortmund, someone said. —They're picking up the diversionary.

—No flak, someone said.

—Piece of cake, Finney answered. —Nothing like the towns we've been rapping. This is a milk run.

And it was. It was. We could see the city ahead of us at least a hundred miles away. It was burning. The fire was one single pulsating thing, not hundreds of scattered separate flames. As we approached, it seemed that the whole world was burning. Even the smoke didn't cover it, and as we moved closer, it was obvious that nobody could pick out markers or aiming points. It was a holocaust down there.

—Fire storm, Finney said casually. —Some first strike. You got to hand it to those Lancasters. Jesus, look at it. Can you see the goddamned river even?

Yes, the river. I could see the river red and shining, a great swooping S curve down there amidst the roaring twisting single flame. I looked for the area marked on my map. It was a built-up residential district. But I couldn't see it.

—I can't find anything down there, I told Finney.

—Wait, Finney said. —I can pick up the Fireman from here. Which was what some of us called the Master Bomber, the man who flew above it all, correcting us, goading us, telling us to try another run, moving us off a target already obliterated, turning us and turning us as if we were mechanical dragons ready to spew death anywhere the Master Bomber said. Then Finney patched me in and I heard his voice. It was Michaelis.

—Phoenix seven, what's the stall? he said, his voice chill as the blue light, detached as if we were all sitting in that wardroom in Pilsbury, Texas. No, cooler. As if this were his natural place.

—Phoenix seven dumper cannot locate markers or target area. The whole goddamned place is for it, Mr. Hots. Over.

—Phoenix seven roger. Take a line across northwest quadrant of town. Hit anything that is unburning. Anything unburning. Try to hit edge of storm area to augment present situation. Clear? Over.

—Roger, Finney said. —Over and out. Okay, deadeye. You heard the man.

—Drop them . . . just anywhere?

—Help the fire, son. We didn't come to put it out. Dump.

—Dump?

—That's what we get paid for, son. Dump.

I dumped. I let the whole load go across that northwest line on the edge of the fire storm and on in toward the center in that strip pattern we'd been using since Kassel. As we crossed the storm, the plane bucked and rose. I couldn't believe it. I could feel the heat.

—Shit, Finney said. —Don't that beat all?

I was still looking down. Down there into the midst of all the hells man ever dreamed of. I wondered if it would ever stop burning, or if we had bombed a hole into the middle of the earth. Then just as we finished the run and began to bank back toward the west, I heard a shattering sound outside. Flak, I thought. There's somebody down there still firing, defending. What is there to defend? God save us just this once more. This is your work, isn't it? Aren't we up here doing your work? I could hear Finney cursing over the intercom. He was trying to cut back the prop on the inboard port engine. It was smoking, the blades spinning crazily. I could hear Finney yelling to the copilot.

—Feather, feather . . .

The intercom was alive with questions and shouts, and then it settled down and for a long time we lurched onward, losing altitude in great falling arcs, then slowly making it up only to lose it again as we went farther west, out of formation now, trying only to get out of Germany, back over our own lines before that engine blew. Because they had not been able to tie the prop down and it was cutting our airspeed, ruining our headway as we ran against a fair wind. We dropped lower after what seemed a long time. I heard Finney again:

—Where are we? he asked the navigator.

—Shit, who knows? Near Weimar, I think. Who knows?

—You're supposed to, you sonofabitch. Ain't that what you're paid for? Goddammit, where's Jacobs?

—Here, I said. —Where I belong.

—Get your ass out of where you belong, Finney barked so loud it hurt my ears. —If that prop comes off . . .

Then, as I turned to crawl back toward the radio section, my eyes moved across the port engine and I saw the propeller shear off from its shaft, and the fuselage of the plane exploded just ahead of me, where I was about to go. I could feel pieces of metal scattering across my back and shoulders as I fell forward and lay on my face in the gangway out of the nose bubble. The intercom went blank. I looked up, shielding my eyes with my hand, and smoke had begun to drift upward from the area back where the navigator and radioman sat. There was a jagged hole rammed through the fuselage just ahead of where the top turret jutted down, and now the smoke had begun to whirl in thin eddies toward the hole. Out there, I could see the glow of the engine on fire, and the instrument lights, still that deadly blue, went out and I couldn't see anything else.

It was the navigator, a man named Pritchard, who crawled up to where I was. His cap was gone and there was blood on his face.

—The cockpit's gone. Finney and Mitchell have bought one. Junk the sight and bail out.

As he vanished back into the smoky darkness, I could feel the plane begin to tilt. I jerked the optical component out of the sight and followed him. Back there, on the far side of the hole where it breached the fuselage at our level, the radioman, young and vivid in his fear, was calling into his throat mike which I think was dead, —Mayday, Mayday, Mayday . . .

The bomb bay was open now, cranked down manually by someone else who had done my job because I was slow. I lowered myself after one of the others, a waist gunner, I think, and held to the empty steel hangers watching the loose wires whip back and forth, hearing the wind roaring beneath me. I tried not to look down. I felt my feet leave their support and I was hanging amid the wires where only a few minutes before tons of bombs had hung, waiting to be released. As the others fell, I jerked off my cap, stared at the golden eagle on it, stuffed it into the neck of my flight suit and let go.

I tumbled over and over, seeing nothing at first, and then finding thin streams of cloud all around me, dark sky, dark earth, and no way to tell one from the other. Up above, I saw the shape of our plane as it began to burn all along its length and started down in a steeper sloping dive, falling wing over wing in slow exaggerated circles. Then my chute opened, and I felt the straps grab at my crotch, my shoulders, like hands from the darkness, rough and unsentimental, determined to bear me up. I was swinging then like a trussed bird, like an ornament on an invisible Christmas tree over the whole world. My eyes were closed and I tried not to retch. I wasn't afraid of heights, not really. But I was afraid. What was I afraid of? Oh, God, don't you see? That wasn't the Texas desert below. I was falling down into Germany.

Michaelis

Moonlight was beginning to slant off the bubble canopy of the P-51 spotter plane so that the bombers below caught in shafts of moon seemed to be bolts of cold fire cutting through light cloud. I tapped the pilot and pointed down. The last flight was passing over now, and I wanted to see what we had done to Dresden.

I saw. From one end of the city to the other, I could see no area that was not in flames. Mile after mile of buildings and roads, trees, even fields on the outskirts were burning. In the center of the city, air currents had joined with the immeasurable heat to start a fire storm, and down there it looked as if we were passing over the center of a sun. There was cold sweat along my spine. I felt no personal sorrow. They were Germans down in that hell, and their criminal pride had blinded them to reality: The great animal forces that rule this spinning world had passed from Europe forever, and the day all Germany had wept and prayed for from the time of Frederick II had come and gone. Perhaps in the seventeenth century. Maybe at the beginning of the nineteenth. But had gone, and the functionary's son from Linz was not mad with the whisperings of destiny, but only a vulgar street-corner bigot whose hatreds were as common among his kind as runny noses among schoolboys. No, I felt no sorrow. But there was another feeling: How should I describe it? As if one were watching the destruction of a great and formidable enemy (not the Austrian corporal; Germany) and realized suddenly and irrevocably that the same awful end would be his, too. I watched Dresden melt and flare and fall into ashes, and I could not stop my mind from announcing like a railroad stationmaster: New York. Philadelphia. Miami. Atlanta. New Orleans. Chicago. Dallas, Houston, Denver, Los Angeles. . . . And behind each name, I saw another shadow image of what I was watching as if second sight were showing me the 1960's or 1970's. I could feel tears in my eyes, and I laughed aloud. The pilot turned in his seat and stared at me. I shrugged. Then I closed my eyes and told him to take us home. As we pulled up and headed west, I glanced over my shoulder and saw a pillar of smoke and deep reddish flame mounting higher and higher, as if at last we had put the world itself on a funeral pyre and set it off.

On the way back, I saw something peculiar that brought the dread I had discovered over Dresden into even sharper focus. We passed over a small village, isolated, somewhere not far from Weimar. The pilot dropped low to see what had happened, because the village was burning, a tiny reproduction of what we had just left. As we buzzed over the broken spire of an

99

old church, past homes and something like a city hall, all in flames, I saw in the beam of a searchlight an old man with a rifle. As we passed over him, he fired at us, and I could see him struggling madly with the bolt, trying desperately to fire again. I could not make out his face, but I did not need to. I remembered another old man describing the evacuation of Constantinople, tears running down his cheeks, mouth loose and quivering. Old men are all the same if they are strong. Their outrage is awful, since there is nothing to quell or ease it. Their hatred is a curse, and it lives when they are dead, I thought, and then, back into my mind against my will: San Francisco, Seattle, Hartford, Tyler, Macon, Brownsville . . . We will all be old one day, I thought, those of us who live. Then I thought, maybe we won't. Maybe it will come before that. But then the plane tilted upward again, and we rose like a balloon, aimed at a lovely wreath of dark-framed cumulonimbus clouds that hung above us glistening white and pure and crystalline as we slipped in among them and lost the earth and all it contained far below.

Jacobs

I passed out there in the sky. I never saw any of the others. I never saw the plane crash. I didn't see the earth come swinging nearer as if I were frozen in mid-sky and the world itself were falling upward toward me at some insane velocity. No, do you know what I saw?

I saw the branches of trees, a tree. And beyond that, lace of branches and leaves. Far distant, the wide dark sky filled with those same stars I knew so well. My neck hurt, and I moved my head and looked down. I could see shadows, bulk. I was only a few feet from the ground. I had no way of knowing how long I had been unconscious. Then, in the distance, I saw the shaft of a flashlight cutting through the darkness, moving toward me. I tried to swing upward, tried to pull my legs up into the shroud lines so that I could climb up into the tree, but it was no use. I couldn't even get started. My body was numb all the way down. Nothing would move. I only made the tree creak and sway a little. I hung there while the light moved along the ground, up into the trees, and stopped. On me.

That's it, I thought. End of the line. Morris should be here. Maybe he'd frown and spread his palms. But I was too tired to care. I heard them calling to one another in that strange rough language that sounds like some alien English spoken far away with words you almost understand coming through now and then. They were standing right under me then with those machine guns they carried in the crook of their arms, staring up, talking casually. One of them laughed and gave an order to somebody named Kraus. You know what I thought of? I thought of reading about Bill the Lizard in *Alice in Wonderland*. Sure, I remembered when the White Rabbit sent Bill down the chimney on reconnaissance. When he got kicked all the way back into the air by Alice. And I thought, Kraus, if I could just shake you out of this tree . . .

Then, from the darkness below, from behind the flashlights, I heard a voice. Only it was speaking English and that was the worst. Don't ask me why. Isn't it good to hear your own language in a far place? Maybe until I heard that voice, its British accent laid over something else, maybe I had believed this was just a nightmare or a movie or something, I don't know.

—Are you comfortable there, American? the voice asked cheerfully.

Then I felt Kraus slowly working his way out on the limb above me. I could hear him grunting, hear twigs breaking and falling as he came out over me. Then he was sawing at the shrouds. And from down below:

—You have about three meters to fall. The ground is even and covered with grass. When you fall, stand quite still. Do not move. There is a dog down here.

The last line went and I fell. Like a log. He was wasting his breath about standing still and the rest of it. I was paralyzed from the neck down. I couldn't move. I hit and sprawled out. I think I moaned a little. Then I just lay there.

—*Ist er gestorben denn?* somebody asked. —*Tod?*

—*Nein,* that smooth detached voice in English again: —You are all right. My people will assist you. Do not be foolish as to

101

run when you begin to feel better. They will kill you. Or let the dog have you.

So they picked me up like a tired kid being carried home from a picnic. They half dragged me along. It wasn't like anything, that trip through the silent sweet-smelling cool woods to their personnel carrier. I couldn't see anybody. Only the beam of the flashlight jolting along in front of us. Then we reached a narrow road overhung with tall trees that had no branches till almost the top. There was a slice of moon above, and I noticed what a beautiful night it was. They pushed me into the back of the carrier, and we drove down the road.

I closed my eyes and tried to understand, to really feel where I was. I needed to be frightened, but I wasn't. No, I opened my eyes again and looked out ahead at the quiet dappled road winding beneath us, patterns of branches and leaves crossing the light dust. I wanted fear and searched for it only to find some kind of a grin on my face, as if this were all some really good private joke that would end with a pint of bitters at some pub that was not too far ahead of us. Maybe these coal scuttle helmets and the man in the leather overcoat sitting in front were all extras hired for the most colossal private joke in history. Sure, maybe Finney wasn't dead. Maybe the whole goddamned war was something Hollywood had rigged.

Then I saw a glow in the sky ahead. We rounded a curve and were driving suddenly not on a country cowpath any longer, but in the back street of some town or village. Out in a field back to my right, I caught a glimpse of some huge barbed-wire fences with concrete buildings behind them, and then we were surrounded by those tall thin old houses and shops that seemed to huddle and hang out over the street. There were no lights, nothing but that deep red glow, and for a moment I wondered why. Then we came out of the narrow street into a square, and I saw why.

It must have been a typical square. What you see in English and French villages. A church, some stores, the post office, the offices of lawyers and the *Burgemeister* and the registrars and all. That's what it must have been.

But the whole center of the town was a smoldering ruin. The front of the church had fallen in, and the bell tower and steeple were lying beside the front door as if they had been placed there by a delivery van. All around the square searchlights were set up on flatbed trucks with their beams playing over the smoking bombed-out buildings, where men and women were digging with picks and shovels, even their hands, in piles of masonry and brick and broken wood. They were looking for people. Soldiers were working with them, and as we made a sharp left turn at one of the square's corners, I could see two of the soldiers pulling something out of a hole amid a drifted heap of rubble. It looked like a bale of rags covered with light dust. Then I saw it was a little girl. The soldiers lifted her carefully, but her head fell to one side, and the way her neck moved was all wrong. A woman who had been scratching frantically farther up the pile stumbled down to where the soldiers were. One of the searchlights from somewhere behind us all followed her down as if she were a star at a Hollywood premiere. When she got close enough to see the child, she screamed. —Lotti, Lotti, she screamed and took the little girl in her arms. The soldiers stood there with nothing to do. One self-consciously adjusted his army-issue suspenders and stared off into the darkness. The other, squatting, blew his nose between his fingers and rubbed his eyes with the back of his dirty hand.

The woman sat down in the ruins and held the little girl as a couple of men came up with a stretcher. The personnel carrier I was in paused and the officer in front, the one who spoke English, called over a noncom with a black smoke-stained face. He told the noncom something in a low voice, and the noncom nodded, glanced at me without any expression, not even hatred, and went off. Up on the rubble, one of the soldiers had seen me. He nudged his friend, who was just standing now looking down at the woman as she rocked to and fro in her agony, not screaming or crying or anything by then, just holding the little girl close in her arms. The second soldier, whose face was a smear of dust and beard, looked down on me as if the blasted building were a judgment seat and pointed to the woman, his hand shaking, fingers splayed. He said something, yelled it at me:

—Look, American sonofabitch. How do you like it?

I turned away, looking for the first time at the soldier who was sitting beside me on the rear seat of the personnel carrier. He was young and blond with a light reddish beard maybe three days old. His eyes were very light and looked as if they had never seen anything at all. His tunic was dirty and open at the collar. He was looking back at me without frowning or smiling, those light eyes as indifferent as a pair of photoelectric cells. Those eyes made me remember Boileau. The soldier shifted his machine gun so that the barrel was lined up with my chest.

—*Raus,* the officer in front said, and we started up again. It was then that I noticed how the people all around the square had paused here and there in their digging and hauling and had started drifting toward where we had stopped. The personnel carrier moved forward slowly through a crowd of them, making two men jump out of the way. We turned right out of the square and drove down another dark side street, turned right once more and stopped behind what was left of the church. We got out and the soldier nudged me lightly with his machine gun and pointed toward a dark door in a wall that still stood. The officer got out and stretched. Right after him came this enormous Doberman. It never made a sound. It just jumped down from the seat and stood right beside the officer who reached down and patted it absently. He was wearing leather gauntlets that seemed to vanish into the arms of his coat so that he looked like a giant totem all made of leather with only a human face. He stood apart for a moment until he saw a small detachment of soldiers coming up the narrow shadowed street in the direction from which we had come. It was led by the noncom I had seen in the square. They were armed with rifles, bayonets fixed. I wondered if I was going in to a summary court and that was my firing squad coming route step up the street.

The officer smiled when he saw the soldiers and walked through the door in the wall ahead of me, his Doberman watching me carefully until we got inside and the soldier with the machine gun closed the door behind us. Inside, it smelled cool and nice. Incense and old wood—and dust. Candles and time. It was still dark in this little foyer where they hung coats and the priest's robes and things. Down at the end of the passage, I could see a large room, and we walked into it single file. It was walled with stone except where there were old wooden cabinets to hold religious articles and things. There was one big stained-glass window showing Jesus doing something in front of a hole with a big stone beside it. Was he coming out or calling to someone inside?

104

The room was lighted with field lanterns, and their glow, soft and reddish, flickered across desks and tables and stools all around. There were men sitting at the desks writing, and several officers standing over a table examining a map and arguing. One shook his head and folded his arms. No matter what the others said, he ignored them. At another desk, a noncom was using a field telephone, and in a far corner near a door that must have gone into the sanctuary of the church, there was a radio set and a man talking into a microphone. The doorway next to him was blocked with fallen timber and plaster and junk.

To one side of the radio operator, there was this bald man sitting at a desk. When he saw us come in, he was the only one who paid much attention. He wore gold-rimmed glasses that sparkled as the field-lantern light pulsed and wavered. He was dressed in a black uniform with silver trim, and I remember thinking it was a shame he was short and dumpy, because the uniform was beautifully tailored. The man got up from his desk and hurried over, as if he had been waiting for me. He kept looking at me, even when he began talking to the officer. He said something fast and breathless in German, and the officer shrugged and stripped off his gloves and took off his overcoat slowly, dropping it on an empty desk. The man in black kept talking while the officer opened one of the cabinets and took out a bottle of wine from beside some gold cups and other things. Who ever heard of an army with gold table service? The officer poured a couple of the gold cups full and handed me one. Then the man in black frowned and started talking even faster. The officer spoke to him for the first time, staring at him hard. Only he spoke in English.

—When this is over, Kurtz, I'm going to make a necklace of your testicles.

The man in black looked at him uncomprehendingly and then kept on talking. The officer, who wore a field uniform with jackboots and a peaked cap, drank his wine, paying no attention. Then he set down the goblet and barked, —Can't you talk English? This man is a prisoner. Talk English before him. How were you raised?

But the one in black shook his head and went on, his voice now low as if he were urging some conspiracy. He kept looking at me as if everything he dreamed and wanted, the whole busi-

105

ness he was talking about, somehow turned on my presence. Finally the officer turned to me. It was the first time I had seen him full face. He was a good-looking man with dark hair and a clean healthy face with a small thin mouth that seemed to have neither softness nor pity in it. I wondered where I stood between him and the other one, the one in black.

—I must ask for your identification, he said. He looked at me closely as I fumbled inside my flight suit and pulled out the tags. I wondered if they thought I was Eisenhower pulling a Hess in reverse. I handed the dogtags to him and he passed them to the man in black who took them back to his desk, arranged his gold-rimmed glasses, and studied them next to a lantern. After a long minute, he looked up at me as if he didn't believe what he had read. What did he expect. Did I look like a picture of Doolittle or Spaatz? The officer who had brought me in reached down and picked up the tags. He smiled at first, then turned toward the man in black and grinned.

—Well, Lieutenant Poole, there was a question of your . . . religion.

—*Jude,* the one in black croaked. His face had fallen, and he looked as if he were ready to cry.

The officer waved the tags in his face triumphantly.—*Protestantisch,* he spat right back at him.—*Verstehen? Protestantisch.*

Poole? Why Poole? Am I with a wizard? What does he know? Then I remembered how we put our stuff almost side by side on the dresser back at the base. Could I have . . . No, I had picked up . . . my tags? No, his? Was black Jacobs back in the mess drinking? Was Hebrew Poole down in Germany?

There was a knock at the door, and when the soldier with the machine gun opened it, I could see the noncom. He looked worried and said something past the soldier to the officer. The officer turned to me.

—It was foolish to bring you here, Lieutenant, he said quietly. —The *Feldwebel* tells me that the townspeople are . . . upset. I think we had best move on.

—*Jude,* the man in black erupted from his desk. He pounded the blotter in front of him and jabbered a lot of things.

The officer turned slowly and smiled at him with great mock sympathy. —*Protestantisch,* he almost whispered. —*Verstehen Sie? Protestantisch.*

Then he was talking in English, talking to me. —Your planes

106

a few hours ago . . . were not expected. On the way back from Dresden, one bomb aimer with an unusual sense of humor dropped his overload on this town. While the people were marching in a church festival. They fail to see what military installation he was aiming at. They think you might be he.

I tried to understand what was happening, really. I was down in Germany. This wasn't a movie I was watching. This man talking to me with a British accent and a faint smile was a German officer. This was a German command post. Outside there were villagers who wanted to . . . lynch me. Because I was one of those beasts in the sky who had killed the little girl and God knows how many others, who had blasted their town and their lives to shreds. —Why, I asked, speaking for the first time, —why?

—The bombing? I have no idea. Terror, revenge. What does it matter now? Why bomb Dresden? There are no military installations there. Why destroy a beautiful old city?

—I only obey orders, I heard myself telling him. —They tell us to fly and we fly.

He smiled and nodded. —Of course. No one asks soldiers anything. It is the same everywhere.

All of a sudden the man in black with the gold-rimmed glasses stood up behind his desk. His face was sweating and contorted.

—*Verdamm ter Judenscheiss,* he began.

I tried to understand the rest. It was as if he were yelling in English, as if I should understand. The officer turned and said something low and vicious to him and he sat back down.

—What? I asked.

—Nothing, the officer said. —He has no power here anymore. He hates the Army because we have the power again.

The officer looked at me for a long time, his eyes straight and direct. —They say two hundred thousand died tonight. It's only a number, but Dresden is dead because of him. My family was in Dresden. Because I thought it was safe.

—Safe, I said after him.

—No place is safe. Except the stalags. I will take you to a prison camp. It may not be for officers, but it will be safe. Then . . .

He paused, and I felt a little faint. —Then? I said.

—Then I will come back here, and if he is still here, I'm

going to kill him. The lines to his headquarters are down and the soldiers obey me. I have to see to you first. Then I will be free . . .

I think there were tears in his eyes, but his voice was still low and settled and cool. —We must go now. You will walk just behind me. Kraus will walk after you. Whatever happens, you will keep walking, do you understand? If the priest were still . . . but he's . . . in there.

He gestured toward the rubble-filled doorway near the radio. Then he started out.

Out there it should have been dark, but it wasn't. They were waiting with torches made of wood with rags soaked in oil or something tied at the ends. There were men and women. Some of them looked very old: men in small hats, women with shawls over their heads and shoulders. And when they saw me, they began at first to murmur, then to talk aloud, pointing at me, shaking their fists. One man held up a little boy so that he could see me over the crowd. On each side of the path, the noncom's men were struggling with the people in the red insane glow of their quivering torches, shoving the screaming people back with their rifles, menacing them with the bayonets.

I thought, how can you blame them? They don't see you. They don't see a man. They see the control unit of a machine that rained death out of a clear night sky for no reason on earth. Something that blew everything to pieces. Which is what I do. What they hate is that there are bombardiers.

What seems funny is that I didn't hate them as I walked down that narrow file between them while they spat and cursed and tried to reach me. I felt as if we were kin, and there was a great awful misunderstanding. I didn't think of Rotterdam or London. I didn't think that these mad people had somehow pulled the whole world into war. I was only sorry. Not simply because I was afraid but because I could still see the dusty tangle of rags that looked like a life-sized discarded doll lying in her mother's arms with soldiers standing useless nearby. The little girl had not worked and prayed for this war. She had not been at Nuremburg or Munich, I thought. But—I—we—had killed her. With malice toward none, far away, impersonal, we had dropped from the dark belly of our 17's the steel and explosive that blew Lotti and her world away. Forever. And these

108

were Lotti's people, weren't they? They had the right, didn't they?

We reached the carrier then, and before I could even get settled, almost before Kraus could get in, we were moving. I reached out a hand and caught hold of Kraus' sleeves as he almost fell backward. He smiled quickly. —*Danke,* he said, and was without expression again. We were gaining speed, honking, pushing angry people out of the way with our fenders. One man threw up his hands, waving us to stop, but we headed right into him and at the last moment he dived out of the way, sprawling in the street. In a moment, it seemed, we were out of town driving along a wide road toward the west. It was dark ahead because of the blackout headlights of the car, with the upper portion of the beams painted black. I lay back in the seat. Kraus had his machine gun slung on the door handle, and he was paying me no mind at all. I could see that under the edge of his helmet, his eyes were closed.

I looked up then toward the stars, signs of my patrimony, and wondered if I would live to see the end of all this. If I would ever set foot on soil that belonged to me. Germany, I thought. America. What are their quarrels? I breathed deeply and folded my arms behind my head while the stars winked and nodded and said that they were from everlasting and no more numerous than people like me; that always some Abraham was in custody, and forever the promise was the same. Then a question occurred to me. I leaned forward and touched the officer's shoulder.

—What? I began.
—Eh? he asked.
—Town was that?
—Town? Oh, that was Buchenwald.

I awoke one morning and stared out the concrete-framed window of the dark dormitory into the gray spring dawn. Down at the wire, no one was walking. There was no guard visible in the tower at the end of the northeast sweep of the fence. I walked slowly down the length of the big room between rows of sleeping Americans and out into the dusty exercise area. From there you could see the gate and the checkpoints beyond. The gates were open. No one stood guard at all. I walked down there, wondering even as I passed through the gates and stepped beyond the tenantless guard shack if it were some kind of trick. Then, down the road where it turned into a forest of larch trees, I saw a tank. There were men in dirty uniforms sitting on it smoking, their rifles at the ready. And when one of them saw me he called out:

—Okay, sonofabitch, freeze. If you wiggle your ears, I'll drop the sky on you.

Which was as near as anybody ever got to saying welcome home. Which was all right with me.

III

Boyd

I came very close to staying in Paris. Very close indeed. I had met a girl who worked as a translator in SHAEF, and it would have been easy to get a liaison assignment. But I had ninety missions, and somehow, even though I knew it was naïve and probably a mistake, I took the recycling and headed back to the States. To be an instructor. To teach men how to annihilate Japan as we had wiped out Germany. The girl in Paris cried and told me that I was without feelings, that the war had destroyed my feelings. For a moment I believed it and shrugged and kept my face cold and expressionless and told her, all right, to fuck off. That it was over like the war was over. Like everything would be over. She left the café where we had met crying, saying that I had left her nothing, and I felt for a moment as if it were true, that the war had found a small crevice in me somewhere and sucked out into the stratosphere whatever sentiments a man should have.

But as I walked up the Champs-Elysées toward the Boulevard Haussmann, I thought of Sandy, thought of her that last winter we had in Idaho, skiing, watching them make that movie with Sonja Henie and John Payne, just before I joined the band.

It happened in Sun Valley,
not so very long ago . . .

And those sentiments, unimpaired, came flooding back, saying it will all be that way again. Nothing happened here to change it. The snow, the evenings by that big fireplace with a toddy. It's another world, and all this is just a vacancy. It didn't mean anything. Go on back and you'll see.

So I did. And before they could check me out as an instructor

113

in the new B-29, someone had done the ultimate job of bombing at Hiroshima and Nagasaki, and it was over. For a little while, I couldn't believe it. The transition was too much, too fast. It was absurd, but I felt somehow that I—no, that we—Michaelis' group had been betrayed, that the Hiroshima job had belonged to us by rights. But who wants to wipe out eighty thousand people? No one, but if it had to be done, it was our job. I was irritable for a day or two. Then Sandy came down from New York, and we ran into Philly and it was very good. There was a new band down from Connecticut—Vaughn Monroe—and we melted together and there had been no Pilsbury, Texas, no Michaelis, no England, no Dresden. It was all now the fragmented memory of an improbable novel I had read once. For a course in literature, perhaps. A novel full of monsters who awoke early in the morning to ride forth and kill thousands of people, to obliterate whole cities, to alter the world's maps. And then came back and drank and fidgeted until it was time to go out again. I remembered that last scene in London when, for no earthly reason, I had shaken hands with Boileau and Poole and said, —We'll have to get together sometime. As if we had ever been together.

But the worst, the silliest, was that night, the night after Sandy and I had been married at her parents' home in Bridgeport. When I awoke in the darkness, heard a passing DC-3 or something and could not locate myself in space and time. I awoke suddenly terror-stricken because I could not feel the chamois bag around my neck in which we kept the optical component of the sight when an early mission was scheduled. I rose from the bed and fumbled with the nightstand until I woke Sandy. When she spoke, I shook my head, still searching for that goddamned bit of steel and glass. I called her Marie Clair and told her I had lost my fucking sight.

Later, when it was dawn, I got up and walked into the other room where I studied, opened something on communications law and stared at it until the sun was fully up and I was already late for a class at Columbia Law School to which I did not go—though I would the next day, and the day after that, and the next.

Krepinski

For a week I was stoned. Started drinking in London and was still crocked when they flew me back to the States. Crocked. Because I was afraid. When it was really over, what am I going to do? Not the Standard New Jersey plant. Something in my nerves had changed, and I couldn't make it. I need to know every minute that just over the hill is something big, something I don't know. I tell you how it feels: It's like there was this bus bearing down on you, coming real fast, and your guts go crazy, you feel ice water where it was blood. This thing has got to hit you. It has got to. Only inside, you know it won't. Because in your hand, you got this grenade. And at the last minute, you throw it. And the bus goes up. You can see the driver, the passengers, coming apart, and that big thing that was going to run you down, it's nothing. It's gone.

Sometimes it was different, but mostly like that. And I wanted it. In the whole war, I never got hurt. Poole got hurt. They hit the nigger. The Jew got his ass shot down. And they almost blew that Cajun sonofabitch Boileau out of the office. It was funny. I wish they had. But being hurt didn't worry me. I needed that other thing and you got to pay for what you need.

They sent me to Japan and had me in this special program. Just me. Nobody else in the group. Me and three other guys. Teaching us to drop from forty to forty-five thousand, using this new sight, up front in the greenhouse of the B-29. They had me ready, even though the new sight felt funny and I didn't do good like in the 17's with the Norden. But I was still good, and I was ready in August. They had us draw straws and I come up number four. On the sixth, they sent out number one man, and I'm waiting in the wardroom wishing the bastard had a dose so I could go. When he come back, his face is funny. Maybe he does have a dose, I think. But he sits down and I buy him a drink.

—How did it go? I ask him.

—Go? Jesus, it all went. Everything. You never . . .

He drinks and gets another one. Boy, did they make a mistake with this guy. He is crackers. They better not send him anymore. Too much Germany.

—Was it fighters, flak?

—Nothing, he says. —They never seen us. When the weather ship sent us in, it was only light clouds. You could have sat there all day. But the . . . that bomb . . .

—Bombs, I said, finishing my drink and starting to go see the duty officer.

—Bomb, Mitchell, this number one guy says. —They sent us to drop one . . . bomb.

I laughed. They had me here for a gag. They wanted specialists who could drop a pencil in a milk bottle from forty thousand feet. Okay, but the feeling is wrong. You need the fighters, the flak. You need the other planes for it to feel . . . good.

—What did you drop it on? I asked, paying for my drink and turning to go.

—On Hiroshima.

—What's a Hiroshima? I asked him. I didn't know the talk. Like Kabuki and kamikaze and that stuff.

—It's . . . was a city. A hundred thousand people. Maybe two hundred. And it's gone. And I dumped it.

So later that day I found out about the new bomb. They had taken pictures. You know the pictures. You drop this one big stubby gadget and it opens a drogue chute at fifteen thousand and blows at maybe eight. And that's all there is to it. Jesus, I'm watching the pictures and I get so excited I'm standing up. Somebody yells, down in front, and for a minute I don't even know he's talking to me. I can't tell you how I felt. It was like Dresden. Only better. Now we don't just hurt 'em, we wipe 'em out. When we finish, there's nothing, nothing at all. Like erasing a mistake on paper in school, only cleaner. It's like nothing had ever been there. It changes stuff like in a fairy story. You come up on this place and point your wand at it, and say SHAZAM, and it's the City of Glass.

That night I couldn't sleep. I had to go out on the next one. I had to. Jesus, the pictures were only in black and white. I had to see how it really was. I wanted to see down into that big cloud and watch what it did. I thought, they know I can put the next one right where they want it, on the money. But then I thought, what's the use? You miss the target by a mile and you still wipe it off the face of the earth. What's the use of being good? So that I never got any sleep at all that night.

Next day I talked to this colonel, told him I wanted to volunteer for the next one, that I had lost a brother on the *Arizona* at Pearl or something. Told him the Japs killed cousins of mine at Wake, on the march at Bataan, that I wanted to even the score. He told me he understood, but that the second flight crew was locked up. He said he would see, though, and later this lieutenant came in and says that I'm set for the third mission, to check with Major O'Reilly, the pilot of a B-29 called Plymouth Rock. So I did, and then sat tight.

We heard the radio transmission on the Nagasaki run, how it went like a watch, not a hitch. And when they pulled away, they didn't leave anything behind but that big cloud. Later, the next day, I see O'Reilly and say, —The next one's ours.

But he just looks at me. —It looks like there won't be no next one. Scuttlebutt is the Japs are surrendering.

They had to pull me off him, and later they put me in this hospital for a while. I don't know, I couldn't believe it. Not when I was next. Jesus, so close. A day, maybe two away from it. And now it would never happen. At least not so that I could be the bombardier. It was all over, and for nothing. They had robbed me of the big one. From now on, it would be some lousy job doing something like routing cabs or checking construction equipment. For the rest of my life. Jesus, I was broke up, and it took me a month or so to get right. No, it took me that long to get any way at all. I never got right. How could I? The feeling was gone. Now it was the feeling that sooner or later that bus would come. And roll over me, and there was nothing I could do. Nothing at all.

Till I remembered what Yancy had told me. About going to Chicago. So when I got out of the hospital, I did. I went there. And I find out that the police department is giving preferential hiring to veterans. So I decide, why not? My people come from near Chicago. They lived in Cicero till Standard New Jersey started hiring. I like Chicago. None of that sissy flop like New York. And not a million-mile sandbox full of snakes and crap like Texas and down there. Then I meet Gertrude, and it's pretty good. Not the way it was. But you got to forget that. It won't ever be that good again. They got United Nations and all

117

this cooperation. Even though everybody sees how it's going with the Russians, they just let it drift. In 1948, they need pilots again. I go to the Air Force Reserve in Chicago. But the guy just looks at me. —We need pilots, not bombardiers.

—A plane crew includes a bombardier, I told him. —I was the best. I was number three on the atomic bomber list.

But he just shrugs. —They don't use none on a C-47. They need pilots.

—You're gonna need bombardiers, I tell him. —When the balloon goes up, you'll need them.

—That's not contemplated, he tells me.

Well, I contemplate it. I contemplate it plenty. And so do the guys I work with. Everybody I know says we have got to go it with the Russians. Now or later, we got to. But try to tell the government that. Then we find out they've got the bomb, too. Now it's in the fire, you see. Now what? Which is when I start having those dreams that Gertrude never understands. And I go on having them for years.

Michaelis

When it was done, they had no use for my skills, they told me, and I was riffed. For almost a year Candy and I traveled. There's still something wrong between us—no, just something. I know there had been men, but that's all right. You want to use my toothbrush when I'm not using it? All right, fine. So long as it's dry when I come back, and I never know. What I don't know I don't have to do anything about. And Candy is fine for me. She doesn't understand anything, and she enjoys everything. We visited Europe and Asia, we spent some time in Athens, but even the ruins are a letdown. I'm a Greek in America, an American in Greece. The wreck of the Parthenon is small and boxy and sad. The Parthenon you see in pictures is a classic of false perspective. Athens must have been the world's premier small town. They thought small. There was no behind, above or under. Maybe I'm a throwback to the Phoenicians. Or maybe my people came from Atlantis, magicians all.

118

Anyhow, the travel and our bank roll wear thin about the same time. And we're back in the U.S. again. To do what? There are job offers, some of them good. One of the minor defense contractors offers me twenty-five thousand dollars a year to advise and consult, which means it is a good thing to have a former brigadier general on your staff. Even if he hasn't got much in the way of current connections, even if he doesn't know anyone in Washington. And there are not enough generals to go around. So I take the job and decide to see what can be made of it. What's the handle? How can I make this world that thinks it's at peace respond to my "skills"? The Russians took care of that in 1948. They blockaded Berlin, and I almost yelled out loud when I heard. Now it begins again. Spells will be abroad soon, and almost before I can get a plane ticket to Washington, I read the first incantation: STATE DEPARTMENT RIFE WITH REDS. A Wisconsin Senator says we are being betrayed from within. Of course we are. Each one of us is betraying himself every minute. That is why we die. But the Senator is a realist: He comes to believe they are after us. And they will get us. Unless we get them. Which is all true, too. Only being a realist, the Senator cannot grasp that one cannot put down a curse by succumbing to it. If your enemy says he is about to transform you into a dangerous animal, is it a proper response to bite and claw him before he can do so? McCarthy feared Communists as if they were warlocks gifted with the Power. Of course, they are only drab vulgar little men enamored with charts and graphs and planning. They are accountants who imagine themselves economists, Catholics who have forsaken the Pope and worship a wax dummy stuffed with revolutionary pamphlets and lying alone in that spotlighted crypt in Red Square. They are like deviants whose peculiar desires and society's resistance force them to obsession. The Communists are like sex offenders. They can think of nothing but their own ghastly materialist perversion. They have cut themselves off from the deep river of terror and delight that should move from person to person throughout the world, and they are drying up, losing belief, losing personal will. They doubt God and fear him. They reject Satan and know that he is stalking through their missile complexes and dining with Suslov—that time and again he came to them as the czar and that they loved and served him then. And will again.

It is ridiculous, but I was glad it came about. To watch McCarthy, the very embodiment of the Inquisitor, from Spain to New England, reassured me of the nature of things. I knew the Senator would go a long way, because this congeries of aliens called Americans are lonely for the God they left behind and could not find room for on the long trip to Ellis Island. They put His name on their coinage and in their documents, claim His protection, visit His various tombs of a Sunday. All of which proves that He no longer breeds even the least terror in their hearts. He was very large once and died many deaths in many places, but like good wine, He traveled very badly. Now McCarthy threw his curses against the Communist unbelievers, working on the principle that the thief with the loudest voice can cast the blame on others, thus escaping himself unscathed.

But I knew also that the Senator would ultimately fail. Because while he was degenerate enough to believe that the Communists were more evil than we, he was not primitive enough to know why. Not that it would have mattered, finally. He had the equivalent of his Sunday morning, and then the aliens tired of him. He became querulous, tiresome. At last he became megalomanic: accused the whole army and so on. And paid the price for trying to make a crusade against a minor vice. He might have studied the fate of Prohibition, but it would have done no good.

He did this much, though. He gave a name and a local habitation to our dread, our inner certainty that we had come to a strange place and had made of it the richest wasteland in history. It was their fault—the Communists. If it weren't for them . . .

So I was in Washington developing unbelievably broad contacts, diplomats, Congressmen, military men. And from that spectrum, drawing the nods and words that gave my firm contract after contract for the hardware we would need when, out of our neurosis, out of that inarticulate horror that others would steal from us what we had stolen, the day of reckoning came. As a sideline, I suggested to the board of directors that we finance a small electronics firm in Indianapolis which was near bankruptcy. We loaned and finally purchased. Its specialty was electronic detection gear: tiny microphones, all the paraphernalia men use to eavesdrop on the intimacies and secrets of others.

The profits surprised everyone but me. Our clients surprised even me.

And we drifted into and out of the humiliation of the Korean police action. Very large for a police action, but a pattern for police actions of the future. We developed a euphemism not only of name, but of thought. We no longer spoke of war. In those days, most of the men I knew believed we were doomed, that sooner or later the Russians would destroy us. I remember a Senator from New England, drunk, sitting in my hotel room weeping. —I'm too old to learn Russian, he said. Then he sobbed and finished his most recent drink. —Anyhow, they'll shoot me. It won't matter. They'll shoot us all.

—Why would they shoot you? I asked, simply to fill the silence.

—Because . . . because I've . . . I've resisted them. They don't like people to resist them. I've said things.

—I wouldn't worry if I were you, I told him and managed to get his support on a new weapons systems contract before I took off his shoes and let him spend the night on my couch.

It never occurred to me that the Russians would destroy us. No, they had their own horrors to contemplate: a cellar at Ekaterinburg, the garrison at Kronstadt, a villa outside Mexico City. We would go our own way at our own time. We would buy and sell, posture and prance and sing of our patriotism until there was nothing left to sell, every posture worn thin, and the music stopped like a broken record.

Then the fifties were over. In January of the new decade, America proclaimed her first royal family and began, in her own way, a posture she had never quite tried before. I was in Washington that chill day, and I remember him, bareheaded, assured, preceded by another New Englander, an old poet who wrote quaint gnomic verses which, saying little, and that ambiguously, managed the illusion of magic. Then he spoke of a long twilight struggle and hinted that there would be no war. And no peace. And I thought, where will he take these people? He is the son and grandson of aliens. Maybe he knows that this continent has become a spaceship, that it is on a doomed journey, and only one will escape—some farmer's son or a sullen miner who is working four thousand feet down when the reckoning comes.

But he did not know. Later his brother came to know, and for him I felt something. I thought, if they make you President, they will have to come to live with what you know. So it will never happen. They will never be ready for that. The war, of course, began that November day in 1963. There was a rifle and some dim fatherless pointless finger behind it. A phantom shot an image, and we began to come apart. A black—one more alien who, knowing everything, signed himself X—said, "The chickens have come home to roost." And himself died an identical death. Then the fat pathetic neo-Nazi, then the black saint. Then the brother . . .

Then it was time for the rite of decision again. We came to the summer of 1968 amid something like a war, with the children coming to know that if paternity is a fiction, so is the state. They came to magic as if they had invented it. Their music, their clothing. I made many trips with Candy, and on each one I could feel the old ground giving way. We were at the Pentagon one day. It was surrounded by proper children and aged ones who had heard the call to let go, to hand themselves to destiny before destiny was taken from them. Of course, there were police and soldiers. Candy asked me, —What's happening, honey? Are they crazy?

—Sure, I said. —They're crazy. They're going to levitate the Pentagon.

—They what?

—They won't. They forget what a pentagon stands for. In whose name it was built. They should try to bring down Fort Knox. That might work. Named for a minor Scottish demon.

—You're crazy, too.

—You bet. But wait. It's only starting.

That afternoon an old Air Corps friend met me at the hotel. He said General Moseley wanted me to drop by, that Curt LeMay would be there. Something political.

—That sounds crazy, too, Candy said.

—All right, fine, I told her. —Do you want the kids to have all the fun?

—I want somebody to make sense, she said, tossing her coat on the bed.

—That comes later, I said. —We may not be around to see it.

—You give me the creeps.

—Stick around, I said, phoning a friend—no, a connection—

122

in Montgomery, Alabama. And while I waited to be put through, I almost laughed.

Boileau

Out on the water it was still as the moment before creation. On each side of the river there were cypresses and a few pines. The cypresses were thick with moss, and they grew out into the water, forming with their roots natural pools for the bass. There were moccasins swimming, gliding like spirits over the mud and fallen leaves and grass on the banks and moving like slow warped arrows out across the water. I would row near the bank and drift in the tall impersonal shadow of the trees, my eyes catching each flicker and dart on the water's surface. Just out from the shore the water lilies grew in thick carpets, small patches of water between the flat leaves which floated, stirring and bobbing as a ripple from my boat touched them and moved through.

Dragonflies preceded me. The sun stood on my left hand, and the river was without current. Almost a quarter of a mile across and smooth as glass. An owl somewhere back in the woods asked and was not answered. Far down, toward the village, in that milky haze where the sun's power lifted up the water's skin, I would see an old man slowly crossing back and forth in an old wooden boat, tending his trotlines, squeezing off catfish to sell in the market.

My line vanished when it hit the water, and I learned again how to let a bait rest for a long time. Then I would twitch it, without expectation, without regret. After a moment or two, I would begin drawing it in and wipe out of my mind any thought or interest in what might be happening down there. Because there was nothing to be known of that world. It was the color of fine port, that water, and six inches below the surface things vanished. Down there were the stumps and dead branches and rotting plants of generations before my own. There was no time down there at all, and hardly any above,

123

where I drifted for hours, resigned to timelessness. No, not resigned. Because I had nothing then to deny myself. There were no alternatives that I might have chosen, wished to choose. I camped back from the shore near the ruins of an old fishing shack and wanted nothing that could not be gotten in the village with a minimum of talk, and that only of the weather, the condition of the water and where fish had been biting.

I felt frequently, sitting out there amid a pool of mottled sun and shadow, on the edge of tears. After a long while, I came to fear God again and even felt mad enough to speak to Him, to tell Him what He already knew and knew I knew: that the world is a very good place indeed and that its fault, its failing, is man. There was no response. A platitude stated requires none. So I would drift, amazed by the sudden apparition of a nutria as he swam from one patch of hyacinths to another, seeking what was everywhere and all around us.

At noon I would go back to my tent and sleep, dreaming of nothing, thinking nothing. I had no books, no radio, no newspaper. There was nothing to know that I wanted to know. How far I had come was this: I did not even want to forget.

I could turn in my mind back to that moment when I was falling toward the flakhole in the bottom of the bomber. I could stop the picture as I tilted, felt myself going, robbed of oxygen, my masked face falling past the stumps of the turret gunner's legs clotted with bright crystals of freezing blood. And with it stopped, I could see how little there had been to lose in that moment. It was proper. In the decorum of things it had been determined that I should fall back into the chaos we had made, end over the flames of Dresden. Not because I had dropped my bombs. I had not. But I might have. I had decided not to, but when my hands moved to that bombsight, I became a part of it and at one with its purposes. Not their purposes: its.

But a blond bucktoothed waist gunner from Kansas, who had never heard of the Lecompton Constitution or Quantrill, reached out and grabbed my flight suit, hanging on till the other gunner came to help him save the sole survivor from that part of the ship. And in the course of time, his Kansas hands and the accident of his coming forward just then had placed me back here, on the edge of a river deep in my Louisiana. To fish. Because it was not allowed that a man should buy a boat and

124

simply row back and forth over a two-mile stretch. It would cause talk, beginning with the old man who ran trotlines, and move on to the village. I understood that, and anyhow, I had to eat. So I dropped those unlikely bits of plastic into the water, sent them spiraling out and down in that familiar pattern that I had mastered. And often enough, the water would explode as if my lure had been filled with TNT; my line would stretch, my rod bend. And I would reel, turn the small crank as the line squealed, turn and turn against some deep alien strength, pulling against something I had never seen. Sometimes the fish would dive, swim to the river's depths, turning one way and another before I could bring him to the side of the boat and net him. Or again, he would boil upward, out of his element, diving upward into the rare atmosphere, shaking, twisting, trying to rid himself of the sudden inexplicable pain of a tiny minnow which bit back and was possessed by some unnatural power that drew him toward the dark mass of my boat.

It would have been pleasant if I could have felt some compassion, some fine liberal pity for those brilliant green-gold fish I caught. But it was not in me. I respected them. The way I had respected those angry German fighters as they knifed through our formation. Because the fish were fine and clean and merciless and ruthless like the river itself, like this swamp and wilderness where there were no debates and no appeals. If I were watchful and careful, I could live out my life on the river. If I made too many mistakes, it would kill me.

And I rested in that. Rested in the river and the swamps and considered what I would do next.

I considered for a long time. I thought, fugitively, of the priesthood. But I was beyond that—beyond even the Trappists, because I wanted nothing. Not even salvation. I wanted to fish, to move on the water, to sit deep in the night with a small fire burning and watch the river out beyond stand like a great mirror reflecting the stars, the moon, the high distant lights of a passing airliner on its way from Atlanta to New Orleans. I would sit thinking of nothing—not paralyzed. No, I had never been more active. It was just that then there was nothing to think about. I had gone from Tulane to Texas to Europe. Now I was back. Being back was a meaning. My father understood. He had given me money and told me to stay out for as long as I wanted to. That there was nothing needed doing. I thanked him and left his law office on Poydras Street and did not go back for three years.

In that time I learned nothing. I mean nothing useful in the world. Oh, I perfected resignation and came to see that dropping that last load of bombs over Dresden would have had no meaning. Any more than not dropping it. Because it is an illusion that we are independent, that our actions belong to us. We belong to movements and to tides and histories. We move among epochs and aeons, turning here and there amid walls so high and wide that we cannot see them. We can change nothing, and only modesty becomes us. That is what I learned. That, and not to be hungry, not to resent the way things are. Not to cry or to laugh, not to fall prey to the Faust in oneself—much less in others. I came to understand what it means to live and how small a thing it is to die, and none of it was the produce of my mind, but came rather from the healing tissue of my nervous system. And when I felt that I could care or not care precisely as I chose, struggle or give way as I wished, I let my mind come to life again to discover how I should pass the time from now until that God I had learned to love and fear again called me to judgment.

And I became a historian. Finished graduate school in three years at Johns Hopkins and returned to study and write, living just across Lake Pontchartrain from my father, who thought I had made an excellent choice, inasmuch as there was no money in my work. It had no commercial value of any kind. I took a small house in St. Tammany Parish, close to the river, only a long walk from Madisonville.

—I was going to suggest you become a master blacksmith, he told me. —But some damned fool would have come to have his mule shoed and that would have ruined it.

But no one came to ask that I unravel the problems of command in the XI Union Corps at Chancellorsville for pay, and so I was safe.

My field was rebellion. From Spartacus through Danton, from Cromwell through Davis and Lee, from Bakunin to Lenin. I studied those who had not been resigned, who had torn the fabric of the world and changed all our destinies. I was a good student of such business, because I did not believe in it. Yet I was not opposed to it on ideological grounds. I recognized revolution as a way of passing time, of occupying one-self—or oneselves—until history came to a close.

My problem as a historian was a rare one. According to my senior professor, I was too detached.

—A degree of detachment, of course, he said. —One has to . . . but . . . this paper on Cromwell at Drogheda. My God.

—Kill the worms, I said, —and you'll have no snakes.

—Butchering children, he began.

—Is it better to wait until they're grown? Until they're old enough to understand what's happening to them?

The professor sucked on his pencil. —It would be better if . . . such things never happened.

I thought of Frank Little, lynched with his leg in a cast at Butte, Montana. Joe Hill tied to a chair and shot in Utah. I thought of the fortunes of Peter and Paul, the Alexis Ravelin, the Bastille, Servetus burned upwind in the name of Jesus, himself nailed to a cross after the manner of Spartacus, who died like Prometheus.

—Such things will happen. There's a poem somewhere. It sounds like Dante, but it isn't:

> Great lovers lie in Hell, the stubborn ones
> Infatuate of the flesh upon the bones;
> Stuprate, they rend each other when they kiss,
> The pieces kiss again, no end to this.

—Ah, the professor said. —Ransom. But . . . lovers.

—Revolutionaries, soldiers are the great lovers, I told him. —Beyond kissing, there is tearing away the flesh to find . . . the essence.

—Yes, but there is no . . .

—I know. No essence. But the flesh of things doesn't suffice. The inquisitors . . . I think Torquemada . . . was honest.

The professor pursed his lips. He felt much surer. —No doubt. But they were . . . monsters. They killed a hundred thousand . . . their autos da fé . . .

I sat back and stared out the window. Let us measure the professor's resignation.

—I was a bombardier in the late war, I told him. —In all modesty, I outdid the best of the inquisitors in a single raid. We killed nearly seventy thousand in one night. Another day . . . You've heard of the Dresden raid?

127

The professor rose and walked to the window.

—And I can assure you I am honest, I said to his back.
—Upright to a fault.

—They . . . the Germans . . .

—Were heretics?

—You know what . . . they did. Dachau. Ravensbrück . . .

—Yes. And I know what we did. Another poem:

> Those to whom evil is done,
> Will do evil in return . . .

—The Jews, the Slavs . . .

—Will have their day and do no differently. And plead what was done to them. It's the flesh. Do you remember what they did to Cromwell's corpse?

—His head mounted on a pike . . .

—He had been dead almost three years. But not being a believer, Charles had to rend his dead flesh.

—What do you expect?

—Nothing. A bombardier expects nothing. He comes to wish . . . He comes to feel better when he's in the air, flying. Except . . .

—Yes?

—Except there may be something above the sky. Something to bomb us in the act of bombing. Cromwell never thought of that. One has to believe in limits in order to . . . smash the heads of infants against walls.

We did not talk again. My article was published in a Northern journal which presumed objectivity as a form of compassion. The editors, blessed with an ignorance beyond their deserving, were right. For the wrong reasons.

I did a piece on Nacheyev and Bakunin, comparing their relationship to that of Verlaine and Rimbaud, Wilde and Alfred Douglas. The point was a fetching one: The old romantic, failing to rejoin society, will invariably be seduced by a young nihilist. It is the natural course of revolution. Only a latent or active homosexual can possibly sustain the kind of hatred and anger at social order necessary to surrender everything to its destruction. If, at last, your hankering queer cannot strike a blow at society, he will give up and practice his milder vice. Neither Nacheyev, Rimbaud nor Douglas was a pederast. They were beyond that. I thought that my own balance had robbed me of revolutionary possibilities. I knew what they knew. But I could not care enough to want to alter the inalterable. So I wrote of folly, of the course by which men hurt themselves and others even more than is inevitable. And by doing so, I became well known in certain quarters. As one might expect, it seemed to many that I was a champion of revolution. I did not argue or try to clarify things. For all I knew or cared, perhaps I was such a champion. I tried to write clearly and accurately, making sure at each juncture that there was no betraying jot of love or hatred in my heart. There was only interest.

I remember, in the late fifties, when I last saw my father in the Hotel Dieu. He was very thin and tired and knew that the next heart attack would be the end of it. And he did not care at all. It was time. I was proud of him.

—I think you're a damned nihilist. He laughed weakly. —What the hell should I do with my money? You'd buy dynamite with it, wouldn't you?

—Not a chance, I said. —I'd buy a life insurance company.

That broke him up. —Same thing, he chuckled. —I can see you doing an actuarial table on the world. That's what you are doing, isn't it?

—You've got it, I told him. It was wrong, but too perceptive to argue.

He lay back on his pillow and looked at me, well pleased. —Tell me, what's coming? What won't I be here to see?

I felt tears in my eyes and thought that, like Cromwell, I believed in limits. I loved my father, so I was glad that he was dying. Dying very well. —You won't be missing anything, I said. —Nothing you'd have enjoyed. It won't be good. There'll be chaos and war, then a Caesar. A world empire. Ours or theirs.

—That won't matter, he said, waving his hand. —Whoever does it will have to . . . to become . . .

— . . . What it takes to rule an empire.

—Do you think this country . . .

—Yes, I said. —It could. Not now. There'll be a last burst of piety. Maybe cowardice will stop us.

—Grace won't . . .

—Remember Mine Run?

My father smiled. —When they do the wrap-up on this . . .

country, we will have been right. Despite everything. The Negroes . . .

—Will cancel out the brutality of slavery with their own viciousness? You can count on it. And the Yankees . . .

—Will be found wanting. How?

—Economically, I expect. The stuff will go out of their free enterprise. It runs on bad faith. And even that kind of faith is a diminishing resource, isn't it?

—Not for me, my father said. —I have plenty. I have faith in you. I loved your mother, I love you. Now . . . the rest is a good clean guess. I guess He's waiting. What do you guess?

And then, right then, dying, without a prayer and in no sense aware of what he had done, my father handed me my patrimony. I must have looked peculiar. He frowned.

—Are you all right?

—Oh, I said. —I'm . . . fine. It's only that . . . Jesus, I see. I see what . . .

I left then for supper at Delmonico's, and when I was roused from my dinner by a phone call, it was over. I was an orphan at last. But hardly alone. Because now I knew what I had been learning since that first day at the Blockhouse when I squatted against the wall determined not to resist what I could not change. It had seemed for so long that I was making do without guessing. But I had been wrong. I had been finding in myself the strength to resign myself to Him, to God. To sit amidst the world expecting nothing and everything, knowing that from out there His things were falling minutely into the world to explode within our hearts, our minds, our freeways, our institutions.

Jacobs

When I got back, it was insane. I came down the gangplank at Pier 82, and there's Morris. He's nodding and smiling like he had told me to go be brave and it would all turn out fine. There's my mother, crying, twisting her hands in my father's coat, but with no expression on her face at all. My father is only standing there looking at me as if I were something that had straggled back from the grave. My mother is not even looking, only waving a handkerchief I know she bought weeks ago for this day, waving it from behind her as if to ward off a spirit returned from the dark place. You wouldn't believe it. When I saw them, I wondered, could they be embarrassed that I had come back alive? With these people, you never know.

Me? Listen, I was always skinny as a spider. Now I'm out of the German stalag *Luft* five or six weeks, and the best, the very best, meal in there was a bowl of leek soup and a heel of black bread. I look like one of those other Jews, the kind who weren't walking down gangplanks back into New York.

There's my life crowded down below behind a white picket fence waiting for customs to release me to it. I don't know. I've been to Texas and I've been to hell. What am I going to do?

What I'm going to do first is get caught by some newspaper people. They hear I was over Dresden, and this is minor fame. I broke the back of the Third Reich. Then they hear I am a Jew who was in one of the German camps. I am, for this one afternoon, a big deal. They take my picture with Momma and Poppa on either side. Morris is just behind my right shoulder. On tiptoe, grinning like a fight promoter whose boy has made it. God, later I see it in the *Post*. I am so skinny it's sickening. My uniform looks like I stole it or like it was washed with its owner inside, and the only thing not Sanforized was me. Even the cap was large.

—What was it like over Dresden? a reporter wanted to know.

—Hot, I said. —Very hot. You should have been there.

Everyone laughs, and for a moment I can't understand why. One reporter is a woman. She wants to know how I feel about the two hundred thousand people who were down there. My mother cuts in.

—You should ask a Jewish boy how he felt about the Germans, she blusters, beginning to cry again. Morris shakes his head at the woman.

—I don't know, I finally manage to get in. —Up where I was, they were killing us. My plane . . . I don't know if anybody else got out. Was it . . . two hundred thousand that died?

Somebody told her to shut up, and then they asked me if the Germans had treated me different because I was Jewish.

131

—No, I said. —They didn't know. There was a . . . mix-up. If they knew you were a Jew, they treated you different all right. No, they thought I was a . . . something else.

Nobody said anything for a moment, and we slipped away. Morris carried my duffel bag, and Momma couldn't keep her hands off me. It was a Friday, and that evening she made everybody go to services. Which became a thanksgiving when people saw me. There was a lot of crying and handshaking. I knew why. I was the remnant, the fragment put aside. So many of them had lost people, you can't imagine. They knew the names, all of them: Dachau, Belsen, Ravensbrück, Buchenwald, and the rest. All of them had died there, naked and helpless and shamed. And they had ridden across the skies of Europe with me in vengeance. As if under the bland white American star there had been painted a shadowy Star of David. I had gone to war and come back. I was Jonathan returned, a solitary warrior, their future and their pride. So it was Thanksgiving and Kaddish all together. Which it always is, isn't it?

After a day or so, things settled down. I had time to walk and think. What would I do? What? The world was open: Jobs for me would be easy. Loans, anything. It was the summer of 1945, and soon the Japanese were out of it, and then it ended. For a little while. Peace. The peace of exhaustion and horror. Hitler burned in the rubble outside his bunker. Mussolini shot like a dog with a little girl named Claretta Petacci beside him by the same dagos who had cheered him five years before. Tojo about to hang. Because he lost. Peace, with a new bomb blowing a new age into the world and the Russians drawing back inside themselves. Europe a huge grave, mined farms, blasted cities, starving people. But what does Jacobs want? Name it.

I named school. College. That's right. Back to where I was before it began. —Be a doctor, my mother said, —a psychiatrist. It's a good job. You can help confused people.

—The hell with confused people, I said. —Who gives a shit for confused people?

So I went back to CCNY and read literature. —My God, my father said, why not politics? —I've been a politician, I said. All over Europe I did politics. Now I'm going to do something useless. So I did the bachelor's in a year and the master's in one more. I learned French. And German. I was obsessed with the German. I read Goethe and Schiller; I read Klopstock. I read

Mann and Broch and Musil. I read all of Musil, myself a man without qualities, without place or purpose. When I was done, I took a place at the Washington Square campus of NYU. I taught composition to kids and some men my own age. No, I taught them literature and we called it composition and it made us both happy. They didn't want to write, and I didn't want to read what they wrote. What we both wanted was to know. So we all read together. It didn't hurt anybody. But it wasn't what I wanted. What did I want? To write? No, I didn't want to write. What would I write about? You know what, don't you? I wanted to read, to learn something. So I thought, be an editor. Start a magazine.

So I did. Only it wasn't a magazine. It was a press. At first, with the GI loan money, I could only do maybe two or three books a year. And they had to make their cost and a little more. I did all right. I published a poetry text and got a few adoptions. I did a volume of translations from Kafka, a selection of Lorca, and in New York there were always a few people to buy books. People from the Village I had met at the Square when I taught. People my family had no use for. A Trotskyite named Landho, some kind of Portuguese, I guess. A Socialist who had known Big Bill Haywood and still corresponded with Ralph Chapman. He was also a fanatic Catholic, don't ask me how or why. Others: thin girls with bobbed hair who worked for Henry Wallace. Boys who studied diabolism and yoga. My God, I had never known how many people were bent out of shape. They went in every direction in those days, Spanish Civil War veterans, Negroes from Alabama who stuttered. A Hungarian who sobbed when he was drunk for having worked very briefly with the Hitler *Jugend*. It was a good place to stay abreast of what was happening in the new writing. In a year or so, I was in the black a few thousand dollars. I wanted to do a really fine book, something as important as Mailer's *The Naked and the Dead*. But there was no such book. I mean, nothing I could get hold of. In 1948 the writers wanted to say something. By 1950 what they wanted was a ten-thousand-dollar advance. One guy who had worked with the Progressives in 1948 told me about his new novel: on the dry rot in the Congress. It foretold the bankruptcy of the congressional system and the coming of an end to parliamentarianism, a progress to people's government.

—Listen, he said, —I'd like to give it to you.

—So give it to me, I said. —Let me read it.

—You wouldn't like it. It's not your kind of book.

—I'll tell you, Maynard, honestly I will. But maybe it is. Who can say?

—No, listen, I mean, look. They want to see it at Random House.

—Do you want to work with Cerf? Is that what you want?

He squirmed. —If they take it, it's ten big ones. Minimum. What are you going to do?

What he was going to do was revise it, cut his book up till it was, as they say, right. Real right. And take the ten and go somewhere and drink and mourn his castrated novel. I saw a copy the next year. It was called *In Congress,* and the hero was a brave, hard-hitting, longsighted stand-in for Robert Taft. It was very well reviewed in *Time* and sold a lot. They were thinking of a movie and bought it for a hundred and fifty thousand dollars. But it was 1952 by then, and before it could get into production, you know what happened. Maynard went to France with his money and died there in the late fifties, leaving his money to his chauffeur, some Italian kid named Agostinelli.

So I kept making it. Very small, very honest. I worked with Joe Friedman and the *Venture* group, trying to keep one of the great little magazines going. I published some broadsides against the witch-hunts, against that obscenity Wisconsin sent to Washington. I put out some of the stuff that came to be called Beat—until the writers got discovered by *Life.* Then their prices went out of sight. One day, when I had lost out on one of the great deviant manuscripts of our time—Putnam's outbid me hands down—I married my secretary.

Which caused mixed emotions all around. A good Jewish girl, you say. What's the sweat? Right, all right, fine. I'll tell you. She was too good a Jewish girl, that's what the sweat.

My mother shrugs and sits down. My father is dead of a stroke. Really dead. Morris lives in my father's old den now. He is old and feeble and doesn't get a haircut anymore and is retired and very religious for an agnostic and still sits and nods. My mother wears thick glasses and speaks through this tiny porthole of a mouth behind which there is no tooth given her by nature. God? She talks like around a peach pit and has absolutely no expression. No, you don't watch her. You watch Morris. You *listen* to Momma. No, you don't listen to Morris. Nothing to hear. You *watch* him. It is what? Stereophoniscopic communication? I guess so. But it rattles the nerves.

—So you marry and don't tell anybody, she said, no expression, voice trembling, but subtones of trying to understand. I'm watching Morris, who has tears in his eyes.

—I want to bring Mariam here. Tonight. I'll take you out to dinner. It's a celebration.

—Look who's celebrating, Momma says. —The lawyer? The doctor? The plutocrat? Who will you dun for the money? Will you forge a check on your mother? Do we do the dishes? Does your wife do dishes?

There was this long pause.

—We don't go out, Momma says. I can tell she wants sympathy because Morris is nodding sadly, looking out the window with a single residual tear trembling on the end of his nose.

Then Momma begins again. —So you marry the agent of a foreign power. That's nice. Is she going to steal the atom bomb? Maybe I'll have a grandson born in the shadow of the galleys.

—Momma, the girl is Jewish. She believes in Israel.

—She should go to Israel. Go be a nomad. Get a tent.

Morris is angry. He's shaking a finger at me. This uncle is a genius. He makes Chaplin look like a blabbermouth.

—This is stupid, I said.

Morris covers his face instantly, and I hear my mother's voice muted, distant, as if over that small, dark, unimpeded cavity in the lower center of her paralyzed face a hand had been raised in pain and surprise.

—So I should love the country, I'm stupid. Go. Leave. Take your wife and go to the sand pile. Pick fleas with the Arabs. You deserve each other.

Morris is pointing at the door, his self-discipline back and in firm pitiless control again. —Go, my mother croaked. I blushed at the melodrama, but I went, Morris behind me, hobbling, pointing, his face twisted, working mutely. As I reached the bottom of the steps, I looked back up to where this ridiculous old man I didn't know stood, arm extended, pointing toward the East River, and a voice his and not his coming to me from far off. —Go. Go to Israel, and I went to find Mariam waiting for me downtown. We went to the Stork Club and ate a dinner I couldn't afford while Mariam talked about her country she

135

had never seen and chided me for not knowing Hebrew, which she could not read or speak.

It was 1955 when I really got started. That year I joined the reform Democrats, went to work as an editor at Putnam's (when they beat you, join 'em. What would Freud say to that?) and fathered a son. Who was named Moishe by his mother and dedicated to the New Jerusalem. The kid was Momma's from parturition onward. Reform was not yet democratic. But I brought *The Deer Park* to Putnam's.

Word was in the trade that Mailer's new one was a bomb. Maybe that Word did something in my brain. But no, because I had read *Barbary Shore* and knew what it was to be a man without memory, pestered more terribly by what he could not know than what he knew for sure. *Barbary Shore* was a book for children, for all of us who had never grown up really and never would because we had all once starred as juvenile leads in a supercolossal movie called the Second World War. *The Naked and the Dead* had been the script itself, with Krepinski, Michaelis, Boyd, all of us. *Barbary Shore* had followed us out of the theater, tracked us as we emerged back into the streets where the permanent war went on, the one we knew nothing about. That book had sent me down roads within myself I had not wished to travel, had shown me how whatever hope a man dares to possess must be founded once and for all on a pure and unalterable hopelessness, a wisdom composed of the certainty that every wisdom is ashes, every truth a sword that waits for us to fall upon it. It drove me to the library to find out about that man, that latter-day Jesus whose name is never mentioned even by his Judas, who died for our sins in Mexico City before they sent me out to help some of his betrayers kill others just like them. *Barbary Shore* lay at the edge of sand, beneath those stars I tried alternately to remember and forget.

And now he had a new book. Which would have to go to the future because there was no place else to go. And I wanted to publish it. So I had to go find him, find Mailer. They said he was a monster, that he took people apart. Or was he, in one mode, a sword for suicides, a living act of charity and justice? Yes, well, I found him. In a bar on Fifty-second Street where a friend who had known him at Rinehart's had said he drank. Alone or with others.

136

It was dark, and I blinked until, at a table, alone, I saw him. Thick in the shoulders, curly hair, eyes tight like those of a predatory animal poised always for those rare instants of action when it lived totally, to which all the rest tended, without which the rest was nothing. He could be a killer, I thought. A fine professional killer. Maybe he is. Only on paper? He was smoking with an empty glass in front of him. I asked the bartender what he was drinking, bought one and my own scotch on the rocks and walked into his field of fire.

I set down the drink and pulled out the chair opposite. He did not look up. The cigarette smoldered between his lips, and he seemed to be looking at my hand where it rested on the back of the chair. I looked at my wedding ring and then sat down. He took the cigarette from between his lips with a delicate gesture.

—Drink some of it, he said, looking at me for the first time.

I picked up his drink and sipped it. —That's enough, he grinned. —You can leave a little.

It was a good grin, and I wondered what it cost him. He looked bad, like a man who had grown up in fits and starts because the rhythms of his mind and emotions and body were not always in phase. Like one of us?

—You can't be too careful, I said.

—Hah. No, I can't. What is it?

—What?

—Did I libel you? Did we fight together in different regiments? You don't look like you need money. Did you train in Texas?

—Yes . . .

—Libel?

—No, Texas. I . . . trained there. I'm . . . I was . . . a bombardier.

—Oh, he said, and looked away as if his interest had died aborning. I thought, he thinks only the infantry did any fighting.

—The new book . . .

—Try your local bookshop. They'll mail it in a plain brown wrapper. You read it with one hand.

—I'm at Putnam's . . .

—That's a nice house, he said. —Go away.

But I didn't. I didn't go away. I am the midwife who delivered Sergius O'Shaugnessy into the world. Which might one day explain everything.

I tell you of *The Deer Park* because it was my triumph. Not Mailer's. He would go on and do more, better things. But it was my reason in those days. Do you know how I felt when I read:

> For do we not gamble our way to the heart of the mystery against all the power of good manners, good morals, the fear of germs, and the sense of sin?

Then, in the night, Mariam in my arms, trying to seduce me always not with her body or even the promise of love, but that vision of hers wherein the Diaspora was gathered in again, where her—our—son might feel all around him the ghosts of genesis. I would close my eyes tightly and say, no, I have to do it here, whatever it is. I have to see the truth told, eyes opened, ears unstopped. I come from the Dark Room. I come from another desert, and I've killed for this place, this people. I would say that to her. And she would put her mouth against my ear and whisper fiercely.

—This is no place. This is no people. What is this? What am I?

—A foreign agent, I told her once, hands on her hips, thrusting, thrusting.

And she laughed, contemptuously, feeling me within her, knowing she had chipped away another fragment of my resolve, promising me with innuendo of her cunt some possession of her, of Moishe, whenever the wearing down should be complete.

So that next year I began what I thought to be my last campaign. I worked very hard for Stevenson, trying to believe that some part of the American world must be malleable. I learned the sorrows of street corners, the doom of doorbells in the Bronx. But I could not be in Wyoming and Kansas. It was not given to me to tell them all that the grandfather they had put in the White House was only good for killing, for crushing. I wanted to say, let the generals bury the generals. Let that movie be over. Let me—us—break the contract. But like *Cleopatra*, it went on and on, budget gone mad, past all hope that profit

138

could justify investment. Bankruptcy at Paris, the Russians shooting our plane, called so rightly U-2, out of the air, and the movie continuing zanily into still one more reel.

It was January, 1960, when I thought that perhaps I had won, pulled an absurd victory through the mute heart of the nation I wanted for a home. They inaugurated John Kennedy, and that night when I made love to her, she said it didn't matter, and I covered her mouth with mine.

—Shut up, I mumbled, giving her my tongue. —Just shut up.

And it was very good. You can't imagine how good it was that night. I was at the threshold of mystery and knew it was there to win.

Kennedy had won. He won and went on to awaken the young, to fill their minds with new images of communion and restitution. I slept that night with no tissue of those old nightmares and waking horrors that I had brought home with me from the Big Movie. He came to make all things new. And three years later the Southerners killed him, gunned him down in Dealy Plaza, there in Texas where the desert invades hearts, where they must keep the Dark Room like a shrine.

Let me sound like a perfect fool. Let me tell you that I cried for over a week. I would be eating or working on a manuscript, and it would come back. I would hear the shots, their wild distant echo, and see him fall forward and then back, his head flying apart, his blood spreading across the country, the people. And another young man said, "The chickens have come home to roost." Then they killed him, too. And amid the agony of those days, I thought again of those missions. When we were the chickens, the great birds called up from ordinary life— whatever that might be—and invested with the mechanics of hell. We laid the eggs of destruction, the payment for what Germany had conjured up and brought to pass. We had believed that we were only technicians—no, we had not. That is what we wanted to believe. That we were some kind of businessmen delivering goods called for. But Michaelis had known better. He had made us believe we were gods, magicians. We had made cities vanish, trains and ships and planes go up in smoke. We had transformed human beings into garbage. We were a generation raised to the magic of violence. Chickens bred to kill. Consider all of it. Which one of us did not carry a fascination with guns, with power, with an enormous capacity to rule and

139

dominate and destroy? I sat and thought that each of us had fought a different war. Poole bringing vast agony to whites, Boileau silently reversing Appomattox, Krepinski mad with the joy of pogrom. Boyd, the team man, bringing down barbarians, another consul ready to report to the Senate and people of America, who existed only in his mind. And I? Had I been Joshua, slaying the Canaanites, giving them over to the sword, destroying them utterly, that the temple might be built in the time and at the place ordained? I suppose so. And each of us lusting backward, even behind those images for some other that had begun to blur before we learned—or were tricked into walking upright.

Except for the war, we might have lived out our lives moving from one small triumph to the next. Couldn't we? Men have. For generations. We are all peasants, and, left alone with our sorrows and our victories, there is no danger in us. But the war had triggered all our images. Things were possible. Now, after twenty years of fitful slumber, those dreams beyond compromise were awakened again. Blacks, Poles, Jews, Southerners, Establishment servitors—all of them and a hundred others were rousing, gathering to their kind, and God knows what the end of it would be.

Then it came to me that I had never wondered what image moved Michaelis. What? Was he avenging himself against the Turks? Or moving eastward to take again the topless towers of Berlin? No, I thought. There was another Greek. Hermes Trismegistus? Surely. He was the warlock. It was his power to raise the dead, to cast off sleep. To figure forth the Apocalypse, to reveal mysteries so long ignored. That was his image. To blast apart the small island of reason that we had built so painfully, trod so uncertainly. To carry us back, each to the magic he understood, had always been prepared to worship if only it were called forth and made to live. And when it was roused, what could lay it again?

For months afterward Mariam and I could not talk. Her Zionism became then a wall behind which only other fanatics were admitted. I could not go in there. Because I knew that her Jerusalem was only a city. And I thought, one day we might be called upon to bomb it. I dared not care for anything that existed. I had cared for Kennedy. I had tried to care for America. What was the use? Everything that existed would finally come

140

under the bomb. The images rolled and turned, and Germany and Japan became our allies, Russia and China our implacable enemies. To love anything larger or farther away than one's own hand would be mad. Either others would bring down the object of your love or you—you yourself—would be called upon to bring it down. Only fantasy was safe. Those who try to make their fantasies manifest are mad. We put them away. Until they are treated, made well. Until they recognize their fantasies for what they are. We could have cured Jefferson. We could have helped Calhoun and Lincoln. Calhoun who saw that war in the distance, and brought it on by saying so—even from beyond the grave. Lincoln who dreamed himself dead so many times that the very strength of his vision called up an actor to make it real.

I saw all this and tried to tell Mariam. Don't dream, I told her. Dreams come true. Then they are ruined. There is no help for it. Just don't dream. Let things go. Let Israel be a wedge of useless sand and ancient memories and a song at the synagogue. If you don't . . .

But it was useless. She couldn't help it. She did it. We had a second son, and she named him David, and when we were riding in a cab back from the hospital, she took my hand. It was the first mark of affection she had shown in months.

—Don't leave us alone, she said. —You know what I mean.

—Yes, I said. —But I don't know what I can do. Don't you see?

—Life, she said, tears glistening in her eyes. —Don't you want it? Couldn't we just pack up, move to Israel?

—They trained me in Texas, in the desert, I started.

—What's that got to do with it? Texas isn't Israel. How can you act as if Texas . . .

I told her that we would see. I told Mariam that we would see. I meant nothing in particular. I was too frightened to mean anything. I thought, if you go, it will happen again. But there, under the stars . . . you aren't Abraham. It won't be Him. You know what will come. Another bombardier. God knows. An Arab commando. A Moslem.

But she took me to mean that I would wait until the elections of 1968. To see what this country was going to do. As if an election, any surface thing, could determine what the country was going to do.

—We can wait, she said. —We've waited so long.

—We . . .

—Your people. Your real people.

And what I forgot to say, what only occurs to me to mention now is that my wife was not religious. The idea of God seemed crude to her.

So that, in order to save myself from whatever might be waiting there in that desert for me, I began to concern myself in politics again. I worked for Robert Kennedy. He became Senator from New York. It was absurd, and once, sitting with him and a handful of party workers, I listened to him and wondered if he didn't feel the same. He spoke of living every day for its own sake. He told us that he made no plans for the future anymore. As if there were no future. As if for him the image of an unbroken succession of tomorrows all came to an end just before noon on that sunny November day in Dallas. We all sat quietly when he had finished talking. I thought he had taken something away from us, and thus he had given us something. Perhaps America was growing old now. Perhaps we would need to learn how to live without appeal to all those shadows which we had brought with us from other countries, other ages. Now we might learn how to value the image of a child's face when you have seen him eat his fill. We could give justice and security to working people, to the poor. We could share what we have with black people and those who had had no luck, no breaks. And maybe we could fall in love with the image of doing right. That was what Robert Kennedy wanted. If we could bring it to pass, maybe I would forget that other ecstasy in the clouds above Germany. And the dead years afterward, examining and throwing away one reason for living after another.

I told Mariam, —Maybe he had to die so that they would listen. To his brother. It's possible, you know.

She shook her head irritably. —You're a fool. You wait and see. They won't listen to anyone. That big horseface from Texas is their style. If it weren't him, they'd take Rockwell. I don't know how long it's going to take you to grow up.

Only awhile, my love. Only until one June morning when you come to tell me that another image has gone down. Then I will be old enough, older than anyone. And where does an old man go? An old man who has tried everything, only to see nothing work except murder. Where does he go?

Poole

When I come back, they didn't hardly let me get off the plane before they dropped it on me. It was a big rawboned captain from Maryland or somewhere thereabouts.

—You go over there, he said.

—Over where?

He pointed at some seats behind a pile of luggage and airfreight. I saw a couple of black guys stooped over in those leftover movie seats or whatever they were.

—I don't like over there. It don't look like officers' quarters to me. I reckon I'll go over with the rest.

He kind of looked like I had hurt him. Here was old Zonk standing on his feet all day, and the first nigger officer he ever saw just naturally has *got* to come on strong.

—Look, he says. —I got my orders.

—Look, I said, mocking him. —I got my pride. I'm gonna sit over there.

He shook his head and then motioned with one white-gloved hand.

I decked the first MP because he was slow, seeing I had them gold bars. But the second one laid me out, cut right through my cap. I wished later I had left in the frame instead of crushing that cap. Only it looked so good with the sides pushed in. It didn't look near as good with my top stove in.

After a while I came around. I was strung out in one of them movie seats. I woke up staring at a blank wall. There was a sailor beside me. He was kind of grinning, but looking away like he didn't want to see me. I rubbed my head. They had laid my cap in my lap and put my duffel beside me. I thought, Oh, them blessed Zonks. Just put me where I belonged. Nothing extra for their trouble. Things has improved.

143

This sailor next to me just has to take a look at last. He couldn't help it.

—Head hurt, buddy?

—Shit, naw, I told him. —Just got my blood to stirring. I'm going back for another time soon as I figure it all out.

—Be the rest of your life, he said. —War's over.

—Want to bet? I asked him. But he paid me no mind. He was talking to himself.

—You just a nigger again, he was saying. —Just a ordinary nigger. In Memphis or St. Joe. In Seattle or Bosstown. Niggers is a dime a dozen. You can find a nigger anywhere.

—Not this nigger, I said. —Last price I went for was half a buck alone. Next time it'll be a good deal more.

—Dime a dozen, the sailor said. And settled down to wait till they were ready to let us go.

Which they did, and I got to hustling. I got me a job at a hotel in Washington. Night bell captain. There I was in uniform. It was all the same. Going up and coming down. Laying the stuff on them Zonks coming and going. Girls and boys. You could look at one of them and guess what kind of appetite he had. You could spot a titty freak or a gumdrop easy. Man wanted chains and leather, wasn't no problem. Stomping and slapping cost more. And I had me a good forty percent all the way around. I built me a stable. I had everything you ever heard of. I even used to go out to drive-in movies to see what was new and then go find somebody who could do it for a price. Nothing easier. I thought of old Michaelis. Should of had him for a partner. Old Michaelis wasn't worth a shit. He had to end bad. But he was all right, fine. He turned me onto that box and I come to see a lot by using it. I come to see how everything on earth is just who dumps what on who. Look at it: Fella dumps it on a girl, and she dumps it in a crib. Boom. Zonk dumps on the black man while the man upstairs dumps on him. It gotta be that way. Whole idea in life is to find a way to swap being a dumpee for being a dumper. Knowing all the time that he who dumps must be dumped upon. Rich dumps on poor. Till he dies. Then guess who digs the grave and dumps it in on the rich man. Love is dumping. Hate is dumping. You *got* to see how war is dumping. It's all dumping, and when you see that, you can move to the next step. Which is learning how to dump and dodge.

I got good. I had some money put up in Prince Albert cans. Had over four thousand dollars in small bills when who should show up? In the hotel? You guessed it. It had to be old Jacobs. The world's great dumpee. Only time in his life he turned the tables was when they flew him over Germany and told him, pull the plug on those mothers.

He come to the hotel on his way from somewhere to somewhere. Working in something about books. I thought he was doing the horses. I thought, shit, this boy is gone straight. He's got him a teeny piece of mob and he can give me a race. Just one. Can you reckon out what twenty to one with four thousand dollars spread here and there comes to? Right. It comes to not being any kind of recognizable nigger anywhere around. But it all come to nothing. This poor child is in the other kind of books.

—Maybe I could do my memories for you, I told him.

—Listen, you're kidding. But, yes, do your own story. It could sell a million copies. The way it really is. The life of a black man in this country. The insults, every day a war from getting up to lying down, the deep-down sick feeling when you see a bunch of white guys on a street corner . . .

He sounded like he was going to write it himself, like he had lived it. I couldn't see why he'd need me.

—That's nice, I said. —Go, lay it on me.

He stopped and studied me a minute. —Would you . . . do it?

—Naw, I said. —It ain't my stool to sit on. Anyhow, who needs to pee in public? I'm all right. I got used to war a long time ago.

He went on talking kind of crazy. He didn't like the government. I mean, shit, who likes the government? He didn't have no use for the social order. Fact is he didn't give a shit for much of anything. Some kind of books I bet he did. Finally he got to thanking me for that mix-up in our dog tags again. Seemed like he'd done that before.

—Forget it, I said. —You done thanked me. In London, huh?

—I didn't . . . see you. I didn't see anybody. You were gone when they let me out.

—That's funny. Maybe you wrote.

So I had to listen to all this shit how my fucking dog tags

saved him from a fate worse than life. How them Nazis wanted just any kind of excuse to fry him. It was all right, fine. So we had got 'em mixed up and good come of it. How can you thank a man for a accident? Turn it around, you gonna hang a man for another kind of accident, huh? Accidents you got to count out. But not Jacobs. Naw, it all means something to hear him tell it. Then he got onto Texas, got to talking about Michaelis and the Blockhouse and the Dark Room.

I don't know. He went on with this silly rapping about how we was bewitched down in Texas. Man took us, just a lot of nice clean boys, and *done* something to us. Now, ten, twelve years later, what he done is still in us. Do you know what they had us do in that raid on Dresden, the one where his plane went down? Naw, I don't know. I mean we bombed that motherfucker plumb *out*. It wasn't enough left to stuff in a gnat's ass when we was done. But that was our job. We wasn't there to bring supplies to them Germans. That come a little later. Naw, I don't know. What?

—We killed a hundred and thirty-five thousand people. Most of them civilians, women and children. It was the worst disaster in human history, I mean more people killed . . .

—Well, that's rough. Naw, I never heard no count on it.

—Do you see?

—Yeah. That's rough.

—No, you don't see. You're just like . . . the rest. Can't you understand what they made us do? God, if *you* don't understand. Of all of them, you . . .

—I don't recollect no MP with a tommy gun nudging your ass into that 17. I remember just climbing in like on the way to work. Ain't that how it was?

—Yes, Oh, Jesus, yes. And that's it: You can't help seeing. Michaelis, all of them. They made us do it. They made us *want* to do it. They stole our . . . souls.

—Horseshit.

—No, no. They . . . turned living men into zombies. They made us . . .

I was kind of tight by then. What you going to do, sugar? I can take 'em on wine. You just ease back and say, yeah, sure, Lord, yes, now you're telling it. Let the child go. Wine's like that. Now you kind of keep your hands free when it's whiskey or gin. Far as a guy who's Horsing, I don't fuck with him any way at all. No price on a gooney bird, son. But ole Jacobs is cold sober and talking like he spiked his wine with Cutty Shark and dust. Yes indeed, he's got him a slit in there somewhere been bleeding like a raw asshole for longer than some folks live. But it ain't my hole. I ain't bleeding there. I don't read no newspapers. I got other problems.

But he's getting mad. Funny sight I swear to you, this little skinny Jew with his hands going, his hair almost gone, his face all screwed up like he was crying. Maybe he needs to be some kind of Catholic. Go tell some priest. Bless, dad. I killed me a hundred thousand people couple years back. Huh? Sure I know that Lord's Prayer. How many I got to say? Ummmm. That's some praying. You say hundred thousand folks choked and burned and blowed apart's a lot? Sure enough. Okay, I'll say 'em. Then I'm off, huh? I won't never die? Oh, I will. Then what? Aha. Comes Judgment. It ain't no way out or around. Which is what's pulling this poor Jew Zonk to pieces. He knows what he knows and it's close as a pigskin purse. All zipped up tight, beginning to end, with all them killings and dyings, birthings and cryings neat inside. Says do not open till Judgment. Why not let it go and walk outside to watch the grass grow? Made me think of Boil-o, that Louisiana bastard. I could see that mean smile of his, watch him watching Jacobs. Him and me should of never missed that talk.

Jacobs is shaking now. Just sits there shaking, and then:
—You're . . . an animal.
—Woof.
—No, it's not funny. Don't laugh. You of all people, after how you've suffered and you can't see what it's coming to, what they've done to all of us, what this goddamned country *is*. They've lynched you, beat you, enslaved you, spat upon you for three hundred years. They've used you, lied to you, cheated you out of . . . everything. And you sit there, just sit there. You're . . . a *nigger*.

I started to slap him. That's what he wanted. Wanted me to slap him, and that would of done for one Lord's Prayer, would of taken off one of them ten-pound thermite bombs he dropped. Every slap, he's off the hook for one of them fire bombs, one more little dead child, one young girl who never got her first kiss cause this here butcher, this Jew avenger, done burned the sweet lips off her. Naw, I don't want no part of that.

147

Fuck him. Let him find a wall somewhere and beat his bald head into strawberry preserves against it. Let him cry for all them babies. I just looked at him with my hands folded in my lap. Stare at him.

And I can see he's gone over the edge. He ain't got no more rope to play out. Last chance. Get that old coon-buddy room-mate of mine to kick the ever-living shit out of me. God creeping down his arm, shaking in his fist. Now that's gone, and he's sitting hunched over with his shoulders quivering and tears rolling down his face. I wouldn't give him carfare to Alexandria. Let him cry. Maybe that's all he wanted in the first place. How do I know? Maybe I should of whipped his ass. Trouble is, I couldn't figure out a good reason to do it.

—I . . . I'm . . . sorry, he chokes out finally. —Listen, I'm sorry, so help me God. Forgive . . . please . . .

I got up then and started walking. Out. Maybe I had carfare to take myself to Alexandria. Or farther. What is it? Fifty cents?

—Forgive . . .

—Naw, I said back into the room. —Naw. I ain't forgiving you a goddamned thing. What do you think of that?

The reason I left D.C. was this: You remember old Passer? That fine chick I carried down to Virginia and got up against the Zonk? Right. Well, in fifty-six or fifty-seven, I hear from her. She's in Philly. Hard times. It's a war, she writes. Right now she's black. She's been black and back, white and tight. She's gone so many ways she don't hardly remember where she started. *I* remember where she started, but that's all right, fine. Anyhow, she's going along now. She's got to be thirty, and she wants to settle. On the far side of the street. Some Zonk just loves what she puts down. He'd go to the dark side for her, she says, but it ain't no way. Yeah. I got a picture of this clerk at a Philly Sears going dark. I can see it on that wide scream with stethoscopic sound. Anyhow, she's going back over, but there's a problem. *Our* problem. Seems she had herself a boy in 1941 after I left town. Now that could be. I hear tell what we done regular will cast a baby. If you're dumb. If you don't get him before he grabs tight. So it *could* be. She says she reckons it's my turn to see to *our* son. 'Cause he just naturally can't make it across. Nice momma. Going not only where little boy can't go, but where he can't even visit. Wanna see momma? Get you a

148

mop and a pail, boy. You can tell her you love her while you're scrubbing her kitchen. Wouldn't kiss her, though. Zonk frowns on child kissing his momma.

So I go on up to Philly on the train. I don't know. I could have wrote on the letter: NOT AT HOME or ADDRESSEE DISEASED. But there was a lot of things. I had loved that girl one time when we was young, and loving makes everything else small. I had done that. I could remember the night we come back from Virginia, and she got over being mad. She got to laughing. Said it was a shame about the Zonk knowing so much, able to pick out a white nigger every time, and him only having twenty miles to use his talent. And I loved her. It was hot and dark in my little old room, and we knew that it would never be that way again, but we loved. Maybe I knew what that Zonk in Philly was going for. Maybe he would come across for her. 'Cause she pulled the stops when she got to loving, I tell you that much. Anyhow, I remembered that girl, and I didn't wish her no ill. She had a long trip ahead, and I didn't wish her no ill.

The boy was something else. I never figured to have a boy. I never thought about it. Having a child is like laying your hand on the block. It's like growing another finger: More fingers you got, the more there is to cut off. But I thought, it would be nice. You can't put that down. Nice to have a boy and see him grow. See him get educated. Who knows? With all this integration shit, maybe one day a nigger will score nearly good as a Jew. If they take to Jacobs, they'll go for anything. I laughed, thinking, Jee-sus, any son of mine could send that poor screw running up a wall. So I reckon there's something to having a boy, going up and saying, —Listen, I'm your daddy. I meant to come sooner, but there was this war. I been in uniform ever since. Promoted from second lieutenant to bell captain. Battlefield commission, son. Well, if he could laugh, we'd do all right. He'd bound to be able to laugh. She said he was fifteen now and still alive. I can see him in there laughing.

So I kind of leaned back in the train seat and thought about the years. Not much to show. Except for that tax-free change Prince Albert was holding onto for me. A lot of women, a lot of time. I thought, a lot to go. Maybe thirty, forty years. My people was from Georgia and they lived a long time. They was strong people. The weak died out a long time ago.

149

When I got to Philly, I bought a deck of smokes. And all of a sudden, holding that white pack in my hands, I thought, Lucky Strike Green, you never came back from the war. Killed on Saipan. Killed in the Hürtgen Forest. Shot down over Schweinfurt, Stuttgart, Munich. Dresden. Poor old Lucky Strike Green went white and never got right. Little by little, the whole world is going white. Less room all the time. And then I got me a cab and went to get my son.

She looked fine. Looked like maybe a year had passed. I couldn't get over it, how good she looked. She shook my hand and smiled, and we talked. Not much about old times. She didn't have much use for old times. All the time we talked, you could see she had that clerk and a house on the other side in her mind. She couldn't help it. Made me think of that song, "Cool Water." She was thirsty, and a thirsty person is crazy. They'll do anything. Even give up their kid for a drink. I wondered what she'd do if I said, All right, fine. I'll take him, but first I got to have me one last piece of what it was got me to make him in the first place. I reckoned she'd come undone. She'd believe I meant it. Hell, if I was to say it, I *would* mean it. And she'd be in between the rock and the hard place. 'Cause I'm her ticket. Not the Sears Zonk. No, he's the train. But I'm the ticket that says she can ride. And you got to pay for a ticket. She knows that. Knows I know it. And all the time my mouth is moving, I'm thinking. Well, she don't *have* to have me. She could just dump the kid. Remember the world is dumpers and dumped. Then I look at her hard. White face. Maybe a little something black around the eyes. I don't know. But what *ain't* there is the look of a dumper. If I turn her down, she's not going. She's not going to leave this son of hers—and mine? She's going to tell Sears to go poke it to Roebuck if I don't come across. I don't think it. I know. The way you get to be a dumper is to know stuff, not guess it. So then I make up the part of my mind that hadn't been all the way made till now. Never mind. Maybe I would have done it anyhow. But now it was easy.

—Yes, I told her, sitting close, letting her feel me across that six inches between our knees. —Yes, I made up my mind to believe you. No, I don't want no tests. Yes, I want to take care of him. No, you didn't say his name was Garrick. Poole? You got to be putting me on. Huh?

150

She showed me his birth certificate. There it was. See? I got to be a dumper, 'cause I know. I just smiled and said, How do you want to ah arrange this?

She called the boy in. He was tall for his age and thin. He didn't look like anything I had ever seen. Light, but darker than his momma. Thin lips, big brown eyes. Only they was kind of slanted. Good teeth. Got his teeth from me. I don't know about them eyes. But what I really like is, this boy comes on. When his momma calls him Garrick, his shoulders bunch up and he kind of smiles real ugly. Like he'd told her about that before. Then he shakes hands with me and says, —I guess you're my daddy. She don't call me Garrick. You know what they call me?

—What?

—Kicky. Just Kicky.

—Beats hell out of Henry.

—She told me she used to call you Mr. Man.

—We let that Henry business drift. You can call me Man, Kicky.

—Do nice, I think.

And we sat there, the three of us, like we was a family. I guess there was some tears. I told Kicky what I had done in the war. It kind of interested him. He liked arithmetic and thought it must have been hard to make them bombs come down right from so high up. I told him we had us a sight, that you just kind of got all around that sight and let 'em go. He said it must have been a shirttail out down where them bombs landed. I allowed he was right.

Until it was time for him to go to bed. We would get started in the morning. We shook hands. And before he went out, he said, —I'm glad you come. I love Momma fine, but I got things I want to do and talk about. Sometimes we argue. Ain't no use for a father and son to argue, is it?

—Like arguing with yourself, I told him.

And thought, this kid has got him a bad streak somewhere. Couldn't be anybody fifteen years old like him.

Then we was alone. I patted her hand and said she done a fine job. That he was a good boy. She was near to crying now for sure, so I got up to leave, to call me a cab. But she stayed put on the sofa. I kind of stood there, and then, still with tears in her eyes, she shook her head.

151

—No, she said. —You going to stay here tonight.

—Well, I said. And thought: You may be a dumper, but you ain't the king of dumpers, son. 'Cause I believe she's just laid a basket of stuff right past you. Ain't she? Or are you getting the wrong idea?

It was the right idea all right. She stood up and kissed me. She says, —I told John Mitchell he would have to trust me to do right. To just forget tonight. That was the price if I had to do this about Kicky. You understand?

I understood she was black, after all. 'Cause no white woman walking around ever saw so much time, remembered love so right. And it wasn't no payoff either. No dump. It was having and wanting, and it was a night without no hours or minutes in it, just all of a piece. Yes, Lord, that was the night Lucky Strike Black got back.

And the next day about nine o'clock, she left a note for Sears in the screen door, and I carried her stuff and Kicky's out to the cab. And after we went by to check out Prince Albert in D.C., the three of us flew to Chicago. And all the way flying, I thought how I wished that DC-3 had a bubble in the nose. I'd like to let 'em know down there that something special was passing overhead.

Boyd

I had to go with McCarthy. There was no choice. Later, it would be easy enough to laugh at us and say, well, that's what you get for following Quixote. But then—that spring and summer—there was no choice. Maybe you liked what was happening, a country coming apart at the seams. I didn't. I talked it over with two of my partners. They were standing off in March. Too many variables. Johnson could change everything with a word. He could pull the plug on anyone, and he could do it any of several ways. Move back from the bombing, move out of Vietnam by stages. Recognize the NLF. Or send armored units into the North. He could do that. And no matter what he did, Jack and Eddie saw that half the American people would back him. And half would border on revolt.

—It's never been quite like this before, Eddie said. —It's always been . . . easier. Either you did or you didn't. But you could tell where the votes were, couldn't you?

—I don't know. In 1860, Jack was saying as he cut his filet. —Lincoln . . . until they fired on the flag at Fort Sumter . . .

—But that was in the country. And the issues that exist today . . . They just didn't . . .

—Civil rights? Abolition . . . Anyhow, we didn't come out of that unscathed. It was right, I suppose. But some people think Lincoln was . . . a bungler.

I turned to my coffee. It seemed a strange conversation. —It made us an industrial power. In four years we built what had taken England four decades. And we freed the slaves . . .

—I wouldn't mention either of those points in front of my son, Eddie smiled. —He'd say the first was a crime. And the second was a farce.

—Eddie junior, I said. —There it is. There's what I'm trying to tell you. Who would he support?

Eddie glanced at Jack and then at me. —He's for Kennedy.

I was surprised. —Doesn't he recognize what Kennedy's up to? Can't he smell opportunism when it's not even concealed?

Eddie smiled. —I think you'd have to talk to Eddie junior. I don't think you quite understand his kind of kid. He's really left, you know. There isn't a taint of tactical idealism in him.

—What do you mean?

Eddie shrugged his shoulders and bit a cigar. —He wants Kennedy nominated because he'll beat Nixon. Because he's the hero of the lowest classes in the country. And because he'll fail. And when he fails, those classes will be once and for all demoralized. They'll have the scales lifted from their eyes. And the revolution will be one step closer.

I stared down at my coffee. I had been at the hospital when Eddie junior was born. In 1948. The year I came out of law school and Eddie senior had taken me in. Twenty years later. I shook my head.

—You're guessing. He never told you that.

Jack leaned across to me. —Look, Al, you aren't up on this thing. Eddie's right. That's what we were arguing about at his house last week. You haven't been out for a while. If you and Sandy had had a kid in the forties, you'd know. That's the way a lot of them feel. The moderates only want to hang everyone over thirty.

Eddie laughed, but there was no humor in it. —You still see things as a bombardier. They've retired all the 17's now. The Crusaders are under the red flag now. If not the black.

—But . . . they don't want this country . . . to go under.

—No. No. They want it to rise. Eddie junior wants the Vietnam thing to go on. He figures if we fight there for another five years, the military will be demoralized. And when they come home shamed, betrayed . . . remember what happened when the Russian Army started going home?

—I remember what a defeated German Army brought on. It only took longer.

Jack lit my cigarette. —Eddie junior's figured on that. It's less desirable, but even a Fascist take-over here would hasten events. A nuclear exchange. With us against a red world. Or a revolution against the Fascists here at home. But it's inevitable the way he sees it.

—You guys are kidding me, aren't you? About Eddie junior?

Eddie sipped a Benedictine. —My son is a full-fledged bastard. I didn't know it until all this Vietnam business broke. Now I know it. One day I may have to shoot him.

Jack snubbed out his cigarette. —That's where we have the edge. The punks all talk political theory. But the old men know how to shoot. I was in the First Marines.

Eddie stared out into the darkness of the restaurant until a waiter came over, thinking he was wanted.

—Sir?

—Bring us three triple martinis. I think we'll talk awhile.

So we talked. About how it had been when we were young. I thought of the Blockhouse, white, solid, standing alone in that desert two thousand miles and a quarter of a century away. It had seemed as if sprung out of bedrock. But there had been only sand beneath it, and at night, at a little distance, it had taken on the pale insubstantial look of an apparition, unreal and distant. I wondered if it still existed. I made a false promise to myself that I would go and see.

Eddie was talking as the waiter brought our drinks. —I was so scared. On D-Day minus one they dropped us behind the lines. Oh, Jesus, right into the middle of the Wehrmacht. I think nine guys in my platoon got out. Two of us managed to walk out. You'll never know how scared I was. But I had it to do. At first because I wanted to be a man. I wanted to show those bastards from Alabama and Arizona what a New York boy could do. But by the time advanced training was over I knew I was as much man as any of them. And I still went on. Because . . .

—Because you loved the goddamned country, Jack said softly.

Eddie looked strange sitting there in his two-hundred-dollar suit, a thick cigar between his fingers, with tears in his eyes.

—My father was a kike, Eddie said. —No, I mean it. They'd hurt him too many times in the old country. All he knew was to get money and put it away. He'd do anything for a dollar. Or a mark or a pound. He couldn't help it. He was a kike. But this . . . country. This country let me be a Jew. A man and a Jew. You know what that means? After more centuries than that little bastard of mine has years, we can stand up and believe what we want. Without hiding, without apologizing . . .

He couldn't go on. Jack and I were embarrassed. But I was

beginning to feel the drinks. I should call Sandy, I thought. But no, she'll be at her sister's. She likes to play with the kids.

Jack was asking me something. —In the Air Corps? A bombardier?

—Yes, I said. —I was that. That's what I did.

Eddie was all right again. He turned to me fiercely. —You know what the bastard would tell you about your war service? That you were only a Nazi in a different uniform. That you bombed German workers who couldn't help themselves. That you should have bombed Washington, the Capitol, the White House. You should have revolted against your officers.

—Is he . . . a Stalinist? I asked inanely.

—If he's anything with a name, he claims to be a Trotskyist. No, he'd wipe out the Russian bureaucracy, too. What is property? Theft. What is the state? A machine for the suppression of all impulses but those of the ruling class. It's all corrupt, to hear him. The stinking little bastard.

Jack waved for another round. —Well, there's a lot of rot. In high places. What was that guy's name? The guy who worked for Johnson. And Billy Sol Estes. And Bobby Baker.

—All crackers, Eddie said. —Texas, South Carolina. What do you expect?

—Then there was the business at General Motors—about Nader. Roche swearing he didn't know they were trying to put a frame on him. And the GE-Westinghouse mess ten years ago . . .

—Say, Eddie said belligerently. —You sound like my bastard. What's with you? This country has been pretty good to you.

Jack drank and said nothing.

—To attack what's wrong isn't to ignore what's right, I said. —But I think we have to do something. Look at the country. Look at us today.

Eddie was drunk. Not ugly. But miserable and wanting to rid himself of it. —I'm looking. I see punks who don't want to fight. Because they're yellow. Finally because they're yellow. And I see a pack of Negroes who've gotten the right to vote, to eat anywhere they can pay the tab. And now they want a handout to boot. And I see grown men who can't tell which side their bread is buttered on.

He was looking from Jack to me as he said this last. A little later we broke it up. I rode home in a cab. Nobody uses the subway anymore.

But I made up my mind that night. And I went to the McCarthy headquarters to volunteer.

—Do you want to work here or out in the neighborhoods? a very fine-looking blonde about eighteen asked me. She was lovely. Young, long straight hair, almost no makeup—the kind you see nowadays. She looked very young to be involved in politics, but she was self-possessed, too. Her clothes were casual, but expensive. So was her voice.

—I don't care, I told her. —Whatever you want. I just want to help him.

—That's nice, she said, and sent me over to talk to some young men in shirt sleeves and horn-rimmed glasses.

—A corporation lawyer, the first one said, apparently bemused. —We don't get many of those.

—Even lawyers have consciences, I joked.

—Sure, he said, not laughing. —Well, let me ask you: Why do you want to work for the Senator?

I shrugged. The others were watching me. One of them was chewing slowly on a sandwich. They looked alike. All Cornell and Dartmouth. Maybe one from Princeton.

—I think what he says makes sense.

—You think we should get out of Vietnam, stop an immoral and unjust war?

—I think we don't know what we're doing there. I think we're over our heads.

They went on staring at me. I remember wondering what might make them laugh. The blonde brought milk shakes. Each one took a milk shake from her without even looking up. I couldn't help following her with my eyes.

—Mr. Carstairs will be along in a little while. Can you wait?

I nodded and found myself a chair. They went back to sorting cards and putting campaign literature in envelopes. I thought what a strange subdued place it was. No joy, no excitement. What kind of politics is quiet? I wondered. Maybe the politics of twilight. Maybe that was what I saw in McCarthy's pictures, heard in his voice. The politics of a man who was morally very tired. Who not only saw nothing left, but was about to commit himself to a campaign he did not want to win, but felt he must contest. For the record. So that history would put

159

down that there was one last voice still speaking quietly, reasoning, as the Republic was divided between Boston and Austin. I could hear what Eddie junior might say about this place. That you could smell the deep stench of aroused bourgeois conscience: a collection of young future technocrats, the daughter of money, and a middle-aged lawyer who vaguely felt something was wrong in the country.

Carstairs was a troubled little man. It turned out he was a professor of economics at Brooklyn College. There was some small particle of pleasure in him. Not a great deal, but enough to see that he didn't belong to this generation.

—Some people think this whole thing is just a rig. That McCarthy will end up a Judas goat—pull some of the Democratic fringe far enough out so that Johnson can isolate them, punish them at the convention. But we're in to the end. This is for real. McCarthy can win. The regulars only propose. The people dispose.

I nodded. But I suspected Carstairs didn't quite believe. He sounded like a man arguing with himself. I wondered if moral indignation, antipathy toward a President and discontent about a war was enough to build a political position on. But I just listened. And agreed to talk to some of my friends about helping, about campaign contributions. I said I would address envelopes or meetings. It felt faintly absurd, but I thought, Eddie junior would shovel crap for his cause. If you want to have a cause, if you even want the right to yell foul, you'd better hang in.

So I went to work. I wore a button and passed out bumper stickers. I spoke to some small groups in private homes. Once they sent me to a union hall along with a Kennedy man and a kind of undercover agent, who grinned at us and reminded the boys what the administration had done for them, how it had walked over the Republican-Southern antilabor bloc. He said he just wanted to speak for the men who were doing the job, not talking about it. He said a lot about Humphrey. More than I would have expected. He got a round of applause.

I kept on keeping on. Sandy thought it was silly. She wondered aloud one evening if I were trying to put down a guilt complex about my war service.

—What are you talking about? That was a different war. A different kind of war.

160

—They're all different, she said. —And all stupid. Was yours a smart war?

—No, I said. —It wasn't smart. It was just what it was.

—Didn't you drop bombs on people? That's what you did, wasn't it?

I put on my coat and took a walk. Yes, Sandy, I dropped bombs on people. I flew so high above the earth that the people down below couldn't even hear my plane. They would be eating or dressing or making love or scolding the children, and there would be a siren, but it was always a little late, and then there would be that cluster of whistles, and then the world would end for some of them. One shoe off, one shoe on. Love never consummated. Dead children who got off with no scolding. That's what I did, isn't it? Yes. But that was a long time ago, and they told us it wouldn't ever have to happen again. We would come home and be home.

I thought I should have stayed in Paris. God knows what I would have done. But I would have stayed with Marie Clair. We would have been real people in a second-rate country. We would have said, —Get out of Algeria, let them alone in Indochina. And that would have been the end of it. No one would have cared what we thought or did. We could have sat over aperitifs in the Madeleine and read *Le Monde,* wondering if the Americans were as insane as the Russians. There might have been children. Claude and Jean and a little girl called Michele.

But I had not stayed in Paris. Maybe because I was an American. Or maybe because Paris is too close to Dresden. Or maybe because in my most private soul I liked being a second-rate part of the most powerful national machine on earth. God knows.

Then it began to rain, and I found I was as near the McCarthy headquarters as home, and I flagged a cab and went over and licked envelopes. This time they gave me a milk shake.

Michaelis

I told him all right, fine. I'll take care of your ideas. But you've got to cool this ideological business. There's nothing in it. They don't even really want it. They don't want the war won and the niggers in their place. What they want is to feel things are like they used to be, that hometown and moonlight and the Stars and Stripes forever are here again. Only with TV and the guaranteed annual wage.

He looked like a bulldog, people said. He didn't. He looked tough and cool, and he was pleasant. I wouldn't have expected it. But he was quiet and never seemed to think of anything but politics. When we flew, he never read or talked. He sat looking out the window. I think my mistake was in not recognizing that he was not a politician. He wasn't. He was not a magician, a manipulator. No, George believed nearly all of what he said, and that is why I was no use to him. A magician is one who masters illusion. There is no name for one who is a prisoner of illusion, unless you like *fanatic*. I came to see that George was much more complicated than I. I came to know a lot of the Southerners around him, and they were all the same. Very complicated. But not complex. They believed the simplest things in the most intricate fashion. I wondered if Hitler's people had been like that: simple of mind and a maze of unarticulated and fugitive emotions. I don't mean the racial thing. Only one or two of them were big for that. It was only a tactic and a taste. But the business about Communism, that was something else. They felt about it—about what they supposed it to be—the way magicians who have lost the knack, who have lost faith in their own spells might feel about a rival dispensation. I wondered how much pragmatic distance separates a populist, an agrarian, from a country Marxist. I decided not too much. But you couldn't sell that to him—not even in veiled terms. He insisted on his own message. Which had no pragmatic value at all

162

and very little magic. One way or the other. But he wouldn't or couldn't.

And finally I determined that George was a new phenomenon: the synthetic hick. The farm was fading, and the plush office and high-level dealing weren't quite there yet. So he was trapped at about the level of a small-town used-car dealer who plays the locals straight and bleeds the out-of-towners for all they're worth. And at last, of course, he gets both reputations, but each in the place where it will do him the least good.

So I left. What was the use of moving from Montgomery to the world with a bushel basket of false positions? The world was beginning to tire of its three-century love affair with rationalism, but the man to carry it back to its heart, back to what lies beneath logic and reason, hadn't shown up yet. And I considered a possibility. Could it be that what I was looking for had nothing directly to do with politics? Could it be a question of religion? Once a reporter asked MacArthur about the basic causes of war. He answered that the basic causes were theological. I hadn't considered that the public, acknowledged aspect of magic is religion—it has always been the front for those impulses that would not square with reason.

I thought of all that, and then I told him, —George, I'm through. It's no good. I'm just not a politician. I'm going to look for a preacher. I want to find God. George studied me for a long minute. He presumed a Northerner talking about God was kidding someone. Then he nodded. He could understand that. I had the impression he would have liked to come along, but there are hungers raised in pine woods, in the heart of a sharecropper that only his grandson can satisfy. Hungers down there, like hatreds, are not personal. They are corrosive in the blood. God runs like a spoiled gene through generations. So does greed.

I flew back to Chicago. There was a lot to consider. His last public manisfestation had been at Hiroshima. Before that, Dresden. Before that, the Nuremberg rallies. Before that? Why at the Finland Station, of course. In 1917. Where next? I thought perhaps in Chicago. In 1968. And I would be there. With a kite and a key. There were a lot of years left.

Jacobs

In June I flew to Los Angeles with him. That was the one that would do it. The New Hampshire primary had been nothing but a curiosity. Indiana, Nebraska—in the election, they might both go for a Republican anyhow. The rest were one thing and another. But if he was to have credibility, he would have to win in California. Even with Johnson out and the charisma of his name, there would be the party types in Chicago to bring into line. A lot of them owed Humphrey, and all of them would feel more comfortable with Humphrey. They had never liked Bobby. Because he didn't like them. He knew they were the tools of political fortune in America, but he didn't like it. Somehow, he said, I'd rather trust the people. Because the only deal you can make with the people is an open one. So anyhow we had to have California.

They had me doing spadework with reporters. I was a kind of psychological warfare man. I made images. Not false ones. No, I had to counter the Humphrey people, the McCarthy people, so that the real image would come through. I had to work against the old charges of ruthlessness and arrogance and against the new one of opportunism. I had to make his positions on Vietnam and poverty and civil rights clear. Not so much to the kids or the Mexicans or the blacks. But to the solid citizens who could make or break any election. I spent time with people from the papers on background. I spoke to college professor types who leaned toward McCarthy and to county Democratic committee people who liked Humphrey because he was a known quantity: a good old-line liberal.

—McCarthy can't win, I told them. —He never could here. Remember what happened to the last Children's Crusade? Anyhow, he hasn't got the name, the strength. Or the drive. Finally, it's drive. Watch his speeches, his whole operation. Never mind what I say. Tell me if that kind of lackadaisical style can run this country in the 1970's. That kind of casual, supercerebral

164

stuff is a luxury. Maybe he could run Monaco. Or Andorra. But we simply can't afford McCarthy today. Look: A good third of your population is disengaged from any feeling of loyalty at all. Now, today, the kids and the blacks and the poor are only questioning the leadership, the administration. But if you put in Humphrey—who won't do anything—or McCarthy—who can't—then those people are going to start questioning the very institutions we live under. They're going to ask if we can afford the slow rate of change, awareness, that is built into a Congress, a Supreme Court, and the rest of it. Do you hear what they're saying in Oakland? Free Huey. Or the sky's the limit. On the campus, they're talking revolution. And the ones who're talking that way can be brought back by only one man. They'll listen to Bobby. They'll give him a chance.

And people listened. They believed. Even some very square types were listening. People seemed to know that we were up against it. That this election, this choice, would be more crucial than any before. That a mistake might make it the last election.

At night in the hotel, I lay back and listened to my brain singing, We're going to win, we're going to win. And I fell asleep to dream that I was flying again. I was in the nose of a plane, with castles of cumulus clouds all around me. We would move into one, and the sun would darken, and I felt safe and at peace. Then we would be out, and I watched all around for those dark silhouettes, the fighters seeking us out, trying to stop this plane of mine as it headed for its target. I was happy in the dream, because we were going to make it. We were going to carry in this one load. And then it would be over. If I were good, if I could lay them dead on the marked coordinates down there, it would be done and the world would be changed.

It was time then, and the plane leveled off. I moved over the sight. I slid in my optical component and twisted to focus. Around us, flak bloomed like gardenias, petals opening slowly, mysteriously, the white turning dark at the center, and then the whole blossom beginning to fade, to disintegrate. In my ears, I heard a voice. But not a pilot. No, it was—what was his name? Boileau. He was speaking very softly, very calmly.

—This is the last city in the world, and when it is gone, so will be the evil that cities spawned. It will be a world of farms . . .

At first I thought he said forms. But I knew he was wrong.

165

Then his voice became Michaelis' who told me to look down there, to see what I was about to do. And when I looked down, I did not see the familiar outline of a city gathered by a river. I saw men and women walking. I saw them in tall hats and Edwardian coats, in long dresses, riding in horse-drawn carriages. And Michaelis said I would change all that, transform the world despite the world, and that they would thank me one day. He told me that the world changes slowly, only against its will, and that some are chosen to make those changes come about. That I was such a one.

Then I heard another voice. Or not a voice. Sounds. As if my intercom had plugged into a bedroom where two people were caught at the rising peak of passion. I looked at the clouds as I listened, unable to pull the headset off.

—Un baby come baby. Left left. Cool cool. Now un un un. Yes man yes you know yes un un. Un-huh. Un-huh. Bombs. Bombs bombs away. Un un un . . .

And the plane was in a black and cloudless sky filled with the immense distance of those cold stars that Abraham could not number, though his children would one day exceed them, if the Lord spoke the wholeness of His mind.

And when I awoke, I was not glad anymore, and I wished that I might be back tonight with Mariam and the boys. I am only a small man who once flew amid the clouds for a time. And did great destruction. And was preserved. I am not large enough to change what the world is. Not nearly large enough to want revenge or fame or power. How can He win with people like me around Him? Does He believe that a pile of twigs bound tightly together is as strong as an iron rod? It is an illusion, a trick of lying physicists. I am only a fagot, and before it is done, I will break, and my bones will clutter one desert or another.

The next evening he won. I was in the ballroom when he thanked us, when he moved us to laughter, to tears, to euphoria. It was too much. I laughed out loud.

—Nobody knows what the Shadow knows, I yelled.

Then we heard what sounded like a couple of firecrackers. I laughed again. I didn't blame them. If I had firecrackers, I'd throw them, too. We had just taken a great step toward the new world. I thought of the proverb his brother liked: A journey of a thousand miles begins with a single step.

But I saw the newsmen running out of the ballroom to the left, toward the passage into which he had disappeared a few minutes before. One of his assistants—was it Steven Smith?—ran to the microphone, called for a doctor. And around me, I heard people begin to moan.

And later I saw the pictures. I saw our hopes and future lying in a dirty hallway bleeding, one eye open, one eyelid fluttering. I saw Rosie Greer and the others wrestling a man down to a table-top. Someone said he was a Puerto Rican, and I told them they were crazy, that there wasn't a Spanish-American on the continent who would—who could—have done it. I was right, Christ, I was right.

It was an Arab.

And he was looking for me. He wanted me and Mariam and Moishe and David. He wanted us. He fired at Bobby to hit us. It wasn't a racist from Alabama or a goon from Hunt's Dallas. It wasn't even an ordinary psychopath riding the chariot of his hallucinated power. It was an Arab. A man from my desert. Coming from the sand, coming from under those alien stars to tell me that the dream could not live. Not even here. That it wasn't the kind of dream for this world. There were no cross hairs, no bullets, no bombs in Kennedy's dream. Only food and medicine and care for those who needed it. Justice and peace.

I closed my eyes against the tears. Mariam had been right. Israel was right. If you dream, it must be of the high places, of a mount to carry you across the sky, over the world booted and spurred to bring it to your will. There is no need of a tongue in this world. You need only teeth. Because they will come for you, the fighters, the pursuits. You have to be ready. You have to bomb. What can you do? If you hold your hand and say, No, I will not, I won't, I'm going to do right, then they'll shoot you out of a car in Dallas, off a balcony in Memphis, in a hotel corridor in Los Angeles.

That night I phoned Mariam. She said nothing about Israel. The next day, when he died, she phoned me. She said, —Come home. We need you. We need you.

And that afternoon I was flying again, the clouds high and massive around me. I looked out the window on the whole flight. I calculated our altitude and listened carefully when the pilot announced tail winds and ETA. And in the evening we came over New York and I was surprised how easy it would be to pick out LaGuardia, the UN, the docks, the industrial areas on the New Jersey shore. Even in the dark.

Poole

We was sitting down to stewed chicken and rice and a nice tomato salad when Kicky tuned in that TV and the screen went blank and the Flintstones which I like went out of sight. It said BULLETIN on the TV screen and this very cool joker says, not troubled at all:

—The Reverend Martin Luther King has been shot in Memphis, Tennessee . . .

I look at Elena, and we both kind of look at the boy without seeming to. He don't say anything. He's eating his chicken and rice like it ain't any more in the pot and no more selling out on the street. But he's thinking.

He never had any use for King. Not really. He was too young to know what them walks in Montgomery and Selma and Birmingham cost. He only knew D.C. and north, and it seemed to him that old King was a born shuffler. He'd tell me,

—Some chalky sonofabitch try to put ketchup in my hair, I'd ram the bottle up his ass. For a start.

I told him, —Easy, baby. It's been a long haul. Old King done his part.

—You can take that nonviolent shit. I don't need no nonviolence, you hear?

—Listen, I said, —you better keep in mind Zonk has got the Bomb. And he's mean.

Kicky kind of cocked his head at me. —You helped old Charlie lay down them bombs one time, didn't you? What you going to do when the day comes? You gonna go black? Or white?

—That day is in your head. It ain't no black air force. It ain't going to be no black army. Just a few alley coons barking at the cops. Hell, they don't even make the cops swallow hard. Did you know that?

We talked like that, but it was close between us. 'Cause we both loved the same woman and knew the same streets, the

168

same rain and sunshine. I had him in school till he was twenty-one. I wanted him to get through college, but he got to wanting money and a job and it wasn't any other way. So he come out and I got him on at the Midland Hotel where I was night clerk. Good money, good hours. He had him a car and a girl. Maybe a couple of girls. If he could hold his mouth, I reckoned he'd be a clerk in a year or so. Same time I kept at him about getting back to school. Told him he could get him a degree at night. Maybe law school.

—What for law school? You going in the rackets? he asked me.

—So you can do all that big jazz you're always talking, I said. —Big black lawyer. Go into politics. Lay all that beautiful blackness on 'em.

—When we go, it won't be with no law degree. I ought to take me a course in marksmanship, he said.

Just then the TV news bulletin cut in again and says:

—The Reverend Martin Luther King was shot and killed tonight in Memphis, Tennessee. He died of a single bullet wound in the chest fired from a high-powered rifle at about . . .

But Kicky was up. He wiped his mouth and grinned at me.
—Got to go, he said. —Got to get out on the street.

—Un-un, I told him.—Bad news on the street tonight.

His momma was crying. She had been partial to old King, had gone to hear him every time he spoke during the Chicago campaign. —My God, my God, she sobbed. —Oh, Lord, why? Why?

—Bad news on the TV, Kicky said. —Bad news all over. Be worse news before they put a stone over him. Maybe he's fixing to do some real good. In spite of himself.

And he made it through the back door before I could get from behind the table and catch hold of him.

—No, Elena cried after him. —Oh, my Jesus, Kicky. You, Kicky, come on back . . . please . . .

I was out on the porch when I heard his car motor turn over and saw the taillights fade in the twilight. Then, just then, I heard the first police sirens and saw over toward what the Moslems call Mecca Street a red glow that grew and grew and filled up the whole sky over there.

We sat for a little while. I had a beer. The news told us about

169

that white Mustang, man running out of the flophouse across from that motel. But Elena just kept her face covered with her apron and rocked back and forth while the news told us what they done to him and then, piece by piece, how the street was going up. In D.C., in Detroit. In Atlanta. In Chicago. Local news tells us how the mayor wants folks to stay home. Something about a tragic time. Everybody stay cool. Extra police called up. Curfew maybe. Then they took us back to Memphis and told it all over again.

And they played this record, this tape they made in some church the night before. Him. Little heavyset black fella with kind of Chinese eyes. He was preaching. I listened.

—It doesn't matter with me now . . . I've been to the mountaintop . . .

And I thought, hey, I been there, too. Over the world, dropping their own stuff back on them. How was it on the mountaintop? Oh, it was good, don't you know? It was solid. It was sweet. Them shooting but not reaching and me with the magic box, the black box, sending down judgment. Listen, King, what do you climb a mountain for? Listen, a mountain is a high place, and whatever you put out falls back and drives 'em crazy, sends 'em crying for Jesus, swearing to do right if you just take it off of 'em. Don't you see now what a mountaintop is for? It ain't no use to call from up there. They can't hear. No use to cry. They think it's rain. You got to carry judgment up with you. And judgment is pain. Ain't that what it says? Weeping and mashing of teeth, eternal fire prepared for devil and his Nazis. Un-huh. Un-huh.

Then I saw the TV had come on to *I Spy* and Bill Cosby was getting bashed by some Zonk with a foreign accent. And Elena just sat listening to them sirens outside.

—All right, I said. —I'll go find him. You stay put and don't open for nobody but us. I'll find him.

She shook her head. That woman loved me good. She didn't want me out. But it didn't matter. It was time I go. Not before. Kicky is a twenty-five-year-old man. But even a man can hear if you tell him his momma is crying like he was dead. Who's your momma? Why, she's just the one who stayed black when the Sears man called her over, that's all. She's just the one who saw black and stayed with it before any wise-ass told her how it was beautiful.

170

And I was in the street. 'Cause he'd stay on the dirt he knew. He wasn't going Northside. He'd move out of Moon's Bar and Grill, where the sports and spivs and pimps stood around fixing their hair and laying on each other how they was going to take out four or five of Daley's bulls when the time come. They talked away the nights and then went and hit 'em a warehouse or burned Zonk's store and called it a big fine time.

But not tonight, no, Lord. I stayed close to the walls, because cars ran up and down, people yelling all kinds of shit. A police car came by chasing an old yellow Edsel. Edsel made a corner, and I thought I saw somebody in it shooting. Cops missed their turn and fishtailed in the street, squealing and skidding and hitting a phone pole. I ran over just as one of 'em managed to climb out kind of weaving with blood running down his face. As I got close, he saw me and backed up to the car. Next thing I know that crazy sonofabitch has got him a sawed-off shotgun and swings it right around on me.

—Hey, I started to say.

—Stand fast, motherfucker. I ain't down yet. Get 'em up on your head. Turn. Don't even breathe deep. Hey, Mike, are you all right? I got one of 'em. Come on. Stand fast, nigger. I want a excuse. Just a wiggle.

Another car is coming, and while I stand, I see a little flame come out of that car window, and all of a sudden the whole front of a store goes up. It's Francis Record Shop. I know the man owns it. A colored fella from San Augustine, Florida. I want to phone him, get him down here.

—Listen, I tell the cop, but the car is still coming. It looks like it's headed right for me. Or the Zonk cop. Or both of us.

And he comes around shooting. He lets go with that shotgun when the car is maybe fifty or sixty yards away. It don't hurt the car, but it scares my balls off. I think, Jee-sus, you didn't get past that peckerwood in Virginia just to get laid out in South Chicago. It's got to be some other plan than that for you, Mr. Man. And I bucked and ran. Cop fired at me, turned and fired at the car, fired his last shot at me just as I ran across that car's path and dived to get out of its way. I lit rolling, and then I heard this scream and some shooting, and when I rolled up on to my hands and knees, I could see the cop laid out on the pavement with his scatter-gun maybe twenty yards away. His partner is shooting out of the wrecked car, but that other car is

171

stopped now, and whoever is in it is shooting back. This is the goddamnedest shit I have seen in a lifetime of shit. I mean all right, fine: You get born with a dose of sunburn and it's a hard row. But it ain't as hard as all this lead flying. I'm back on my belly and scooting up onto the far sidewalk thinking, you was a lot safer with the goddamned German Air Force coming at you loaded for bear. You come out of that with a whole ass all except that clout on the head welcome home, and now they're going to kill you in your own country. Either some crazy Zonk cop or a drunk nigger who heard they killed the King and says, Hey, this'll do. It's as good as ninety-five degrees in July.

At the end of the block there was this little ratty park, and I crawled to it, wishing to hell I was back at that bus stop in Texas trying to get me a beer. I come out of that with fifty cents. It looked like I might come out of this dead. I wondered whilst I crawled if it was a civil right to get dead in the middle of somebody else's quarrel.

I made it and started walking. Moon's Bar was just down the street maybe two blocks from the park. All the sirens and noise seemed to be behind me, so I reckoned on getting that far anyhow.

And I did. I wanted to call Elena, but there wasn't no time. I found Moon's with a lot of boys standing around. Cars kept coming up and going off, people getting in and getting out. Inside, it was dark and loud and noisy. People working like maggots in a dead dog. In the front, they're watching the city burn on TV and drinking beer and laughing and cheering. In back, they got guns and somebody has drained a car's gas tank and is filling empty beer bottles with the gas. One of 'em grins up at me. Yellow guy named Hill.

—Says they're nonreturnable, he's laughing. —That's what ole Honkie thinks. They are returnable.

I kind of smile at him and poke past. Then I hear him.

—Hey, Mr. Man, where you at?

Kicky has got him some kind of little machine gun that looks like what the commandos was using in the war. Like a pipe with a wire stock and a clip of .45 slugs fitted in the side where you could hold it whilst you sprayed around. Kicky turns this thing toward the back door and pulls it back and forth real slow.

172

Kat-kat-kat-kat-kat, he says, and grins at me. —You come to join the family, Mr. Man?

—Family is back at the house, I told him.

He kind of shrugs and puts down the gun. He hefts up what look like a pair of concussion grenades.

—This is the place. We're going out in a few minutes. We're going to visit Charlie.

I just looked at him. —Them grenades ain't fragmentation, I said after a minute. —They ain't worth a shit except in a hole or in a bunker. Outside, you'd have to push it down some fella's throat.

He shakes his head and winks at some of the others.

—How about inside a car? A police car?

—Oh, I said. —Reckon they'll roll down the window for you?

He rose up then. I had said the wrong thing. Don't piss this child, I said to myself. You didn't come down to piss him. You come to carry him home from Moon's and off these goddamn streets.

—We'll shoot their windows out for 'em. How about that?

—I seen some of that on the way. Time I left, looked like a draw. Cops got guns, too.

—Aw, shit, man, one of the other ones puts in. —Not like this they ain't.

He was holding up an old Browning automatic rifle. Jee-sus, I thought. These sonofbitches meant it. You could cut a car in half with one of them things. They shoot straight. I had one day on BAR in basic.

But I got to scoff this cat. He's tall and black with dark shades and a little bitty nothing of a beard. Makes you want to pull out his tongue and tie it around his ass. —They got M-16's when they call for 'em, I said. —You ever seen the track one of them things leaves?

But he just went back to pushing shells in those big BAR clips. And I thought, the longer you stand around watching, smaller the chance that boy is coming out. Move or forget it. I took hold of Kicky's arm.

—Come on, I said. —Let's us go find a beer somewhere.

He shook off my hand and looked at me square. —Right out there, he said, pointing with one of them green-brown grenades. —All you want. It's on the house tonight. They gonna send the bill on down to SCLC. Slip it in amongst the cost of wreaths, hearses, embalming, stuff like that.

—You never give a damn for that man.

—That man was black, you hear? He was black, and he was big. And Honkie shot him. Pulled the plug. Last train. People used to pray every time he showed on the TV. Now some of them Jesus shouters done give it up. They're coming over and we got to move. Now or never. Now lemme alone. I'm going out and I'm going to kill me a couple people for sure.

Un-huh, I thought, sick all the way down. You're going out and they're going to be there, ready for you and that little silly-bearded bastard and every two-bit nigger in this place.

—Listen, I said, trying to say real careful. —Do you know what they got out there? They got tanks. And a whole fucking army. They got flamethrowers. They got planes and bombs. There ain't a thing you ever dreamed of they *ain't* got. And they'll use everything they got. All on you.

He just grinned kinda like he was humble. —Aw, Mr. Man, you think they'd put all that expensive stuff on dis year wuthless lil ole pickaninny?

I turned and started out front. I been in and out, and I knew when the talking is done and finished. I reckoned to have me one of them free beers on the reverend. And think. Whether to cold-cock him with the bottle when I had emptied it. Or follow him and hope I could get in if it went up tight and started to come down on top of him. Or to just thread me a way home between all them cops and leave it lay. And pray.

I got to the counter, and this one fella behind the bar set out a Busch for me without even asking. I drained it, still thinking. I dumped number three right off. I wasn't built to walk off and leave him. Didn't have them kinds of guts. Wished I did. But I couldn't do it. Not for me without even thinking about Elena and her face and what would have to pass in her mind behind that face that could be white even still if it wanted. Left my baby. Your baby. Child needed bread and you left him a scorpion. Another gulp of Busch and I let go number two. Wasn't no good. Sooner or later, all these hard sons had to find 'em the riot squad. Longer it took 'em, meaner the cops was going to be. One had near killed me just for helping him. Before morning, they wouldn't let nothing black run, walk or crawl away in one piece. White cops, black cops, it wouldn't matter. I

174

couldn't do nothing that way. By then I hit the bottom of that brew, socked the bottle into my left hand and had all the answer I could see. I walked off from the bar and started back to the rear when all the lights in the world come on outside, and there come this great big voice sounded like it was from outside, inside, above and below, close and far. It had the natural true word, and when it started, wasn't a person in Moon's moved an inch.

—Inside Moon's Bar and Grill. This is Captain Edward Tomaselli speaking. You will begin filing out the front door one by one, hands above your heads, palms out in plain sight. If you are wearing a coat or jacket, take it off. Walk slowly and directly into the light. Do not stop or attempt to turn to either side until an officer stops you. This is your only warning. All exits are covered . . .

Then it was quiet, but nobody moved. All those black faces, turned upward and outward toward the light. White eyes big, and woman kinda whimpering, and somebody saying, —Oh, Jesus, Oh, Jesus.

I thought like a fool, All right, fine. Saves me tapping him. They can't go to shooting fifty to sixty people. Once we're in the wagon, it's going to be all right. Not all right, no. 'Cause here goes my job no matter how I explain it. But it ain't going to be all right again for a long, long time. But better than that child dead in a box with his hands crossed over his chest. Better than that.

So I dropped my bottle, and the sound of it breaking on the floor started everything. Woman calling for Jesus, she really cut loose:

—Jesus, Jesus, they done come for us. They done killed him, and they come for us. Oh, sweet sweet Jesus, don't let 'em do it to me. No, don't let 'em . . .

—This is Captain Edward Tomaselli . . .

And the people started moving. Like rats, like roaches, like some kind of people in a movie. Throwing over tables, pitching chairs around, falling down, cursing, praying. Like people hearing the planes coming over, like that captain's voice was the siren. One woman went for the door, but the light was too much, and she fell down and crawled right between my legs, crying and asking somebody to help her. But all I could think was, You and your goddamned beer bottle. Why couldn't you?

175

Out back, somebody had tried the back door, but I heard the big hollow sound of a shotgun, and the door slammed, and I thought, sonofabitch, it's that cop they run down. He's done followed me and this is going to be judgment. Then one of them nuts in the back slipped the doop open and flipped out a grenade. You could feel it more than hear it. It kind of squeezed the walls in at you, but you just knew it hadn't done nothing but put the wind up the cops. As if they didn't already have enough to sail Lake Michigan around.

That was when the big voice on the bullhorn just stopped and you could hear the dago say, back from the horn, just before he cut it off, —All right, let 'em have it. And the windows went. Right through the glass, knocking down the curtains. Gas bombs. One hit up against my leg and went off, putting out that bad smell and making you ready to run on out, taking a chance they might miss. Then somebody pushed me out of the way. It was Kicky. He grabbed that thing and threw it through the broken window and went to scrambling after the other one, yelling, —See, Mr. Man, that's what you . . . do with a bomb.

Then he stood up, and I saw he had that damned machine gun. I went for him, but he was already shooting, out into the lights, out where the cops was waiting, praying somebody would shoot. I had me one second to think, though, Boy, it's like shooting flak at 'em. It ain't a chance. Too many. Too much. I hit him behind the knees just as they let go, but I was maybe a piece of a second too slow. It was only one bullet hit him. But it hit him in the head, and he was dead when he fell back over me, before I could twist around and lift him up. He was dead, and his eyes was open and his mouth all twisted up and not any kind of frightened. He was dead, and I had him in my arms screaming something and not even noticing that they was still firing and dropping in gas. Because it didn't take no gas to make me cry. Never mind the bullets.

When they stopped, I was still sitting there. The gas and the plaster they had shot off the walls made it so you couldn't see anything. The dust was settling on my boy's face, making him look like some black clown wanting to put on he was white. I wiped his face with one hand and mine with the other.

They come in then. They come in the back and front, and pretty soon they was marching people out. They had all of them with their hands on top of their heads and all them guns and grenades left behind for the cops to pick up in boxes and bags and take away. Then it was only the boy and me left, and a cop come and laid a shotgun on my shoulder.

—Go on, I said. —Get it over with. You been after me since Virginia.

But another one come and got me on my feet and some fellas in white coats with a cot you pull by a handle come in and picked up the boy. Last sight I had of his face, it seemed to me he looked mad and lost, like somewhere he had missed a turning and now would have to back up and find out where it was he had missed. Like he wanted to say, is that all there is to it?

Power, I told him in my mind. You just a dumb nigger boy didn't never understand power. If you seen what I had seen . . .

They handcuffed me. They put me in the wagon and took us to the lockup. Asked if we wanted a phone call. I didn't pay no mind. They had me in a cell, with that ratty-assed burr with the glasses and the beard. His head was bleeding, and they had took away his BAR. He kept saying, —Black power, black power, like it was a magic word, a conjure to lift him out of this jail and put it all right. I come close to getting up and going over and whipping on him, but I thought, no, he didn't do it. The boy was grown. He did it on his own. And it was Zonk shot him down. It's between us. Always was between us.

When they took me to the judge, I just stood there. He asked me what a workingman was doing in that place. I just stood there. It was an old room full of wood benches with wood walls and people walking around. Some little sawed-off Zonk with glasses asked me if I knew my rights. I said, —Fuck off. I got no rights. Nobody got no rights. He kind of shrugged and went off, and the judge went to talking to me again. He was kind of fat where his chin come down over his collar, and his robe looked like it was rusty under the black. It was a ugly black. I looked at the flags and out the window where you could see other buildings out there. Once in a while you heard a siren. They was still in the street out there.

—Aren't you a veteran? the judge asked me.

—I was over to that war, I said.

—Were you in combat?

I looked up at his fat dago face. I kind of smiled. I saw something. I said, —I bombed for youall. I dropped bombs on people. I killed women and little children for youall. I killed

177

folks' sons and daughters. I blew up babies in their cribs. Killed dogs and horses. Blew up cars and trucks. Raised shit over there for you.

He didn't look any way at all. Not mad or funny. He just looked out of them brown pockets in his face where he kept his eyes. I saw he had real smooth oily skin. He ate good and lived good, and you knew he made him deals and was good to a lot of girls. Maybe he had a son. Maybe his son was a cop.

—If you fought for this country, how do you explain taking part in . . .

—I never fought for nothing, I said. —If they had put me in another place I would of cooked food. In another place I would of rolled bandages and emptied bedpans. Most colored did that. I bombed. I never fought. They paid me and I bombed. It was a job.

I never told him about the Blockhouse and the Dark Room and the sight. Or how the sky looked before dawn over the Channel. I never told him how in my mind I was glad those Germans was white and glad I was dumping on 'em.

He just looked at me and whispered over to the one with glasses. Then he hit his table with a mallet and said something about bound over for trial and named some bail I couldn't hope to make, and they took me back to the lockup.

I laid down on my bunk and rubbed my wrists where they had those cuffs so tight. I thought about the boy. I hoped at the home they would clean his face, wipe off the plaster dust or whatever it was. I hoped they would. But leave his face how it was. Don't make him look peaceful and content. Don't make him smile. Don't cross his arms to say, —Hoping in Jesus. Because it wasn't no hope. Not in Jesus or in the law or anything. Except, I thought, in a 17, in the sight. In five-hundred-pound HE. Wouldn't any number of concussion grenades do no good. Nor fragmentation either. It needed bombs. Great large flights of bombers. V for victory, keep 'em flying: bombs and people who knew bombs and how to dump. I went to sleep thinking of bombs, figuring to dream. But I slept sound, no dreams at all. I didn't have any dreams.

They told me she had come, and I got up like a machine, threw some water in my face and went out to the room where they have visiting. It was a great big cage, and there were black people all up and down the length of it in little cubbyholes separated by a piece of plywood from the next. Outside the wire at one cubbyhole, I saw her. They had her in black. I mean she was wearing black. She looked light against those dark clothes and I felt tears in my eyes. First tears since the gas. I hadn't done no crying for the boy. Why cry for your own self? I felt 'em now and thought, See where you brought her? She'd of been better with Sears. She could of lost him then, said good-bye to that boy and walked off and, when she got a telegram or a call, said to Sears, —Oh, look Mr. Jones, that little boy I had over there got himself hurt so bad he died. Oh, that's so bad.

Then I was sitting looking at her through the wire. We just looked. Like one of us was a person looking in at a animal, only you couldn't say which was which. Just looking without smiling or looking sad or anything at all.

—I buried him this morning, she said. —Some of the folks in the neighborhood helped.

I nodded and didn't say anything. There wasn't anything in me. I was just meat growing cold and stale. It felt like I had been in prison for life. I guessed I had, only this time there was wire and bars and I could see it for sure. I tried to say something, but my voice give way. She reached out like she'd take my hand, but then she pulled back. Maybe it was the wire.

—They killed Mr. Francis. You remember the man owned the record place? They killed him. He went down to stop the fire they started, and they shot him. Nobody knows who. Just found him in front. Shot dead.

I tried to say something again and couldn't believe what come out.

—We thought we'd got away from him. Said all he had was that twenty miles in Parker County, but we never got ten yards from him. No, 'cause it's all that twenty miles of back road, that's all there is. With hell at one end and confoundment at the other. If I loved you, I would have lied to him and said, Yes, man, she's a white college girl out for a thrill now what you gonna do and he'd of shot me and killed the boy right then, shot him while he was still in me and you could of gone over and stayed over and then . . .

Her face never changed. —Stop it, she said. —Just stop it. It's over now.

Then I laughed. I laughed so loud the guard come over and

179

kind of sniffed at me. 'Cause in that place didn't anybody laugh. They cried or they sat still or they cursed God and their momma's womb. But they didn't never laugh.

—Over, I said, looking back at the guard, wondering how come they had changed his uniform since he drove that old Plymouth car down in Virginia. —It ain't nothing over. It ain't even started yet, honey. It ain't even taken the lid off yet. It is still rattling in the can.

And when they took me back to my cell, I saw how the Zonk locking me in was a spitting image of that captain in New York when I come home. Somewhere was that MP, too, and I minded to find him. And then see. See what come next.

Boyd

While I worked for McCarthy, I came to know the kids. Not understand them, I don't claim that. Just know them, experience them. I began the hardest part, what for me was really the hardest. I started turning on to their music. It had been noise. From the middle fifties on, it had all been noise to me. A bunch of musical illiterates and primitives smashing on guitars, using circuitry to replace talent. Screaming so no one would notice they couldn't sing. The last things I had enjoyed were Stan Kenton's late work and some of Les Brown. Once in a while I listened to Sinatra or the Four Freshmen. Until one evening, on the way home, I found that the barbarians had taken over the whole waveband and I flipped off the radio. For ten years. Once in a while I played the piano at home. Not often, because I was still doing what I had always done, and I knew what would come out before I ever touched the keyboard. So why bother?

Now the kids had me listening. *Listening.* I was beginning to hear their sounds, and they were good. The lyrics were a light-year ahead of the rubbish that had limped along twenty-five years ago masked by our instruments. I listened to the Beatles and heard the perfect blend of truth and put-on that was their early stock-in-trade. I heard Dylan and saw why they loved him

and his flat fantastic Okie voice telling them that however bad
it was, there has to be a song for them somewhere:

> . . . Mothers and fathers all over this land,
> Your sons and your daughters are beyond your command . . .
> For the times they are a'changin'. . . .

No bravado, no malice. Only that fine drone saying how it is,
matter-of-fact as a decision from an unappealable bench. The
Doors, the Jefferson Airplane, Herman's Hermits, Simon and
Garfunkel. And after a month or so, I even found some of my
own: Stone Pillow, Peter Starstedt; I came across an LP by Joe
and Eddie, bought some acid rock nobody had ever heard. It
was a very strange thing, like losing your ears to find them
again. I could hear it now, feel where it had to go. I even wondered if I could play it on the guitar.

> There's a meeting here tonight,
> There's a meeting here tonight,
> I can tell by your friendliness
> There's a meeting here tonight. . . .

What came to me suddenly one night as some of us sat
around at the headquarters late at night was that this underground music rising, taking over, had brought with it singular
sadness flitting behind its blare and easy freedom. It was as if
they had all at once no trace of hope and boundless dreams of a
tomorrow cleansed of all the horror we had been willed, had
willed them in turn. It was strong music, original and driving
—far more than most of ours had been. But its roughness was
not truly barbaric; it was more nearly the electronic equivalent
of rococo: a music meant to alter moods and fill in intolerable
silences. Not to be listened to, simply to be heard. Even able to
hear it, the vestiges of my old ear and my musical brain per-
sisted. After I heard it, I went the next step, which, by un-
spoken rule, they forbade themselves for the best of reasons:
self-preservation. I listened and turned each phrase over and
over in my mind. It was a heartbreaking music by people who
were determined to feel, really *feel*, no matter what. I tried to
remember the last time I had had an authentic unhung feeling.
Before Sandy? Before law school? No, before Dresden.
  Was it that all of us were, long before the occasion, born for

bombardiers? Given to thinking before feeling, to the rapture of infinite space, machines, abstractions, a deep and secret hatred of the flesh, of the dark places where life is made, of the limits, the edges, the palpability of our bodies, the scent that identifies us to ourselves? Deodorants and sprays, a hundred mouthwashes and toothpastes and foot powders designed to carry us as far from ourselves as possible. A music which declined from the sweat of jazz through the brief equipoise of Miller and Shaw and the Dorseys—down to Lawrence Welk and Muzak. A way of pausing always between thought and act, weighing ends, distant places, heights, something unhuman where we could escape death and self and stink and dwell like blind gods plucking dooms from that original tree near always to our hand and throw them back down into the world on the poor, the incapable, the black, the alien. What if the war against Hitler and the endless contest with the Communists were no more or less than rivalries, a series of campaigns, semifinals, to see which national beast would bestride the whole world with the sole right to bomb, to ravish, to annihilate any state or gathering or single human being who should dare raise a flag or a cry—much less an army—against us?

It was the music—their music—that made me go down within myself, tear up pavements in my mind and what was left of my heart, and probe what was beneath. Guilt? No, worse than that. Because there is in guilt a high and awful pride, the certainty of a doom that springs from the nature of the universe. Guilt will be punished. Won't it? But what I found was not guilt. Nothing so real and personal and fine. What lay beneath the accreted layers of spiritual asphalt almost a quarter century collected was complicity. I was one of the tools. I was part of things. I was not the leader, the cutting edge of a ruthlessness old as the Vikings, cruel as Attila. No, I was a cog which, on certain occasions, had meshed with others in order to produce effects that no one of us was guilty of. Wheels within wheels, a web, a galaxy of single irresponsible actions which added up to a complex of horror that could not be laid to any man or men, nation or nations. At Dresden, I had taken part in the burning of one hundred and thirty-five thousand men and women. And children. And, God help me, I was not guilty.

Now I came to understand the music, the crudity of it, the animal simplicity of it. The kids were unkempt; some were dirty, their hair long and snagged. They had no interest in what we called morals, in the clean order of their parents' lives which hid beneath the sprays and douches and underarm pads the gangrenous suppurating memories and present knowledge that there had been at least a hundred million empty seats at Nuremberg that might have been filled with—us, the complicitors, who had followed orders, done what was called our duty, purposely ignoring the question of how one distinguishes between gassing Jewish children and bombing German children. We had known—known for certain by the raid on Dresden—that we were no longer hitting military targets. And we had followed orders. And now, saying nothing, the kids were saying it all:

> Yes, and how many times must the cannon-balls fly
> Before they are finally banned . . . ?

They were dirty and crude because young animals find in themselves, the glory of their strength, the joy of their animality, the antidote for dreaming of a flight above the world at twice sound's speed to bomb those who remain below. They had turned from being counterfeit gods. Their trips to the sky were taken on pot and acid, and they could hurt only themselves; only they themselves were at risk. And they hated those who still bombed, who, recidivist, still listened without hearing and dreamed above the clouds of the final conquest of infinite space, of the world brought to silence, of an order that, once achieved, might last for a thousand years.

So much from a guitar strummed over cold coffee by kids who, without believing, were making one last bid within the structure of our politics. Before some of them went out. For good.

Krepinski

We were working Southside when the word came that they'd want a special detail for the convention. They had talked about moving the convention to Miami Beach. But one of the boys on the Cook County Committee just laughed.

—They're kidding themselves. Nobody takes anything from the mayor. He gives, maybe. But they don't *take*. And he's not giving. He's keeping. They'll name the next President right here. Count on it.

—Who's it going to be? somebody asked.

He just laughed. —That's up to the delegates, ain't it?

Everybody laughed.

Welch and me went back on the road. After we volunteered for the special duty. It's a few bucks. And from what we hear, it could be action. I'm driving and Welch is reading the *Tribune* out loud. About these punks coming from California and New York—all the beards in the world. Jerry somebody, this wild queer, is saying they'll bring the town to a stop. They'll break up the convention. I kind of laugh.

—You think he believes that? I ask Welch.

He shrugs and puts down the paper. —I think I want him to try. I want him to try hard. I ain't shot anybody since I left Tulsa. I want him to come at me with something. I want to shoot him once in the nuts. Then I want the next one to really hurt him.

We both laughed.

—You ever shot anybody? Welch asks me.

—You mean kill 'em? No. I shot a guy in a warehouse a year or so ago. Took his knee joint out for him. Tried to let me have it with a flashlight.

—Why didn't you take him out?

—No way. I'm an expert with everything they use. If I kill a guy, they know I shot to kill him. I'm on the tactical emergency unit. When they get a nut up in a building, they give me a rifle with a 35X sight.

Welch whistled. —A regular gunslinger. Were you in the Rangers?

Welch is new on Southside. He worked the lakefront till they transferred him. I don't ask him about his transfer. He don't tell me anything. —No, I say. —I was a bombardier.

—Sock it to me, Welch laughed. —That was a good job. They had me wrapped around a rifle. I got to Belgium in December of 1944. Just when the Krauts headed west. Jesus, they hit us. In the Ardennes. I was listening to a radio in the mess

184

tent. It must have been twenty below. It was Artie Shaw playing "Begin the Beguine." An eighty-eight shell came right through the tent. It begun right then. Some beguine.

—I don't know what they hit you with. We were taking them apart every day. Once we made two missions in one day.

—They got it somewhere. They damn near drove Troy Middleton and the Eighth Corps back to London. I wish they had.

—You like London?

—No. I wish the fucking Germans had run us out of Europe. Then they could have creamed the goddamned Communists, fixed the Jews. There'd be one place with no niggers in it.

I didn't say anything. You don't get promotions coming on with your own ideas. Sometimes you get transferred. But Welch was right. We bombed the wrong people. We handed half the world away. Not next time though. Not next time. You don't say anything. You just fire twice a week and keep the eye sharp and the reflexes good. You do that and wait. Because sooner or later, they'll try. Maybe at the convention. Maybe the beards would try to put the arm on the police. That would be nice.

We drove along the West Side. Nigger shops and a whiskey store or two. Juke joints and rib joints. Lots of these skinny Afro creeps with frizzy hair and long dresses on. Shades, too. They can't even see where they're going. Man, they can't find their own asses. When you pile out on them, all that wise crap they lay on the newspaper jokers is gone. They freeze. Here's the heat: duck, cover your burrhead because we got a license to break you apart. Go tell the City Council about police brutality. Show 'em your bruises. Show 'em nothing: A pile of BB's in a canvas cover don't leave any marks if you're careful. Once in a while you break one of them up just to keep the word out that the cops are strong. Let 'em smell you up close. They like it. It helps 'em be niggers if you're there to remind 'em. No big noise. No shooting. Just stop and frisk, a tap or two when you get one alone. It's good for everybody.

Now this is my end of town. I work sometimes with nigger cops. I don't mind. They know how it is. They got to live, too. We hold an end of the sheet up, so it don't fall and spill anything. We got a piece of the numbers, something on a couple of keno banks. We got some hags forking over, and there is a deal cooking for a few house jobs that we oversee from a block off for twenty-five percent. It cuts their risk ninety percent. It's

185

worth the price. Hell, it's worth thirty percent, but you don't push. And the nigger cops are in all this. They fence; they front. They collect. It's all right. And the rake-off is according to grade. I make another bill a week. Sometimes a bill and a half. A big nigger sergeant keeps our books. I don't worry about him. He wants all this—and his pension, too. And what I want to say is the nigger cops whip up and down the street, too. It's not nigger against white. It's not that easy. That later. First, it's us against them. We're in and we're staying in. You want in? Apply. We'll let you know. You want to push? If you say so. But it will go real bad. This town is very solid. There ain't any holes, any vacant places. You can't pick an orange peel out of the gutter without getting into somebody's spiel. There's a guy who owns the gutters and whatever is in them. There may be an orange peel man who splits with him. There's threads on everything in the street, and they connect to a string in the neighborhood. Which gets to be a rope in the ward. And a cable as it goes to City Hall. And the threads and the string and the rope and the cable all wind up on one desk. The mayor's. There are others who have a say. But nobody tries to break the web. The town is too solid for that. Everybody is taken care of.

That night we break up some trouble between a spade and his wife. We bust a crap game that has been going since 1962. We pull in eighty bucks and let people run. What can you do in the dark? It's no sweat. They've already passed ten or twelve thousand. The last pot is left there as a kindness. It means we come in next time with the siren on. It's quiet. No bad stuff.

And the next morning there is an inspection at district, and they call off the men for the special detail. They call me out. Then the captain tells everybody to walk easy for the rest of the week on Southside. No hard busts. We don't want any minority trouble, because we can't use another riot there while we're welcoming the beards and the sandals at the Loop. And we have delegates to protect. We got the future of the country in our hands. This is where Hubert Humphrey is going to walk off with the big ticket. In a nice quiet atmosphere.

The special detail people are pulled together, and we go in for these training films on crowd control. We know all this stuff. We got a look at the kind of crowds you have to control last April when they shot up that nigger preacher down in Memphis. The shades went ape. Burned, shot, looted. Nice peo-

186

ple. But this time it will be different. Somebody from Intelligence says they are making solid deals with the coons. This is not your action, they tell them. This is a bunch of Charlie punks with rich daddies who are coming because it is vacation from college and they want to find some fast kicks. You keep your people cool, and there will be some jelly roll. The other side is bringing in the tanks and parking them on top of you. This comes down from the top, and they are all believers. They heard that shoot-to-kill order in April, and when the stinking reporters and fag politicians finished doing the bad-mouth, it stood with the force. The word is, even a suspension or dismissal for blasting a bomber will be sweet. Enough lump sum to make the pension loss hurt good. And a little job somewhere. Stock-control clerk in a city warehouse on the Evanston line. Foreman of a sanitation crew. At a detective's salary. When you own a house this big, there are cubbyholes, little rooms, nice places under the stairs, out of the rain.

So we are ready. And this time I'm not standing third. I'm right in the front line. I tell Gertrude, —Shut up. I'm not going to get hurt. What's hurt? If they behave, it'll be the easiest week in history. If they come on, we'll bomb them back to Berkeley and New York. They'll think the whole world is falling in on top of them.

Boileau

—I think you're overdramatizing it, I told Patrick Foley. But through the overseas static, he kept on talking.

—You're too close to see it, he said. —They drove your Texan to the wall. They're not going to let his heir apparent walk into Chicago and out with the prize. Kennedy's dead. McCarthy is a ghost without a house to haunt. I want you there. It's our money. All right?

So I said all right, fine. It was their money. The London *Examiner* would pay me one thousand pounds for a series of dispatches from Chicago. On the second American Revolution.

Recorded on the spot by a student of revolution. It seemed absurd on the face of it. My articles on Cromwell, on the Peasant Revolt and on that whole spectrum of madness called, after Joachim of Flora, the Third Realm had been well received. My book on post-Comtean scientism and Positivist political thought had even drawn attention from the newsmagazines. I was an authority on revolution and totalitarian mass movements, and the *Examiner,* a newspaper noted for not writing down to its audience, saw the Democratic Convention coming as a matter for my attention. It disturbed me. I didn't think it had come to that. I had thought our 1905 would be a bit more dramatic. I was waiting for Prynne, for Praise-God Barebone, for a cold day before the Winter Palace with Father Gapon bringing his sheep on, a Judas goat in spite of himself. I wondered if Foley saw more in Wallace than there was. Could he believe that Montgomery was the next Nuremberg? I dismissed that. No, it had to lie elsewhere. The American Gracchi were dead, though there was a third brother whose mere presence must inevitably evoke all the desperate love and insane hatred that his kin had inspired. No, America would never go down in a welter of conscience, making a monarch to lay so many ghosts. That was not the American style. America knew that ghosts are laid not by acts, but by will. The mind of the Republic, whatever its first response to assassination and martyrdom, was too accustomed to living with its sins to have a sudden fatal attack of remorse. It lived with Nat Turner and Elijah Lovejoy, with Chief Joseph of the Nez Percé, with Sacco and Vanzetti, with Wesley Everest, with Lincoln, with Leon Czolgosz, with the dead, just and unjust, wrong and mad. With the Haymarket rioters, Albert Parsons, late of the Confederate cavalry, calling out for a chance to speak before Chicago hanged him for a bomb he had not thrown. With the Scottsboro boys and the Rosenbergs. Every last one a revolutionary in his way, and every one bomber and bombed. No, shadows were part of the Republic as it existed, and Malcolm X to the contrary, the chickens still pecked and strutted in various corners of the yard. The mix was not right yet, and the man to bring that three-hundred-year-old brew to a boil was nowhere in sight.

I made my plane reservations and then went out to fish. I could not help thinking how apropos it was for me to have found my field, my metier, in the study of modern mass movements. I who had been part of one, the controller of long-distance horror. Who had never seen a bomb explode at ground level. Who had killed thousands and who once had planned to hold his hand and had been balked even in that gesture by German antiaircraft.

That day I used a fly rod, whipping a yellow bug among the lily pads, into the small patches of open water, where, as I twitched the bright bait, the surface would explode as a bass dragged it down. Then there would be the silent struggle, the brutal tug from below, my own play of the rod and the line. The bass might go deep, or flash suddenly into the air, shaking his golden-green body, trying to rid himself of the hook concealed in the painted wood and feathers of the fly. And sometimes the line would go slack. He would have won. Down there he would be swimming away, still shaken by his sudden meeting with the supernatural up above the atmosphere. Where the gods dwelled. Where once, long ago, certain of the fish had dared to go, creeping up into the air to mysterious apotheosis. Once fish and men had been of a single kind. What had happened to us was called history. Or time. Or evolution. What happened to the fish who stayed where they belonged? What was that called? Eternity, grace? Now we sent down our lines and chose victims blindly in the dark water. I wondered if we were fished for, too. And if, down below, there were fish who declared the millennium, the imminent coming of the Final State of Things. Would the gar rule, the hunter-scavenger? The grunnel? Not the bass. He was too brave, too single-minded, too shy and too careless all at once. Danton was a bass. He had no chance. Kerensky was a bass, striking at the obvious. Until the scavengers made their play.

It was sundown as I moved up the river toward Rainey's camp. On both sides the deep green of midsummer cypress began to cast shadows over the darkening water. Soon they would be trees no longer, but high walls marking the path of the river. The moon would rise early, an enormous presence turning the water at first to gold, then to silver, making of the river a wide magical highway that would seem to flow off the earth and onward through space to the very surface of the moon itself. At that moment, I would cut the motor and let the boat drift, let my wake pass by and exhaust itself among the lilies and roots and grass along the shore until there was no movement at all, only the unstirring surface of the water and the distant questioning of owls as they prepared to fly, to soar above the trees and fields, looking below for mice and rabbits, small birds who did not realize that the moonlight was as lethal as the day.

I would sit for a long time there thinking of distances and grace. Of the moon's secret force that made flood and ebb and ruled our women. Somewhere beyond the face of creation, even beyond this place and this moment, ruled a reality capable of reconciling us all. We tried to hear it, to find it, to serve it. All of us stumbling out of pasts and into futures, pretending to be sure of the one, confident of the other. I shivered and felt what must be compassion. Because I knew that the mystery of Sazonov's heart, of L'Ouverture's mind, of Liebknecht's intention, was impenetrable. And that the future lay beyond even the pathetic speculations we call history. We swim in this river called existence, bumping into one another, dreaming of far countries and fairy cities emerald and cool and filled with singing and the odor of justice. We flounder for a while, somewhere between green Eden and the New Jerusalem, dreaming, dreaming, then we go down.

It is taught that the Virgin was assumed into heaven. That night I felt a pity for her. A mermaid rising against nature, higher, higher, out of our element. Into the far dark freezing cold of intergalactic space. Shall we all swim there one day? Is it no farther than from the water to the shore? And will there be no swift death, no brutal stroke and counterstroke, no scavengers waiting to take advantage as we fall back, drift downward from our latest assault on misty divinity that lies even farther on? Will we be happy?

Then the moon stood high, a heavenly body, the closest of billions, riding across the night sky, across the orchestration of stars which I would never see closer. But where I did not doubt man would one day stride amid other agonies, sadnesses I could not imagine, thinking of the sad track left by those who could not rest and did not know.

Then I started the motor, seeing that it was later than I thought and that my plane would be leaving from New Orleans almost before I could get there.

And as I pulled up to the scattered lights of Rainey's landing,

190

someone's transistor was blaring small and tinny from a dark cabin:

> . . . do you know the way
> to San Jose?

Nor Chicago either. We ride at the front of an impulse, naked and certain amid our bubble, protected from the cold until the blast comes. We cannot hear the pilot or the navigator. But we hunch forward, gazing down on the earth, believing that our act will alter the flow of things. We are deceived, and the target is forever our own home, our own people, and we will one day have to land, to walk in the deserts we have made, amongst the ashes of Carthage and Hiroshima, of Dresden and Mine Run.

V

Boyd

There was no reason for me to go to the debate at the Lasalle Ballroom. Afterward I wondered if there had been any reason for me to go to Chicago. I satisfied myself on the second point by reference to the first.

Because if I had not heard them all, Humphrey, McGovern and McCarthy, I wouldn't have believed it. We went to hear the climactic confrontation on the war, to watch Humphrey either step away from the wreck of Johnson's policies or go down under McCarthy's essential rightness. Of course neither happened. Because in American politics, I came to see, nothing is ever pressed to its limits. There is always a pulling back from the abyss, a refusal to say precisely what one feels and everyone knows. Because, goddammit, the rival, however wrong he may be, will still be around tomorrow. You won't shoot him, and you can't extirpate him from political life as they did Khrushchev. No, he'll be there, and a thrust at his jugular today will be, must be, repaid with a slash at your crotch tomorrow. There are limits. And because even if you cared nothing for those tomorrows stretching out beyond to an infinity which is no more real than that posed in physics but just as essential, you would have to realize that politics carried beyond any limits stops being politics at all. It is called revolution or anarchy or something.

So anyhow Humphrey said it all again. He told of the rightness of the war and the bombing, explaining that aggression had to be made profitless and how a democratic South Vietnam had to be preserved. There were boos. A couple of McCarthy's boys were with me. Clyde just bit his fingernails. Newton kept looking at the faces around us as if each word Humphrey uttered were part of a lie so monstrous, so evil in conception and in speech, that surely the lectern would dissolve if the people didn't rise to beat him from the ballroom.

And that's what it would have taken. Because McCarthy said nothing . . . let it go.—The people know my position, he said. And that was it. I had come a thousand miles to hear five words. I couldn't believe it until McGovern was before the mikes, speaking well, saying what McCarthy should have said, but with that sweet forceless style that made you wish he could be just a bit phony. For the sake of truth.

I shook my head. I wondered if I had had a tiny stroke, a momentary failure of the synapses, during which McCarthy had obliterated not only Humphrey but the whole poisonous administrative apparatus that he represented, that had grown on us since the outbreak of my war, that had begun like a secret tumor to grow and burgeon in the nation, beginning there in the Blockhouse in Texas—naturally enough—had carried us outward to a war made even more horrible than it needed to be by our demand for unconditional surrender from all our enemies, to that courtesy raid on Dresden with which we had placated our future enemies at a catastrophic cost in human life, no less human because it was German.

But I had missed nothing. The limits were fixed. Neither McCarthy nor McGovern was about to tell these people that we had gradually become a little insane, that what our arrogance required of the world was impossible and that in our rage at this closure of the world's possibilities before our desire we were becoming a nation of two hundred million cowboys, recidivists all to Dodge City and Tombstone.

I felt as if I were back in the nose of a 17 again, only this time I was an unwilling passenger, an observer strapped in a seat and about to be forced witness to the destruction of Manhattan. This continent was becoming itself a gigantic instrument of destruction, its will, its purposes as grandiose and hopeless and unswerving as ever the Bolsheviks or the Tsars or the hoard of the khans had been. But even so, the tactics had not changed from my day. There were men who talked of tossing an H-bomb into the men's room of the Kremlin, of an "acceptable casualty rate" in nuclear exchange of fifty million people, of "interdiction" of China, and on and on.

But the limit had been reached, and when we walked from the room, I knew two things: McCarthy not only could not win, but had no business winning. Somehow, in some sense, he was not a serious man. Maybe, I thought, it's because of that damned mad Irish Catholicism. Maybe, pressed, he cannot care if, before Armageddon, there is a training exercise so vast and catastrophic that the final judgment will be anticlimax no matter what God thinks of it. The second thing I knew was that we would not be turned, that the country, whatever its purposes two hundred years ago, had lost its appetite for change and growth and that some secret gland within us had atrophied, no longer poured forth the juice that makes people say, —Well, this is wrong. We have to change it.

I was sorry for Newton and Clyde. They knew what I knew. The difference was that they were heartbroken. They would not admit it yet, not until the balloting was over, but something had cracked within them when McCarthy did not, or could not, or would not say it all one more time, say it to Humphrey's face—and with all stops out like an ancient prophet whose least concern was that the king might order him stoned or dragged through the streets behind a chariot. The difference was that they were heartbroken; I was frightened. Maybe now the craft was on automatic pilot. Maybe America, unrealized by any of us, had sometime in the last four years pulled loose from the world altogether, had circled like a space capsule and was headed now, a kamikaze bomber nose down, directly toward the earth. Pilots of the divine wind, they had called themselves, and someone who worked for the *Times Book Review* had once lent me a book of last letters sent by those boys, my exact contemporaries, to their families before they were bolted into their cockpits and sent after our ships in the Pacific. I remembered one especially, from a Catholic pilot who invoked the Virgin and the saints to give him courage and aim him straight. The mixture of Christian language and the absolute fanaticism of his words had shaken me then. Were we like him now, uttering the formula words of freedom and justice as we prepared to crash-dive into the world, the guts of our national craft stuffed with the greatest destructive power the world had ever possessed? I remembered one of the first heroes of my war, one Colin Kelly who, they said, crash-dived his crippled plane into a Japanese ship. Had his act become, through subterranean decades, a national pattern? I remembered the Alamo, the Texas holocaust, itself part of a dubious military effort, and was not

197

comforted. They would not believe it if I told them, but Clyde and Newton could be enriched by this disaster. They would grow up depending on nothing marginal, only on themselves and what they had safely in hand. I knew too much. There was no new wisdom in all this for me. There was only confirmation of my worst imaginings. I did not want to go home to Sandy. We would have to talk, and I didn't want that.

Jacobs

Mariam said, —What is it? You've got a taste for acid rock? You're meeting halfway a *shiksa* from the Fillmore.

—No, I told her. —I ought to go.

—You ought to go east and you want to go west. Wrong-way Cunningham. Look, he's dead. He doesn't need you. All the bishops and popes are praying for him. In Tel Aviv they need you.

—There's only one Pope, I told her.

—There's only one homeland.

I'm thinking, goddamn homelands. They're all deserts, aren't they? With a Blockhouse or a Kaaba or a wrecked temple. And inside something terrible to teach the boys when they're old enough. You know of any exceptions?

—So go, she told me. —Go and see them cast two votes for this other man from Kansas.

—McGovern is from Dakota, I said.

And I went. To be there. Not for anything. To be there. And it was good I went. If I hadn't gone, maybe I wouldn't be going.

When I got to O'Hare, the children were coming in. With guitars and blue jeans and long hair. I'm sorry, I say they were children. But they looked at me looking at them and one began to play on his guitar:

. . . for the times they are a'changin' . . .

198

With that nobody can argue. And when I found out how little was going on with the Kennedy forces—only backbiting and still tears and confusion—I said, —You've wasted the price of a ticket. Go home to Mariam and the boys. Tell her you can't go anywhere because you are like a man sitting in a lousy cheap movie: It's terrible, but you have to see what will happen next. Even if you know what will happen next.

So I went to Lincoln Park and took off my coat and tie and settled in. The music was very bad, very loud, the small speakers distorting it even worse than it needed to be. There were many speeches. I didn't know so much was wrong with the country. Me, I knew there were bad things, but who knew there were so many? My God, nobody is free, they say. They want drugs and public screwing and an end to war. They want Reagan dead and Huey Newton free and nobody to eat grapes and nothing bought from Southern textile mills and the poor people to get millions. I thought, nobody wants that much. They just say it. Maybe they just want a good job and a car. They want not to be drafted and go die in somebody else's desert.

It got dark, and the police who had been patrolling in pairs all afternoon seemed to grow in number. There was an announcement that the park would close at midnight. People laughed and jeered. A girl with big round glasses told the fuzz to fuck itself. I laughed. Because it was a shock, and I guess because I'm forty-five years old and wanted to say that to police myself. To tell them to take their chrome-plated pistols and handcuffs and push them up their asses. To drive their red-lighted cars up an alley and gas themselves. But I never did. I who had dropped bombs on dozens of cities, surely killed thousands in another country, had never had the guts to say what I felt to these puny amateurs with their toy weapons. If I had a 17 and a crew, I thought, and blushed considering that forty-five is not old enough to excuse the spinning of sociopathic fantasies.

The police passed on, their eyes front, their jaws tight. They're storing it up, I thought. They can feel the weight of those pistols riding their hips like spare dicks, and so they can bear it. They're storing it up like current in a battery. Sooner or later they'll have to let it go.

I remember one of them. His uniform didn't fit. He liked a tight shirt, but he was running to fat so that the skintight shirt

199

only revealed a wide rim of excess flesh that moved like liquid when he walked, that lapped over his gunbelt almost obscuring the cuffs he had clipped to it. I remember thinking that he moved too smoothly for a big man, an almost fat man. He moved as if he were onstage. Really, he moved like a woman, and I had to hold back a laugh, curb it back to a giggle. His ass moved in half circles as he came abreast of us, and it was a revelation telling me something frightful about men who found their life's work within the aura of guns and police stations, investigation and interrogation. A jail, one of my authors had said once, is the asshole of the society. You can see what gets eaten there and what gets dropped. I thought of Genet and what he discovered in prison as that cop passed.

His face was younger than his body, heavy and strong, dark of beard. He had taken off his helmet for a minute and carried it in his left hand. His right hand moved up and down, back and forth, hovering over and brushing the butt of his pistol without settling on it. He paused for a moment a little way from us under a light, and I could see in his face some muffled outrage, some stew of hatred and disgust for the human offal he was walking among. Jesus, I thought, who can say what he'd do? There was none of the control, the distant blood-disciplined objectivity I remembered seeing in the eyes of that German officer. He had been an aristocrat, one of those nearly vanished things who, dying, laughed and left the ruins of the world to the scum which, breeding unendingly, had at last bubbled up into power. The cop's eyes turned and fixed on me for a moment, and I thought he looked familiar. But his eyes passed and then he walked on and became one more of them again. No, I knew no one like him. He was from some other place. Maybe a place I had once bombed.

I should be leaving, I thought, but I couldn't. I couldn't leave yet. The music sounded better now, and somebody had offered me a drink of grapefruit juice. A speaker was telling us that it was five minutes to midnight, and probably we should leave, that this wasn't the time or place for a confrontation, that it would be irrelevant. But everybody booed him and began to huddle nearer singing those songs they learned from the Negroes in Alabama. A boy and girl sprawled in the grass near me, and even in the dark you could see what they were doing. Others gathered closer around so the police couldn't see, and

I wished I had somebody who cared so much about me that they didn't care who saw it. I thought of Mariam and laughed out loud.

Now it was past midnight, and there were no more police to be seen. You could still hear them far off saying to clear the park, but I knew that they were only doing it to make an excuse. Everybody knew they would come. That's what made me loose and tight. Something was coming and I couldn't know what or when or where. They were singing a song I had heard now:

> . . . I'd hammer out love between
> my brothers and my sisters . . .
> all over this land . . .

But you can't hammer it out, can you? Love does things its own way, doesn't it? It uses lips and time and smiles and kindness. You can't hammer it. It breaks.

Then the first tear-gas canister fell almost on top of me. It hit and rolled, spinning out a pale cloud that stood out against the darkness. One of the children pulled me away, onto my feet. I lost my coat.

—Come on, pop. You don't need that haze.

We stumbled away with the others. But then another one hit nearby and stopped against my foot.

—Shit, chief, the boy who was guiding me yelled. —You're a gas magnet, aren't you?

I laughed. I wanted to laugh, to free the adrenalin building in me. —Cops eat shit, I yelled, and the people around laughed and clapped as we all headed toward a kind of bridge or passageway.

But there were police there, most of them wearing masks.

—It's bad, the boy beside me told two long-haired girls in short skirts. —Look. No badges, no name plates. They're here for blood.

I didn't understand. I thought they would try to channel the people, try to move them out of the park along certain routes. They wanted us out of the park, didn't they? That's what they said.

But the people ahead of us came up to the bridge, and as they did, I saw one of the police strike his club into his left hand over and over again. I knew what the boy meant. The charge in the battery was about to be released. Every remark, every sneer, the day's frustrations were about to be purged. Then those first people reached the line of police and the purging started.

We stopped and watched. A cop leaned forward and hit a girl in blue jeans and a sheepskin coat across the head. She went down as if she were dead, and he hit her again. A boy tried to pull her clear, and another cop knocked him down. He twisted and tried to kick, but when they hit him again, both of them, he stopped and lay still like a doll some child has dropped and left out in the grass when mother called him to come in because of the dark. It went on like that, with the police beginning to move out, hitting, kicking, cutting a swath through people like a reaper through grain. They came closer, leaving people on the ground behind them writhing or motionless, some with their shoes off, purses and coats lying here and there.

—Got a handkerchief, pop? the boy with me asked.

—Here, I told him.

—Keep it. You may have to pee in it and hold it over your face. Look, we got to move over to those bushes before the pigs get here. We hang in there till they're well off; then we head for the bridge. And don't fall down. And if you do, you better stay down.

The girls and I nodded. Then when the pigs passed to our left, we started to run. I heard a muffled yell behind us, and I took a look. Two or three of the pigs had broken off from the rest. Under the dim park lights, I could see them—no, not them, those disembodied blue helmets bobbing in the darkness, headed for us. I was running good. I was surprised at how good I was running.

And thinking. Thinking, they didn't want us to leave the park. They wanted us to stay. They want to punish us. They want to hurt us for everything that's happened in the last twenty years. They want to kill these children for not going along, for telling them that everything they've made is dust and ashes, arrogance and brutality. They hate the kids. And the kids must be right, because if they weren't right, why would they hate them so much?

Then I made the bridge and was over and found my way into the streets of Chicago again. The boy and the girls were gone.

202

I was by myself in my shirts sleeves, coat lost, pants dirty and grass-stained. Alone in a town I didn't know, a town where the police had gone crazy, where the whole country's future was being decided. My God, I thought. This isn't my country. Who does it belong to? What am I doing here? I looked at the dark building fronts and tried to find street signs so I could find my way back to the hotel. I half expected to see crude signs splashed on the filthy brick walls in whitewash: JUDEN RAUS.

No, this didn't belong to me. I had nothing to say about it. They didn't want to hear from me in this town. I couldn't go and say, Listen, I was born and raised here. I went to public school in the Bronx. They gave me a scholarship to City College because I was clever. Listen, over Germany, I killed for you. I bombed thousands of people in your name, and if this isn't my home, holy Jesus, what does that make me? Do you want to make me a mass murderer? There's no proscription on murder, you know. Not in law, not in the mind. Who did I kill for? You're taking away my country, my reason, my excuse.

I got to my room, and I began to pack. I thought, you did it all for them, for your people. Now they need you. They're calling to you. You should have known that in Texas, that night in the desert. You can't be forgiven for anything by anybody. You can only forgive yourself. Can you forgive yourself? No. So go to your own people, and after you make up for wasting twenty years, you'll be all right. You'll die forgiven. It doesn't matter how you live if you find your way at the end. There's plenty of time now, you'll be all right.

At last they put through the call, and as I lay there on the bed, breathing hard, reeking of gas, eyes full of tears, and so tired that I felt as if I were floating, I could hear the great emptinesses of space as they were bridged electronically, as this small space was welded to another hundreds of miles away. The operator, whose voice acknowledged nothing, neither place nor time, home or age, came back. —I have your party, she said.

—Pack, I told Mariam. —Get things together. Call a realtor. I'll be back tomorrow and we'll get passports and find out about emigration. Check with El Al.

—What? she asked, her voice suddenly lax, without that edge, that brittleness of the fanatic resisted. —What is it?

—It's nothing, I said. —It's not anything. That's the point. Don't argue with me. We're going home.

Krepinski

You look out at the world from behind the eyepieces of the mask, and it's a different place. Everything is all of a sudden hostile. Trees and buildings look different. You're locked into a kind of special world, almost like being up front in the office of a 17. You're looking out and down, and it's all enemy territory. It may be a brick or a bullet or somebody coming down out of a tree on your back with a nine-inch blade. You're in a spaceship, and your only friends are the ones who drift past in helmets and masks, looking like huge grasshoppers or something in a science fiction movie. I thought of that as we moved in at Lincoln Park, and I laughed. It hurt my ears, laughing inside the mask. It ain't made to laugh in. It's for business. We moved into the gas, and it got hard to see where you were going. All you could see was the others in masks, and out in front the trees and something moving this way out of the trees.

Then they started getting closer, picking up edges. You never saw such a bunch of human junk. Long dirty hair, clothes like they'd found 'em in a dump. Some running with guitars or carrying bags or baskets. One guy is no kid at all. He looks older than me, with his coat off, his bald head shining in the dark, running toward some bushes with two or three of these garbage kids. That's mine, I think. He's mine. I want to tap him a little. I want him to feel what it costs to live it instead of staying home to see it on TV. He never got this close to anything real in his life. He never will again. He ought to have something to tell his old lady. I could hear it, see it. He's home in bed with a bandage over my gift, telling her, —It was awful, terrible. This thing came at me. You couldn't get away from it. It looked like a monster. It got me, kept hitting me. Jesus, Lorraine, you don't want to get mixed up in nothing like that. You want to stay clear.

Which is all anybody had to do. Just stay clear. Just go to work and go home and go bowling or out for a drive and leave running things to the people who get paid to do it, who know how to do it. But you know how it is: Everybody has got this thing in him. He wants to mess around with what he doesn't know anything about. A doctor wants to be a lawyer once in a while. A lawyer wants to operate on somebody. And everybody wants to run the country. It ends up with fucking kids wanting to run the country. Like in high school where they make it so some kid gets to be mayor for a day and tells the police chief and the commissioner of public utilities what to do. And they put his picture in the paper, this kid. And everybody says maybe he'll make it one of these days. No, he ain't going to make it one of these days. If he was going to make it, he wouldn't be messing around. What he'd be doing is out in the street, hustling, picking up a buck and making a friend where it counts. Which is how you get up there. Not getting citizenship awards in some lousy civics course in high school.

So I moved a little out of line and headed for this bald guy in his shirt sleeves. But he was with some smart kids. Because as soon as we moved into the crowd coming, as soon as we got off station and started popping a few skulls, this old guy and the punks he was with made it past our flank and got away. It pissed me. Now when he got home, he'd sit there with a beer, smiling, saying, —It's easy. They're dumb. It don't take any brains, Lorraine. Naw, you just hang in there till they make their move, and then kind of slide around. It's nothing. This town is run by clowns. Nobody calls me a clown. I turned and started back, made it over the bridge and ran real quiet as I reached the street. Once they made the street, they'd slow down, walk, laugh, tell each other how cool it was to fox the fuzz. These people have got to be punished. You can't run a country with people laughing at the law. Jews, niggers, punks egging each other on.

Then I saw him. By himself now, walking alone, easy to spot walking along in front of some dark buildings. I stopped for a minute. It was almost a block to where he was. I'd have to run. He'd hear me. Then I'd have to run back. What could I tell the captain—who wasn't my captain anyhow? Yeah, I left ranks to go whip on one broken-down old guy with a bald head and fat shaking when he ran. No, it wasn't worth that. He was only one. There was plenty more.

So I ran back, and like I thought, there was plenty. We handled them for maybe two hours. When it was over, I was sitting at this all-night lunch place drinking coffee with five or six of the other special unit guys from all over Chicago. It was good to be out of the mask, but I left it hanging around my neck. The way we used to let our oxygen masks hang in the old days. It was like the old days. We ate hamburgers and drank coffee and talked. Like after a raid. Everybody had been in service. Europe, the Pacific, Korea, a few young guys in Vietnam. It was all the same, we agreed. One of the young guys had a bottle, and we poured it in our coffee. It got to me quick because I was hot and excited, and when I felt it hitting, I told them what a fine bunch of guys they were, how this country would be fucked without them. They laughed, and the kid who had brought the bottle was telling us that this business in Lincoln Park reminded him of counterinsurgency in Nam. Which was like herding cattle. You swing a big tight net around 'em and pull it closed. Then you take care of what you've caught.

—Zap, the kid said, laughing, pulling another bottle out of his musette.—Zap. Like fish in a barrel.

—How do you tell your people from theirs? somebody asks him.

He stopped and smiled. —Hell, none of my people are yellow.

Everybody laughed. He went on saying you get 'em gathered; then if in doubt, zap.

—It's easier here, he said. —Anything in that Lincoln Park after twelve belonged to us. No mistake possible. Listen, this is an elite unit. I don't make mistakes.

We laughed and agreed, and people talked about how their wars had been. The guy from Korea won hands down for tough duty.

—That little bastard from Missouri, he said. —I wanted to kill him. So help me Christ. We pushed those gooks all the way across Asia, and all we needed was bomber support across the Yalu. You give us that and we'd have eaten up the whole Chinese Army. But this little turd from Missouri . . . you don't know how many good guys got chewed up. They buried a lot of Chicago boys because the politicians were yellower than the gooks . . .

I told him we could have interdicted the Chinamen with 17's. We could have pulled off the pressure.

Then somebody cut in and says, —These punks are worse than the Chinamen. They're worse than the fucking Nazis. They want to wreck the country.

—What do you mean, want to? They're doing it, the guy from Korea says. —The only way to handle this is with force. I don't even know if it's a police job anymore.

Somebody agreed. Said the trouble with policing is that they let you swing just hard enough to get 'em moving, but not enough to keep 'em running. —It's all halfway on the force. When we went back into Mindanao, they got the whole load. We paid back Wake and Corregidor and Bataan. Buddy, when we were done, the Japs didn't have any problems.

—No problems?

—No Japs.

—How about the ones who surrendered?

The guy from the Pacific just grinned. —Didn't you hear how crazy and fanatical they were? Why, they was all crazy. You tried to get 'em to surrender, but they just wouldn't.

That was funny. It was the way I figured it must have been.

—Naw, he said. —What we didn't get the Filipinos got. I bet we didn't take fifty prisoners all the way across the island. If they wanted to surrender, they had four years to do it in. They could of just not stabbed us in the back. It was too late when we got there.

We got back to the stuff at the park. The guy from Korea shook his head.

—This ain't going to get it. Every time we go in, they pull our fangs. They stand over us, making sure we don't hurt anybody. You call that police work? When they move out on the street, you give it to them. Let them know they better keep that stuff in their dormitories or whorehouses or whatever. Not on the streets. The streets belong to us, he said.

—The streets belong to us, I said, and after a while we broke it up and went home. Tomorrow would be a big day.

Boyd

I found myself walking past the Midland Hotel, suddenly, ravenously hungry. Recovering on my feet from some kind of cerebral or spiritual hemorrhage, how could I be hungry? Can you believe that I thought, have you no decency? Would you eat a hot pastrami sandwich over your mother's barely dead body? And before I could brake the workings of my mind, I thought in answer, yes. Yes, I think I would. Those who mourn most deeply spend their sorrow at a wake.

So I found myself before the café called the Berghof. I walked in and downstairs, already rested amid the wood, the steins, the heads of stags and still lifes full of hares, pheasants and fruit. A waiter motioned me to a table amid mock-Gothic decoration, and I ordered a double martini. I closed my eyes, squeezed them with my fingers trying to clear my mind. When I opened them, my martini was before me. When I raised them from my drink, I saw a man eating alone at a table close by. He wore a small Vandyke, and his hair was short and heavily gray, but I knew him. I knew him and could not place him and yet felt some peculiar, almost unnerving wish to speak to him, to ask if indeed we knew each other, or if it was just one more oddment of my brain generated by the fiasco of flying halfway across the country with kids to see our mutual dream fade like a half-doped filly in the stretch. He looked up just then, and I knew who he was. Boileau, the Louisianian, another one of the bombers. He looked at me and nodded. For no reason I could imagine—we had never been more than civil—I took my drink and joined him.

Oddly, the preliminaries were brief: more like reports, given quickly, precisely. He told me why he was in Chicago. I told him the same. He grinned.

—How do you like your man? he asked me. —Is he your choice? Or your excuse?

—Neither, I said. —I just came from the debate.

—Ah, Boileau said. —I left. I waited while all the prima ballerinas tripped in late. But Humphrey's little lecture was too much.

—You like McCarthy?

—Not a bit. He grinned. —No better than I liked Kennedy. I shrugged. —That leaves you out of it, doesn't it?

—Yes and no. We've been out of it for a long time. But we'll have to live with whatever the democracy pukes up next.

I knew what he meant. He was still the Southerner, the ironic outsider who watched the antics of the Yankee gorillas in stoic amusement.

—I hear you've had a little trouble down there in the past few years, I said, almost instantly ashamed of the pettiness. I needn't have worried.

—Yes, he said. —But no Watts. No Detroit. No Newark. Seems down home they still kill people one by one. They haven't taken to killing forty at a whack. By the way, you might enjoy a book I read recently. On the New York draft riots of 1864. Very modern, actually.

I finished my beer. Time had done nothing. We still had nothing but idiocies to exchange. Still, I wasn't quite ready to walk away. Boileau lit a long thin cigar and offered me one. I took it, not surprised that I had to bite off the end. Then through the smoke, he smiled at me.

—Have you ever wondered, he asked softly, —how many places like this we obliterated?

I had not. Only then did I realize a connection—that people around us, the waiter, the cashier, any of them might have left part of their families in the hells we made of Durlach and Stuttgart—and Dresden. —No, I said coolly, —I don't think much about the old days. So much has happened.

Boileau winked. —Right. Fine. None of us thinks about it. That's why we become involved in this particular convention.

—What's the connection? I asked.

—Perhaps you get the idea that the whole country is being pushed into the Dark Room?

—Jesus, I said. And knew why McCarthy had let it go. Because, surely, he had come to see that what we were about in Vietnam, in the cities, on the campuses—all of it was foreordained. It could not be changed, because there are rhythms to things. You don't choose the level of your resonance; you obey it. You do not choose to like blondes or small breasts or electric-blue dresses. Or war for the Cause of Liberty. You just do. The nerves establish themselves in train: even the nerves of a nation.

—All right. I think of it a lot. More all the time. And you?

—Ah, he said. —It's my profession. Come on up to the Hilton. I've got to see someone with Reuters.

—I have a room there.

We had some supper in my room after Boileau had made contact with his man. Over the intersection, we heard the sounds of the hippie types in Grant Park. Boileau nodded toward the window.

—Last night the police beat them and gassed them. In Lincoln Park. Tonight in Grant. I like that.

I laughed. —Some irony.

Boileau raised his eyebrows. —You see it as ironic?

I felt that old anger rising. I wondered why we were here together, yoked to one another by some false and hypocritical Army-buddy meeting, pretending common interests over antipathies a quarter of a century—or was it a century?—old. —Well, what?

—Logic, he said, finishing his coffee. —As the kids down there might say, you people got hooked on organized, institutionalized violence a long time ago. Under Lincoln—and his enforcer, Unconditional Surrender Grant. Now the chickens are finding their way home. I wonder if Daley will demand Unconditional Surrender. In the grand tradition of the U.S.?

I said nothing. It was only rhetoric, not logic. I walked past him to the window. There was a police line across Michigan at Balbo. They were letting some kind of sideshow through. Mules pulling wagons. I thought at first it must be a convention gimmick. Obviously Humphrey. God, I thought. Then Boileau stood beside me.

—Abernathy. His poor people's crusade. I talked to some of them. They don't have a candidate either. They lost their candidate and their king to the same malady. Don't you wonder where their loyalties will light?

But before I could answer, it happened again. I was looking down at the people pouring out of Grant Park into the intersection of Michigan and Balbo, and there was that peculiar sensation I had felt at the debate. As if I had had the smallest of strokes, an instant's—or was it an hour's—aphasia. Because as I watched, apparently without reason, the line of police, straight and virtually static, swayed a little backward like a bowstring and then fired a portion of itself at the demonstrators who pressed up to them. They were beating people, kicking them, and when they fell or tried to back off, the police did not stop or withdraw or move on. No, they kept it up. They were beating people indiscriminately, smashing them, stomping them with their boots.

—Jesus, I said. —My God, what are they doing?

Boileau's jaw was tight. —They're punishing their children, I suppose.

Then he looked at me with contempt and anger and over it a compassion I had never seen in him—or in anyone else, I suppose. —How should I know what they're doing? How can you expect me to understand this?

Then we were moving to the elevator, speechless, descending. Going not as gawkers, but because something rooted in our blood that quarter century ago forbade us to stand in quarters when the planes were lifting, when there was, so close, action total and inexorable to which we were joined by . . . something. Boileau would have called it history. I think it was death.

No use to tell what happened down there. I was hurt, my ear cut, my hands almost broken by a billy club. Boileau was pulled away from me at the hotel door, moving outward on a tide of terror-stricken people who were not demonstrators or politicians or militants, but only people caught in the bowstring, dragged outward into the mounting darkness of Chicago in August where swirling lights and screams and blood and injured people clubbed senseless by their countrymen all swallowed him up. I did not get so far before I encountered those local police we are told to support. No need to tell it in detail. The whole world was watching.

Later someone helped me to McCarthy's headquarters upstairs in the Hilton where they had set up a kind of aid station. They tied a piece of shirt around my ear and kept it wet. Then I got hold of my pain and my anger and began to help the others. After what seemed a long time, they brought Clyde in. He was cut up and unable to stand. Someone said it was a concussion. I remember the someone. It was a girl. A little girl about

211

seventeen in a mini-skirt whose face was much older and very self-possessed.

—I've seen it down in Oakland. When the pigs beat us at the induction center. He'll be all right. The cuts are superficial. You can tell when it's bad. I almost lost a guy down there, she said.

Just then Clyde came around for a moment. He smiled beatifically, gave us the V sign as his eyes lost their focus.

—Peace, he said, and passed out again.

We stayed at it while they nominated Daley's choice at the amphitheater. I lost hold once and felt sobs wracking me as I tried to wipe the mouth and lips of a boy who had been hit across the face with one of their clubs. My seventeen-year-old, whose name was Cindy from San Jose, passed me a cigarette. Not a Pall Mall.

—I hardly ever use it, she said. —But there isn't any whiskey. It'll give you distance. You need some distance.

It did. It gave me that and a strange certainty that I was in the most important place in the world. Eddie junior stopped cutting tracks in the recessed marshes of my mind. So did Eddie senior. So did Boileau and his anger and mockery and those soaring escapes, those cop-out flights we made in formation so long ago to visit upon others the wrath that should have been ours as well as theirs. It carried me through the cuts and cries of pain from children who could have been my children, and much later it carried me back to my room. With Cindy. Who made warm and sweet and unashamed love to me for reasons that she understood completely, that I could only guess, hope, at.

And the next morning, when I awoke, I did not think until much later of what we had passed through, into, the night before. Nor of the wreckage of values and stances and denials that I had carried like chains for more than half my life. No, I kissed Cindy awake, and sober, unstoned, we made love once more: a charm of breasts and slender tanned thighs, a conjure of youth and age melding, annealing at least for an instant the abyss that gaped all around us like a deep spread-lipped wound in the nation's head.

Something else: How to say it? I was, in the midst of that sweet drifting night, ahead of Cindy. Do you know what I mean? I anticipated. I felt her need, her desire, her loneliness. I

212

found myself, on the other side of that cigarette, reading the currents of her mind, the ways and means of her wanting before she realized them herself. And as we concluded, in the distant ruins of memory there rose a stage softly lighted. With a piano under amber lights near an old-fashioned bar and an enormous smiling black man in a derby hat whose hands moved with the precision of baroque machines across the keyboard. There he was, called back from the dead, but not to taunt me this time. Because now, in the midst of my dream, I knew where he was going, could have played each phrase before he invented it, could imagine alternatives to each block of chords, each declension of melody. The Café Rouge was gone forever, and that magnificent big band, that team that I had ceased to be a part of at last. I knew then, at that moment, what joy was, why there was music and how it belonged to its maker. I knew how it felt to create, to own some portion of yourself truly by putting it beyond yourself without help, without others to make it partly theirs. To be great, it had to be completely yours—and then you could give it easily to others.

And, mirror image, I knew why I—we—had become such marvelous bombardiers almost a quarter century before. Not because of what we could do. But because of what we could not. Each of us had been—what? Can there be a whole nation, a generation of failures, people lost to themselves and one another? No, not that. Only a nation, a generation that had forgotten first and last things, had lost the capacity to go beyond here and now to find the future instead of waiting for it. The teams had captured us because we had lost faith, lost confidence in ourselves. So only by losing ourselves among others could we function at all. A big band, a bomber crew—always collective weakness joined together, and the result had to be endings, not beginnings. A big band, a bomber crew—a law firm?

From Chicago I took away certain things I had not brought with me. I cannot name those things, but I am very good at my profession, resourceful, I am told. And whatever my profession is now, I mean to use it for Newton and Clyde. For Cindy from San Jose.

Michaelis

Snorts Reinhart and I were good friends. Which is why I was sitting with the Illinois delegation as the nominating speeches were given. The amphitheater seemed, from my vantage so near the podium, a very small place in which Carl Albert contended against the elements: a great wind, thunder and stirrings of the earth.

He contended very well most of the time. He was a small man of no particular talent, virtue or importance. He was, one could see, one of those who brought the heartland of America into the halls of Congress. Brought the fears and the anxieties and the tiny hatreds of those spiritual refugees who had been displaced without even being removed from their land, their place. Albert was that hybrid who looked as if he should have ramrodded a small beef cattle spread in southwest Oklahoma, but had, as his juices dried and his size diminished the inward man, fallen in love with powers: with those raised up by Henry Ford, Rockefeller, Carnegie. And moving from small-town car franchise to lease buyer to stockholder, ever further into an undeclared exile he did not even recognize as such. Loving power, he became such power as he could. And this was his reward for the regularity, the dependability of his transmission. Like a light bulb which has burned continuously for twenty thousand hours, he was mildly remarkable to the party. It was of no account, really, that he illuminated nothing within the twilight that was beginning to lower on us all. He functioned. And he was thankful to the party for the opportunity, the right to function. Conceivably he lived in an endless sweat of relief that he had been assumed, lifted from those deadly Oklahoma wastes into the glory of Washington and drawn into the party.

I had talked to Snorts about the party. He grinned. He was that rare and marvelous combination of ignorance and nerve and faultless observational skill, of complete party loyalty and regularity without the faintest tinge of belief in anything. Not even power or money. Snorts had been in the old Air Corps. His serial number was only four digits long. He had flown guns in the late twenties until he knew the mud flats and sand beaches and strips of Central American highways as well as these Chicago streets. He had flown in the late thirties with Claire Chennault, then in 1940 with the RAF. He had accepted a direct colonelcy in the Air Corps in 1942 and had become a top planner in TAC. Then when it was done, when the last cymbal clash sounded and the F-51 became a training plane for boys who would ride jets the rest of their lives, in and out of uniform, he retired. Retired and came home and found another service in which he was comfortable. The mercenary's happiness is a love of form without respect to content. A tight organization engaged in a steady quarrel is the mercenary's proper home. He charges higher to work for chaos-prone idealists and even then does not work well, because he senses that idealism is the root of all evil, against nature, the beginning of disorder and the evoker of spirits and powers neither steady sense nor raw force—the mercenary's prime properties—can cope with adequately.

Snorts grinned at me and tipped half a pint of bourbon into my glass. Wild Turkey. Mercenaries either invest it or slough it off. Snorts did both. That is why he was a mercenary officer, not one of the troops. He was Daley's hand and mouth, arm and thumb, in the Southside. Not the club or the gun. Snorts was a tactician. His office was large, low-ceilinged with concealed lighting, paneled, deep-pile carpet. With an enormous map of Cook County behind his desk, and wing panels of cork, upon which were survey maps and aerial photos of the amphitheater area, the Loop—and late additions—Lincoln and Grant parks. He had been called up from Southside for this action, this convention. He might well never go back.

—Some people got God, some family. Some people have themselves a business or a woman or even the country. I've got the party, Mike.

—You put a lot of goods on that train, I answered.

—It's a good train. It can pull anything. It does things. All kinds of things. You wouldn't believe. The Republicans have some banks. The Democrats have a party. Look, Mike, what do you want? The party can give it to you. The country can't. There are laws. But the party can. Women, power, a place to do

215

whatever you want to do. All you have to do is go along. Go along and you'll get along.

—From each according to his ability, to each according to his need?

Snorts slapped his leg. —That's nice. Maybe we should have that on the campaign literature.

We talked about the campaign—after the nomination. There was nothing to say about the nomination. McCarthy was not even a cute suicide. Simply a bad-tempered type who had never been of the party, only in it. Mean, hallucinated by the stark and bony vision of his own rectitude playing over and over, scene after scene in the cramped cell-like theater of his mind, the gothic blur of his memory. McGovern was stand-in for a ghost who had been ten times his size alive and was larger now. But the virtues of the dead are rarely transmissible outside the line of blood. That ghost would speak. But not here, not now. It was Humphrey.

—But Nixon will chip him, Snorts told me. —The federal system needs some work. When we get one man, one vote, then you can have a federal fix. Not the way it is. The electoral system keeps the big towns down. And big towns are where you plant the fix. No, Nixon will shave him. He had to play the rubes in the South even though Nixon and Wallace will split them. He had to talk to the Midwest knowing Nixon will carry what he doesn't ruin. And the East is not going to be out. They'll sit on their hands. Listen, except for city employees and the Southside, I wouldn't guarantee him Chicago. And even with them, I wouldn't give him fifty-five percent. It's gone, Mike. This wasn't a fight for the country. It was for the party. Let them have the country. In the shape things are in, it'll strangle them. But we own the party. That's where the goods are carried.

So we were sitting with the Illinois delegation watching the nominations with a big Italian dressed in a black silk suit so high-sheen that he sparkled as if seen through an inch or so of clear water, as if he were covered with sequins. He wore tinted glasses, and his hair, not combed or even polished but molded to his thick head in heavy waves like shiny basalt, lay in the contortions of its cryptozoic upheaval, small sweaty curls above his ears, along the back of his neck. He was a trooper, perhaps a noncom, and the perquisites of service were stamped into his pleasured flesh, his small hard mouth, so that there was no need to see his eyes in order to know how cruel he was. He was the modern incarnation of those Sicilian knights so long corrupt that worship of the Virgin had become the cult of kidnap-rape, the search for the Grail satisfied in service to whatever spangled hoodlum best wielded terror and silenced the perpetual moaning of the countryside. He could only be his own man by being owned. He worked for Snorts. Who worked for the mayor. He was absolutely trustworthy up to a five-year stretch for aggravated assault or attempted murder. Beyond that, between arrest and arraignment, it would be wise to send a man to reassure him. He would not cost so much, but he would have to be reassured. The agony of a mercenary *in extremis* is that gutrending fear that since he is unloved, he will be replaced without consideration. There must be consideration. Attention must be paid to the troops whose silken-cased shoulders bear the weight of the party's business.

He whispered into Snort's ear, one hand guarding his mouth from me as if I were a lipreader in one of the many enemy camps. It was a full hand, Flemish fingers, a two-carat diamond on the third one: mark of a journeyman mercenary, upper grade. Still expendable and probably not wily enough to ever handle the Southside, but certain to hold a ward, a neighborhood, or move forever on the streets, liaison between the cells of the beast that was Cook County.

—Let 'em through, Snorts told him, his accent losing its polish altogether, lapsing into the argot of command. —Don't fuck with the poor people. Wait a minute.

Snorts sat and stared down at the floor for a moment, his brow furled in concentration. Then he looked up at the trooper. —Where are the cameras?

The trooper said something about the Hilton.

—All right, all right. Let the poor people through. Then stop 'em. Stop 'em cold. But I want it over with in twenty minutes—thirty at the outside. You tell those people of yours they had their fun in Lincoln Park. Tell 'em to get back to work.

I paid no particular attention then. It was only later, when I saw the television reruns that I realized what kind of two-front war Snorts had taken on. I grinned then, thinking how easily he might have been checked—or mated. If his opponents had not been children and political cretins. Suppose the business at

217

Michigan and Balbo had been only a diversion, a demonstration, while the main force had made for the amphitheater in a suicide attack on the convention, on the exposed, beating heart of the party itself? Snorts had been lucky. I wondered if, in common with planners who have luck, he might have pushed it too far. After all, the battle in front of the hotel might one day prove to have been the turning of a corner.

—Sure, Snorts told me the next night while we waited for them to crank up the movie honoring that ghost for which McGovern had gathered 1461½ votes the night before. —Sure, it could have been a turning. I knew that.

—It was a strategic decision, then. Shouldn't the mayor have made it?

—As far as the convention is concerned, it was a tactical decision.

—What about later? I asked.

—Later. Snorts smiled and shrugged. —Later is for who comes later. I'm sixty-four years old, Mike. For me, this is later.

—Do you figure those hairy kids will come later?

The amphitheater lights dimmed. —Not a chance. Snorts' voice came out of the gloom. —No, they'll pave the way, Mike. They'll do that for sure. They put the last straw on Johnson, so they'll be around. If they want to call that victory, I give it to them. But they may not like what they pave the way for. It could go lots of ways.

—They sow mosquitoes—to reap dragons?

—You're full of them, Mike. I figure the guy they eventually hand it to may spend his first hundred days hunting them down with machine guns. Not sticks or Mace.

—And?

—That's later. That will be strategic. No, I'll leave it to them. And him.

Then there was the movie. I seemed to stand back from it, and as I watched that man grow, in the shadow always of his father who knew a dollar, how to trap it, and how to use it on others as if it were a pair of pliers; in the shadow of his eldest brother, no particular hero by the standards of those who have seen heroism, but a big, healthy phantom going down in my war; in the sudden shade of John. It brought tears to my eyes. Not because I had loved him. I loved almost no one, least of all

218

politicians, but because in him and with him I saw the birth and death of what they had once long ago called feeling, or the Christian impulse, and later liberalism. I saw the end of an age which could believe in science and sense, in square deals for workers and "others." I saw the last rationalist of the bourgeois West as he strode clear-eyed toward a fatalism that fulfilled itself. The fade-out brought actual sobs, chokings, from those in other delegations. Not from Illinois. Casualties are expected by mercenaries, and if the mayor had liked the Kennedys, it was not a weakness of the affections that had numbed the mind. Calculations continued. For the mayor and his kind, the decline of the West would be just another hassle. After all, the barbarians are already inside.

But when the movie ended, something remarkable began. Spontaneously, without planning, delegates began to sing. It was the "Battle Hymn of the Republic." And more than suitable, I decided even as my mouth twisted in a sneer. Of course. Because all republics have three civil wars. The one they rise in, the one in which their identity is set and the one in which they go down, choking on their own blood as the aliens watch and wait to move in. A good choice, and a warning.

But what was remarkable was that it continued, went on and on, while Albert tried to stop it, force a return to the kind of order he had foisted all week. But for twenty minutes business was stalled by a collection of soloists who had somehow gotten into the wrong show. The dance of labor and hood, bourbon and ward heeler, the props of democracy could not go on. Until the outsiders had finished their hymn. There was, amid the convention, for a brief space of time, something resembling a camp meeting, an adumbration of what was to be the tone of future politics. Trouble was, the preacher was dead.

While the commotion went on, Snorts and I went upstairs and stepped into the television booth. One of the producers must have known Snorts because just for a second his face opened, and I could see fear and uncertainty in his eyes. Were we there to simply cut the coverage? Were we going to unplug a major network? Were we that tough? Had things gone that far? It was possible to see, as in an instant replay, how the man, a graying sport-shirted technician who had not seen force in twenty years except on his monitor screen, was calculating odds, possibilities against random occasions like those which had killed two brothers in five years. Then he had decided: No, we were not so tough. We would have sent troopers, anonymous men who could be connected with nothing more than the city of Chicago and the madness of this place and time. No, things had not gone that far. We might beat and maim reporters and children in the streets, terrorize delegates, eradicate every pretense that democratic processes were working here. But we would not actually pull the plug on fifty million television sets. His medium had too much *virtu*. We had not yet retreated so far that like those so-called barbarians who burned the library at Alexandria, we could coolly slice away the transmission of information, await the cries of dismay and liquidate the criers. Our numbers were not yet right, the producer thought, and took what pleasure and relief he could from that rough calculation.

So he turned back to his board, prodded his lower echelon technicians, cut from one view to another. While at another bank of monitors, a pair of technicians were running a reel of film or videotape, watching the intersection at Michigan and Balbo as it had been the night before. They paid us no mind, and Snorts and I reverted to type, a pair of old officers watching an operation that should have been surgical.

But which wasn't. It was impossible, given what we had, bits and pieces, runs of blank film and film shot into lights or blurred by movement or gasoline flames, to determine what had gone wrong, how a punishment had degenerated into an orgy. But there it was. Enough visual evidence to convince anyone—everyone—that police procedure on this evening had been a matter of wholesale brutality. One would make the best of things later. One would claim that some of the demonstrators had had razor blades, flung sacks of excrement at the officers. Cornered, certain officers would claim amid a show of virtue unmatched since Ribbentrop claimed to be a simple diplomat that they had been *cursed* by the demonstrators.

Just then, however, we watched. Watched and did not need to talk because we both knew everything the other knew. And we watched in utter silence broken only by the distant heavy breathing of the air-conditioning system and the occasional clipped orders of the producer. There was no sound on the film. Images passed, faces twisted in rage or agony, a police car burning or racing down a slippery street. A camera followed a

220

disorganized bunch of demonstrators down the street, a pack of police close behind, their clubs rising and falling almost in rhythm. On another monitor, a girl fell, and one of the police skidded to a stop and hit her once, twice. The film snapped off, while on another monitor there was a sudden burst of flame which lit up the front of a building on what appeared to be a deserted street. On the monitor next to it, a long shot of a police car afire, its screech light outlined dark against the sudden brightness. Then, as I backed up a step or two, blurred film reached up, up the building and transfixed the figure of a Negro, a tall black in work clothes who stood colossal and rigid against the façade of the building holding for a fraction of a second a dark mass in his hand with a tip of flame. On all the monitors almost simultaneously he appeared in long shot, close-up, telephoto zoom lens, right profile, nearly head on, his mouth wide, lips working, eyes white to vanishing. He heaved the fire bomb, dipped and rose with another already lit as if he were drawing it from an endless supply or had been handed it by one of a host of invisible confederates who stood behind, out of sight, urging him on and supplying him with the infinite stuff of their rage and their frustration.

Snorts breathed in deeply, and I heard him whisper almost below hearing, —Hit him. Goddamn you, take him out. But there were, I thought irrationally, too many of him. He was on every monitor; he was legion. The films were out of phase now again, so that when he threw the fire bomb, he threw it not once, but time after time. When he leaned down and rose again, there was no end to his going down and rising once more. Even the producer had turned to see his booth full of insane blacks determined to incinerate the world. Then the films fell away, back to the street, to the figure of a single man in police uniform raising a rifle, his body jerking as he fired. And an instant later he vanished in a cloud of flame that filled the monitors for a second before they moved on to find police wagons being filled, windows broken by the weight of people being pushed through them and the rest of the visual debris of an operation that had gone sour.

Snorts and I turned away together, exchanging a single look. —Some of 'em you win, he said.

I shrugged. —How much room did you have?

He shook his head with a lopsided smile. I saw then for the

first time how old, how tired, how mired in time and certain assumptions he was. —Not that much, he said. —Would you like to go down to the lounge and wait to see what it looks like when they've finished editing it?

—I don't think so, I said, and we walked down through the ranks of security guards and silk-suited troopers until after a long time we reached the street and the August night.

As we walked, we could heard the working out of the libretto: Muskie nominated to commit suttee with his feckless party husband. They will go down, I thought, in flames, in the middle of their own fire storm, searching for a political Dresden as if it were the New Jerusalem.

Krepinski

I figured the creeps running the kids would push for the amphitheater Wednesday sometime. But nothing. They had us walking the wire and driving up and down the streets around the stockyards, but the place was buttoned up like a vest. I stood around. There was nothing else to do. It was like in the afternoon at the Blockhouse after Michaelis had finished with the lessons and stuff. You just stood or sat or laid around in that stinking Texas heat, feeling your guts boil. It was that way in the city now. The summers were long and hot, waves of heat rising out of the concrete and asphalt as if the source of it was underground instead of in the sky. And everywhere there were things like rattlesnakes ready to let you have it. Go out on a call about a man beating his wife and you could find yourself in the middle of a riot with everybody trying to kill you. You couldn't tell anymore. Not by clothes, not by anything. The niggers were dangerous; the whites were dangerous. The punks, the people with steady jobs. You name it. A guy in a Cadillac might try to run you down or shoot at you.

It was near dark, and they were going to let some of us off when the call came through. It was hotting up at the Hilton.

The punks were in Grant Park and ready to move out, to march here.

—Oh, no, the captain said. —We'll hold them right there.

And he grabbed ten of us. —Get your pieces, he said. —Bring 'em with you.

Mine was in the car. It was a sporterized 1903 Springfield with a nice polished walnut stock. All reblued and fixed up real good. It was lighter than an M-1, and you could kill anything a foot square at two hundred yards without even aiming. They had this 10X scope on it, which was bad. You need more resolving power for a clean hit. But sometimes you had to work fast, and a 35X or something can be tricky for a fast shot. Another thing I didn't like was that it was a set scope. You couldn't swing it out of the way to use the leaf that was under it. I thought maybe I should buy my own piece, but the captain said no, it looked bad. Like police only thought of nothing but guns. Like who was willing to spend his own money on something for the job. Something he might never get to use.

—I'll get to use it, I said. —Sooner or later.

He just grinned. —We took that .03 off a sniper last year. Off his body.

—He wasn't no pro, I said.

—You better be glad they're not pros, he told me. —No, they're just punks. If they ever get some pros in with them, we'll have to have M-16's.

Which is the Armalite invented in California and made now by Colt. Just a little more than .22 caliber, but it goes through like a tornado. You can kill a man hitting him in the shoulder. Maybe the punks will get us some.

Anyhow we got downtown, and they strung us out. We was all up and down Balbo and Michigan. They didn't station us, the guys with rifles. They told us to rove, to keep our eyes on the roof line, on the windows. They said not to shoot until we got orders, but to spot, to get a sighting on anything and hold it till we got orders to take it out. They gave us walkie-talkies, so we could check in if we saw anything. The captain was edgy. He pulled me over.

—They're mean down at the intersection. But you don't want to figure they're dumb. Some of them could have infiltrated. Into the buildings before they closed. They could be up there waiting. You never know. So stay awake.

223

Then I started walking. It felt good. I like to work alone. It felt good walking along with that piece in the crook of my arm, looking at the dark windows, up and up, then down again. Back at the intersection, there was trouble. You could hear the yelling and the chanting. But down here the traffic was blocked off and it was quiet.

I never saw him until the first bomb hit the street. He wasn't throwing at a car or at one of the other buildings. He was throwing at me. It hit right next to me and went up, the fire washing over my boots. I had to jump clear. But when I looked up, there was nothing. Just a building. No lights, no open window. It was black up there. I called the captain and told him. He said to lay low; he'd send some people. I got behind some kind of delivery truck and stayed still. All you could hear was the noise back at the intersection. Then here come a patrol car with its lights off. I waved, and it stopped right beside me. The Captain was in it. He looked over at the burning gas.

—Threw it right for you, huh? Okay. If you spot him, shoot to kill. We got that from all the way up.

So we played the car searchlight along the building, story by story. It was some kind of place with offices upstairs and a dress shop or something downstairs with one of those awnings like they use for funerals or weddings so the people won't get wet. On the second story was a ledge, and we went along that with the light. Nothing. Then we went up to the next floor. Closed dark windows.

And just then comes a whole bunch of people running toward us from down in front of the hotel. With a TV truck following and some of those guys with portable cameras taking pictures of everything in sight. Somebody says, —Cream 'em.

—Hold it, goddammit, the captain says, trying to keep an eye on the building, an eye on the people coming—and an eye on those TV cameras. —Hold it till I say . . . goddammit.

Then, right then, out of the corner of my eye, I see this flicker, this little worm of light, like a reflection only brighter, up along the face of the building. So small it's nothing except I make a place for it in my brain even as I look down the street at those people who are running now, trying to get away from the police units down at the intersection. Later I know what my brain was telling me: It's him, there he is. It's got to be. But the commotion coming down the street was too much, and I've got an eye on the TV cameras shooting backward at the people running. Then the bomb hit the patrol car. It blew and spewed gas all over the captain and one of the special unit guys with him. I jumped back and swung up the rifle, slipping a round into the chamber. The back of the car was burning, but I grabbed the spotlight and twisted it over and down to play on that second-story ledge about where I had seen the little rift of light—which now I figured must have been a match or a lighter—and there he was. Standing, beginning to yell something even as the light hit him. Some kind of foreign stuff or else it was that goddamned accent of his. It was a nigger. He looked tall, but you couldn't tell because he didn't stand still. He moved out of the light still yelling while the captain rolled on the pavement trying to put out the flames on his uniform, while this other special unit guy ran into the street like a human torch and got mixed with the people running, who by then were around us, yelling, screaming, trying to get away from the unit—and running right into this mess. Jesus, you never saw anything like it. I twisted the light again, but before I could fix him, I saw that little flicker again—here came another bomb. It spiraled over and over at me as if the nigger had thrown it with me in mind. It came on, and I dropped down, but it went over my head and over the car and I swung up my rifle, put my eye to the sight, hearing this nut yelling something like, Zonk Zonk Zonk. And when I had him centered, just as he lit one more bomb, I zonked him. But as I did, that nutty black bastard let go with his bomb, and it hit on the top of the hood and I felt the fire all over me. I tried to run, to pull it off with my hands, to roll, but nothing did any good, I couldn't breathe, and my hands and face were on fire, and I passed out.

While I was out, I dreamed. Nothing much, but it was kind of crazy, kind of shook up. I dreamed that I was in this town, drinking beer, kind of giving the barmaid a bad time. I was with these other guys, and it was war and we were sitting out on the sidewalk under a kind of awning and laughing because we were on leave. It was night, and the stars were big and flat like little plates in the sky. Then there was this loud howl like some kind of big animal was dying or had lost something it could never find again. And I knew it was a raid, and I got up and yelled at the other guys, but they just laughed and lifted up their steins and yelled back, *Sieg heil, sieg heil*—and all of a

225

sudden I saw they were wearing those other uniforms—not us. One was *Einsatzgruppe,* another was *Waffen SS*—and one was in the black and silver of the Gestapo. And I was yelling, *—Raus, raus mit uns, um Gottes . . .* I looked down. I was one, too. I saw I was one, too. Which didn't bother me. I mean, what I thought of was, What's up there? What's coming? And I looked up and saw the searchlights coming on, probing the blackness, trying to find them. And they were there: high, so high you couldn't hardly see them. But they were there, tiny and above the flak they were sending up. Seventeens—hundreds of them, thousands maybe, flowing across the sky, already beginning to dump, and I looked down, hearing over the sirens the first far-off crump crump crump of bombs hitting the edge of town, and as my eyes came out of the sky, they hit this black and gilt signboard out over the café that read DAS DRESDENER KREUZ. And I fell down on my knees, praying to something, to somebody, and I woke up. Hurting, my hands and face bandaged, thinking, they'll shoot me as a spy, I'm not a German, I'm not. They'll know. Or else they'll burn me, my own planes. Then I remembered the car and the nigger on the ledge and the people. But I couldn't figure what was the dream. The stuff in the street seemed like a dream, and the sidewalk café was like the real thing. I mean, was I an American in 1968 who dreamed he was a German in 1944—or a German who dreamed he was an American? I was thinking in English . . . wasn't I? I mean, what you think in isn't a language. Maybe it was German. *Nein,* I thought, no. And then this nurse comes over and says, —Are you feeling better, Sergeant?

And I feel the chill again. It sounds like English, she looks American, but I'm not a sergeant. Not on the Chicago force I ain't. Maybe in the German Air Force, the *Luftwaffe.* I remember I am a bombardier. I know that. Whatever, I am a bombardier. But if I try to say it, what will I say? *Ich bin Bombardier?* The word is the same, ain't it? Maybe it wasn't Karlsruhe and Dresden I hit. Maybe it was London and Coventry and Southampton. Maybe Rotterdam and Cracow. Why not? All I know is I have bombed. I am a bombardier. The places I have hit, like all in a dream, could have been any places. I remember what they told me, but maybe I lost my memory and dreamed. Jesus, what is all this?

Then, past her, I saw the captain. He had some bandages on,

226

but he was in uniform and smiled at me. But even so, I couldn't stop it coming out:

—I'm a bombardier, I said. —I'm a bombardier . . .

—Wrong war. The captain grinned. —In this one, you're a sergeant.

And it was true. In a little while Gertrude comes in saying that everybody thinks I'm some kind of a hero, and the mayor says I did my duty in the best tradition. This is all a lot of crap, but the stripes are worth a couple of bills a month, and what you take on the side goes up, too. It's nice. It's going to be very nice.

The only thing that bothers me is that nigger. The dream doesn't bother me anymore. I mean, so I'm a German soldier laying under a slab of concrete with the 17's going over, and all this is a dream. Okay. What isn't? You play the whole deal like a dream. You can't go wrong. But the nigger is like that nameless village in Germany. They never found the nigger. And that bothers me.

Poole

The judge let me out. No bail. Just recognition, he said. On account he had checked out my war record and I had done a lot of good. Said he didn't know what come over me, I had been a good soldier.

—Wasn't you a good soldier? he asked. —Your record is exemplary.

And by then I had something on my mind. I thought, it can't nothing grow on your mind in jail. Give him a dose. Let ole Zonk have what he craves. One more once. So I give him a turn and a shuffle. Kind of grinned and showed some teeth. I believe I could of got a beer if I had done like that at the bus stop going down into Texas. I believe I could of. And I said:

—Yessah, I said.

—Well. What possessed you to be in that place? Didn't you know Moon's Bar was a good place to find trouble?

I look kind of stupid and smile, and give him some of dis year ole nigger stuff. —Doan know, yo' honor. Jes' doan know.

Something new in me says, —Nigger, it's too broad. Don't you know this Zonk going to see you're making a fool of him? But something older, something else says, —Naw, you can't go too much on him. 'Cause that's what he *wants*. He wants to know you know you're a nigger. He don't even know he wants it, needs it. But he does. And when he's satisfied in his soul, then he's going to say, —All right, boy. I believe you've done got hold of yourself. Now you go and don't sin no more. You hear? That was what the old part of me said, and it was right. He did him a take on dis year ole crossed-up bad-luck nigger, and there I was. Out. Out and walking. With six dollars in my pocket and a April day all spread out in front of me like a dead child.

Oh, I thought about that judge. What a good thing to set a ole nigger back on the right track. Ain't that something else? Ain't that enough to season a poor tired meal out in Oak Park or wherever ole judge lives. See him coming home full of good feelings, and all his children—his living children—say like on the TV, —Here come the judge, here come the judge. And he presiding at dinner, belching a little, saying, —All right, what come to pass today? And dealing out justice and mercy in equal parts, hand to hand, among those children. Like they was little niggers, and that's all right.

But I ain't one of his children. And that new thing in me says, —Walk home, nigger. You ain't hardly unscrewed the cork yet. There's lots more to drink. And even the old part of me says, —There's something in that, Mr. Man. It got to get worse before it gets better, and that's a fact, ain't it?

Yes, Lord, and when I come to my house, come through the buildings burned and still smoking and the furniture all out on the sidewalk and people sitting on the curbstone crying, when I come through the national guardsmen with their carbines and helmets and white eyes looking like the wind was up 'em, and the pigs with their pork all wound in gunbelts and with helmets and goggles, when I come home through all that, the boy's momma is gone.

No note and the neighbors don't know a thing. Cab come and she got in. No suitcase. Nothing. Just gone.

Maybe now she's looking for where Sears, Roebuck has got

to. Or maybe not. Maybe she just don't reckon to live side by side with the nigger got her boy killed. I see that, and all the time I'm in the parlor crying, I say, I see that. I can sure see that.

And the new part of me says, —Well, nigger, what's your excuse now? You're close on fifty years old. You got no woman, you got no job. You got no chick nor child. It's up, ain't it? Now what's your excuse? But the old part says, —I like a cool drink of water. I can bait a line and throw it in. I want to sit on a porch swing and watch the cars going into the city. I can still do that. I can still take a good deep breath.

New part just swears. —Motherfucker. You wasn't ever anything. You knew when you was twenty, it would come to this. You knew Zonk was born with one foot on the ground and the other on your face. It ain't no never mind, is it? You a born slave. You are a sure enough nigger.

I slapped at myself like a man with a mosquito bothering him. But I was in the habit, and I couldn't break it. No use to try to break it. I had come to arguing with myself, found I was a house divided. Come to wonder if I had ever been any kind of man. Or just a common coon. Jig. Burrhead. Spook. That old part says, —Forget it. You been up there, up in the high places with them fighters and that flak all around you. You been there. It's no man walking can question you.

Right. No man walking. Then I knew what that new part of me was, where it come from. It was the boy. It was Kicky. All that was left. All they left of him. It was his voice, his words. Words I hadn't never heard him say, but words I knew he would of said sooner or later. If they had of given him even that much time. He was in me, and when I saw that, I went out on the steps and watched the sun go down and laughed till I had tears in my eyes. Thinking, he was in me before. He was there in 1941, and I sent him out to his momma, out into the world. And now he's back; only now he's got him a voice and he ain't going to leave me ever. Everything I do and think and feel, he's going to have him a say. It won't never be over till I am. It won't ever be a time when I'm free of him again. Not ever.

What you going to do? Eat for two? Pregnant with a dead boy and you a fifty-year-old . . . nigger. Man you going to hurt, honey. You going to question every breath, and what you used to ignore, put off, you going to have to handle, consider, fool with. It makes your head hurt. But that's what it comes to. You got it to do.

So I sit out on the stoop. Feeling old, you say. No, young. No, I'm feeling all kinds of young. And it's awful. You feel old and you're tired and your bones hurt and your eyes are gone and your hands got calluses and feel like old broke-up leather. But it's done and you're through with it, and truth to tell you don't give a shit what happens so long as they make it happen two blocks away. What for? It ain't yours. You're old, and you got all you're gonna get. And you don't mind. 'Cause you're tired, and even if there was more to get, maybe you wouldn't step down on the street for it. 'Cause it's the same. It's all the same, and nothing is going to ease your pain. And that's all right. That's all right, fine. On account you've had that pain so long it's like a uncle who drinks or a friend can't hold on to a dollar. It's like dirt and rain and old shoes and creosote. It's there. And that's being old, and I been there now, and it ain't so bad.

But young is something else. Young is knowing it's out there, knowing it ought to be yours, feeling in your body and in your soul that they're keeping it from you, keeping what belongs to you. You can feel all the good in you, and you know it's going for nothing, that what could be big and fine is withering in you, turning to dust and crumbling away. And knowing it drives you crazy. It drives you plumb crazy. You see all the world out there, and you see what somebody could do. You see that. But not you. Anybody but you. And they keep saying, —Sure you. Come on and try. Listen, we ready for you. Come on out. And you seen what going out will get you. You can be the house nigger. They need 'em some good boys for that. They got to have some nice clean light bucks so that if anybody says, —Hey, now, they can point and answer, —There's our nigger. How come you say we ain't got any niggers? What do you call that over there? If that ain't a nigger, what do you reckon it is? That's being young. And more. And it all hurts because you've still got something inside, and it ain't no way to let it out. Except maybe a couple. A couple the MP and the judge and that Zonk down in Virginia ain't got blocked. And that's what I'm carrying inside me sitting on that stoop. It's what my boy left me. And it's gonna just have to find itself a way. I see

230

that. It's just gonna have to find a way. Then this fine-looking young thing comes by in a short skirt with her hair piled up natural. And I says, —Where you off to, honey? Reckon you want to take somebody along?

Way it turned out, she wasn't going nowhere. Stopped in for a while. It sure felt funny. But it felt good, too. Felt good cause I had give up thinking about what was past and gone. That old Poole had got himself lost. Strayed or stolen. What you had now was the New Nigger. He wasn't sweating who was dead, who was gone. He had him this new chick and some stuff cooking in the back of his head—nothing sure, nothing set down. But something. You think I'm crazy, but that night, with this girl, I never felt so good. So long, everybody. So long, Elena. So long, Kicky. Oh, Jesus, when you lost everything, when there ain't anything left for them to take away. Never was a man so free. I thought, reckon you was back on that road again? What would you do? No Elena, no child. Nothing ahead of your black face but a black street. What you gonna do?

Easy, I thought, turning that girl from up to down, riding her like a circus pony (wasn't nothing but a nigger girl, see). I could feel Zonk's face under my fist. My knee dredging a place between his nuts. Shit, every time I dropped it in that girl, I was feeling that towheaded motherfucker on that back road in Virginia falling, giving way. All his skin and meat and bone coming apart. I got gentle then. You want to get gentle lest you kill him. Can't kill him. He's got hundreds of years to go. Can't grow new balls, a new head. Got to preserve him, keep him like a bulldog for pits he can't never win in.

—You nice, girl says to me. —You real nice, daddy.

I laughed and swatted her sweet ass. Good brown ass. All I had in the world—except that little idea, something pecking and scratching like a Plymouth Rock hen back in the barnyard of my head.

Girl went on away next morning. I laid in bed for a long time thinking, it's coming for you. All this freedom shit fixing to melt away, and it's a black hole going to open up underneath and swallow you whole. It's coming, and you know it. So I laid and waited like a woman laying quiet for her time. Nope. Just like last night. I was free. Sorry about everything, but shut of it,

231

too. All but that voice in there that had took to calling me nigger. When they cut it off, it's gone. It don't hurt. You sorry about that leg or them fingers. But gone is gone.

So I got up and went on to the hotel to pick up my stuff. Nothing worth much. I didn't have anything like that anymore. But whilst I was cleaning out my locker, the personnel guy come down. He went to talking to me. Said he had talked to that judge. Said he heard about my boy and he was sorry. Said all them riots was awful, Mr. King dying was awful. But what you going to do?

—I don't know, I said. —I just don't know yet. I got to give it some thought.

He just looked at me. Didn't understand. Wasn't the right answer. So he kept on talking.

—You still got a job here, he said. —Judge said you was a victim of circumstances.

—Hey, I said. —Is that what he told you?

Says I had a good job record and that my Army time and owning a house and never being in no trouble all went in my favor.

—Once, I said, —there was this Zonk down in Virginia . . .

—What can you expect? he said. —Southerners . . . down in the South . . .

—Aha, I said, and stopped pulling my stuff out of the locker. I reckoned to eat. Whilst I was thinking.

—You nice, I told him. —You real nice.

He kind of grinned and patted my shoulder. Like it was something we knew together and then walked off. I didn't know shit. He didn't know that much. I thought, hell, one day you going to cut his throat. For being nice.

Summer come, and the girl come most nights. I never heard anything from Elena. Never heard where she put the boy. Never tried to find out neither. Just let it ride. It would all come out.

One night I was sitting on the steps with the girl. We sat in the dark listening, looking. Nothing to hear, nothing to see most times and we would go in. But this night that no-good little burr with the shades and the high hair come up. He walked right up and stood with his hands in his back pockets like he was window-shopping. I never said anything. After a minute the girl kind of laughed, and I poked her quiet with my foot.

232

—Well, reckon you ain't going to do a thing.

I let him stand. —May go buy some fried fish, I said. —Girl, you like some fried fish?

—Ummm, she said, hunching her shoulders.

—We gonna settle up with 'em for Kicky, he said, jerking his head like he had some kind of sickness.

—Tell them, I said. —Don't tell me.

—Some got to die so the rest can live decent.

—All got to die, I told him. —Ain't you heard? Done been tried and found wanting. Sentence of death. One hundred percent.

—We gonna lay for them pigs. We gonna roast us some pigs.

—Go shit in your hat, I said. —And throw it at 'em.

—He was my friend, the little burr says. He looks so small he's fragile. It's that BAR missing. He needs that piece in his hands for anybody to hear him decent.

—Wasn't no friend of mine, I said. —Anyhow I hear he's dead. You let them dead folks alone. Don't want to mess with haunts. Drive you crazy.

Girl laughs and laughs like somebody told something funny. In my head, I can hear the boy laughing. 'Cause dead, he knows. He knows it all, and sometimes he sends it on over to me. We don't talk. I just listen. Where he is they ain't no pity. They got no pity over there. What they going to do with pity? They know it all. Nothing to pity, huh?

So the little old burr walks off. And that idea comes nuzzling in the back of my head again. —Un-huh, I says. —Un-huh. And we skip the fish and go inside out of the night.

And come August they bring the Democrats to town. They going to have 'em a convention. Going to elect a President from among the survivors. You got short and fat, tall and holy, and some other something don't quite know how to go seeing he's standing for a ghost and keeps listening but don't hear. I work nights at the Midland, where a bunch of the little no-account Democrats come. They drink and smoke cigars and sit around saying why it got to be one thing and not another. I don't pay no mind. Till I see on the television late one night where they gone to whipping the children out to the park. No sense in that, I think. What good to do that? And it come to me, come across in that new voice in my head, they got to put down the

233

children 'cause the children have got 'em on their uppers. They going to make samples of the children.

Good. Better it ain't any children left. Shouldn't be anything young left in the world. But I know better. I know that. So I went down in the basement and found me some bottles. Old whiskey bottles, a wine bottle left by some janitor or maybe somebody just wandered in to be warm near the furnaces. Somebody who had got over being young but never got free. And I took me some cleaning solvent, and I filled 'em and tore up some rags and stuffed 'em real tight in the necks of those bottles. And set 'em up on the back of a shelf. Where they could wait.

It was near morning when I got home. Girl waked up. She didn't leave anymore. Hadn't moved in. Didn't have anything to move but her ass. She just didn't go off. I climbed in the bed, and when she woke up, she woke breathing hard and crying out to me. Woke the best way you can. The way that makes you sorry you got to go and die and leave your body behind. And when we was done, that's how I fell asleep.

Next day at work the word kept coming in. Man bringing in the towels and sheets had a cup of coffee in the kitchen with me.

—They whipping those kids, he said, shaking his head.

—White kids, I said.

—Sho' white kids. You reckon that makes it all right? I mean, some folks does. Man told me over to Tom's Sho-Bar he didn't give a shit how many of their own they killed. Fewer for us.

—I don't know, I said. —How come you asking me?

—I don't know, he said. —Seems wrong.

—Yeah.

He kind of laugh and sip off his coffee. —They had 'em a pig, he says. —Ole pig on a leash. Said it called Pigasus. Gonna run it for President. Nice-looking pig.

—Yeah, I said.

—Gonna run 'em a pig for President. Seems nice kids. One of 'em asked did I want part of his sandwich. Had a ham sandwich. Said it was a relation of the next President. What do you think of that?

I didn't say anything. He finished his coffee and went on off. Later they had news on the TV. Same stuff. Then this guy

234

come with groceries and stuff. I knew him pretty good. He said they was out in Grant Park singing and running around.

—But they got the Army out there.

—Army?

—Got 'em some Army out there. Rifles with bayonets on 'em. Never seen the equal.

—Reckon they'd shoot those kids?

He kind of shrugs. —They got guns. Army supposed to shoot. Ain't that what Army does?

Then it come, and it wouldn't let up. That voice, him, talking over and over. Not saying *daddy* cause he knows wherever he is that I can't hardly take that. Naw, it's nigger. Saying, —Nigger, you gonna let 'em go with children killing? Well, yes, I think. I got some kind of idea but. But I see then what my idea is. Old idea. Twenty some-odd years old. From when I was Army and they had me bombing. Kids. Anybody. I did what they told me 'cause I was some kind of nigger. Niggers is people who do whatever you tell 'em to do. A man is somebody does what he needs to do. It ain't what you do. It's how come you do it.

So I went down when it was getting dark. I got them bottles and put on a old pair of coveralls and went out in the street headed for Michigan Avenue. I come in the back of this building breaking the lock and started climbing. Up on the third or fourth floor I broke another one and kind of groped my way to a window. You could look down into the street where they had the police and the Army. Down in front of that big new hotel they had 'em drawed across the street, and people was yelling and screaming. So I got me a window open and climbed out on the ledge. It was wide, and down below was the street and one lone police walking up and down right under me. It was like in the war: them down there and me way up. No sight, but I saw I didn't need one. You don't need it flying so low. Maybe you don't need one ever. I saw how it must have looked down below my plane. I saw the street and the buildings and off to my right those people all hating the police and Army. Only this time I knew what was going on, and I sighted in on that one police, turned a little and held my lighter close to my chest till the rag in one of them bottles was going, and I come around real smooth and didn't even throw, just let that bottle kind of go. It sailed up and out and down and hit almost on top of him. I

235

dropped down on the ledge and watched him jump back and kind of go into a dance getting that fluid off him. He was scared. Kind of hunched down with his rifle pointed across toward me. But he don't see me. He knows I'm here, but he can't shoot down the whole world. No, he got to wait, and I got time. I got all kinds of time. I'm too old to hurry. They say time is with young folks, but they're wrong. The old has got all the time because they got nothing to do with time. They lost everything already, huh? So I just lay there and watch him talking into his radio, wagging his head up toward me. He edges over like a crab and eases in behind a bread truck peeking out from behind it now and then. But I hold still. Not yet, Mr. Man. Let Zonk sweat. Let him reckon on how many of me they got up here. Let him just lay there.

Pretty soon a car comes rolling up the street real quiet. Pulls in behind the bread truck like if they was quiet, nobody'd see 'em. Zonk laying in the gutter with his radio motions like he'd found him a dollar among the cigarette butts. In a minute he's alongside the car on the offside. They got the door open to duck behind, and somebody turns on a light. It come cutting up through the dark just like over that last town in Germany, like a blind man's finger feeling its way along, trying to make out what the empty windows and blank stone meant, trying to find me. Stay off, blind man, I thought. You can't find me. No way. You got to know where I am.

So I lay and watch 'em work along that floor down below me. Stopping, going back. I get me another bottle ready and slide it up right next to my chest. Fluid smells real bad, but that's all right. Then they put that light up one floor and bring it right across me. But it's no use. I shut the window coming out and they can't get that light flat enough to spot me. When it moves by me, it's a good six inches over my ass. If I lay low, they got to come up into the building to find me. And them new cops are wondering if that number one Zonk is so scared he got the wrong building. They know it's something 'cause what's left of that first bomb is just burning out right in front of 'em. But where am I? What am I? One of them kids? Some kind of crazy man? Naw, I'm a bombardier. Been out of work for a long time 'cause while I was a nigger, I thought only the Army could hire a bombardier. But now I knew a man could go into business for himself. Man can go back to bombing on his own. I kind of gig-

236

gle, thinking, join the Army and bomb the world. Fine trade for old men. What if every old man took him out a cop or a city when he went? To let them know he been unhappy in his life.

Then I see people coming. Breaking past police and Army. And some kind of truck with a camera and people on it. They coming right at the cops, where they all hunched down across the street there. Well, shit, I think. I got to get on with it so as not to hurt them folks. So I lit me another one, kind of got up to one knee and laid it right on their car. It was fine. Blew wide and scattered, and that car was burning good. Wasn't no use to try putting it out. Direct hit. Getting to be what they called a good mission.

They put the light on me, and I kind of shifted down the ledge a few steps and stoked my next to last one. I see a couple of them down there on fire and think, it's coming back, it's all back. That's how they looked down there a long time ago. On fire and running or laying down trying to get it out. But it's judgment fire. You can't put out judgment fire, Zonk. No way to put out hellfire. Comes up and down on you for judgment, Zonk. And I hear somebody yelling and I reckon it's them cops or them people and the light comes across me again and I throws that next to last one at the light and it's a clean miss and the yelling goes on and the people are coming and I can see 'em looking up, faces white and far off, and here I am up high, going to save 'em from police and Army and somewhere there's screams and glass breaking and judgment coming down all around and I light up my last one and see lined up against that burning car one of them with his gun up, and just as I let the bomb go, I see that fire from his rifle, but I see it after I feel the flak sizzle along my side and the searchlight goes sailing up the side of the plane and I feel myself letting go and beginning to fall, fall, but right then down there before I jump, that sonofa-bitch goes up in flames and I see it was a perfect hit and the plane is falling away from me and the lights burst all over, new lights and the people down there running to the shelters and the yelling is my voice and I'm falling falling falling down into Germany.

Then I dreamed. 'Cause I was worked up. I don't know what did happen. But the dream was strange. It was a conjure. I was

237

back with the group again, but it was still Chicago. I don't know. I dreamed like this:

Somehow or other when I fell, I never hit the ground. It was like I was all wound up in the chute. I come down on this canvas and then I was rolling and somebody stepping on me and I thought, Lord God, they told us how them civilians might try to kill us on account of what the bombs do. Man had his baby girl blew out of her carriage might stomp you to death. Boy whose daddy died driving his cab might put a broken bottle in your neck. But all I felt was that pain in my chest and side like somebody had drew a razor across me there. That, and all my breath was gone. There was light and yelling and all kind of hell busted around me and then somebody had hold of me and I was trying to remember my serial number but I couldn't even remember my name. I am a nigger bombardier name Mr. Man, I tried to yell out, but whoever had hold of me didn't give a shit. He never hurt me, just pulled and dragged me till pretty soon it was dark and quiet with all them civilians still back in the street yelling scared and hating. I rolled over on my back and looked up. It was black. Disadvantage of black is you can't see nothing. But I tried to say something. Something they taught us.

—*Was machen Sie?*

—Shut up, you crazy nigger bastard, somebody said. Then he lit a match, and I could see him.

—Well shit, Boil-o. They brung you down too. How we gonna get out of here? How we gonna get us back to the U.S.A.? You can even drop me in Virginia . . .

—Jesus Christ, he said, and put the match down close to my face. He looked older, had him a beard, and there was blood running down his forehead. He kind of shook his head at me and just squatted there not saying anything.

—They gonna kill us if they catch us, I told him. —You know what Michaelis say. We done killed too many of 'em, Boil-o. We got 'em crazy. We got to get out . . . he say if we can get to Switzerland . . .

—They'll intern us . . .

—Yeah.

—There ain't any more Switzerlands, he said and kind of put his arm around me to lift me up and set me against the wall of this alley I see we're in.

238

—You ain't going to leave me here, are you? I can travel . . .

—Shut up, he said. —Hell, no. I'm not going to leave you . . . Wherever you think we are. Because you're probably right and whatever you've been up to was probably right, too. Wasn't it?

— . . . done what we was supposed to do . . .

— . . . fight to freedom . . . ?

— . . . you said it, coon-ass.

He grinned real big, but I could see tears in his eyes, and I wondered if it was that cut on his head or if he had took some fragments somewhere else. I asked him where the rest was.

—Rest?

—Rest of our crews. People we flew here with.

—Oh, he said, trying to help me up, —gone. All gone down. Three thousand miles and twenty years ago.

I couldn't follow him. —Long way, I said. —Reckon they'll catch up with us?

—Not this time, he said.

Then we started walking in the dark with him leading me around trash bins and kind of watching as we crossed open streets. I passed out now and then in the dream, and I was afraid he might think I was dead and leave me there for 'em, but he never did. I'd come around again and he'd be pulling me along. Old Boil-o wasn't no Zonk, I thought. Naw, he's a bombardier. He knows. He might know most of what I know. You got to ride the nose of a 17 out over the world with nothing but a inch of plexiglass, and the Sight between you and thirty thousand feet to really know.

—They got Kicky, I told him. —Took him out with a machine gun.

He just grunted and kept walking. Then I passed out for good, and when I come around again, I was laying in my bed with my ribs bandaged and the girl sitting beside me listening to her little transistor radio. When she sees me come to, she got me a beer, and I lay there for a long time thinking of that dream, trying to pick out what was real and what was just a vision.

I couldn't say. Except for the pain along my side and the bandage, I would of thought it was all a dream. Maybe Virginia and Texas and England and them missions and Philadelphia and Chicago—maybe I had been dreaming always, dreamed my

239

whole life away. I kind of held up my hands, and I saw they was black. That wasn't no dream. Whatever I had dreamed, it was a black man dreamed. Now, I thought, when I get all right, the dreams is over. I got to do. Make like the dreams was telling me something and now time had come to do.

—Honey, where we at?

—Hee, hee.

—Sho.

So I finished my beer and eased over on my good side. Next time I go out it's going to be all the way out. When you rode the lightning and dreamed such dreams, it's time to go on out. The boy don't talk to me no more. I do the talking now. And what I say is I got to go. Girl tells me she got a kid in her. You might know. Yes, I have a dream. We got to get out of Germany.

Michaelis

After Muskie was safely settled in the place appointed for him, Snorts and I went into town. Around the hotel, there was still the odor of gas and a tension among police and guardsmen that one could feel. As if they were not sure that it was over for now, that the next act would be a little later—days or months. Or years. It was twelve years between 1905 and 1917.

We drank until very late, Snorts and I. For old times' sake. Because it was the end of something. I remembered the last night I had spent in London in 1945. I had bought some things for Candy, had seen them packed and gone into Soho looking for friends who liked a Spanish restaurant in Greek Street. There had been this same feeling, this release, this note of elegy and conclusion. There had been troops in the streets and of course much rubble. An Intelligence colonel was with my Air Corps friends. He was drunk and could not share our feelings. No, he was telling us about the next one, about Russian perfidy, about their enigmatic abilities, their brutality, their determination to take things over. We were not set for it, and after a while the colonel staggered off looking for an audience he would not find for some four or five years.

But Snorts and I drank alone. I suppose we both felt we might not drink together again, and we had been over much of the same territory together or at different times. We spoke of men we had known. Who had died carrying mail or trying to pick up a dinner flying in local races at Akron, Ohio, or Madison, Wisconsin. Men who had gone down over Hickam Field or Wake Island. Men who had died over every city and hamlet in Germany. Men frozen now in that vast mosaic where the living catch and keep the dead lest their immense past kineticism infect life itself; that frieze where Immelmann and Boelcke and the rest dive and soar forever in their fragile planes against foes no more substantial than themselves.

In that run-down Chicago bar, it came to me that I might yet live to see a coronation. To see the next manifestation of those forces that were rising from such long sleep. The spells I knew were old. They had yammered in men's hearts for five thousand years and were shrieking for release again now, to be broken from the brittle bonds of reason in which they were chained. It would take time. But not much more.

We drank, and before I caught my plane to go home to Candy, I toasted Snorts in all sincerity. I toasted him and the mercenary in him which required no Blockhouses, no Dark Rooms, no magic bombsights to do his job. And who, however things might go, was never disappointed. It is no small magic to avoid that final feeling, that long fading of self when it turns out the age has betrayed you. It is a spell worth learning even as the sun declines: the formula for avoiding belief in everything. In order that one may serve anything. If I had it to do over, I would try that dark manipulation, using an apparent appetite for some portion of money and power to mask my real intention. Which, I toasted in Snorts, was to have no intention at all, to escape time by standing loyal to space. To do whatever and however and let it end there. Which, as I finished my last drink, I saw was where it ended anyhow.

But beyond that, I was not yet done. I still possessed treasures looted and gotten honestly: genes and dreams and certainties that can be transmitted if their holder, waking and knowing, should encounter his own image unaware, hungry for something that has no name, no time, only a place.

241

I had seen one such, I thought. A most unlikely one, but already possessed of half my store and very nearly knowing it. He had owned a brief moment of the convention, had joked and spoken and captured certain neural tracks in people who did not yet know that they had been opened to him. He was, by any measure, a very long shot, but the intensity of his control was epic, and, after all my specialty was long shots. It would not be hard to arrange a meeting through my contacts. Could we talk? It seems quite likely. And given that, the ceiling and floor of our time might be made to alternate. It would be quite a gambit to end on, but the young, when they become wise, are ready to gamble all because they know that there is really nothing, nothing whatever to lose. And as he had pointed out only hours before, he was too young to be Vice President.

Boileau

The first dispatch was not much. It was a most personal résumé of a nation *in extremis,* quoting D. H. Lawrence on America:

> They came largely to get away—that most
> simple of motives. To get away. Away
> from what? In the long run, away from
> themselves. Away from everything. That's
> why most people have come to America, and
> still do come. To get away from everything
> they are and have been.
>
> "Henceforth be masterless."
>
> Which is all very well, but it isn't freedom. . . .

No, it isn't. But in lieu of freedom, for a while at least, vast supplies of money, diverting new technology, spanning first with rails, then with highways, finally with airlines a vast empty continent, and grinding down any opposition will do. Mastery will do in place of freedom to those who have escaped all mas-

242

ters. For a while. But America is running out of diversions now. She has destroyed all internal and peripheral opposition: Indians, Southerners, Latin Americans. She has broken the continent to her will. She has woven the densest web of commerce and communications and transportation across and up and down. Now what? Foreign adventures are proving most costly and other powers have the means to punish her for large miscalculations. So, in Malcolm's words, the chickens have come home to roost. They have flown distractedly, pecked here and there for three hundred years, and now they are lighting on the ridgepoles and crosspieces of the American structure. They are enormous fowls, heavy and beyond numbering. Hens named for the Salem witches and Mrs. Saurret and a little girl age nine killed at the corner of Peachtree Street by one of Sherman's first shells—and women and girls without name and number who vanished in flames in the streets of Schweinfurt and Hamburg and Tokyo and Hiroshima. Roosters named Nat Turner and Wesley Everest and John Pelham, the boys of Chapultepec, the cadets of VMI, Frank Little, Chief Joseph of the Nez Percé, Geronimo, Cochise, the Haymarket martyrs, Spies and Parsons and the rest—Leon Czolgosc, not simply executed for his madness, but annihilated, quicklime poured into his casket, the Scottsboro boys and Sacco and Vanzetti, the lynched, the maimed, the purchased, the broken, the silenced: all created equal, all smashed in the headlong attempt of the masterless to find some essence of freedom, an abstraction hypostatized, and settling, on a continental scale, for money. For power. For the privilege and the subservience that masters have all required.

Men are free when they are in a living
homeland, not when they are straying
and breaking away. . . . Men are free when
they belong to a living, organic, believing
community . . . not when they are escaping
to some wild west. The most unfree souls
go west, and shout of freedom. . . . The shout is
a rattling of chains, always was.

And in Chicago today, those who have shouted freedom are at bay. It just may be that the last of the American illusions is going to die. Here and now.

243

It was not good history. It was a newspaper piece. From which tomorrow's history will be written, if I am correct. And I am correct, but it will take as many years to prove it as I have spent coming to realize it. It will be a history of those who ran together for a little while and then ran apart. A history of those who shrieked for freedom and never dared permit it, those who dedicated themselves to equality in word and created a society of slaves and serfs and victims. It will be a history of brag and pout, of cowardice and cynicism; of cant and pretense and broken promises; of brutality and false superiority. Was it Carlyle who said,—There is only one truth in the universe: that a lie will not stand forever. Nor will a liar, whether it be a man—or what passes for a nation.

I spent time with many people. I listened to a luncheon conversation between two young men from Boston as word circulated that McCarthy was prepared to back Ted Kennedy. It was obvious that, whatever Kennedy's decision, it would be made on grounds of expediency, not principle. I talked to Humphrey people—who wished that it was all over—the convention and the election. Because they knew that the only thing worse than losing both places might be winning either.

And there were the McCarthy people. Who told me American politics would never be the same. As if a system developed under Andrew Jackson and perfected in its corruption and insanity for a hundred and fifty years could be changed by Minnesota's answer to Clark Kent. Who, when he removed his shirt, revealed that he was, whatever else, not Superman. Prufrock, perhaps.

I talked to the outsiders, the young, the disaffected, the aliens who had discovered over the past four years that they had no country. One was a leader in the revolutionary student movement.

—They don't have enough prisons to hold all of us, he told me.

—They can build them, I said.

—We'll fight.

—You'll die.

—But not forever, he said.

—No, not forever. But it will be worse. When you've smashed them, who do you expect will take over? Not Sazonov. Not Kaliayev. Not even Trotsky.

244

He gave me a lopsided grin. —You're the expert on revolution. Stalin?

—More or less. For a while.

—You'd lay off, then. You'd go with Hump?

I stoked up my pipe and tried to look reasonable and professional. I do that when I'm going to talk sedition.

—No, I said. —I wouldn't go with him. I wouldn't lay off. But I'd know that can of worms I was opening.

—Let the worms hang out. He grinned. —All power to the worms.

—That's what it comes to, I said. —I believe a Southerner named Poe said that.

We parted in good spirit. We might see each other again.

Later I came across Boyd. It was too bad. I had put the Blockhouse out of mind. Or maybe it wasn't too bad. Maybe the Blockhouse was what I needed to remember. And how I had been raped in it, no—had been accessory to my own deflowering and even managed to walk like a man afterward and look at my right hand and the thumb which had killed so many. I remember laughing, half-drunk one night with a Houston reporter, telling him it was a Roman hand, that my thumbs down had once been deadly as Nero's. He thought I was something other than half-drunk. He may have been right.

But Boyd. Still a Yankee Bourbon. Who, even slumming, had done it in an internationally famous band. Who had learned nothing, forgotten nothing. A McCarthy man, teetering on the crumbling edge of his conscience, terrified that some word, some act about to take place would subtract him from the ornate and stylized world of a New York law practice and send him hurtling out again into the thin air at the edge of space, to make new decisions, new commitments. He could not imagine being a bombardier with an independent command, a man who chose his own targets, briefed himself, and bore the whole responsibility of his acts. Our conversation was polite as such things go in the North. Neither of us was much reassured by it, though. I suppose we each came to know how much space and time stood between us still. That our common servitude to Michaelis' black art twenty-five years ago had made us neither kinsmen nor fellow citizens. There was blood between us, true. But it was the blood of those others we had butchered impersonally, not blood we shared. We were aliens, too, for all our

245

neat suits and clipped hair, our briefs and books and stake in, I believe they call it, society.

On the way downstairs in the elevator, I glanced at him. His face was heavier, hair stylishly—but honestly—gray at the temples. The old snobbery I remembered had changed subtly to an expression of earnestness, a tightness along the jawline that spoke of a deep and perhaps growing disgust with the world as it is and a matching obdurate refusal to grasp even intuitionally the degree to which he, Boyd, contributed to the very condition he had come to despise. I smiled, wondering if disappointed snobbery, snobbery crushed or shamed, or in some way outgrown becomes in its new incarnation moral rectitude. There was a connection with the essence of McCarthy in this, but before I could sort it out, we were in the lobby. And just outside, things came apart like a slow-motion movie of the *Hindenburg* over Lakehurst.

Out there, a crowd of screaming people surrounded us. It took me a moment to realize that they were trying to escape from some police who had apparently gone mad, who were running onto the sidewalk striking everyone in reach with their nightsticks. They knocked down women, pushed others up against the plate-glass front of a bar that occupied the street side of the Hilton. They were attacking a bunch of middle-class people who had been standing near the hotel entrance watching the demonstrators—as if the very presence of witnesses to their betrayal of duty enraged them even more than that of the ragged youngsters. Suddenly, under the pressure of people trying to avoid them, the plate-glass front of the bar caved in, and people fell inward, as those sitting around the bar turned to see the amazing spectacle of police in riot helmets leaping through the blasted window, beginning to hit them, too, chase them around the bar. One man, quick-thinking, threw his whiskey into the face of a charging officer just as another knocked him down. It was like a film clip taken from something of Mack Sennett's, reshot in modern dress. Only the comic police were in deadly earnest.

Boyd and I were pulled apart, and the last I saw of him was that hard, polished, upright face turning and turning, hardly shocked, as people milled screaming between us. I saw a woman knocked down by two police near the wall, and Boyd leaned over to help her up as they moved on, flailing, hitting like windmills driven mad by an invisible tempest. As he turned to look back down toward the intersection one last time, his lips were tight as if somehow the very core of ethics were to avoid an expression of surprise. How far is it, I remember wondering inanely, from the Hilton to the Pennsylvania Hotel? Then I was dodging a plainclothesman, apparently an agent provocateur, who looked as if he had last worked on Frick's goon squads at the Homestead strikes: bent ears, eyes glazed, breathing hard, either from uncommon exertion, sexual excitement— or both. I still had Boyd—both Boyds—in mind and paid the police little mind, simply sliding out to the edge of things. In the years to come, Boyd would be hard pressed to maintain that expression, I thought. This is, at most, the Girondist. Wait till he sees the living face of our Robespierre.

Then, as the crowd carried me down the street away from the intersection, the beatings, the screams of a city in agony, I looked up for some reason. Above the broken plate-glass window of the bar there was a brightly lit sign. It said, whether you believe it or not, THE HAYMARKET INN. On the sidewalk below a few people lay curled or sprawled, and a police captain with a bullhorn was trying to direct—no, to control—his men. He seemed a little absurd, like a Tsarist officer trying to rally his forces as they drifted away from the German front, pulled like tiny bits of iron filing toward the magnet of Petersburg, where, it was said, strange things were happening.

The people around me began to break into small groups trying to outrun the police. It was surrealistic. There were middle-aged businessmen and long-haired boys and even one black in a leather jacket with sunglasses, all of them running together. The black stumbled and almost fell, and a man with a calf briefcase grabbed his arm. I began to trot, watching over my shoulder as they came: vandals inflamed by a decade of frustration, somehow aware that the tide had swung around, that thirty years of liberal posturings and pretensions had finally reached ebb flow and that things would soon be as they had been before: the gloves off, violence against violence—the American way. Which is to say the way peasants have always resolved their quarrels. With rope and tangles of barbed wire, gasoline and broken bottle. Klansman and American Legionnaire shaking hands over the bleeding bodies of Mac Parker and Wesley Everest.

247

I was far enough ahead of them to really watch, to see that stories of police brutality were mostly true, that stories of prejudice were liberal lies. The police beat anyone they could reach. Without regard to race, color or national origin. The job of police is to beat, to hold down, to suppress, to make order—which, in their estimation, is a species of death. American police see themselves as successors not of Robert Peel's Metropolitan Constabulary, but of the Tombstone gang, the Earps and Doc Holliday. Disagreement is sedition. Disorder is a capital crime. Redress of grievance is accomplished by payoff. Or not accomplished at all. And tonight they were doing their duty, fuck the Supreme Court and the queers and the niggers and the Jews and the bleeding hearts.

It was the Wild West, and things are easy there. If his hair is over his ears, if he wears a beard, if his accent is odd, he's one of them. Except that in the new Wild West, only the deputies had guns and clubs. That, I thought, will be remedied. And I wonder how the cowboys will like it when the objects of their instant justice shoot back.

I turned forward again, and as I did, a police cruiser behind and on my right went up in flames. In the street, there was another patch of flame, and then I saw two police, their uniforms burning, trying to slap out the flames. Behind me the people were closing with more police pressing them. Was there some kind of fight developing here? I moved to the far sidewalk on my left. To hell with the ones on fire. Whatever was happening, they had stoked the flames themselves. Then, at the side of the car, I saw another one, rifle in hand, twisting the searchlight of the burning cruiser up, sweeping back and forth along the front of the building above where I was standing. I dropped to my stomach, realizing that the fire bombs had come from this side of the street, that if he saw me standing alone, he would open up. Not maybe. Certainly. An axiom of combat is, when in doubt, open up. Those who take a different view are not around long enough to argue for it.

When I hit the pavement, I saw that there was a cardboard box of shavings and junk at the curb. Not much protection from a 30-30, but as much as a car door would have provided. So I looked out quickly and saw it—saw a bottle, neck afire, looping through the air from behind me, going over the burning car. The rifleman brought up his piece, leveled it, and even as he fired, another bottle, on a much flatter trajectory, smashed into the street where he was kneeling. He vanished in flames, and I saw, coming on my right, those fleeing from the Hilton, and behind and above me I heard for the first time something like a voice, a screeching howling sound that might have emanated from one too often laid rack in Spain, tortured often but slowly, who had at some past moment given up the tension of remaining human and surrendered to some other impulse dragged from his nightmare agony. It sounds, I thought in that instant, like the scream of a star going nova, like energy trapped in wire, pounding for ages against a resistor.

I lowered my head to the pavement involuntarily. Too much to see, to hear. For that instant, it seemed that things had stopped. I heard only the hiss of fires and saw nothing but the vague afterimage of flames and lights on the inside of my eyelids. There were no abstractions, nothing plaguing me. But when I raised my head a second later, the American world had begun again. I heard something hit only a few feet from me, something that sounded like a sack of concrete dropped from above, and directly across from me, the rifleman had abandoned his piece and was rolling in the gutter, howling, both hands tearing at his burning clothes. Then he vanished as other police surrounded him, and the crowd from down in front of the hotel flowed between us, some of them almost trampling me on the sidewalk. At the rear of the crowd, police were still beating, a little wearily now, and arresting those who fell.

It was at that moment that I looked to my left and saw him lying on the sidewalk, back up against the front of the building. Just above him, extending out to the street, was one of those canopies used by apartment buildings, restaurants and the like to protect patrons from the weather. It was torn, a great hole in the center, one of the metal supports bent, part of the canvas in strips hanging like a tattered flag. It was as if he had appeared from another dimension. A Negro, decently dressed, hair a little gray along the edges, lying sprawled on the sidewalk like one of those improbable suicides who dives out of a plane at thirty thousand feet, dreams a lifetime on the way, and appears smashed and miraculous on the pavement of a city he has never visited before.

249

They'll kill him, I thought. The way they are, they'll beat him to death. So I grabbed him under the arms, pulled his left arm around my shoulders and moved down the street in the same direction as the crowd. A boy came up beside me, blood running over his forehead and ear.

—They busted the spade, huh? Lemme help you.

Between us, we got him down a block or two and into an alley. —I got to keep going, the boy said.

—Thanks, I told him.

—Nothing. From now on, we got to hang together, huh?

I looked at him. No way to know what lay behind him. He was homeless, classless, without a party or a place—without even a world.

—That's right, I said. —We'll come across each other again.

—You bet.

And he was gone. I sat down in the alley, lit a cigarette—my pipe was lost, dropped somewhere along the way. So I smoked the cigarette and regarded the motionless nigger I had appropriated from the Chicago police. Not Prynne or L'Ouverture or Bronstein. Just a crazy nigger who had been bombing police. What the hell had I been thinking to pick him off the street? I looked down at my hand. There was blood on it. His blood. Then I checked in a hurry to find out if I had dragged a corpse so far. No, he was alive. With a long sear down—or up—his ribs, maybe half an inch deep. I tried to get off his shirt, wondering as I did why it is that all Negroes seem to remind you of other Negroes. Then he began coming out of it, opened his eyes. I kept working off his shirt, ready to hit him if his craziness was aimed broader than just at police.

—Goddamn, Boil-o, he said, —they got you, too.

And I saw it was Poole. We were in the Blockhouse, in that ratty pub near Maidstone, standing on the tarmac trembling, after a mission, from fear and awe, knowing somehow that all reality was being bent around our acts, that we inhabited the past and the future simultaneously. And just possibly only Poole and I even sensed it. Unless Michaelis . . .

I don't know what I said. I lit another match and studied him. He looked the same. He was one of those Negroes whose age, after thirty, becomes moot until he reaches eighty.

—They coming for us, Boil-o, he said, his eyes misty and

fixed on something behind me. I almost turned to see if the police had come this far. Then he said: —'Member what they say the Germans do to a man? What you reckon they do to a black man? Lynch?

—Nobody's going to do anything to you, I said.

—If they catch us . . . them Germans . . . look what we done to their town . . . Jesus . . .

—They won't. Fuck their town.

Poole laughed. —You right. Fuck their goddamned town. If we had more bombs. If we had our planes . . .

He went out again, and I got him standing and we moved again. He thought we were back there. In 1944. He thought we were down in Germany. Insane nigger. Then why hadn't I told him, this is Chicago? This is 1968.

I managed to find his wallet and make out an address on his driver's license. A block or so farther on, I found a bus. I pulled Poole's coat close around him and paid our fare. The driver looked at us. I grinned back at him like a fool. A pair of drunks. Who were trying to get out of the war zone. Because his madness had infected me, and the whole time we rode the bus, I was making up German phrases in my head—as if my ability to ask or answer a question in German might be the measure of our survival.

When we got off the bus and began walking again, he came to. He looked at me for a long minute while I rested.

—Ain't no use asking me nothing. I won't say.

—Ain't a goddamn thing I want to know, I said.

—You know it, don't you? Poole said, grinning without humor. —Some Zonk, you.

—Whatever I didn't know, I found out tonight.

Later he passed in and out of consciousness. We finally got to the address on the license. A big stone or brick house jammed in among others identical to it. Shades moved back a hair's breadth. Negroes watched us. As we reached the house, a girl came running onto the sidewalk. I let her take him and almost fell down on the front stoop, the concrete stairs that did for a stoop.

—He's shot, I told her. —Police. Get hold of some nigger doctor who don't feel he's got to report it. Because when they shot him, he was bombing them . . .

251

Later the house quietly filled with Negroes. There was a doctor and some women. One of the women brought me whiskey and water and a bowl of sugar. I smiled at her.

—Tennessee style, I said.

—Is that so? she answered kindly. —Georgia, too.

And this little skinny boy with dark glasses who told me about Poole's son. And wife. Then he got cold, asked me why I had got involved.

—If it's anything to you, because he was in my way on the sidewalk and I was too tired to step over him.

There was low laughter around us, and the boy froze. Good. I wanted to smash his face. Much hatred, few guts. No talent. His great gesture was to buy a dollar ninety-eight pair of sunshades and then forget to take them off when it got too dark to see.

Then I was ready to go. I went by the bedroom to see Poole. He was still going in and coming out. As I came in, he fumbled on the night table.

—Here, he said. —Here's your fifty cents back.

I took it and flipped it into the air, caught it and dropped it in my pocket.

—All right, fine, I said. —Thanks.

—Now we're slick.

—All right, I said. —We're all slick.

As I moved toward the door, he spoke again.

—Except we got to have us that little talk sometime . . .

—I'll see if I can't fit it in my schedule, I said.

—Sometime when they get us back . . .

—?

—Back to the States . . .

—The States . . .

—See you, Loosianne . . .

—Hang in, Virginia . . .

It was almost evening when I awoke, turned on the television to hear that Humphrey had chosen his running mate and saw film clips of what I had lived through the night before. I could recognize at last that chant they had been yelling up at the intersection while we lived a century in three minutes just out of camera range. They had been shouting, —The whole world is watching. Which, I thought, is different from saying, —The

252

whole world is seeing. Then there was word that McCarthy, who had not joined McGovern with Humphrey after the nomination had been rammed through, was still hedging. Why bother? I thought. Either Humphrey doesn't need you, or you won't be enough to save him. Probably the latter.

The next day I did my last dispatch. It was a cheerful report that the old American settlement—whereby even the most alienated were tossed at least fragments of a bone, might well not weather the seventies. Perhaps those whose interest was represented by remaining within the parties—or even the nation— were becoming relatively fewer every four years. Just possibly the right and left would go out simultaneously, shooting at each other across the middle. Preservation of the Union, I said, depends, as it usually has, on the diminution of virtue. If selflessness and honesty and compassion can be held to a minimum, all may yet be well. Maturity in America is determined by one's capacity to absorb vice cheerfully for profit. The young will have to learn this, or the country is finished.

Or would the country then start? Is it idiocy to believe that once, in Philadelphia or Richmond, amid provincial squalor or Confederate revolution, there was a chance to begin making the Declaration of Independence more than a bombastic preface to individual barbarism and collective bureaucracy? I know that man is imperfectible. But isn't he at least improvable? Does every cry for freedom and justice from the Declaration of the Rights of Man to the Communist Manifesto have to serve as one more introduction to tyranny and corruption rearranged, established on a new plan, but tyranny none the less?

That night I left Chicago. You could still smell the acrid stench of tear gas in the air. There were still police and national guardsmen in the streets, and litter, trash, rubble in Grant Park and along the sidewalks. It is said that the morning after the Decembrist uprising in St. Petersburg in 1825, there was not a sign to reveal to the Russian people that dozens had died in Senate Square the night before. In their name. The Romanovs at Chicago had not done so well.

There is a train which leaves Chicago, fleeing south across the flat prairie of southern Illinois, down through western Kentucky, down to Memphis, falling on south through those humid steppes of the Mississippi Delta, across the toe of Louisiana's

253

boot until, flashing through Hammond, it pulls up short in New Orleans, huffing steam, shuddering as if ready to go still farther south, pausing only a few hours before it begins its tortuous journey north again, retracing the miles of track almost unseen except from coach windows by those inside who cannot at any moment say just where they are until, with perfect assurance, the conductor walks unsteadily through, ancient, stentorian, proclaiming Memphis, Vicksburg, Natchez.

And the passengers say, —Ah, we are in Tennessee, Mississippi, Louisiana. But the children are not sure. They ask, —Where is Tennessee or Louisiana? and the adults can only say, —South of Kentucky, north of the Gulf. Along the way from Chicago to New Orleans. And the children subside, knowing no more than before, but unable to ask their question better, to demand an answer that will satisfy.

I lay back in my comfortable seat, a copy of some magazine lying unread in my lap. I watched evening come, twilight fade, stars rise above the bulk of the hurrying trees. From beneath me came the regular, distant clatter as our coach crossed each splice of the rails. Outside a tiny crossroads town flashed by. I saw it only for a moment, but I can remember an Esso sign, a huddled cheerless drive-in hamburger dump, its name small and inconsequential on the great expanse that announced Coca-Cola. And the string of cold bluish streetlights, awash in an orgy of August insects, light falling on the dry fevered dust of the street below where one man or boy—or girl?—stood alone, white or black, I could not tell, stood alone waiting. Either for a person or event or possibility that he—or she— could prophesy, or for whatever the night might bring.

And for the first time in my life, I was lonely. Not for myself or in myself, but lonely as one out of many. I sat on the thick upholstery of the coach's seat, separated from that world, those two hundred million fractions that supposedly made one, distanced from them not only by velocity and a pane of heavy glass but by ages and memories.

Of when, detached even more, I had ridden the unpadded seat of a bomber high above the clouds, carrying destinies, denials, endings, epochs, renewals, cancellations in the belly of that 17 whose purpose in being was me and my mission.

I looked up again then and saw above me the clouds, the stars—above me now and still, as they had been long ago. Still turning according to some immutable law. Or fiction which we cannot read. Once, when cloud cover was total, we had read those stars to find Hamburg. Or was it Dresden? Had we found it? I only remember the navigator's voice on intercom, speaking to the pilot. —I'll have to shoot a star, he said, and through my fur jacket, warmed by the filched skin of some beast other than my kind, I had shivered.

When I awoke, it was dawn or thereabouts and as quickly as we arrived, I cleared New Orleans and got home.

Where the lying jocular sun raised steam from motionless bayou water, and a swirl near the roots of a distant cypress told me the bass were feeding. So I loaded my boat, fired my engine and headed out on a mission again.

St. Tammany Parish, Louisiana, 1969